VIC' BRIGHT DAWN

Siobhan Dunmoore Book 4

Eric Thomson

Victory's Bright Dawn
Copyright 2017 Eric Thomson
Second paperback edition November 2018

All rights reserved.
This book, or parts thereof, may not be reproduced in any form without permission.

This is a work of fiction. Names, characters, places and incidents either are the product of the author's imagination or are used fictitiously, and any resemblance to actual persons, living or dead, business establishments, events or locales is entirely coincidental.

Published in Canada
By Sanddiver Books
ISBN: 978-1-545465-97-4

— One —

The battle stations siren yanked Siobhan Dunmoore out of a deep sleep and sent a surge of adrenaline coursing through her arteries. She jumped out of bed before her brain caught up with a body already tensed for action and reached for her clothes. Dunmoore took a few seconds to regain a sense of reality and recognize surroundings that had not yet imprinted themselves in her muscle memory. She was aboard the Q-ship *Iolanthe*, her new command, an armed cruiser disguised as a bulk freighter whose sole purpose was to attract hostile ships by posing as a ready victim before dispatching them with superior firepower. The Fleet had decommissioned her previous ship, the frigate *Stingray*, retired the ship's bell and posted her former crew to new assignments.

If the officer of the deck was calling *Iolanthe* to action, it meant that the trio of Shrehari Ptar-class corvettes plaguing human shipping in this sector had taken the bait, and not before time. They had been sailing along the most obvious star lanes for longer than anyone wanted. There were always more marauders to exterminate in the vast chunk of contested space between the human Commonwealth and its alien foe, the Shrehari Empire, and never enough naval vessels to keep civilian shipping safe. Moreover, after eight years of war, other non-human species were feeling bold enough to nibble at the edges of the conflict while the giant interstellar polities had their eyes fixed on each other. Even outer colonies far from grasping Shrehari hands and once thought safe from alien depredations had come under increasing threat.

Dunmoore pulled on a midnight black tunic with the stripes of a merchant captain on the collar and ran long, bony fingers through short copper hair shot with silver strands. She grinned at her reflection in the cabin's sole mirror, amused by the feral glint she spied in her gray eyes. The thrill of the hunt always excited her, but in *Iolanthe*, it had another dimension.

She made her way to the Combat Information Center, dodging crew members running to their stations, trying to keep a steady, if not a stately pace. Warship captains never ran.

A charged atmosphere of repressed excitement greeted her the moment she stepped through the doorway. *Iolanthe*'s combat systems officer, Lieutenant Commander Thorin Sirico, rose from the command chair and stepped aside.

"We picked up three simultaneous emergence signatures one and a half million kilometers aft," he said. "Preliminary analysis of their power curve makes them Ptar-class with ninety percent confidence. They're on a direct pursuit course."

Siobhan took the throne-like seat and studied the three-dimensional schematic at the center of the CIC showing their immediate surroundings out to one light minute. She touched a control surface on the arm of her chair and rotated the image, examining the intruders' projected course from every side.

"It's them, Thorin," she said after almost a minute of silent contemplation. "They're maintaining the standard Shrehari echelon formation."

"It took them long enough to notice us," Sirico replied with a fierce grin that lit up his dark, ascetic face.

One of the petty officers of the watch raised his hand to attract her attention. "Captain, the first officer confirms we're at full battle stations. He has the bridge."

"Excellent," she replied, touching the chair's control surface again. The miniature holographic image of a slender, blond, one-eyed man with a patch over the other eye shimmered into existence by her right elbow. "How long did it take, Zeke?"

"Four minutes," Commander Ezekiel Holt replied. "We shaved ten seconds off the earlier record. Not bad for a bunch of scruffy wannabe privateers."

"Who still remember they're in the Navy."

"Combat systems are active," Sirico reported from his station to Dunmoore's left. "Standing by to retract covers."

"Not too early," she warned. "I don't want to spook the buggers."

Dunmoore still felt a vague unease at commanding her ship in battle from the CIC while her first officer sat on the bridge. Her previous ships had been too small, or in the case of *Stingray*, too old for separate command nodes. However, in *Iolanthe*, mostly thanks to the automated systems that allowed the Q-ship to sail with a frigate-sized crew, it made sense to separate control of the fighting from that of the systems needed to keep her in the fight. Here she could focus her full attention on destroying the enemy while Holt dealt with everything else.

"I'm picking up faint sensor pings," the combat systems chief said. "They've locked on, but aren't targeting us yet."

"Do you want my ship," Dunmoore murmured, running a gloved finger along the scar on her jawline, "or do you want to create wreckage?"

Iolanthe seemed harmless enough that she might tempt the commander of the Shrehari flotilla into a boarding operation, which would bring his ships within point-blank range. Bringing home a captured freighter would not only mean a bounty for him but a measure of fame. After years of war, seizures had become increasingly rare, and transport ships a valuable commodity.

"I suppose we'll know if he comes within missile range and doesn't fire," Sirico said, having heard her musing in the stillness of the CIC.

"That we will." She gave him a quick smile. One thing she missed most about *Stingray* was the atmosphere on her bridge when going into battle, not in small part because of the banter, especially that between her former first officer, Gregor Pushkin and her coxswain, Chief Petty Officer First Class Guthren. Pushkin now commanded his own frigate, *Jan Sobieski*, while Guthren sat at *Iolanthe*'s helm under Holt's eyes, having transferred over to the Q-ship with her.

She enjoyed the calm professionalism of her CIC crew, but they were a different bunch. Sirico was pleasant enough, even if his mustache and goatee gave him a piratical air, while the sensor chief, Marti Yens, had turned out to be a woman of few words.

She stared at the schematic, willing her opponent to show his hand. If he intended to take *Iolanthe*, Dunmoore would let him come almost within visual range before unmasking. However, if his plan was to destroy what he thought was a freighter, he would open fire from much further out, forcing her to unmask on his schedule and not hers. The soft whispers of conversation in the CIC and the sounds of a warship ready for battle barely reached her ears. Her new command did not just have a quieter, less rambunctious crew; it also did not generate the background noise only an ancient ship, rebuilt once too often, could muster.

Then, the three icons representing the Shrehari corvettes changed position relative to each other, transforming the echelon formation into an inverted arrowhead. Her opposite number had decided what he would do. He would attempt to board.

"Looks like we'll soon hear a summons to heave-to," Sirico said, confirming her thoughts. "He's come close enough to read our fake emissions and conclude we're nowhere ready to jump out yet."

"It's a mistake he won't make again," Chief Yens said in a low growl.

"Let's not sin through overconfidence," Dunmoore replied. "Their commander could be smart enough to smell a rat and abort. We're not the only ones who've learned over the last few years."

Yens, a compact, middle-aged woman with a hatchet face and dark almond eyes beneath a mop of jet-black hair nodded. "True enough, sir. Yet I have the premonition that his one's had his last bit of schooling, and I'm rarely wrong."

"From your lips to God's ear," Sirico grinned at his chief.

The minutes ticked by as the three Shrehari corvettes closed the distance, passing optimum missile range while the strength of their sensor signal grew. Then, one of the sensor techs seated in front of Yens raised his hand. "They've switched to targeting sensors."

"Any signs they're about to fire?"

"Negative."

Sirico scrutinized his screen, then said, "At this distance, they figure we'll pick up their weapons lock with our civilian gear and panic."

As if on cue, the signals tech called out, "Incoming message from the Shrehari, sir. Text only, in Anglic.

Prepare to be boarded. If you resist or try to escape, you will be destroyed without mercy or hope. If you cooperate, you will be treated honorably as prisoners of war and live to return home one day."

"A rather wordy message," Sirico said. "I've always figured the boneheads to be more concise in an 'obey or die' fashion."

"If we were a genuine merchant crew, we might be inclined to surrender and save them the trouble," Dunmoore replied. "As I mentioned earlier, they are learning. Respond, via text, that we will obey." Turning to the holographic Holt, she said, "I trust you heard that, Zeke. Shut down the reactor spoofing, so it'll seem like we've aborted the hyperdrive spool up."

"Consider it done," the first officer replied, nodding.

"Now, we pretend we're nothing more than a clapped-out behemoth with the firepower of an aviso and none of its speed."

The signals tech raised his hand again. "We've been ordered to maintain our current course and velocity, and we've been warned that at the first sign of weapons powering up, we'll be destroyed. Further instructions concerning the boarding party will follow in due course."

A cruel smile tugged at the corners of Dunmoore's mouth. "Step into my lair, said the spider to the fly."

Though she missed *Stingray* and her crew, commanding a Q-ship was turning out to be even more of a joy than command of the frigate had been. She enjoyed wielding the element of surprise more than anything else, and with *Iolanthe,* she could make it fatal in a matter of moments.

"Two of them are decelerating," Yens reported. "Maybe the enemy commander has a pricking in his thumbs."

"He's playing it safe," Dunmoore said. "They'll only need one to provide a boarding party. The others are keeping their distance just in case something goes wrong, such as *Iolanthe* self-destructing or should a Navy ship show up unannounced."

"When do you intend to go 'up weapons,' Captain?" Holt's tiny hologram asked.

"Soon. I want the one designated to board us as close as possible but still far enough so we remain beyond the danger zone if his reactor core has an explosive failure."

"I'm glad to hear it," the first officer replied with a chuckle. "For a moment, I had visions of our gunners firing over open sights. If we had manned gun turrets that is."

"Too old-fashioned, Zeke. I would rather my combat systems team fire over close circuits. We achieve more first round hits that way."

"Sir," Chief Yens said, "the two ships that decelerated have now matched our velocity. They're keeping a steady distance, though it's still well within our missile and gun envelope."

"In theirs as well," Dunmoore replied, "but we hold the upper hand. How's our optimist doing?"

"If by optimist you mean the ship detailed to take us into custody, he's approaching point-blank range."

Dunmoore dialed up the three-dimensional schematic's resolution. Sirico had overlain a Ptar-class corvette's self-destruct danger sphere. The ship was still at a sufficient distance, but closing fast.

"Do we have a tentative firing solution?" She asked, knowing until *Iolanthe* went live, her targeting sensors would not be able to reach out and lock on.

"As good as we can make it, sir," Sirico replied. "We'll need twenty seconds after 'guns up' to confirm the lead ship, thirty for the others, based on range and velocity."

Siobhan let her instincts reach out, eyes still on the icons floating in the holo-projection. Chief Yens' voice snapped her back to the CIC. "The lead ship is decelerating at a greater rate than necessary to come alongside. I think he's decided that something wicked this way comes."

"Close enough. Up systems, ID signal on," Dunmoore ordered, "up guns and get me a firing solution on the three in equal measure. I think the chief is right. They've made us."

Almost instantaneously, a series of low rumbling sounds permeated the Q-ship, signaling that the camouflage plates hiding the massive plasma gun turrets and the gaping maws of the missile launchers were sliding aside. At the same time, Dunmoore felt an almost palpable electric aura permeate *Iolanthe* as her energy shields snapped into place. No longer the lumbering, superannuated freighter, her ship had now revealed itself as a high-powered killer. She tried to imagine the surprise felt by her Shrehari opponents and failed. The inability to adapt fast enough to changing circumstances was not only a human failing.

In the days of ocean-going navies, she would have run up her true colors. Here, in interstellar space, she had to settle for activating her naval transponder, identifying *Iolanthe* as a Commonwealth warship.

"Shields up," Sirico reported, "ID on transmit and targeting sensors locked on. Ready to engage."

"Fire missiles."

Iolanthe had four launcher bays, two per side, each of four tubes fed by automatic loaders. The first salvo, from the port bays, sent eight birds at the rearmost corvettes while the starboard launchers shot their ready loads at the closest ship. Within moments, the loaders cycled through, filling the tubes with a fresh salvo. Lieutenant Commander Sirico glanced at Dunmoore, expecting the signal to send another brace at the enemy. She held up her hand, enjoining him to wait, while her eyes tracked the missiles' path in the holo-tank.

"Enemy has opened defensive fire," Yens said, "and I'm getting a lot of coded chatter on their frequencies. The lead ship is altering course." Then, "The enemy has fired missiles. Four birds per ship for a total of twelve."

"Second salvo, Mister Sirico, if you please," Dunmoore said. "Stand by with the guns."

The closest Ptar fired at the oncoming missiles with everything it had. One exploded in a flash of light, then another, but the third and fourth evaded the continuous stream of plasma erupting from the Shrehari calliopes. Even before seeing if any of them would strike the enemy's shields and either weaken or collapse them, Dunmoore ordered the main guns to engage. The enemy commander was not the only one to feel a pricking in his thumbs.

Iolanthe's close-in defense guns opened fire first, laying a curtain of plasma across the Shrehari missiles' path. Then the Q-ship's main turrets, designed so they could turn all the way aft, spat out heavier streams to take advantage of a missile's direct strike on the Ptar's shields. Seconds later, one exploded at point-blank, creating a power surge that sent a bluish green aurora dancing around the corvette, weakening its defenses.

The first large-bore plasma blobs hit seconds later, sending a howling feedback through the unfortunate starship's circuits. That strike failed to overload them, but the second and subsequent ones ate away at the bow shield until it collapsed, its generators overwhelmed by the Q-ship's massive firepower. A further salvo splashed against the pristine hull, digging divots into the hardened metal until it failed in one spot, allowing the next burst from *Iolanthe*'s main guns to wreak havoc on the corvette's interior. The Q-ship had the guns of a battle cruiser and the Shrehari never stood a chance.

The other two corvettes, mere spectators so far, now faced their own existential crisis. Each had a brace of

Mark Thirty anti-ship missiles aimed at it, every bird backed by a gun turret ready to exploit a weakened shield. While they fought off the initial assault, the first Ptar to suffer *Iolanthe*'s wrath broke apart — not in a spectacular fashion but by bits and pieces, leaving a widening trail of wreckage in its wake. The flash of a miniature sun put an end to the disintegration when its antimatter containment failed.

"One down," Sirico said, smiling with glee.

"We'll have a second kill at any moment," Yens replied, "I make two hits on the one to starboard." A moment later, she continued, "Forward shield failure; she's toast."

The Q-ship's own defensive guns opened up just then, swatting aside the less capable Shrehari missiles, but her main plasma cannons never ceased firing, hammering weakened shields before eating through armored hulls once the former collapsed. Corvette number two vanished in a blaze of fury and then *Iolanthe* gave the third one its deathblow.

Silence descended on the CIC as realization set in that they had destroyed three starships, killing hundreds of Shrehari spacers.

"Did they send a final message?" Dunmoore asked, breaking the spell.

After a few heartbeats, the signals petty officer shook his head. "I didn't pick up a transmission on any of their known frequencies, captain."

A sigh of relief escaped her lungs. "Good. It wouldn't do for the enemy to figure out that some harmless-looking freighters aren't actually prey. Secure from battle stations and turn her back into an honest civilian transport. Department heads to the conference room for the after-action review in one hour. Resume cruising stations."

"What about our report to HQ?" Holt asked.

"Send the following, along with our coordinates — engaged three Ptar-class corvettes; destroyed same." She climbed to her feet and gave Sirico a wan smile, feeling tired now that the adrenaline rush of battle faded away. "You have the CIC. I'll be in my day cabin."

— Two —

The shipwrights had wedged Dunmoore's day cabin between the bridge and the conference room, with a private door to each, though wedged was a relative term. It would put more than one admiral's office to shame and made her ready room aboard *Stingray* seem like a linen closet. She had placed the old ship's clock with the silhouette of a gaunt knight on its face, and the leather bound tome that inspired the drawing, in this compartment rather than her sleeping cabin. Both items and her other antiques seemed to fit this space as if it had been designed for them.

She tapped her ever full coffee urn and filled a mug with *Iolanthe*'s crest on its side. The emblem, a winged woman brandishing a blazing sword seemed far removed from the mythical fairy that had inspired the name. However, few would know about the actual *Iolanthe* story and even less recognize that the Fleet, in a fit of remarkable whimsy, had named all Q-ships after ancient comic operettas, stories in which things were never as they seemed. Whimsical, but fitting, in her opinion. Smiling as she sat behind her desk, Dunmoore wondered how the captain of *Pinafore* felt about his ship's name.

Almost exactly fifteen minutes later, her door chime sounded, announcing that Ezekiel Holt had finished placing the ship at cruising stations, held his own after-action review with the bridge crew and was now ready to share his views on the engagement, ahead of the meeting with all department heads.

"Come."

The gray panel slid aside with a soft sigh, admitting a tall, one-eyed man who still walked with a faint limp, courtesy of a regenerated leg that had replaced the prosthetic he had worn since losing the original in action years earlier when he had served as Dunmoore's first officer aboard the corvette *Shenzen*. He would receive a regenerated eye, to replace the one lost along with his leg in due course, but since it would mean almost a year in an undemanding shore posting while the war still raged, he preferred to style himself a pirate aboard a ship one step up from a privateer.

After helping himself to coffee in a mug with the furious fairy emblem, he dropped into a chair facing Siobhan. "That was interesting," he said, raising the cup in salute before taking a sip.

"How so?"

"Without pre-judging, I'd suggest something gave us away at the last moment. Fortunately, or if you were the Shrehari commander, unfortunately, it was a few minutes too late."

Dunmoore nodded. "That's what I thought. Chief Yens called it before I did."

"A touch of the second sight, that one," Holt replied with a crooked smile. "It's just as well she's working combat systems, where she can supplement the sensors with her intuition."

"I'll wait until the after-action review to decide, but I think we might want to send Chief Yens and someone from the engineering department, perhaps Renny himself out in a shuttle to take a new baseline reading on our 'covert' emissions signature." Lieutenant Commander Renny Halfen, *Iolanthe*'s chief engineer, took great pride in his ability to make the Q-ship seem inoffensive to all who scanned her until that is, she became a raider's worst nightmare at Dunmoore's orders. He would take any revealing leaks personally. "Mind you, the Shrehari commander might simply have felt, as Yens put it, a pricking in his thumbs without enjoying the privilege of a combat systems wizard on his bridge, unlike me."

"Is there such a thing as intuition in the Shrehari psyche?" Holt asked.

"Perhaps. I've told you about Brakal. It wouldn't surprise me if he had their version of second sight. Thank God there's only one of him. Otherwise, we might be looking at the shitty end of the stick."

Holt raised his mug again. "Here's to boneheadedness. The Deep Space Fleet can strike three more corvettes off their order of battle without ever knowing how they disappeared. I'd like to see your Brakal suss that one out."

"Hopefully their loss will have the Shrehari admirals rethink this latest obsession with deep raids, but I won't hold my breath. They adapt all too slowly."

"We should be thankful. It's a double-edged sword." Another sip, then the first officer asked, "When do you think you'd like to take a break from patrolling and top up our stores? After today, we have little more than half of our missile stocks left, and the fresh food is down to a quarter."

"With that Ptar flotilla gone, I suppose we can head for the Sigma Noctae Depot any time we want. Shame we don't qualify for replenishment underway." Though she tried to sound indifferent, it failed to fool her first officer.

"Not keen on revisiting the scene of what almost turned into a disaster, both for you and the Fleet?" A mischievous smile creased Holt's face.

"Some memories are best left untouched." She shrugged. "Unfortunately, it's the closest naval supply point, so my tender sensibilities will have to take a back seat to practicality. We can't afford a long trip to the Sigma Draconis depot, and I'm not even thinking of what the Admiralty might say about my sanity if I head inward, wasting time and fuel."

"The depot staff will have changed, never mind that many of the culprits are still rotting in the stockade."

"But not the people behind the embezzlement scheme. Most of them escaped punishment. They'll have no reason to remember me with any fondness."

Holt grinned at her. "Yet once we're in orbit, you'll hold the power to obliterate all human life on Toboso in the palm of your hand. She who can destroy a thing at will commands its destiny."

Dunmoore cocked an eyebrow at him. "Please, Zeke, you think I'd use the threat of *Iolanthe*'s firepower to get my way with the folks controlling the colony's destiny?"

"In a nanosecond."

"Not even in an eon," she replied with a dismissive shake of the head. "Your time in counter-intelligence has turned you into an unredeemable cynic."

"Merely into a realist. All of us are venal to some extent. Only the ones who resist temptation might save humanity from its fate. Sadly, there's all too few of them, when weighed against the bovine masses or even against that segment of society dedicated to seizing power at any cost."

"You'll find that Toboso has its own, scaled down version of that latter group and they're not impressed by a naval uniform."

"After what you did to their nastier elements, I wouldn't be so sure about that."

"They've had a few years to forget, Zeke. Human nature being what it is... Yet we have little choice in the matter."

She touched the comlink embedded in her desk. "Bridge, this is the captain."

"Officer of the watch here, sir," a feminine voice replied a second later. Just the person Siobhan wanted – her sailing master, Lieutenant Astrid Drost.

"Plot a course to Cervantes. We're paying the Sigma Noctae Depot a visit."

"Aye, aye, sir. Any idea of when you'd like to go FTL?"

"As soon as we're ready. There's no point in hanging around this place, watching Shrehari corvette debris spin out in an ever widening cloud."

Holt raised a finger to catch Siobhan's attention. "What about the emissions check?"

"We'll do it after the first jump. Yan and the engineers can use our time in FTL to check for anything else that might have betrayed us."

The first officer nodded. "Fair enough."

Dunmoore turned her attention back to the comlink. "Astrid, once all departments have reported ready and you're satisfied with the astrogation, you may call the ship to jump stations and execute."

Iolanthe's officers had proved to be a cut above the average, not unexpected aboard a special operations man-of-war, and needed a lot less prodding and hand-holding than most of her previous crews, though *Stingray*'s complement had almost much reached that level near the end. Dunmoore knew Drost would have her junior, Rin Pashar, work out the numbers, so she could be the second set of eyes checking the results, rather than kicking the proposed course up to the first officer or the captain for approval. A crew with a high level of initiative and experience to spare left her with less to do on a daily basis, but after eight years of fighting the Shrehari Empire and sundry star lane scum, she did not mind.

A quarter of an hour later, the call to jump stations echoed through the Q-ship, followed by the usual one-minute warning klaxon. Then, Dunmoore's universe twisted sideways as FTL nausea threatened to expel her guts through clenched nostrils.

— Three —

The moment of silence following *Iolanthe*'s emergence at the edge of the Cervantes system dissolved as the crew recovered its senses following the shift between hyperspace and their own universe. Status reports flowed to Dunmoore's command chair display as the duty watch probed space in an ever-expanding sphere, searching for threats, both natural and sentient. The debris of the Shrehari flotilla lay many light years and many days behind them.

While reading the messages pushed to her bridge console, she heard a male voice behind her mutter, "That's strange. Where are you, my pretty?"

Turning the command chair to face Lieutenant Theo Kremm, her information systems officer, Siobhan cocked a questioning eyebrow, waiting for him to elaborate. His first duty upon emerging was to set up an encrypted link with the system's subspace relay buoy and use it to warn Sigma Noctae they were inbound, attaching a list of needed supplies to the message.

"The relay's gone absent without authority, sir," he said. "I'm not picking up its carrier wave."

"Is it in lockdown?" She asked. Buoys sometimes slipped into stealth mode if their AIs sensed a hostile presence within detection range, or if human controllers had ordered them to go silent for that or any other reason.

"That's what I first thought, so I ran a visual. The charts say we should be within half an AU of its current position, close enough for the sensors to pick it up, but that area of space is empty. I've sent out a coded query on the emergency subspace channel, ordering it to respond, but got nothing more than static in return. We're around four light minutes away, so it'll be another five minutes before we can get a reply to my query via conventional radio."

Hostile forces sometimes destroyed subspace relays, if they could find them, to cut a system off from the rest of the Commonwealth. However, Cervantes was far from the war zone and had little to commend it as a target for Shrehari raiders when there were more strategically vital systems closer to their own forward operating bases. Marauders, most little better than opportunistic pirates, seldom had the ability or even the inclination to hunt down, let alone destroy relay buoys that did not want to be found. Why risk damage from its automatic guns and trigger an alert that would warn everyone with a working subspace receiver within a parsec when your most useful asset is the element of surprise.

Dunmoore's eyes narrowed as she contemplated the ramifications of Kremm's news. There had been no reports of marauders in this sector, let alone Shrehari raiders – *Iolanthe* had taken care of those who had penetrated the furthest into human space almost a week earlier.

"Are you getting anything from Toboso itself?"

Kremm shook his head. "Negative, but that wouldn't be unusual. The newer setups use tight-beam technology to connect the orbital transmitter with the outer system relay to avoid signal spillage, and it's not beyond the realm of possibility that Toboso's comm facilities received the upgrade already thanks to the presence of a Fleet depot. Do you want me to try pinging their orbital?"

Dunmoore hesitated, and then said, "No. Not yet. If things are off kilter around here, it's best we don't advertise our presence until we know more."

"Are you having one of your gut feelings, Captain?" Ezekiel Holt asked.

"Yes and no." Her lips twisted into a brief grimace. "Keep in mind that my time as Sigma Noctae's deputy commanding officer has left me with less than fond memories of this system, and that's bound to affect my perception. I can think of many legitimate explanations for the relay's failure to respond. However, one of the things I've learned over the years is why take chances when there's no extra effort involved in being cautious."

Holt chuckled. "I never figured I'd live to see the day when Siobhan Dunmoore used the term cautious when speaking of her actions."

She gave him a pained smile, all too conscious that his injuries stemmed from a lack of caution when Dunmoore drove the corvette *Shenzen*, with one Ezekiel Holt at her side as first officer, to ruin under a Shrehari flotilla's guns. Her expression only increased Holt's mirth. Where Gregor Pushkin, her number one aboard *Stingray*, had been guarded, if not taciturn, Holt was a fount of good humor and held not so much as a shred of resentment at her condemning him to years ashore and many painful rounds of regeneration. In fact, at the court-martial for *Shenzen*'s loss, he had testified on her behalf, endorsing all of her decisions, including the one that had sent the corvette to its doom.

"Cautious it is," he said after regaining a modicum of seriousness. "I assume we're keeping up the false flag until we're in contact with the depot?"

"We are. Until we've established the lay of the land, we're a big, fat, and dumb freighter."

"Aye, aye, Captain," Holt replied with a twinkle in his single eye, "setting *Iolanthe* to big, fat and dumb."

"As soon as Mister Kremm has confirmed that the subspace relay isn't responding to a radio query either, we can head in-system."

"Course laid in for a jump to the hyperlimit," Astrid Drost confirmed.

"Thank you." Dunmoore touched her screen, calling up the CIC. "Anything of interest?" She asked when Sirico's foreshortened holographic image appeared above her command chair's arm.

"Strangely, no. We're not picking up any traffic, not even around Toboso, though they might be experiencing a lull. The register shows no off-planet installations in this system, other than the automated fueling station, and it's not a shipping hub."

"How is the fueling station?"

"It's still where it should be, in orbit around the inner gas giant, Benengeli. We have a lock on the beacon, and it's telling us all is well. I'm not seeing any customers."

"Hmm..." Dunmoore, in an unconscious gesture that her new crew now recognized as showing deep reflection, ran a gloved finger over the scar running along her jawline, a souvenir of a battle gone wrong. The gloves themselves hid another souvenir, reactor coolant burns suffered when the cruiser *Sala-Ad-Din*, in which she served as second officer and thus responsible for damage control, took the full brunt of a Shrehari broadside. "What's that thing they say in those corny stories that seem to clutter up the entertainment services?"

"It's quiet — too quiet?" Holt suggested.

"No, wrong cliché, but it'll do."

"You maybe thought you had a bad feeling about this?" Chief Guthren offered over a hunched shoulder, his eyes on the navigation plot, preparing to helm *Iolanthe* deeper into the Cervantes system.

Dunmoore snapped her fingers and pointed at the coxswain. "That's the one."

"I prefer mine," Holt replied, smiling. "It's less theatrical."

Guthren snorted. "No arguments here. Besides, everything we're seeing, or not seeing, as the case may be, might have a reasonable explanation. Paranoia's an ugly thing."

"But it saves lives," Sirico's tiny hologram said. "If your instincts are bugging you, Captain, we can put the ship at battle stations without unmasking before our emergence at the hyperlimit."

Siobhan glanced at Holt who, after a moment of reflection, nodded. "Concur with Thorin's suggestion. If nothing else, a little drill to drive away the last of our FTL daze wouldn't hurt."

"In that case, make it so. Set us at battle stations ten minutes out."

Several minutes ticked by in silence as the bridge crew prepared for the final micro jump that would take the Q-ship as close to their destination as the star's gravity allowed. Finally, Lieutenant Kremm slumped back in his chair and sighed. "Nothing from the relay on the regular radio frequencies either, Captain. It either vanished into an alternate dimension, a rogue wormhole sent it ten thousand years into the past, or it suffered a fatal incident that left no trace we can find from our current position."

Dunmoore repressed a smile at Kremm's quip about wormhole time travel, something he and most of humanity, except for the former crew of a now decommissioned frigate, believed to be an unproven theory advanced by a few of the more adventurous astrophysicists over the centuries. The data *Stingray* had carried back concerning a human society that had established itself on a distant world two thousand years before the first spaceflight, thanks to a rogue wormhole throwing their ancestors' colony ship back in time, had vanished into the memory hole.

"How about a detour to check?" Holt suggested. "In the interests of paranoia."

"No. If something happened to it, we're more likely to find answers on Toboso. Set the ship at jump stations if you please."

*

"I think we can cancel battle stations," Dunmoore said after almost half an hour spent scanning the inner system once they had dropped out of hyperspace within a day's travel from Toboso at maximum sublight speed. "This time I'll wholeheartedly agree with the first officer. It's too damn quiet."

"At least the orbitals are still there." Holt pointed out. "I'd have been far more worried if they had vanished into the same rogue wormhole as the subspace relay."

"Perhaps, but I'm still not getting a response from the communications platform," Kremm said. "It may still be spinning around Toboso and its own axis for all we know, but refusing to acknowledge my attempts at establishing a link, whether I try subspace, radio, or laser. That's worrisome enough, I'd say, sir. At this point, the only thing left is a general broadcast to announce our arrival and hope that someone will pick up the communication."

Dunmoore shook her head. "Not until we're in orbit, although if someone reaches out, we'll reply. Stand her down, Mister Holt."

Moments later, an announcement echoed through the ship, sending its crew back to cruising stations, although the sensor watch in the CIC would maintain full vigilance and continue to probe the system for anything unusual.

She stood, tugging her battledress tunic down and repressed the urge to stretch like a cat. "I'll be in my day cabin. Officer of the watch, the bridge is yours."

Kremm jumped to his feet and came to attention. "I relieve you, sir."

"I stand relieved." She caught Holt's eye. "Coffee, Number One?"

"A quick one, sir. I've promised our chief engineer a moment of my time to discuss the new shielding ideas he's had."

Once ensconced in the privacy of the captain's office, Dunmoore, after taking a sip of the fresh hot brew, sighed. "Admittedly, it's been a few years since I last graced this system with my presence, and the appointment as second in command proved to be short, but I don't recall a near total absence of orbital and supra-orbital activity, not to mention the silence. Sigma Noctae has an operations center linked to the geosynchronous communications platform, which also serves as one of the long-range warning satellites. If the duty shift isn't passed out drunk on the deck, they'll have seen us by now. God knows *Iolanthe* has a big enough emergence signature."

"Does that happen often?" Holt asked with a feigned air of innocence.

"Does what happen often?"

"The operations duty shift passed out drunk?"

Dunmoore's lips twisted with revulsion. "The state of the place when I took up my billet would have appalled you. Alcohol abuse while on duty was only one of the many dysfunctions enabled by the late and unlamented commanding officer. It helped make sure he had a free hand with his many criminal dealings. Unfortunately, it also made the depot vulnerable to attack, which eventually happened."

A spark of understanding lit up Holt's single eye. "And you're afraid history might have repeated itself, but without a Siobhan Dunmoore to pull off a surprise turnaround."

She tapped the side of her nose with a finger. "Exactly. My memories of that time are coloring my instincts right now, and that's not something I'm keen to share in public — at least not without evidence."

"I thought you gave the place a thorough cleaning out."

"The Depot, yes. The colonial administration and those colonists who were making hay off the Navy's back, not so much. A few of them joined the CO in an early grave, but most escaped the consequences of their perfidy. By the time investigators showed up, they'd reformed ranks, and I was on my way out. They're still on Toboso, or at least I assume many of them are, in particular the colonists. I'm sure the governor at the time and her staff rotated out long ago."

"No wonder someone buried the real story so deep even I wasn't able to find your report during my time with counter-intelligence."

"Oh, it gets better, Zeke. I'm not supposed to talk about it, but later, when I'm not fretting as much, I'll tell you the entire story."

"Fretting?" He gave her an alarmed look. "First caution and now anxiety. The war hasn't been generous with you."

"It isn't really the war's fault. I used to think I had to hide my deepest thoughts and fears even from my first officer. I know better now."

Holt contemplated her for a few heartbeats, and then asked, "Pushkin?"

"Yup." She nodded before taking another sip. "He figures he learned much from me. What he doesn't know is that I learned valuable lessons from him as well."

"Perhaps he does." Holt raised his mug in salute. "I misjudged Gregor Pushkin back then, so count me as someone else who learned a lesson from him."

"I wonder how he's doing. We've not heard news of Jan Sobieski's exploits since he took command."

"That's a good thing," he replied. "Fleet gossip is amazingly swift and vicious when a starship captain screws up, but we have to wait for an official communique to learn of victorious battle runs."

Dunmoore snorted. "I suppose the good thing about being captain of a special operations vessel means that my screw ups won't become gossip quite so fast."

"Considering you're one of the few in this war who brought a ship home and decommissioned it with all due ceremony after racking up a solid combat record, I wouldn't worry." He drained his mug. "Now if you'll excuse me, Renny's waiting, and I'd rather get this over with before we enter Toboso orbit. Replenishment, especially from a dirtside depot, turns cheerful first officers into unpleasant grumps, and that doesn't much help the relationship between bridge and engineering."

*

The intercom's soft chime yanked Dunmoore out of the intense story of one of the Second Migration War's most infamous battles. Having wrapped up any ship's business that still awaited her attention, and with nothing else to do but fret, something best done in the privacy of her day cabin, she had plunged head first into her on and off study of humanity's dark history. Compared to the billions who had died in that most murderous of civil wars a century earlier, the fate of a small colony world such as Toboso seemed almost risible. Yet the inexplicable radio silence permeating the Cervantes system felt ominous enough to prevent Dunmoore from napping, let alone withdrawing to her quarters.

She placed her tablet on the bare desk and touched the comm screen. "Dunmoore."

"Chief Yens, sir, in CIC. We've entered visual range and are getting images of the surface."

"Pipe them up to my day cabin, Chief."

"I think you'll want to see this on the main screen." Yens' inflection sounded matter of fact, but it conveyed an undertone that caught Dunmoore's attention more than her words.

"On my way."

The sensor chief must have called her department head right after Dunmoore because Sirico, off duty at this hour, entered the CIC on his captain's heels. Both came to a sudden stop when their eyes took in the grainy image projected on the large tactical display.

"Oh, my," the combat systems officer whispered. "I guess now we know why Sigma Noctae wasn't answering our hails."

"Aye." Yens nodded. "It's no longer there."

— Four —

Little remained of the naval installation at the base of an imposing cliff. Where once there had been an extended runway big enough to accommodate the largest landers, a circle of defensive ordnance emplacements and a cluster of aboveground buildings for operations and crew quarters, nothing remained but a series of craters. Only the part of the landing strip closest to the underground warehouse's massive doors remained intact, though Dunmoore had no doubt they would find the entrance to the cavernous underground facility blown wide open and most of the valuable ammunition, food and spare parts gone. This time, someone had managed to carry out a successful raid.

"Sir." Chief Yens' voice intruded on her thoughts.

"Yes?"

"I'd like to show you a picture of Doniphon."

Her gut clenched at hearing the name of Toboso's capital, a few kilometers south of Sigma Noctae. Yens would not have brought it up unless...

"Go ahead."

The grainy image of the ruined depot faded, replaced with an equally rough one of a small town on the banks of a slow-moving river. It had sprouted a small cluster of craters at its center.

"They took out the colonial government complex as well," Dunmoore said in a flat voice after her memory had dredged up a mental map of Doniphon. "What about the other nearby communities, specifically Stoddard, Valance, and Duke?"

"No craters, but that doesn't mean they didn't also suffer an attack. We're still too far out for any sort of detailed images. The remaining settlements on Toboso aren't in visual range right now."

Dunmoore's eyes shifted to a side screen where, among other navigation data, a display of their time to orbit showed the minutes ticking backward. The laws of physics being what they were, she would have to stifle her impatience for a few more hours, but that did not mean they could not prepare. She reached out to the comm screen embedded in the command chair's arm.

"First and second officers to the CIC."

While she waited, Dunmoore fought to suppress the urge to look over Yens' shoulder. The chief would have seen this as the lack of patience it signaled, and might even take it as a sign the captain thought Yens could not do her job. When new data came in, Dunmoore would be the first to hear. Lieutenant Commander Emma Cullop, a slim, prematurely gray woman in her late thirties showed up first. Like so many in the expanded wartime Navy, she was a former merchant officer who joined up days after the outbreak of hostilities, along with most of her old ship's crew, and had proved invaluable in helping Dunmoore and the others maintain the Q-ship's cover identity when in port.

She studied the image of the depot once more and whistled. "Someone did a real number on the place. I doubt it was an ordinary marauder raid. I suppose we're still too far out to know if there are any survivors."

"Aye," Yens said, nodding.

"They hit the government buildings in town as well," Sirico said.

"Who hit what?" Holt's voice asked from the threshold as he entered the CIC. Then, he too assimilated the overhead view of Sigma Noctae. "Wow. Your gut feeling was right on the mark, Captain. Things aren't just off kilter — things aren't anymore, period. Kinetic strikes from high altitude or low orbit?"

The combat systems officer nodded. "That's what I'd say. Cheap and nasty if you don't mind risking collateral damage."

"Except these strikes look precise," Dunmoore said, "in particular the ones that took out the five government buildings at the heart of Doniphon without damaging the structures bordering them."

"As far as we know," Sirico replied.

One corner of Siobhan's mouth went up in a half-smile that acknowledged the point. "As far as we know. The landing party will give us a full report, which brings me to my next point."

"You wish me to form a landing party and head for the surface the moment we're within range," Cullop said in her precise, clipped tone. "I want to take two shuttles with the landing party armed and armored. Did you wish me to bring the surgeon and a detachment of medics as well?"

Dunmoore glanced at Holt who shook his head, then said, "Take a physician's assistant and one medic. If the situation warrants Lieutenant Polter's skills, we'll either send him down with more folks or bring any casualties up. I dare say *Iolanthe*'s surgical suite beats anything the colonists have, especially since I seem to recall that the Doniphon clinic was in one of the government buildings replaced by a gaping crater."

"What about our flag?" Holt asked. "If Emma goes down with full naval accouterments, we might as well put on our big, fat, and dumb Navy transport identity. The folks planetside might find it strange for the crew of a civilian freighter to come in hot."

"Agreed. Activate the appropriate transponder and have the crew put on their uniforms. It looks like we're rejoining the Service for the duration of our stay around Toboso."

Holt leaned over and said, in a low voice, "I trust you're not thinking about heading down until Emma's declared the area secure."

A burst of ironic laughter escaped Dunmoore throat. "No worries. I received an earful from your predecessor after the last time I put myself in a bad situation without adequate reconnaissance. Considering he had to send Guthren at the head of a raiding party to retrieve us under enemy fire, the guilt trip he laid on me afterward has left a permanent scar."

"Ah yes, the mission of which no one can ever speak." Holt winked at her. "Anything else, Captain?"

"As a matter of fact, there is. We should think about how we'll relieve a humanitarian disaster down there. We can only see the largest wounds inflicted on the colony, and they appear to be concentrated on the centers of authority, but Emma's landing party could come face-to-face with a situation requiring every resource we still own."

"Of course." Holt's earlier roguish expression gave way to a more solemn one. "If there's nothing else, I'll have the purser figure out what we can spare, assuming our next replenishment is ten light years away and we don't want to become the latest version of the Flying Dutchman."

*

"Other than the depot and the government precinct in Doniphon, Toboso didn't suffer any visible damage, Captain," Chief Yens announced soon after *Iolanthe* entered orbit. "We're not picking up any signs that might show whoever raided the place is waiting for fresh meat, but this might interest you."

A live view of Sigma Noctae materialized on the main tactical screen, showing small figures moving around the ruins.

"Part of the garrison survived."

"Aye. Lord knows what they think they're guarding, bless them, but I'm referring to the emission readings on the craters. The heat signatures show that the strikes happened only a day or so before we dropped out of FTL on the system's outer rim. Bastards who did this got away under our damn noses, and no, I didn't find any trails leading away from Toboso. Their spoor has dissipated."

Dunmoore touched the intercom screen. "Bridge, Captain here, I assume you see the feed from the CIC. There appear to be survivors within the depot's perimeter. Try to open a communications link with them. Identify us by name and registration number as a Fleet unit, using the current transponder data."

"Acknowledged," the officer of the watch replied. "Stand by."

The minutes passed as Siobhan worked hard to keep her fingers from beating an impatient tattoo on her thigh. *Iolanthe* was braking to assume a geosynchronous orbit above the depot while on the hangar deck, Lieutenant Commander Cullop was completing the preparations for their flight to the surface.

One of the duty ratings raised his hand to attract her attention. "Sir, hangar deck reports that the landing party is ready to go."

She studied the tiny, ant-like figures among the ruins for a few moments, feeling her impatience at getting answers warring with caution. Impatience won out. "They may launch. If we can't open comms with the surface, they're to exercise extreme caution."

Moments later, another data stream appeared on one of the status boards, proof that the shuttles had left the Q-ship's embrace. They were as unmarked as their mothership, and though armed, they had a distinctly civilian appearance. Only their transponders identified them as naval units, though with the destruction of all aboveground facilities at Sigma Noctae, there would not be anyone listening for the beacons. She would have liked to link up in advance with what was no doubt a very jumpy bunch of survivors before two unidentified spacecraft crossed their gun sights, friendly fire being anything but welcoming. However, Cullop and her party would have to chance it. If the survivors had casualties requiring medical treatment, time would be of the essence.

Moments after *Iolanthe* assumed her orbital parking slot, the shuttles dipped into the atmosphere on a long, spiraling glide designed to shed both altitude and speed high above Toboso's equatorial ocean, before turning north towards their target, yet they still had no contact with the people on the ground. The tension in the CIC, though not at combat levels, was high. Then, the first images transmitted by the lead shuttle reached them.

"Those folks are wearing Fleet armor," Sirico said. "They're Commonwealth ground forces, either Army or Marines. There's no National Guard on Toboso."

Dunmoore nodded. "I'd say Army. By the time I left, they were planning to establish a garrison to help deter raiders who had more greed than sense."

"It doesn't appear to have worked." A pause, then the combat systems officer frowned. "Mind you, I don't know of any star lane scum who uses kinetic strikes from orbit, let alone manages this degree of precision."

"Indeed, Mister Sirico, and therein lies but one of the mysteries we're facing."

Before he could reply, the duty rating said, "The shuttles are on final approach to Sigma Noctae."

— Five —

Lieutenant Commander Emma Cullop, born to a spacefaring family aboard the sort of freighter *Iolanthe* pretended to be, though it had little more than a few small-bore guns for self-defense, had followed both her parents into the Merchant Guild, never expecting to spend a single day in a naval uniform. Then, war broke out, and the Navy requisitioned the ship in which she was serving as the third officer. Instead of looking for another berth in a commercial fleet shrinking by the day, Cullop joined up for the duration plus six months and received a direct commission as a lieutenant. To her surprise, she not only took to naval life with surprising ease but also discovered that she enjoyed the adrenaline rush of combat.

Leading a boarding or landing party into an ambiguous if not downright dangerous situation came a close second. However, that did not make her rash. Eight years of war spent aboard three different ships, including a narrow escape from her first one after the Shrehari ambushed and wrecked it, had taught her to distinguish between boldness and recklessness.

She nudged the petty officer at the shuttle's flight controls. "Take us over the runway at five hundred meters, nice and slow, then peel off towards the south for a one kilometer loop before approaching at a running pace while shedding altitude. We'll land as planned in front of the warehouse where our ground-pounding friends have set up camp. I think they'll understand we're not the enemy and hold fire."

"I hope your optimism isn't misplaced, sir," the pilot replied, grimacing. "In my experience, folks who've taken a beating are more trigger happy than usual."

"Cheer up, Purdy. I see no surviving aerospace defense ordnance, and small arms fire won't bring us crashing down in flames before we fly out of range."

"You hope."

"We both hope." She grinned at him. "Remember, my ass is sitting right next to yours."

Someone had spotted *Iolanthe*'s shuttles because the troops on the ground scattered to emergency fighting positions prepared after the unknown attackers had demolished the depot's permanent defenses with surgical precision. They came within plasma cannon range, but no one fired, bolstering Cullop's hopes that someone on the ground was keeping his or her cool. Helmeted heads stared up at them through blank visors as they wafted over the full length of the ruined runway while weapons, none larger than a twenty-millimeter squad support gun, tracked them. The shuttle's threat board showed several targeting sensors had locked on to them.

"Give them a waggle," Cullop said.

"Waggling, aye."

The pilot made their shuttle sway from side to side by firing the attitudinal thrusters. It was the closest thing to a friendly wave they could manage from five hundred meters up; then he banked to the right, aiming them at Doniphon's low skyline. The second spacecraft followed suit, still without a shot fired from the ground. They looped around, then came straight at the gaping hole in the cliff where massive doors had once protected the extensive underground warehouse, flying so slow and low they made perfect targets for anyone inclined to open fire. Once across the perimeter berm and over the edge of the tarmac, Cullop raised a hand and gave Petty Officer Purdy the signal to land. Both spacecraft settled side by side, the whine of their thrusters dying away in the breeze.

Cullop unfastened her safety harness and climbed to her feet. She motioned towards the rear of the shuttle. "Drop the ramp."

Then, she gestured at Chief Petty Officer Holger Henkman, *Iolanthe*'s gunnery chief, in charge of this half of her landing party. "Let's you and me say hi on our own. I prefer not to startle them with a bunch of armed naval yahoos erupting through the aft hatch." Turning back to the pilot she said, "Tell Lieutenant Pashar that he and his folks are to sit tight until I give the general disembarkation signal."

"Consider it done."

Chief Henkman held up a hand, preventing her from exiting the shuttle. "I suggest we take off our brain buckets, sir. If we want to come across as friendly visitors, maybe showing we're harmless gray-haired old squids will help."

"Good point." In an instant, both had removed their helmets and handed them to the nearest ratings. She grinned at the bosun's mate who took hers. "If I find something in there that didn't come from the top of my head…"

The rating smiled back. "If you think I would dare mess with an officer who controls my every waking moment aboard ship, sir, you're mistaken."

By the time Cullop and Henkman stepped out onto the tarmac, a cluster of armored troops, weapons at the ready, was approaching them.

"Let's let them come to us," she whispered at the chief, before stopping level with her shuttle's nose and assumed a loose version of the parade rest position, imitated by Henkman. Although the spacecraft carried no markings, their passengers wore naval rank insignia and name tapes on their chests. One of the approaching soldiers, with the three four-pointed stars of an Army captain on the chest, held up a hand. The others fell back while the officer kept on walking, raising her helmet visor to show a narrow female face, deeply creased by fatigue and worry. Her eyes met Cullop, and she came to attention.

"I'm Lieutenant Commander Emma Cullop, CSS *Iolanthe*, armed transport. This is Chief Petty Officer Henkman. We came to top up our larder, but perhaps we might have to top up yours."

The woman stopped a few paces from them, then gave them a twisted smile that oozed both relief and weariness. "Sir, you're a sight for sore eyes. Captain Tatiana Salminen, Company Group 31, Scandia Regiment, in command of what's left of Sigma Noctae."

"Although my skipper will have plenty of questions for you, Captain, do you have any casualties requiring medical care? I brought a physician's assistant and a medic with me, and we're equipped to evacuate those needing more than first aid to our sickbay."

"I'll gladly take whatever you have, sir. My own medics have barely been coping, and with Doniphon taking a hit, we've pretty much been on our own." The smile became a sad grimace. "Half of CG31 died in the attack, along with most of the depot's naval personnel, but we have over a dozen injured inside, mine and the Navy's." She jerked a thumb over her shoulder at the warehouse entrance.

Cullop glanced at Henkman, who nodded once, before jogging around the shuttle to order the landing party ashore. Salminen glanced back at her troops.

"Sarn't Major, they brought medical personnel. Take 'em to the first aid post." Turning to Cullop again, she said, "Since your CO is now the senior Fleet officer in the system, I guess you'd better put me in communication so I can deliver my report. We have ourselves a big mess. Toboso no longer has a colonial government and what's left of their leadership is in shock — at least those I've been able to contact. I don't know what happened to settlements on the continent's far side. The bastards who did this took out our long-range communication gear."

"Doniphon's government buildings are the only installations besides Sigma Noctae to have suffered an attack, but we still had no contact with the ground by the time I left orbit. Do you know what the situation on civilian casualties is?"

Salminen shrugged, a difficult gesture while wearing a battle suit. "The Doniphon people evacuated their injured to Stoddard, the next settlement downriver. A bunch of colonists bugged out too, afraid the raiders might come back to finish the job. What's left of the colonial administration's moved to Valance, even further away. A lot of them blame us Fleet folks for attracting the attackers in the first place, so they've not been communicative or helpful. Mind you, it hasn't been two days yet since they hit us and I don't expect civilians to work it through as fast as we can."

Sub-Lieutenant Pashar and the medical personnel jogged past them with half of the landing party hard on their heels. A stocky figure in combat armor waved them over, then fell into step beside *Iolanthe*'s junior navigator, leading them towards the gaping wound in the cliff side. Chief Henkman deployed the rest in a defensive half circle around the shuttles.

"Why don't we step aboard," Cullop suggested, pointing at the nearest craft, "and link up with the ship. If the attackers struck recently, we might still pick up an ion trail from their drives and be able to pursue."

The moment she spoke the second officer realized she said too much. However, Salminen did not react at the bizarre notion of an armed transport chasing marauders. Sometimes dealing with the Army had its advantages. A Marine captain would not have missed it. Instead, she removed her helmet, revealing short, matted black hair that made her look younger than Cullop had thought, based on her tired features.

"Lead on, sir."

Once aboard, the pilot opened a link to *Iolanthe* and set them up to use the passenger compartment's rear-facing screen. After a brief flash of the ship's badge, Lieutenant Commander Sirico's face swam into view.

He nodded. "Nice to see you made it in one piece — hold for the Captain."

Ten seconds passed, and then Siohban's face appeared. "Sorry for the delay, Emma. Who have we here?"

"This is Captain Tatiana Salminen, Company Group 31, Scandia Regiment, the senior surviving officer on the surface."

Dunmoore inclined her head. "Captain, I'm Siobhan Dunmoore, commanding the armed Fleet transport *Iolanthe*. What in all that's holy happened down there?"

Upon hearing the name, Salminen's eyes widened for a moment. "Are you the same Siobhan Dunmoore who was Sigma Noctae's acting CO a few years back? There's plenty of mention of your name in the records." Then she remembered she was speaking with the most senior Fleet officer in the Cervantes system and tagged on an apologetic, "Sir."

"I was the deputy commanding officer, but took over for several weeks when the CO died, but that's ancient history. Let's deal with the present, shall we?" Dunmoore replied, feeling uncomfortable at the notion that her exploits still resonated. The Official Secrets Act had ensured that most of the real story would stay forever beyond reach. Commander Jole's suicide when he discovered that Dunmoore was preparing to arrest him for running a regime of corruption and treason, abetted by most of the depot's senior noncommissioned staff, had been decreed as a non-event.

"Yes, sir." Salminen understood she had stepped on uncertain ground. "What happened here? Where to start. Sorry, sir, but I'm still coming to grips with it."

Siobhan smiled at her. "Just tell it in your own way, at your own speed."

"Two days ago, mid-morning, a salvo of kinetic penetrators slammed into the base, taking out the entire defensive array, the operations center, the barracks and the communications array. I had taken half of the company group out into the mountains on a few days of training — you know how it is with garrison troops. If they sit on their butts for too long, they become useless. We were in the next valley, so we both heard and felt the impacts. Then we heard more distant ones. We later found out they struck Doniphon. Within maybe an hour, while we were double-timing it back to base, a pair of smallish ships, I guess you'd call them sloops, along with a freighter, landed. They were on the ground for just under ninety minutes. We made it to the crest overlooking the depot when they lifted, one by one. I have video, which I'm happy to share if it'll help you find the bastards. We saw no markings on them. Once they vanished into the clouds, another bunch of penetrators rained on the depot, ruining the runway along with the rest. We took a while to get back. We found a handful of survivors, folks who dodged a direct hit and a few wounded left to die in the warehouse, but they killed half of my company group, those who weren't up in the mountains training with me, and destroyed most of our heavy weapons, commo gear, and vehicles."

Though her voice betrayed repressed emotions, Salminen continued, her face remaining expressionless.

"I sent a platoon on foot to Doniphon to find out what happened there while we treated the injured and tried to salvage what we could. Whoever they were, they emptied a fair chunk of the warehouse, taking the most valuable stuff from what I could see. They left the food behind, for what it's worth. We've been working on cobbling a new transmitter together since then, to call for help, but haven't gotten very far, I'm afraid to say."

"It wouldn't have done much good," Dunmoore replied in a soft tone. "The system's subspace relay buoy has vanished. Someone either took it or destroyed it. The communication platforms in orbit are still there but are refusing to accept any link-ups."

Salminen's eyes hardened. "That fits with my theory, sir. It was an inside job of sorts. I've done plenty of shifts as duty officer in the operations center. No one can approach Toboso without detection, and no one can fire on us from orbit without the sensors raising the alarm. We should have been able to shoot the penetrators down before they came within five kilometers of the surface. Heck, if anyone tried to mess with the commo orbitals, sirens should have been going off at every ground station, including the depot's operations center."

Cullop made a disgusted face. "Yet someone circumvented Toboso's defenses while cutting it off from the rest of the Commonwealth. Subspace relays aren't defenseless and will scream for help when someone tries to take them over or destroy them. This one vanished without a peep."

That someone had betrayed Sigma Noctae again represented the sum of Dunmoore's fears since

Iolanthe's failure to link with Toboso's communications array. Perhaps whoever tried the last time had finally succeeded. The Fleet had never found all of the Toboso-based perpetrators, let alone the identity of the raiders and those who had backed them.

"Lieutenant Commander Cullop said something about picking up the raiders' trail and heading off in pursuit," Salminen said jarring Dunmoore out of her contemplation. "If that's your intent and you need good troops, we have nothing left to protect here and a more than a hundred comrades to avenge. We might be Army, but I'm sure we can be passable ersatz Marines. That's provided you have room on your ship, Captain."

This time, Dunmoore smiled. "I have room, and I've always fancied having a company's worth of ground pounders aboard my ship. As a wise man once said, well before humanity stepped off Earth, the Army should be a projectile to be fired by the Navy. Let me figure out what we need to do next, and sort out the logistics. First order of business is taking care of the casualties. Emma, I want you to survey Doniphon. Establish contact with the colonists and find out who's running Toboso if anyone. They're the folks I must speak with at some point."

"Sir Edward Grey," Cullop said.

"Pardon?" Dunmoore looked at her with surprise.

"The thing you quoted about the Army being a projectile. The wise man was Sir Edward Grey. Political type. I had a lot of time to read history while standing watch aboard a merchantman in deep space."

"I've met someone who did just the same before joining the Navy as a wartime augmentee, except his thing was Kipling and other classical writers of that era. Last I saw him, he was in command of a corvette."

Cullop chuckled. "You must mean Hayden Gulsvig. I spent two years under his tutelage when I first struck out to become a merchant officer. He was a great teacher and a good man."

"And he's an excellent starship captain. If you have no other immediate issues, it's off to Doniphon with you Emma. Captain Salminen, I look forward to hearing more concerning this attack when we meet face-to-face…" Dunmoore broke off as her eyes shifted to one side. Then she said, "It seems someone in Valance has a working transmitter and knows we're in orbit. Until later. *Iolanthe*, out."

— Six —

"Hello starship in orbit," a disembodied voice rang forth from the CIC's speakers. "This is the provisional Toboso government in Valance."

Dunmoore turned towards the petty officer operating the communications console. "Do we have visual?"

"No, sir. Audio only."

"Give me a link." When he gave her thumbs up, she said, "This is the Commonwealth Navy ship *Iolanthe*, armed transport. I'm Captain Siobhan Dunmoore."

"Praise the Fates!" The unidentified caller's voice exuded relief. "My name is Anton Gerber. I am, or to be more accurate I was the governor's chief aide. With everyone higher up in the chain of command gone, I suppose that makes me the acting governor of Toboso. Someone attacked us two days ago. They destroyed the government buildings and the Sigma Noctae Depot from orbit before landing to plunder the warehouse. We've been unable to contact anyone until now. The orbital communications platforms are refusing to respond."

"I've just spoken with Captain Salminen, of the Scandia Regiment, who gave me a report on the attack. Two of my shuttles are on the ground at Sigma Noctae right now, and the officer in charge has instructions to survey Doniphon. The system's subspace relay buoy seems to have vanished, but the orbitals are still there, just not playing nice. My engineers are scanning them as we speak and if we can bring them up again, we'll do so. I can't help with the subspace buoy, but I've sent a message to the nearest Fleet unit, advising them of the attack."

"It's comforting to know the Navy's here to take charge."

A message appeared on the command chair's screen, confirming that the latest Colonial Office staff directory listed an Anton Gerber as the late governor's aide, along with the image of a middle-aged, bookish looking man.

"I'm not taking charge, Ser Gerber," Dunmoore replied. "My responsibilities are military, which means my authority extends only to matters surrounding the Fleet depot and the surviving Fleet personnel, although the Toboso government can ask for humanitarian help and we'll do our best between now and when I break orbit to pursue the raiders."

A long silence followed her statement, making Siobhan wonder whether Gerber was a man overwhelmed by the situation who had hoped that the Navy's arrival meant he could shift the burden of picking up the pieces and putting Toboso back on an even footing onto someone else's shoulders. Dunmoore's shoulders.

"I see," he finally said. "That certainly makes sense. Might it be possible to meet, Captain?"

Dunmoore glanced at Ezekiel Holt, sitting at one of the combat systems consoles. Their eyes met, and he nodded, raising one finger.

"Of course," she replied. "I'll be there in an hour."

"Thank you, Captain. Valance has a small landing strip along the river. I'll be there to greet you."

"If there's nothing else, Ser Gerber, I'll sign off so I can prepare. We'll resume our conversation once I'm dirtside."

Once the signals petty officer gave her the all clear, Dunmoore grimaced. "Anton Gerber sounds like a man out of his depth."

Holt nodded. "That much is clear. For the governor's aide to be in the hot seat that means everyone in an executive position is dead or incapacitated."

Dunmoore stood, tugging her tunic down and sighed. "If the bad apples I dealt with a few years ago are still up to their usual tricks, Gerber won't know whether he's coming or going. By the time Earth appoints a new governor and colonial staff, there might be quite a swamp to drain."

The first officer cocked an eyebrow. "Really?"

"In fact, it wouldn't surprise me to find a few of them behind this mess. You heard Salminen utter the words inside job." Dunmoore hesitated for a moment, trying to decide how much of the classified information stemming from her earlier involvement with Toboso she could share. "When the Fleet posted me to Sigma Noctae as second in command, I found evidence that several prominent Toboso colonists, well-connected and involved in the planet's more lucrative business ventures, were involved in theft and attempted theft of Fleet property held by the depot. All with the connivance of my CO. I suspected they were behind the abortive raid as well. Sadly, with Commander Jole dead and the attack repelled, the Colonial Office declined to prosecute and ordered that part of my report thrown into the memory hole."

"Fleet HQ went along with it?" Sirico asked in an incredulous tone.

Dunmoore gave her combat systems officer a tired smile. "The primacy of civilian authority, Thorin. We cleaned up the depot, but everything beyond that wasn't within the Fleet's purview."

"Of course. Sorry, sir."

"I felt just as outraged at the time, but if the Fleet interferes with civilian rule, we'll end up no better than the Shrehari Empire. Some would even argue we're already partway there, with our Special Security Bureau picking up bad habits from their *Tai Kan*."

Holt stood as well. "I'll make sure the pinnace is ready for you, sir. May I assume that you intend to ignore the rules concerning captains piloting their own craft again?"

"Of course I will, but out of the best intentions. Two of our pilots are already on the ground, and I'm sure we'll need the rest soon enough to transport humanitarian aid down and bring our ersatz Marines up."

"Who do you want in your entourage? I assume Joelle for starters?"

"How could I discuss aid without my logistics officer? And Vincenzo, of course. He wouldn't allow me off the ship without him."

Holt grimaced. "Aye. It would be more than my life is worth to exclude him. Add one bosun's mate as his winger. Perhaps you should take the cox'n too. I'm sure he'd like to stretch his legs and give your bad apples a once over."

"Five of us should be enough. Battledress with the proper naval insignia, but sidearms only and no armor. If for some reason, I need backup, I'll call Emma. Valance is a fifteen-minute shuttle flight at most from the depot, and it seems I now have half of a company group to augment my landing party."

The first officer nodded. "Fair enough, and speaking of which, I'll have the personnel pod activated. It should hold what's left of Company Group 31 with plenty of room to spare. Though I'm sure I'll hear complaints from engineering about adding another hundred or more breathing, eating, and eliminating humans to our environmental cyclers without warning."

"*Iolanthe* can manage twice that without burping. On the theme of eating, Salminen said the raiders left food behind. I'd like us to bring up as much as possible."

"Will do. If nothing else, when we run out of ammo for the guns, we'll be able to fire rat bars at the enemy."

Sirico made a face at the mention of the barely palatable emergency rations. "I think doing so would be against the laws of interstellar warfare, Commander, but better that than us eating them."

*

Chief Petty Officer Third Class Mariko Shigata, physician's assistant, emerged from the warehouse, medical bag slung over her armored shoulder, helmet dangling from it by a strap. She headed for where Emma Cullop was giving Chief Henkman his instructions before leaving for Doniphon.

"We'll need a medevac to the ship, sir," Shigata said, once she was within earshot. "Five of them should be in sickbay stat, and another seven will heal faster and cleaner under Doc Polter's care. I'd like to see the dozen walking wounded scanned in depth. The Army did a decent job, but much of this was beyond them, other than stabilizing the worst cases."

"Can your medic keep an eye on them during the flight?" The second officer asked.

"Aye."

"Good. You'll be with me for the hop over to Doniphon while Chief Henkman organizes the medevac. The attackers hit the colonists there almost as hard, and they might need your magic."

Shigata signified her understanding, then turned around and raised her fingers to her lips, blowing a loud whistle. In a voice that belied her slight frame, she shouted, "Move 'em out, folks."

Within moments, a line of Army troops, two to a stretcher, filed out of the ruined warehouse entrance, carrying the worst of the injured. A slower line of walking wounded followed them. In a matter of minutes, they had filed aboard the shuttle and settled in for the flight up into orbit and *Iolanthe*'s waiting surgeon. Most wore Army uniforms, but a few were naval personnel, the last survivors of Sigma Noctae's complement. Once the last one was aboard, the rear ramp closed and the craft's thrusters spooled up with a whine. It rose above the tarmac in a slow, graceful movement until its engine nacelles cleared the other shuttle and banked over to one side, gaining both altitude and speed. Cullop watched it disappear into the clouds, glad to have dealt with the most important issue, then turned back to the others.

"Chief Shigata, you're with me. Chief Henkman, you're staying here with Lieutenant Pashar. I'll take half a dozen troops. Captain Salminen, I suggest you get your company organized for departure. My CO will most likely send transport to bring you up before nightfall."

"Should I have the food they left behind made ready?" The Army officer asked. "You may not have enough rations for another one hundred and thirty mouths for however long this will take."

Cullop smiled. "Good thinking. You'll do well as our new major of Marines."

When she saw Salminen's quizzical expression, she chuckled. "There's only one captain aboard a Navy starship, the one who controls its destiny. Marine and Army captains receive a temporary, unpaid courtesy promotion to major the moment they step aboard. It avoids confusion."

Salminen nodded. "Understood. Are there any other protocol minefields waiting for me?"

"Plenty, but I'm sure Captain Dunmoore will cut you some slack. You'll be the first Army unit to board

Iolanthe. If no one has questions or wants to point out something I may have forgotten, I'll be off to Doniphon."

As one, the officers and chiefs snapped to attention, though none saluted. Cullop turned on her heel and climbed aboard the remaining shuttle, followed by Shigata and the six members of the landing party detailed to go with her.

Once it had lifted off, Salminen caught Lieutenant Pashar's eye and nodded towards the rapidly receding craft. "A bit of a whirlwind, your Lieutenant Commander Cullop."

"Being a whirlwind is part of the second officer's job. She gets all the fun assignments, such as boarding enemy ships with a gun in one hand and a sword in the other."

Salminen snorted in disbelief. "I may not know much about the Navy, but I thought sword fighting went out of fashion long ago. Next, you'll try to convince me that your first officer has an eye patch and a peg leg."

Chief Henkman's smile turned into outright laughter. "As a matter of fact..."

*

Cullop's shuttle crossed the distance between Sigma Noctae and Doniphon in a matter of minutes, overflying the gaping holes where Toboso's colonial administration once held court before landing on the town's airstrip, beside a small industrial park. They had seen people moving in the town, but no one came to meet them. Leaving the pilot to button up his craft again, she led the way into the settlement, intending to examine the damage at ground level. Beyond the cluster of warehouse-sized buildings adorned with signs denoting ownership and function, Doniphon appeared to be a typical frontier town, with single and two-story prefabricated buildings set a few meters back from the streets. Dust lay everywhere, along with an increasing amount of rubble as they neared the impact area. The few colonists they encountered avoided them though they received more than one angry stare.

The bird's-eye view during their overflight had not done the damage justice. Though the colonial administration complex once sat in the center of a large square, separated from commercial and residential structures by wide strips of grass, the force of the multiple impacts had created a ripple of destruction that marred and in some cases collapsed building facades all around the periphery.

Two dozen colonists seemed to be digging through the debris, even though nothing living inside the compound could have survived. One of them, an older man, stopped working and, shovel in hand, approached the landing party. The expression on his sweat-streaked face was anything but welcoming. He stopped as soon as he came within speaking range and, having identified Cullop as the leader, speared her with his eyes.

"What do you want, Navy?"

"I'm Lieutenant Commander Emma Cullop of the armed transport *Iolanthe*. We entered orbit a few hours ago to find someone had attacked Toboso. I'm here to see what help we can offer, be it medical or otherwise."

"The best thing you can do for Toboso, Lieutenant Commander Emma Cullop of the Navy," he spat out the words, "is to sod off and take what's left of that pirate magnet disguised as a naval installation with you. If it hadn't been for Sigma Noctae, we wouldn't have become a target, and almost a hundred good people wouldn't have had to die. Not to mention all the injured. If you want to help, leave Toboso. We don't need you."

The force of his anger felt like a physical slap in the face, and Cullop almost took a step backward when he raised his shovel. She had encountered dislike for the military before, but never with this intensity. It took the second officer a few moments to recover her composure, during which the man turned his back and walked away.

"That was... interesting," Chief Shigata murmured. "I've never met a colonist who refused our help with such naked hatred."

"Nor I," Cullop replied. "Relations between the depot and the townies must not have been fantastic before the attack. If this gentleman is an example of the locals' attitude, we're wasting our time here. Much as I hate turning back empty handed and confessing failure to our beloved captain, I don't see us spending more time trying to find someone who doesn't want to shoo us away."

"Concur, sir. You can't force someone to accept help, not even of the medical kind. I suggest we take the long way back to the landing strip and look for more welcoming folks."

"Good idea, Chief. Let's make it so."

They walked around the ruined area, under the baleful gaze of the locals working their way through the debris, and took one of the wider commercial streets, passing storefronts whose 'open' signs mysteriously switched to 'closed' at their approach.

"The folks here seem to dislike us," Shigata said after the fourth such occurrence. "Makes you wonder whether it's more than just a reaction to the raid."

"Aye." Cullop grimaced. "And having folks cross the street to avoid us isn't giving me the warm and fuzzies either."

After half an hour of fruitless crisscrossing the small settlement, they passed through the industrial park again, on their way to the shuttle. A low voice called out from the shadows of a factory door.

"Hey Navy."

Cullop checked her step and turned towards the source of the hail. A small man of indeterminate age and a week's growth of stubble on his sunken cheeks waved her over to where he stood. She nodded at him, then wordlessly ordered her bosun's mates to set up a security perimeter by pointing at them and the alley, after which she focused her attention on the colonist.

"I'm Lieutenant Commander Emma Cullop…"

"Of the armed transport *Iolanthe*, yeah, I heard. Word gets around fast in Doniphon, especially when it concerns the Navy. I'll keep my name to myself if you don't mind. Plenty of folks wouldn't take kindly to me giving you the time of day."

"Understood. What can I do for you?"

A cackling laugh escaped his cracked lips. "You can't do anything for me, but I once wore the Navy uniform so I can't just let you go without at least trying."

Cullop nodded again, waiting for him to continue.

"Some people aren't heartbroken that the depot and the colonial government turned to dust. People with business interests, you savvy?" He pointed a finger upwards, at the sky. "They told everyone around here that when the authorities showed up, we were to shun them. Those that don't cooperate, well let's say they might find trouble getting by."

"You don't seem concerned," Cullop said.

"I'm already on Andy Devine and Strother Martin's shit list." When he saw she did not understand, the man cackled again. "The buggers fancy themselves the real power on Toboso. Tried to mess with the Navy a few years ago and lost. They managed to weasel their way out of legal troubles nonetheless. Now that the governor and most of them from the Colonial Office are dead, they'll try again. Devine has a chokehold on off-planet trade while Martin runs Valance, the largest and richest settlement, which he figures should have had the colonial administration, anyway. Now he'll have his chance. I hear whatever survived scooted down there."

"What happened with the Navy a few years ago?" Cullop asked, although she already had an inkling he was referring to Captain Dunmoore when the latter was the temporary depot CO.

"Officer a lot like you, same rank too, blew away a couple of pesky raiders and called Devine out in public. They almost went at it gun to gun, old school, before cooler heads prevailed. Dunmoore was her name if I recall. She tossed Devine, Martin and a few others in the brig on charges of corruption and attempted murder. I figure one of 'em had friends back on Earth because the next thing I know, Dunmoore's posted out, a new set of officers are running the depot and everyone sitting in the brig goes home with a kiss on the cheek."

Out of the corner of an eye, Cullop saw Shigata's mouth opening and knew the chief was about to tell this unknown colonist that Dunmoore had returned. She grabbed her by the arm and said, "Do you have any idea why this raid might have happened."

"Same reason they always do," he replied. "Some nasty bugger's too lazy to shift for himself, so he goes and steals off the taxpayer."

"That explains the depot, but not the destruction of the colonial administration complex."

He laughed again. "If you want my opinion, look to Valance. You'll find an answer there. It might not be the one you want or expect, but when it comes to Devine and his cronies, there's always something evil brewing."

Then, without warning the man vanished through the doorway, leaving them to stand in the alley wondering what had just happened.

Cullop shook her head in semi-disbelief. "The captain will love hearing about this."

"Why?" Shigata asked.

"What we may have here Chief, is a bit of history repeating itself. Since there was no reason for anyone to expect our arrival, let alone Captain Dunmoore's, perhaps we're on the verge of tossing a left-handed spanner at a right-handed monkey."

— Seven —

"Pinnace, this is *Iolanthe*."

Holt's voice filled the silent cockpit, breaking Dunmoore's concentration. She was flying the small shuttlecraft without the benefit of the AI to keep her piloting skills fresh, as she had told Guthren after he had taken the right-hand seat instead of joining the others in the back. The tiny spaceship was not designed to be graceful within an atmosphere and possessed the flight characteristics of a large, metallic brick and watching her work the controls fascinated the coxswain.

"Pinnace here," he replied. "The captain's a tad busy right now."

"As long as she can hear me. We've just had an update from Emma on her survey of Doniphon. It's something you need to know before landing."

"Fire away," Dunmoore said between clenched teeth as the pinnace bounced through upper atmosphere turbulence.

When Holt finished recounting Cullop's report, a pained expression replaced that of intense concentration. She returned control of the craft to the AI and slumped back in her seat, eyes shifting to the video screen where the first officer stared back at her with his one good eye.

"Wonderful. I almost shot and killed Andrew Devine back then. He's a through and through crook, greedy, amoral and vicious. I'd hoped he might have found Toboso too small for his overweening ambition, but no such luck, though I'm not surprised Strother Martin's still gravitating around him. He has more ambition than brains, explaining why he follows Devine's lead in almost everything. This should be interesting. I beat the living tar out of Martin the last time we met before I tossed him in the brig."

Guthren gave Dunmoore a surprised look, and she snorted.

"Martin's a small man, not just in intellect but in stature, and I seem to recall that a long, solid wood implement was involved, something he liked to use on his entertainers for fun. I'm not sure I should confess this over an open frequency, be it ever so encrypted, but I experienced something close to a berserker event at the time - red curtain before the eyes, uncontrollable rage, the works. If Chief Moulens hadn't been there, I would have faced a murder charge."

"Note to self, never piss off the captain when there's a bat at hand," Holt said. The first officer did not quite sound as if he was suppressing an outburst of laughter, but there was an amused lilt in his voice, nonetheless.

Dunmoore snapped her fingers. "That's what it was. A cricket bat. Strother Martin's tool of choice to prove his status as a big shot. Shame I don't have one with me. It might make an interesting conversation piece if either of those two notables pokes his nose into my talks with the acting governor."

"Maybe we should have worn battle armor," Guthren said, then added, deadpan, "since we don't have bats."

Siobhan stared at him with cold eyes. "I'll never live this down, will I, Chief?"

"Expect a bat-shaped gift from the Chiefs' and Petty Officers' mess soon, sir."

"From the wardroom as well," Holt's disembodied voice said, equally deadpan. "That way you can display crossed bats in your quarters — symbol of good triumphing over evil. Or an inexplicable addition to an incomprehensible sport, or a mystical achievement, I suppose. Whichever works best. I hope I need not tell you to be careful down there. It sounds as if a coup could be under way, involving people who have no reason to remember you with fondness and every reason to avoid a repeat of their last encounter with you, cricket bats notwithstanding. Shall I order Emma join you in Valance with half of the landing party, backed by a platoon of our soon to be Marine complement?"

"As much as I would enjoy marching into Strother Martin's little empire with enough firepower to flatten the place, there's no point. With a naval vessel in orbit and troops on the ground, no one will try anything stupid."

"I will reluctantly agree with you on this, for now, Captain," Holt replied. "Please be careful and if the cox'n or Vincenzo tells you to duck, don't question them — hit the deck immediately."

Dunmoore smirked at him. "As if he'd give me a choice. I doubt anyone on Toboso will try to harm me, even as revenge for what I did four years ago. The Devine clique are bullies, and that makes them cowards at heart. They'll put on patently insincere smiles, pretend to cooperate and hope we bugger off as soon as possible so they can keep running their schemes undisturbed."

"Will we? Bugger off and leave them to do whatever they're doing, that is?"

"Unless the acting governor declares martial law on Toboso, our job is limited to providing humanitarian aid and chasing the marauders. A few colonial big shots playing games doesn't justify troops in the streets, Zeke. It's not as if they're in a position to commit treason, such as handing Cervantes to the Shrehari Empire."

"My views may have been thoroughly warped thanks to the time I spent working in counter-intelligence. But treason with a small 't' comes in many more forms than that, Captain, and most of it involves greed or lust for power rather than ideological conviction."

"How did we shift from discussing Emma's findings to contemplating martial law on Toboso?" Dunmoore asked with an amused shake of the head.

"Via the tale of how you dealt with Toboso's finest citizens the last time they got frisky?"

"This is why I don't speak much of my past misdeeds, Zeke. You have a knack of using them to suggest actions well beyond my authority as starship captain." She glanced at the navigation screen. "Amusing as this conversation has been, we're almost on final approach, and I haven't practiced landing this thing by myself for a while. I promise I'll behave and listen to my armed escort in all matters, but I won't involve myself in local politics. Once we're done here, I want to start hunting the scum who attacked Toboso."

"Chief Yens and her crew are working on it. The hanger deck is also preparing a flight of shuttles to fetch Company Group 31 and all the food we can carry. That means by the time you're back, we should be almost ready to break out of orbit."

"That's what I want to hear. If there's nothing else, I'll speak with you once we've met with the acting governor."

*

Valance had metastasized since the last time Dunmoore saw it, sprawling along the lazy river in an undisciplined jumble that seemed to go on for kilometers. The war did not appear to have affected Toboso's growth rate, with most of the increased profits accruing to Devine and his entourage, no doubt. She took them over the entire length of the town at low altitude. Then, she banked hard to starboard and aimed her nose at a long airstrip surrounded on three sides by warehouses and low-slung industrial buildings, shedding their remaining altitude as she came closer.

Once her forward momentum had evaporated, she brought them to a hover over one end, where a small structure served as the control center, then touched down with only the slightest thump. Several large wheeled cars sat at the edge of the tarmac, their skins covered with mud and dust. A thin man with a receding hairline leaned against one of them, arms crossed, watching *Iolanthe*'s pinnace with obvious interest.

Guthren nodded towards the cockpit window. "Anton Gerber, acting governor of Toboso, I presume?"

"Yep. Looks like his picture, only a lot more tired." Dunmoore nodded before focusing her attention on the post-flight checklist.

"That's one unhappy bureaucrat, if you ask me, Captain."

Guthren slipped out of his seat harness and stood. He left the cockpit for the passenger compartment and made a great show of checking his sidearm, imitated moments later by Vincenzo, his mate Alyss and Lieutenant Joelle Biros, *Iolanthe*'s logistics department head, a title she found infinitely more suitable than purser and tradition be damned. No one carried purses anymore.

The port hatch swung upwards, allowing a gust of dry, dusty air, underscored by a hint of organic fertilizer to enter the pinnace. Without waiting for an order, Vincenzo climbed out, Alyss on his heels, both scanning their surroundings for anything resembling a threat. Then, one took up position by the shuttle's nose and the other by the tail. Guthren made a sweeping gesture towards the opening, inviting Dunmoore to exit next, as per naval protocol — a starship captain was always last on and first off, unless when, as now, there was a security detail.

She stepped out onto the tarmac and inhaled through flared nostrils, the familiar scents of Toboso stirring old memories. Her eyes drifted over a monochromatic terracotta landscape and faded structures that could have spent the last few years in stasis, for all she knew. If someone had told her a year ago she would be back, facing another crisis, Dunmoore would have laughed them out of the room. Standing here now, she had to accept the truth inherent in the proposition that although lightning didn't strike twice, history, even writ small, had a tendency to repeat itself and not, as that intellectual fraud and ridiculous con artist Karl Marx had so glibly stated, first as tragedy and then as farce. It was a truth, and often a curse, as old as humanity.

The acting governor pushed himself away from the car, uncrossing his arms, and started towards them, an unsure smile tugging at his lips. Dunmoore was identifiable thanks to a Navy captain's four gold stripes on the tunic collar, and his eyes met hers. Once within earshot, he said, "I'm Anton Gerber, Captain, and I'm so incredibly pleased to finally meet you. I don't know if you understand how good it feels to know the Navy's in orbit, standing guard over us."

Dunmoore tossed off a crisp salute as per the regulations entitling colonial governors to military courtesies, then said, "A pleasure, sir. I've taken the liberty of bringing my logistics officer, Lieutenant Biros and *Iolanthe*'s coxswain, Chief Petty Officer Guthren. Both will be invaluable to our discussions."

Gerber nodded at the others, clearly puzzled by the presence of a man-of-war's senior noncommissioned officer, but was too much the polished gubernatorial aide to ask questions.

"If you'll follow me," he said, "we'll take my car to the temporary Government House provided to us by Strother Martin, the mayor of Valance. It's one of the municipal buildings, but considering what little remains of the colonial administration, Ser Martin and his people have been invaluable in helping us reestablish services."

I'll bet, Dunmoore thought. More likely, the little weasel is trying to figure out how to turn this to his advantage, such as induce a permanent move of the capital from Doniphon to Valance and create more opportunities for graft. She touched the slim device on her wrist, and the shuttle's hatch slammed shut, securing it from any unauthorized access, then she smiled at Gerber, one hand waving towards the parked cars.

"We're at your disposal, sir."

— Eight —

Renny Halfen, *Iolanthe*'s chief engineer, dropped into a chair opposite the first officer and raised a freshly filled mug to his lips. The wardroom was quiet between meals and Holt often used it as his office instead of conducting ship's business from his cabin. For one thing, he had immediate access to the coffee urn and snack dispenser. Halfen, who sported one of the more luxurious salt-and-pepper beards Holt had seen over the course of his career, wore the faded coveralls favored by the entire engineering department.

"I assume you climbed up from the depths of your mechanical dungeon because you had something to impart," Holt said dropping his tablet before sitting back with an expectant air.

"Aye." The ursine chief engineer nodded with vigor. "I can't find a thing wrong with either of the communications platforms or with any of the other satellites based on the scans Chief Yens provided. There's no apparent damage, no fried circuits, nothing physical that doesn't come from regular use and abuse. They're powered up and under AI control. My best guess is that someone tampered with the AIs, ordering them to refuse incoming links until a particular condition is met or they receive an override command."

"Which means that whoever tampered with them to blind the garrison wanted to make sure Toboso could get things up and running at the drop of a command line." Holt nodded, rubbing his chin with one hand. "Then why destroy the subspace relay?"

"We don't know whether they destroyed it," Halfen pointed out. "The sensor crew has found no debris, meaning the attackers might have kidnapped the buoy. If they made sure not to damage anything other than Fleet and Colonial Office property, they might have towed it to a new position after doing to its AI what they did to the others."

"That adds proof to Captain Salminen's suspicion of it being an inside job."

"Captain who, now?" Halfen asked.

"She's the CO of the surviving garrison complement."

"Of course. The mob of ground pounders who'll be giving my environmental scrubbers a fit. She'll have it right. It takes someone with override access to convince an entire constellation of AIs that their duty has become refusing to do their duty. They're all linked, or at least they should be, so an outsider tampering with the first one will trigger the others and cause a ruckus."

"What if they're not linked?"

Halfen snorted with derision. "Then whoever's controlling the orbitals is a damned fool. For another, it would mean taking control of each one in turn to reprogram the AI, but that leaves the rest to record it happening. Even without being linked, the things keep an eye on each other. I'm not saying it didn't happen that way, but an attacker sophisticated enough to manufacture a denial of service that doesn't harm hardware would have thought of something that obvious. Mind you, the only way to know is open one up and root through its brain."

"In other words, provided your guess is on the mark, someone who didn't want to deprive Toboso of its satellites and communications facilities over the long term engineered a temporary blackout, and we queered the pitch by showing up unannounced before they could return things to normal and leave behind an even bigger mystery."

Halfen gave him a grim smile. "Good thing our job is to queer the pitch for scum. But now we not only have to hunt down the raiders and turn them into wreckage. We also have to find the bastards who helped them. Where I come from, we call what they did treason, and in wartime, that's a capital offense. The captain declares martial law on Toboso, and we can hang them high ourselves."

Holt chuckled at the engineer's bloodthirsty enthusiasm. "Whatever you do, don't mention that to the captain. Otherwise she'll treat you to a discussion about the primacy of civilian rule."

"Here's a man who speaks from experience." Halfen drained his mug and sighed with satisfaction. "Good stuff, the wardroom coffee. Better than what my folks brew behind the fusion reactor. I try to teach them, but they want scorched and salty goo. Do you wish me to send a team to the main orbiter and have a look? It would take maybe three or four hours and could confirm my theory, which in turn could provide evidence of foul deeds by colonists or, God forbid, Fleet personnel."

Holt mentally calculated how much time would elapse before everyone was aboard to prepare for departure and nodded. "You should have approximately five hours. The moment the last flight leaves the surface finished or not, you're done."

"Fair enough." Halfen rose to his feet and tossed Holt a mock salute with his empty mug. Then, he lumbered off, whistling happily.

The first officer touched his communicator. "Bridge."

"Officer of the watch," a voice replied almost immediately. "What can I do for you, sir."

"Prepare the other pinnace. Engineering's sending a team to examine the closest communications platform."

*

"There's enough edibles in here to stock a battle group for six months." Cullop stared at the endless container stacks filling one of the warehouse's vast underground rooms.

"More than that," Salminen said. "It's a major industry around here — producing long-storage food for the Fleet and civilian customers. One of the guys the old man in Doniphon mentioned, Andrew Devine, runs the largest agricultural co-op on the planet. Most of this comes from him. The garrison used to buy its fresh stuff from the co-op as well, and not a piece of vat meat in sight. Every piece of it real and recently on the hoof."

When she noticed Cullop's lips briefly tighten in distaste, the Army officer chuckled. "Not a fan, I gather."

"No. I was raised on a deep space freighter. We grew most of our own food, so I never developed a taste for meat, vat or otherwise. My one and only experience with a real beefsteak didn't end well. But don't worry. *Iolanthe*'s galley serves animal protein regularly for those who want it."

"Good to know. That means I won't have to smuggle a butchered carcass aboard your shuttle." Salminen nodded at the containers. "You want to tag those that'll go with us? I'll have them moved out to the landing strip."

Cullop pulled a tablet from her combat harness and flicked it on, calling up the list that Holt had sent in response to her suggestion they take what they could and scanned stack after stack. Half an hour later, she had selected enough containers to fill one of *Iolanthe*'s holds, and Salminen summoned Sigma Noctae's surviving storekeepers to shift them.

The two officers watched as a trio of Navy ratings in coveralls, under the supervision of a petty officer third class, now under Army command, their own leadership dead in the attack, maneuvered a set of antigrav sleds into place. Using an exoskeleton, a fourth rating picked up the cubical containers, each the height of an average adult human, and piled them on the first sled. As soon as it was loaded, the petty officer dispatched it and its handler to the landing strip. The second sled followed, and the third, by which time the first had returned.

Cullop nodded towards the ramp. "Time to head back into the sunshine."

"Agreed. I've seen this show many times before, and it gets old fast."

They barely had time to take a few steps when the petty officer shouted a warning seconds before a loud detonation echoed through the warehouse. The shock wave bowled them over, and then a rain of atomized packaging, food, and human flesh covered everything within range of the explosion. Ears ringing, Cullop pushed herself up on her elbows and glanced at Salminen, who was equally dazed, but unharmed. The Army officer's lips moved, but no sound came from them. When Cullop tried to respond, Salminen shook her head and pointed at her ears. Of course. Blast deafness. They helped each other up and turned back to the chamber where moments earlier the petty officer had been directing the transfer of the crates.

A twisted exoskeleton lay meters away from a stack turned into confetti, the man inside shredded. No trace remained of the petty officer. The blast had blown the third rating into the next wall of containers along with his sled, but one glance at his ruined face showed that he too was dead.

Moments later, Chief Henkman and Sergeant Major Haataja came running down the ramp at the head of a mixed platoon of soldiers and spacers. They skidded to a halt beside their officers when they saw the sorry spectacle that greeted them.

"Booby-trap," Haataja said. "Fuckers left us a few presents. I can see what's left of Yee and Klaas, but where's PO Sorne?"

When Salminen did not respond, the sergeant major tapped her on the shoulder. Startled, she stared at him for a second or two before pointing a finger at her ear. Haataja nodded. He tapped his own arm with three fingers, to represent the three stripes of a petty officer and pointed at the devastation before them. Salminen shrugged, before saying, "No idea. Probably vaporized by the explosion. No one goes in there. Block the entrance and mark it as containing unexploded ordnance and human remains because Yee and Klass will have to stay. I'm not risking anyone else."

When Henkman examined Cullop for any apparent injuries, he noticed the spattering of gore on her armor and caught Haataja's eye. "It looks like your PO Sorne is all over the place, including on them."

A volley of harsh sounding words in a language Henkman could not understand erupted from Haataja's mouth, but his feelings towards the sort of subhuman scum despicable enough to booby trap a food store were clear.

Iolanthe's gunnery chief gave the soldier a feral grin. "Don't you worry. We'll find the assholes who did this. We always do. Few of them survive the experience, and you'll get your chance at revenge."

Haataja considered him for a moment, then shook his head while a skeptical expression replaced the earlier mask of rage. "You're not off an armed transport, are you?"

"Technically, yes, but since you're about to join us, let me ask you a question. Do you know what a Q-ship is?"

"As a matter of fact…" Sergeant Major Talo Haataja returned Henkman's bloodthirsty grin.

*

"Charming." Ezekiel Holt lips settled into a hard line once Chief Henkman had finished reporting. Emma Cullop, still deafened, sat beside him in the shuttle's aft compartment. Chief Shigata had checked both her and Salminen's ears and found no permanent damage. Their hearing would return soon enough. "Of course that means we're not taking any of the containers on board. After what happened, I'd prefer not to take the risk that the bastards tampered with any of them, poisoning the food or whatnot."

"Agreed, sir," Henkman replied. "Sergeant Major Haataja has isolated the containers already on the tarmac, and his sappers are fixing it for destruction when we leave. Shame, but if we need food, we can always contract directly with the cooperative that produced the stuff in the warehouse. Haataja tells me they raise good beef on Toboso."

"I'll keep that under advisement, and yes, I'm aware the Chiefs' and Petty Officers' mess prizes real steaks."

"That we do." Henkman grinned at the first officer before asking, "Any idea when our rides are coming?"

"I'll know once the captain calls. She's in Valance by now, meeting with the acting governor. Once we have confirmation of what, if anything he needs from us, we'll pull you out." Holt stopped speaking, glanced away, then looked up at Henkman again. "Tell Captain Salminen that the injured have arrived safe and sound and are on their way to the sickbay."

"Aye, aye, sir. She'll be glad to hear."

"If there's nothing else?"

The chief shook his head. "Nothing and I hope it stays that way until we're back aboard ship, sir."

"You and I both. *Iolanthe*, out."

Holt tapped the command chair's embedded screen. "Bridge to chief engineer."

"Aye?" Renny Halfen's tone indicated that the first officer had interrupted something.

"The landing party came across a nasty IED dirtside. Three casualties from the depot's surviving complement. Emma and the Army captain who were close to the blast are temporarily deaf but otherwise unharmed."

"You're afraid the bastards might have rigged the orbitals. Understood. My folks will go ahead with all due caution, but I doubt they'll find anything nasty. Remember, we're operating on the theory that this is a temporary denial of service. That means it's unlikely they'd risk damage just to blow someone's limbs off for shits and giggles."

"True, but treat this as going aboard a hostile ship, nonetheless."

"Acknowledged."

"Bridge, out."

— Nine —

Downtown Valance looked much as Dunmoore remembered it. Perhaps more rundown. The war would have done to Toboso what it did to many other colonies relying on exports to fuel growth. With so much of the interstellar shipping reoriented to support the military effort, when it wasn't destroyed outright by the Shrehari or other marauders, bulk commodity producers had become increasingly isolated.

Now, with the Sigma Noctae Fleet Depot all but destroyed, the colonists had lost another major customer. Dunmoore doubted that the Fleet would rebuild it anytime soon, if ever. This sector was a backwater of the war and the ships patrolling it required nowhere near the amount of stores the ones facing the Empire needed, except for those such as *Iolanthe* who trolled for enemy targets and expended ordnance at several times the average rate. Unless they recovered the stolen supplies, they faced the long trip to Sigma Draconis, or a replenishment underway, provided the Fleet gave its authorization.

"It's been hellish, you know," Gerber spoke without taking his eyes off the controls. For what was no more than a minor frontier town, Valance had a surprising amount of traffic, including, to the astonishment of those who had never set foot on Toboso before, horses.

"What has, sir?"

"Witnessing all that death and destruction when we're so far from the war zone. Then, trying to restore a measure of governance when there's only a dozen of us left."

"Ah." Dunmoore nodded, even though Gerber could not see. "How did you and the others survive? The attackers wiped the entire colonial administration complex from the surface of the planet."

"It was my day off, and I hiked up into the mountains to look for Toboso snipe. They're a rather unusual avian, with fascinating behavior. I returned to find myself the senior surviving member of the administration. It was much the same for the others. Not the snipe hunt of course, but they were also away that morning. It was harrowing to come back and find my colleagues and friends gone, just like that. Then I had to deal with the panic that had spread among the colonists. The satellites were out, the naval base destroyed, and we had no way to speak with anyone beyond the reach of our long-range radios."

"I can reassure you that your satellites and communications platforms are still there, but unresponsive. My crew will try to revive them, but, I'm afraid the system's subspace relay has vanished."

"Heavens above." He turned an owlish stare at her. "You mean we can't communicate with anyone?"

"At this point, my ship has the only subspace transmitter capable of reaching other systems. We've already sent a message to our HQ advising them of the situation. Hopefully, they'll be able to deploy a new relay buoy in a few weeks."

"A few weeks?" Gerber's voice rose by an octave. "We can't stay out of touch that long. Lord knows what might happen to us."

Dunmoore did not have the heart to tell him that before the invention of the subspace radio less than a century earlier, avisos handled interstellar communications. A breed of small FTL starships they were no more than a personnel pod attached to outsized hyperdrives, and no colony died on the vine because it sometimes took weeks, if not months to deliver a message. In fact, many thrived by not having to check every decision with the mother world.

"I'm sure you'll be okay. If there's anything you want to send, we'll serve as your relay while we're nearby. Besides, I'm sure my orders will be to stay in the vicinity until we find and destroy the marauders who did this, something I intended to do anyways."

A measure of relief dampened his earlier agitation. "I'm gratified to hear you say so, Captain."

They pulled off the main street and onto a gravel lot beside a gray two-story building clad with quarried stone. It bore a hastily produced sign that said 'Government House.'

"We're here," Gerber said.

Dunmoore thought she might have heard Guthren mutter, "We can see that," but elected not to follow-up.

The acting governor ushered them through a front door that would not have seemed out of place on a prison and up a broad granite staircase to his office. Dunmoore ordered Vincenzo and Alyss to stay in the corridor, confident that both would keep their ears and eyes open for anything that might interest their captain. Knowing Vincenzo, it was a given he would take a stroll around the floor.

Gerber invited them to sit at a table made of dense native wood then asked, "Can I interest anyone in a tea or juice?"

Dunmoore shook her head. "Nothing for me, but I appreciate the offer."

When both Guthren and *Iolanthe*'s logistics officer, Joelle Biros, demurred, Gerber said, "Perhaps another time then. Please excuse me while I make myself something. I find that a nice cup of strong tea helps me cope these days."

Once he had served himself and joined them at the table, Dunmoore gave Gerber an expectant look and asked, "What can we do for Toboso? Other than getting your satellite constellation back in operation, then track and punish those responsible for the raid, I mean."

The man suddenly seemed uncomfortable, hesitant even. "I wasn't expecting you to come with a delegation, Captain. Toboso as such doesn't need any humanitarian aid, and though the Doniphon medical facilities were destroyed along with the rest of the government complex, we've been able to transfer the injured to other clinics, and they're coping well."

"And we're already solving your technical problems as best we can. Might I infer that you'd prefer to speak with me alone, sir?"

A smile of relief made a brief appearance. "Would you mind?"

"Not at all." Once the coxswain and Lieutenant Biros had joined the ratings in the corridor, she placed her elbows on the table's surface and leaned forward. "What can I do for you?"

*

"We're docked with the communications platform," Lieutenant Yulia Zhukov, *Iolanthe*'s information systems engineer reported. Her voice came through the link loud and clear even though she and the two ratings accompanying her, wore pressurized battle armor, capable of withstanding vacuum. "It's still not responding to commands, but I'm not picking up any signs it intends to deny us access. Power levels remain consistent with a dormant state, and it is depressurized."

"Acknowledged," Holt replied, eyes on the video feed showing the inside of the pod. "You're authorized to examine the entry port."

He bit back the temptation to recommend caution. Zhukov had been briefed on the booby-trap that killed three of the depot's survivors, and like most engineers, especially those commissioned from the enlisted ranks, caution was second nature. She had witnessed too many mishaps in her twenty-year career to take any short cuts.

"Depressurizing the pod," she announced moments later. Then, "Opening airlock."

Holt's view changed to show the platform's entry hatch beyond the airlock followed by several minutes of Lieutenant Zhukov, battlefield sensor in hand, examining every square millimeter with utmost care. After five minutes of scrutiny, she stepped back.

"All appears as it should. My sensor isn't picking up unusual readings, and the power levels remain as they were."

The first officer said, "Go ahead."

She gestured at one of the ratings. "Unlock the hatch."

He took the large wheel in both hands and slowly turned it while Zhukov concentrated on her sensor's display, alert for any changes to the platform's state. After one full turn, the wheel stopped.

"Unlocked, sir," the leading spacer reported.

"I detect nothing that might indicate tampering. Ready to open."

Holt nodded, even though Zhukov could not see him. "Proceed at your discretion."

"Acknowledged." She motioned at the other rating, who attached a cable to the locking wheel, then stepped out of the airlock, leaving Zhukov alone with her sensor. Those watching understood she wanted to be the one taking the brunt of any booby trap triggered by opening the hatch. "Pull, but gently."

Holt realized he was holding his breath when the thick portal swung outward without triggering anything lethal.

"No change in the platform's state," the engineering officer reported in the same flat tone she had been using all along, giving further credence to the rumor that reactor coolant flowed through her veins.

"You're authorized to board."

Zhukov stepped over the coaming with exaggerated care, stepping out of the pod's artificial gravity and into the platform's zero gravity. Her helmet light slashed through the darkened compartment, illuminating bare metal and dormant displays. Her eyes switching from the sensor display to her surroundings every few seconds, she moved with deliberation, letting the magnetic soles of her boots grip the deck at each step. One of the ratings followed with a portable power generation unit while the third remained in the pod. Holt's view changed again, but this time he saw the satellite's interior from the same perspective as Zhukov, thanks to the video feed from her suit's built-in camera.

"So far, I detect nothing," she said, stopping in front of a large console whose screens were as dark as the rest of the satellite. After tucking the sensor into a pouch at her waist, she ran her gloved hand over each control surface in turn, without result. "Whatever they did to this unit, it cut power from the primary interface. I will connect the auxiliary power generator now."

"Proceed," Holt replied.

Zhukov waved her assistant over and pointed at the input port near the base of the console. The first officer knew it would be the next hurdle. An apparently dormant system could easily be rigged to do something lethal when an intruder connected a portable power source. So far, Renny Halfen's theory that the saboteurs wanted to preserve the satellite constellation had proved right. However, there could always be layers within layers, such as the trapped food containers, which might not have been triggered until weeks or months after the attack.

After a bit of fumbling, partly due to the zero gee environment and partly due to the thick armored gloves, the rating hooked up his auxiliary power unit. Zhukov ran another scan, confirming that nothing had changed due to their opening the input port. She waved the man back to the pod before switching on the APU herself. After a few moments, the central display screen flickered to life, but nothing untoward happened, and Holt forced himself to relax.

"The emergency response subroutine has been activated. It is prepared to accept commands."

"All right, then. Let's see if you can boot up the platform." Hurdle number three now loomed.

Zhukov tapped the control screen, and after less than half a minute, lights came on while the other displays woke from their slumber. She scanned her surroundings once again.

"Power levels are rising, but remain within normal parameters." A visual alert flashed on the screen, calling her attention back to the controls. "The AI is back online and restoring normal functions."

"Excellent." Holt tapped his communicator. "Bridge, this is the CIC. Have signals establish a link with the communications platform. Let's see if that puppy wants to play."

"Acknowledged," the officer of the watch replied. Then, a few moments later, "It has accepted the link."

"Confirmed," Zhukov said. "It indicates that it's back in contact with the ground stations."

"All of them?" Holt asked.

"All except Sigma Noctae, for obvious reasons. The Doniphon ground station must not have been located within the colonial administration complex."

"Do you think you can convince it to cough up the log of events before the moment it went down?"

"If no one has changed the override code we have for this system's satellite constellation, yes. I shall enter it now." Ten seconds ticked by, then another twenty before Zhukov spoke again. "It has accepted the override code. The log appears to be present. I'm ordering the AI to transmit a copy to *Iolanthe*. Stand by."

"Confirmed," the officer of the watch said. "I'm routing it to tactical."

"Thank you," Holt replied. He caught Sirico's eye and said, "Over to you for analysis, Thorin. If they haven't tampered with it, we might just find something connected to the attackers. Other than what the ground pounders recorded, we have nothing."

"Will do."

The first officer turned his attention back on Zhukov. "Do you think you'll be able to wake the rest of the satellites from where you are?"

"Perhaps. If the colonists used the standard configuration and slaved all of them to a prime platform, such as the one I'm on, the AI should be able to assist, especially if the attackers, or whoever they had on the surface, used it to send all of them into dormancy."

"Good. Sending you to each, in turn, would take more time than we have."

"It is something I would rather avoid, sir."

Before Holt could say anything further, Yens raised her hand to attract his attention.

"Please tell me you found a trail, Chief."

"Aye."

— Ten —

Gerber's eyes dropped to the polished tabletop. "I'm not sure how to say this, Captain, but I fear certain leading persons on Toboso might use the almost total eradication of the colonial government as an opportunity to gain power, and honestly I have no idea what to do. I'm no politician, nor am I an administrator of any note, but by law, I am the governor until relieved by Earth. However, without communications, I can't ask for orders or assistance from the Colonial Office. Since you're the senior Commonwealth official in the system now, I'm throwing myself at your mercy. I — no make that Toboso needs your help."

When he glanced up at Dunmoore, she saw the pleading look of a man overwhelmed by events.

"What makes you fear that these leading persons are seeking to usurp the colonial administration?"

"I lost most of my colleagues and friends only two days ago, but I've already been under heavy pressure about the matter of establishing a legislative council that could create a new colonial administration, drawing on Toboso citizens, rather than Colonial Office employees."

"Would that even be legal?"

Gerber nodded. "Toboso is an early stage Class Two colony, which means the governor can foster limited home rule institutions, but Judy LaSalle — the late governor — has always believed the socio-political foundations here haven't matured enough to allow for responsible self-government, something with which I agree. However, I fear that those pushing for it might take matters into their own hands. This place is still a tad rough around the edges if you get my meaning. On top of that, I'm hard pressed to restore authority with only a few survivors, and increasingly forced to hand bureaucratic functions over to the various mayors — until a new colonial administration is in place, you understand, but it's a delicate balance. Having the Navy to back me would be of immense help."

While he spoke, Dunmoore felt her stomach tie up in a knot as the memories of four years ago merged with the events of the present. It was not exactly déjà vu, but the similarities were eerie enough to give her pause.

"Those leading citizens of Toboso are?" She asked in a soft tone, both knowing and dreading the answer.

"Andrew Devine, Strother Martin, and Kila Vanclef. They're the ring leaders, the most powerful ones who style themselves Toboso's future. Another dozen or so lesser notables follow their lead in everything. All together, they represent most of Toboso's wealth."

Dunmoore took a deep breath, then exhaled slowly. "It pains me to admit I'm more familiar with those individuals than I want to acknowledge, sir."

"Strother Martin intimated as much when he found out I'd spoken with you."

"The last time I saw those three was through the bars of the Doniphon jail after I put them there. Unfortunately, Devine has powerful friends who pulled strings back on Earth and had the charges dropped. Otherwise, they'd be spending quality time in a penal colony."

"I see." Gerber seemed, if anything, even more at a loss. His already pale face had lost what little coloring it possessed.

"You can appreciate that enlisting my help to deal with these individuals might produce results you likely don't wish to see. Besides, my duty is to pursue the raiders before they attack another colony and hopefully recover what they stole while I bring them to justice. The Colonial Office will be apprised of your situation in a matter of days, now that we've reached out to our HQ. I'm sure they'll send a new governor along with adequate staff as quickly as possible."

He stared at her for what seemed like a long time, while a faint hue of color returned to his cheeks, then he shook his head. "Actually, I'd venture to say that since Devine and his clique have already had a taste of your determination, backing me in resisting their attempts will be all the more effective."

Devine's oh so arrogant, oh so sneering face swam before her mind's eye. Immensely wealthy by the standards of a frontier colony, with fingers in every business venture, control over the ranchers' cooperative and utter contempt for anyone associated with Commonwealth authorities, he had almost cost Siobhan her life back then and was indirectly responsible for the deaths of many under her command. She would have gunned him down in Doniphon's main street if Chief Petty Officer Second Class Joshua Moulens, the depot's long-suffering coxswain and one of the few among the leadership who had retained his professionalism and loyalty to the Navy, had not stopped her. Instead, she had arrested Devine with as little gentleness as possible and tossed him in a cell. Not long after that, a heavily bruised Strother Martin and their crony Kila Vanclef, second in wealth and influence only to Devine and one of the most poisonous individuals Siobhan had ever encountered, joined them.

Emotions, long suppressed, rose from deep within, demanding she relive that day, long ago, when she had almost died at Devine's hands. As she fought to send the memories back into the dark recesses of her consciousness, a detached part of her mind wondered how she would react if any of them crossed her path. Would she be able to keep her hard-won self-control, or would she lash out?

When Dunmoore noticed Gerber watching her with a mixture of curiosity and alarm, she realized that her thoughts must have shown in her eyes. It was enough to extinguish the fierce, but mercifully brief flare-up of emotions.

Pleased that her voice remained steady, she said, "Governor, you may tell whoever you wish that the Navy is committed to supporting you until the Colonial Office dispatches a new administration. I will, in all likelihood, leave Toboso within the day, to chase down the marauders, but will return as soon as I can. If you want to remind Devine and company of the last time they and I crossed swords, feel free to give them my regards. Perhaps that will suffice to keep their schemes in check long enough. I would also recommend that you decline any further hospitality from Strother Martin and return the seat of government to Doniphon. If you can find a few colonists who aren't fond of Devine willing to become temporary Colonial Office employees, so much the better."

"What if they decide to form their legislative council anyway and force obedience from the colonists? They have most of the municipal police forces in their pockets, and Toboso has no other law enforcement agencies, something Governor LaSalle wanted to change as well."

A cruel smile twisted Dunmoore's lean face. "Then the Colonial Office will send an Army battalion along with the new governor and Toboso can forget about self-government for another generation or two. Earth takes a dim view of breakaway colonies, especially in wartime.

I'm sure Andrew Devine knows this, which is why he's attempting to enlist your support. You need only stay strong and resist his blandishments. Toboso will mostly continue to run itself over the short term."

Her wrist transmitter vibrated at that moment, indicating that the shuttle's AI wanted to link up. *Iolanthe* was attempting to contact her via its more powerful radio.

"If you'll pardon me, sir. My ship seems to have news that might interest you."

She accepted the link.

"Dunmoore."

"Holt here, Captain. Is this a good time?"

"I'm with Acting Governor Gerber, Zeke."

"Then he'll be happy to hear the primary communications platform is up and running, and has linked up with all ground stations, meaning all parts of the colony can now talk to each other again. Once Earth ships them a new subspace relay, or we find the missing one, they'll also be able to speak with the rest of the Commonwealth. Lieutenant Zhukov is working on the remainder of the satellite constellation and is confident they'll come up within a few hours. We've also downloaded a copy of the communications platform's log for analysis."

Gerber visibly brightened at the news. "That's wonderful."

"I have more," Holt continued. "We have a definite trace, about forty-eight hours old and quickly dissipating, which could only be the raiders, but we must follow it soon, or it'll be gone."

A brief burst of adrenaline coursed up Siobhan's veins.

"In that case, bring everyone up from the surface and prepare the ship for the hunt. The colony doesn't need aid as such, but we can discuss it later."

"With pleasure, sir. If there's nothing else, I'll put our preparations for departure in motion."

"Make it so, Mister Holt. Dunmoore, out."

She looked up at Gerber. "Finding a trace doesn't guarantee we'll catch up with them, but it will give us a general idea of where they're headed. Space is vast, but we humans tend to prefer hanging around solid objects such as planets, and there's a finite amount of those where pirates can hide from the Navy while they work on disposing of their booty for profit. Unless you wish to discuss other matters, I must go. Please consider my recommendation that you leave Valance. With the Doniphon ground station hooked into the system again, you can run Toboso from anywhere, preferably somewhere that's not here."

He bobbed his head. "I most certainly will, Captain. Thank you. I'll drive you back to the landing strip now if you wish."

"Please." She rose and tugged her tunic into place. "If I may give a final piece of advice. Don't share what you just heard with Devine and his cronies. Better he wonders where my ship and I are."

"That makes eminent sense. I shall be as quiet as the proverbial grave." He ushered her out of his office and into the hallway where they found the others waiting with varying degrees of boredom.

"We're off, folks," was all she said, pointing at the staircase. "Governor Gerber will return us to our shuttle."

Guthren gave her a questioning look, to which she replied with a minute shake of the head. They emerged from the temporary Government House into Toboso's bright afternoon sunshine, but before they could make their way to Gerber's car, a tall, well-dressed patrician-looking man in his late fifties barred their way. The deep-set dark eyes that speared Dunmoore shone with unsuppressed malice.

"Well, well, well. The rumors are true then. The redoubtable Siobhan Dunmoore has graced Toboso with her presence again, and as a post captain at that. Will wonders never cease? I'd welcome you back, but then, I do remember your distinct lack of hospitality towards my friends and I. Fortunately, cooler heads prevailed on Earth." When he noticed Vincenzo's angry expression, he raised his gem-topped walking stick and pointed it at the bosun's mate. "Do restrain your gorilla, Dunmoore. A Navy uniform won't protect him from prosecution for assault."

After Siobhan's initial surprise had passed, the heat of anger rose in her gorge again, but before she could speak, Guthren growled, "Steady, lad." Though ostensibly aimed at Vincenzo, she took it to include herself and imagined a cascade of ice enveloping her. The rage receded as quickly as it had come.

"Ser Devine." Dunmoore inclined her head. "I won't hide that I'd rather you were enjoying the comforts of a penal colony, but here we are. Now if you'll excuse me, I have the governor's orders to carry out. Have a good day."

Devine stepped aside with an ironic bow, but his hard, dark eyes locked with hers, promising retribution for past humiliations.

"And a splendid day to you, Captain Dunmoore."

*

"For a moment there, I thought you were about to rip his living heart out, Captain," Guthren said once he had strapped himself into the copilot's seat aboard the shuttle. "Not that I'd have blamed you, considering I saw the classified report you filed back when I was with special operations. A nasty customer that Andrew Devine."

"He's also very good at provoking folks, Chief. He almost had me ordering Vincenzo to take him down."

Guthren snorted, then said, "Bull. You'd have reached out and done it yourself if you had a mind to get physical with Ser Devine. You'd have never let the lad compromise himself."

"Your confidence in me is touching, cox'n," Dunmoore replied, eyes on the controls while she ran through the pre-flight check. "However, since I'm not a fan of courts-martial, I prefer to let the law take care of Devine and his like, accepting that now and then, scum like him manage to escape justice."

"Sure, skipper. I'll go with that."

Dunmoore turned her head as if it was a battleship gun turret and locked eyes with her smirking coxswain. She smiled, shaking her head. "Oh, ye of little faith."

Then, without warning, she gunned the thrusters, shoving all of them deep into their seats while the small craft rose straight up into the sky.

*

Anton Gerber, acting governor of Toboso, watched until the shuttle, after dwindling to a tiny speck, vanished from view altogether.

"You keep dangerous company," a man's voice said from the shadows of the airstrip terminal.

"I keep the company I must, Strother. Now that the communications network is back in operation, I'll be returning to Doniphon, the designated capital of Toboso. You have my thanks for your hospitality."

Strother Martin, mayor of Valance, stepped out into the waning light of day. Short, balding, and resembling nothing so much as a strutting peacock, Martin followed his patron Devine's taste in clothes, if nothing else. "She's a viper, that one. I wouldn't take her advice to breathe in deeply if I were choking."

"Yet she has a starship at her command, and that's more than I can say for anyone else on Toboso."

Martin made a dismissive gesture. "An armed transport. Hardly something to impress the yokels around here, let alone marauders capable of wiping out an entire naval base."

"I wouldn't be too quick to dismiss her. She still seems to carry a lot of anger for whatever she experienced her last time here. It might not be wise to underestimate what that could entail."

"So what?" Martin shrugged. "Even the captain of the most powerful battleship can't do much to influence planetary matters. Earth frowns on the Navy bombarding human-occupied worlds."

— Eleven —

"Nice of the Army to give us ground troops to play with." Holt, arms crossed, stood beside Dunmoore by the large hangar bay's inner door. Both were watching Company Group 31 disembark, the soldiers forming up by platoons under the sharp eyes of their sergeant major.

"The Army doesn't know yet that we've shanghaied one of their units. I doubt they'll let us keep them for long."

"If it's long enough to help us sort this mess out. I'll be happy."

Eventually, one of the armored soldiers removed her helmet and headed towards them. She came to a crashing halt three paces in front of Dunmoore and saluted.

"Captain Tatiana Salminen, Commanding Company Group 31, Scandia Regiment, reporting with one hundred and twenty-five effectives, plus ten naval personnel from the depot staff."

Dunmoore returned the salute with a smile. "Welcome aboard *Iolanthe*, Major," she replied, putting an emphasis on the courtesy rank to remind the soldier of her changed circumstances. "This is Commander Ezekiel Holt, my first officer."

Salminen saluted again. "Sir."

"Once you've offloaded everything, my bosun, Chief Petty Officer Second Class Dwyn and her crew will settle you and yours into the barracks and show you where to stow your heavier gear." Dunmoore pointed at a dozen spacers standing behind a stocky, short-haired woman wearing faded black coveralls with a chief's silver starbursts stamped on the sleeves. "I intend to get under way as soon as possible. We've picked up a recent radiation trail left by several starships, but it's dissipating fast."

"Yes, sir. We'll sort ourselves out as quickly as possible, so we don't delay you." Salminen hesitated for a moment. "Sir, pardon the question, but this isn't an armed transport, is it? Your hangar bay looks more like something I'd expect on a carrier."

Holt chuckled. "Well spotted, Major. In reality, we're a Q-ship, a heavy cruiser disguised as a freighter. Our job is to troll the star lanes for bad guys and give them the biggest and last surprise of their lives."

"The disguise gives us more internal space than a regular cruiser, which allows us to take you on board. They fitted us with barracks for a Marine contingent but forgot to give us actual Marines. It won't be luxurious, but you won't be cramped either. And," she swept a hand out to encompass the hangar, "it affords us the ability to carry a squadron's worth of shuttles, which can be armed and turned into gunships. You mentioned naval personnel among the survivors..."

"Yes, sir. Ten came up with us; four went up with the injured. In all, fourteen survived. It would have been seventeen except for the booby trap. The most senior among them is a chief third class by the name of Trane. He's in your sickbay right now."

Dunmoore gave Holt an amused glance. "More people to shanghai, except, in this case, we'll formally add them to the ship's company. I'm sure we have enough spare billets to fit all of their occupational specialties. By the time our friendly career manglers at Fleet HQ figure it out, we can present them with a fait accompli."

"Aye. That must be them, forming a separate platoon on the side. If you'll excuse me, Captain, I'll go round up our newest crew members before they stray too far and stumble across the cox'n by mistake." He nodded at Salminen. "We'll speak later, Major."

Once Holt had gone, Dunmoore said, "Your quarters will be in the barracks module with your troops, but you and your officers will mess with the ship's officers in the wardroom. The cox'n — our equivalent of a sergeant major — will invite your senior noncommissioned officers into the Chiefs' and Petty Officers' mess."

"Only one other officer survived, sir, Lieutenant Puro, who's now my second in command. What about my soldiers?"

"The barracks module has its own eating and recreational facilities for the junior ranks, but they're welcome to mingle with the crew."

"I suppose my eating with the troops is out of the question."

Dunmoore nodded. "It's discouraged. We spend our waking moments in such close proximity to each other that it's custom to let the junior ranks enjoy a few compartments that officers and senior noncoms don't enter other than for duty reasons or if formally invited. Even I, as captain, enter none of the messes without invitation, unless it concerns ship's business."

"Not even the wardroom?"

"Not even the wardroom, but fortunately, its president gave me a standing invitation, one I don't abuse, needless to say."

"I suppose that makes sense." Salminen sounded dubious. "It's a lot for me to absorb, Captain. My only time aboard a starship has been as a passenger, not as part of the ship's company."

"Don't worry; no one will take offense if you violate one of our more arcane bits of protocol. I'm sure you and your troops will adapt soon enough."

The soldiers, now formed into six tight blocks of varying size, had stopped moving. An armored figure stood at the head of each while another stood in front of the entire contingent.

"Would you like to speak to the troops before I dismiss them, sir?" When Dunmoore did not immediately reply, Salminen said, "It's custom in the Army that when we come under a new commander, she says a few words of welcome. They're expecting it."

Dunmoore smiled. "We all have our protocols to observe, I guess. How would you like to do this?"

"I'll take the formation from Lieutenant Puro, then hand it to you."

Within a minute or two, Dunmoore found a hundred and twenty-five pairs of eyes locked on her while a hundred and twenty-five sets of ears were ready to listen.

"My name is Siobhan Dunmoore. I'm captain of the Commonwealth Starship *Iolanthe*, your new home for now. Welcome aboard. I don't know how long you'll be serving with us as our ground component, but I can promise you we'll see action together. I intend to break out of orbit within the next few hours and head out on the trail of the bastards who attacked Toboso and killed so many of your comrades. Once we find them, and we will, I promise you that, retribution will be swift and deadly. Hunting marauders is what *Iolanthe* does, and we do it well. Don't let the ship's appearance fool you. Our motto '*We Strike Without Warning*' is entirely apt. She may look like a bulk freighter, but beneath the camouflage, she has the armament of a battleship and the moves of a cruiser. All we lacked until now was a Marine complement. Thanks to the fortunes of war that job now goes to Company Group 31, Scandia Regiment.

Over the next few days, my second officer, Lieutenant Commander Cullop, who you've seen planetside earlier today, and her division will train you in boarding party techniques so you can function just as well as any Marine company when we catch up with the scum. In the meantime, the crew will help you settle in and answer any question you may have."

She turned to Salminen, who had been standing beside her since handing the formation over and said, "You may dismiss your troops to their barracks, Major."

*

Dunmoore stuck her head into the CIC on her way to the bridge and found the charged atmosphere it always generates when the ship prepared to head out on a hunt. Lieutenant Commander Sirico made to relinquish the command chair, but she waved him back down.

"Anything new?"

"Lieutenant Zhukov is in the final stages of rousing the rest of the satellite constellation. She figures another thirty minutes at most, and we've finished analyzing the commo platform's log."

She took a seat at an unoccupied console and gave Sirico an expectant look. "And?"

The combat systems officer touched the screen embedded in the command chair's arm and the image of two innocuous, ordinary seeming sloop-sized starships appeared.

"Item one, the platform was able to capture this before it went dormant. I suppose the timing was just a tad off unless they didn't care about appearing on a wanted poster. No registration number to be seen, of course. We're running a comparison check with what we have in the database to figure out who or what they are. Item two, the log shows the AI received a command from

Sigma Noctae to order the constellation into dormancy before switching itself off. There's no identity tag attached to the order, but someone used a Navy override code."

"So it was definitely an inside job."

Sirico nodded. "No doubt about it. Someone who had high-level access. It doesn't necessarily mean Navy or Army for that matter. The commo platform is mixed military-civilian use, but the transmission came from Sigma Noctae's ground station."

"Might it have come from another station and been routed via the naval terminus?"

"I suppose that's possible. Theo's the one with the answers. I'll run it by him."

Dunmoore chewed on her lower lip, then said, "We'll have to interview the depot's surviving naval personnel one by one."

"That's what I figured, Captain. Perhaps the cox'n could handle that. If I recall, he received interrogation training during his stint with the special ops teams."

"He did. Make it so, but wait until they've settled in. The first officer is sorting them out into their assignments as part of the crew. Anything else?"

"Other than clamors from the surface to use our subspace transmitter as a relay since Yulia brought the commo platform back up, no. We're up to fourteen packets by now, each with a dozen individual messages. We've kept a copy of each, in case there's something related to the attackers. Theo said he'd do the analysis once we're under way."

Dunmoore knew it crossed the bounds of legality, but anything going through her transmitter was fair game. "Excellent." She stood and, with a last glance at the image of the mysterious ships, left the CIC.

*

Dunmoore looked up from the conference room's navigation display when the doors hissed open admitting Ezekiel Holt. She turned to Lieutenant Drost and said, "I approve the proposed course. You may prepare for departure."

"Thank you, sir." She slipped past Holt and out into the corridor.

Holt dropped into a chair with a weary sigh. "I've assigned our new crew members to their respective divisions, though we're not dealing with an overjoyed bunch here."

"How so?"

"They're not unhappy to be off Toboso. Surviving that sort of bombardment leaves a psychological scar. On the other hand, to say they're not thrilled at being pressed into service aboard *Iolanthe* would be an understatement. I get the impression we've inherited garritroopers who prefer life ashore."

Dunmoore made a dismissive face. "Tough. They're in the Navy and serve where they're told. Too bad for them, but we're at war, and that means the option to resign doesn't exist, although the mindset shouldn't surprise. Much of the garrison was like that in my day. What specialties do they have?"

"Four supply technicians, which will thrill Joelle to no end; four bosun's mates, though I'm not sure Emma will be happy to inherit spacers who haven't set foot aboard a man-o-war in years; one communications specialist and one engineer's mate. I still need to sort out the four in sickbay."

"You heard the command shutting down the entire satellite constellation came from the depot, right?"

Holt nodded. "I did. Inside job, just as Salminen figures. We must consider the possibility of a traitor among the folks we brought aboard. The fourteen depot staff members would be at the top of the list, though it's more likely that whoever betrayed the garrison left with the attackers."

"Guthren will interview the naval personnel about the attack once we've broken out of orbit."

"What about the Army folks?"

"I need to discuss the matter with Salminen. The soldiers who were with her in the mountains are obviously in the clear, but not necessarily those who were at the depot during the attack."

"Most of them are in sickbay, from what I understand. They'll have to wait. Our esteemed surgeon will offer to perform a colonoscopy with a high-powered laser if we try to interview them without his permission."

Dunmoore winced. "Ouch. Best not to tempt him. He sadly shares the temper of my former chief engineer aboard *Stingray* although his bedside manner is…"

The intercom chimed. "Bridge to the captain."

"…better." She touched her communicator. "Dunmoore."

"Officer of the watch, here. Lieutenant Zhukov and her team are back. The personnel pod is secure, and we're for all intents ready to leave."

"Excellent. Put the ship at departure stations. I'm on my way." Siobhan jumped to her feet and grinned at Holt. "What are you waiting for? Let's go hunting."

— Twelve —

"Now hear this, all hands to departure stations, I repeat, all hands to departure stations."

Sergeant Major Haataja gave the deckhead a baleful stare. "If they announce everything, down to the captain's bowel movements, this will turn out to be the most tedious posting in living memory."

Salminen smiled. "Different service, different protocols. We're here, and our only choice is to adapt. Besides, it's our best chance to kick ass and kill assholes."

CG31's top-kick and Lieutenant Puro, Salminen's second in command, did not quite crowd the company commander's small private cabin, but she sensed the gentle touch of claustrophobia brushing the outer edges of her consciousness, nonetheless.

"No arguments, sir. Can't say I hate the setup either. We didn't even have the luxury of individual squad bays on Toboso, or separate rooms for the noncoms, so it's a given the troops won't start bitching until they get totally bored."

"Which will happen any moment now," Puro interjected. "Still these shipboard barracks are better than I expected."

"Give 'em the benefit of the doubt, Lieutenant. They'll need a few more hours to realize there's no way to take the liberty bus into town for a bit of fun."

"Can't recall finding much of that in Doniphon, Sarn't Major."

Haataja winked at the younger man. "That's because you had no idea where to look. I never had a dull moment there."

Salminen snorted. "I'll bet."

One of the platoon leaders stuck his head into the cabin. "Thought you might like to know they locked us in."

"Pray tell us, Command Sergeant Saari," Haataja growled, "which fine specimen of humanity ignored the orders to stay within the barracks module until further notice?"

Saari grinned. "The fine specimen is one of mine, and he's already been suitably chastened."

"Let me guess," Salminen said. "He told you he forgot something in the shuttle that brought him here."

"More or less, Captain. But we know he just wanted to satisfy his curiosity about something or other."

"Once we're allowed out, I will ask permission to hold a formation on the hangar deck, and we can discuss how we need to behave because I'm suddenly getting visions of a few of our less than brilliant troopers finding their way into the engineering compartment or any other sensitive areas. God knows, we have our share of anti-geniuses in the ranks."

"Actually," a familiar voice said from behind Saari, "I'm here to tell you I'll be briefing your folks on several matters once we're under way, including which parts of the ship are out of bounds." Emma Cullop's face replaced that of the command sergeant, who had wisely retreated down the corridor. "That way we won't have to confine you to quarters whenever we're executing a maneuver. And I'm here to give you a few of these, so we don't have to send a runner here every time we want to talk."

Cullop held up a box of personal communicators.

"They haven't been keyed yet, but that's easy to do." She passed out three of them, took a fourth and showed how, then said, "I'm not sure how far down your chain of command you think we need to issue these, so I'm giving you two dozen. If you need more, tell me, but we definitely don't carry enough spares for your entire unit."

Salminen turned to her second in command and sergeant major. "Opinions?"

"Depends on what we're expected to do aboard the ship where we won't be suited up," Haataja replied. "If we're suited up, we have our own network to link everyone, and there's no reason we can't patch that into the ship's net."

"Two dozen means we can pass 'em out to the platoon leaders and platoon sergeants for starters," Puro said. "Once we're settled in and start earning our keep, we can figure out if the section leaders need their own."

Cullop nodded. "Fair enough. How about you form up on the hangar deck in fifteen minutes. If there are any changes, I'll call."

Then she vanished.

Salminen examined her communicator for a few moments before clipping it on. "I guess we're part of *Iolanthe*'s crew now."

Haataja followed suit, saying, "I guess we are, Major."

*

Emma Cullop's lecture to the assembled soldiers of Company Group 31 was concise and straight to the point so that even Salminen's 'anti-geniuses' should have no problems remembering what they could and could not do. Her announcement they would be subjected to regular daily drills which involved suiting up in full battle armor, followed by boarding party training and, equally important, how to repel boarders, drew a few soft groans from the rear ranks. However, her description of how

Iolanthe operated as a Q-ship, including the use of merchant uniforms, resulted in many more smiles of anticipation, especially when she announced that CG 31 would have to occasionally pass for a mercenary unit and remove all Army insignia from their battledress.

When she opened the floor for questions, one of the soldiers, the one Salminen suspected was Saari's earlier culprit, asked, "Corporal Vallin, Commander. I was wondering if you expect us to come up with our mercenary unit name and crest."

"Trust Vallin to seize on the trivial," Puro muttered in a tone so low only Salminen, standing beside him, could hear.

"That would be up to your CO, Corporal. But if ever we have to deploy you off the ship in a situation where we don't want to give the bad guys evidence the Fleet's hitting them, then it would be useful."

Salminen nudged Puro. "Not so trivial after all," she whispered back. Then in a louder voice, "I'll discuss the matter with the command group, Vallin. Your platoon leader will let you know my decision in due course."

"Yes, sir."

When the questions petered out, Cullop asked the sergeant major to divide the company into small groups and assigned a bosun's mate to each for an orientation tour of *Iolanthe*'s areas open to them. She personally took Salminen, Puro, Haataja and the platoon leaders around the ship, showing them parts that were off limits to the rest of the soldiers but which they would have cause to enter during the regular course of business, including the bridge, CIC and finally the conference room, where the department heads were assembling for the daily status brief.

Cullop pointed at a chair, marked 'Major of Marines,' and said to Salminen, "Since you're now one of us, you'll be attending the dailies, or if you're unable to for some reason, Lieutenant Puro will attend in your stead." Then she turned to the others, "Sergeant Major, the cox'n will want to speak with you top-kick to top-kick once we're done here, so don't wander off too far. I'd suggest waiting in the mess. We rarely go over fifteen minutes, but with a new face at the table, that might stretch out longer. The rest can return to barracks."

As one, the soldiers snapped to attention, then except for Salminen, pivoted on their heels and marched off. Since they had a few moments before the captain took her seat at the head of the table, Cullop introduced their new major of Marines to the other department heads. Head swimming with information overload after a surprised-filled day punctuated by more deaths, Salminen sat in her designated seat and found herself a beat behind the others in rising to attention when Dunmoore entered the room.

"As you were, folks." She smiled at Salminen. "Welcome aboard, Major. You and your troops are probably feeling a bit dizzy by the sudden change in circumstances, but I'm sure you'll find yourselves at home in *Iolanthe* as much as the rest of us in no time at all. I don't know if anyone has explained what the dailies are supposed to accomplish…"

"Sorry, sir, I didn't make the time to do so," Cullop said.

Dunmoore waved the apology away. "No matter, Emma. The last few hours have been hectic. Have you made the introductions?"

"Aye."

"In that case, Major," Dunmoore continued, "even though I sit at the head of this table, the daily status update is not primarily for my benefit, but to give each department head the chance to inform the others of matters that might cross departmental responsibility lines. It's also pretty much the only time in any given day when we, as *Iolanthe*'s command group, can come together, since we're rarely all on the same watchkeeping schedule."

"Understood, sir."

"I'll leave you for last today. However, I think we would benefit from hearing the story of the attack from your point of view, and get a quick overview of CG31's strengths, abilities, equipment and the like, and the issues you face as a combat unit that's lost a considerable part of itself to enemy action. It needn't be detailed at this point since several of the department heads will sit down with you and your executive officer over the next day to formalize your integration with this ship." When Salminen nodded, Dunmoore turned to Holt. "First officer?"

*

When Dunmoore dismissed them after Salminen had told her harrowing tale, she held the soldier back with a raised hand.

"Why don't you join me for a coffee in my day cabin next door? I usually take the time for a welcome chat with a newly posted officer when he or she reports aboard, but things have been more than a little unusual today."

A crooked smile briefly lit up Salminen's tired face. "It's a practice our two services share, Captain. I'd gladly go up against a dozen Shrehari Marines for a good cup of coffee right now."

"You certainly look like it." Dunmoore let her through the connecting door and pointed at one of the chairs in front of her desk. "Please sit. Do you take anything in your coffee?"

"No. I prefer it black as a reiver's soul."

"As do I." She handed Salminen a steaming mug, then raised hers in salute. "Once again, welcome. Consider *Iolanthe* your home as much as the rest of my crew consider it theirs. You might be here for a while, knowing how slowly the Fleet moves on matters when things work fine as they are. Besides, the idea of Army units serving as Marines aboard warships isn't as unusual as you might think, not even in recent memory, let alone in the days of wet navies on Earth."

"I know. If I weren't so tired, I'd consider it a nice change of pace. We've been on Toboso for over six months now and other than field training exercises, there's been little to keep the troops from battling boredom. Once they're over the shock of losing so many of their comrades and ending up aboard a starship, I'm sure many of them will find this assignment downright thrilling, especially the part about undercover operations while masquerading as mercenaries. When I get back to the barracks, I'll probably find myself drowning in name and crest ideas."

"No doubt. I wouldn't worry about it too much in the immediate. We won't hunt down these marauders under a false flag, at least not when the plasma starts flying."

"Knowing my troops, they'll make it a priority." Salminen suddenly yawned. "Sorry, sir. Fatigue seems to have crept up on me."

"Understandably so. A touch of this caffeine will help you through the rest of the day, though when we're done here, I suggest we head to the wardroom for a meal, and after that, you can catch a few hours of shuteye. I won't be calling any drills for the next twenty-four hours, to allow your company a chance to rest, and I don't expect to stumble across anything that requires going to battle stations. After that..."

"I appreciate it, sir." Salminen yawned again. "Unfortunately, I have company business to take care of before I can call it a day."

"In that case, why don't we drink up and see what the galley's serving tonight."

*

Guthren poked his head into the Chiefs' and Petty Officers' mess to find Sergeant Major Haataja, beer in hand, surrounded by half a dozen off-duty chiefs, including Henkman, and talking up a storm. A slow grin split his broad face. Trust a pongo to head straight for the booze. He entered, and the cluster around Haataja broke apart.

"Glad to see you settling in so, Sarn't Major. I'm Kurt Guthren, and for my sins, *Iolanthe*'s cox'n."

"Talo Haataja."

The men shook hands, testing each other, then Guthren said, "I'll get myself one of those as well, then we should talk, top-kick to top-kick."

Taking a table in one corner, away from prying ears, they examined each other for a few moments, then the cox'n asked, "First time serving aboard a starship, Talo? By the way, among chiefs, when we're off duty, it's first names, and an Army sergeant major is equivalent to a chief second class."

"First time, Kurt. I've always been an idle git of a passenger before this."

"It'll come to your lot quickly enough. Pay attention to the bosun and her folks, and you'll be fine." He took a gulp of his beer. "You know something about how the Navy works?"

Haataja shrugged. "Not much more than what they teach you in basic and whatever I picked up over the years."

"Okay. When it comes to our kind, consider me the regimental sergeant major. I'm the disciplinarian for all enlisted ranks aboard, and the captain's left arm — Mister Holt is her right arm. That means on discipline matters, you and me, we're joined at the hip. You're a department chief, like the bosun, the engineering chief, Holger Henkman, the combat systems chief whom you've already met, etcetera, etcetera. I'll be looking to you for anything that concerns the soldiers aboard, officers included."

"Understood."

"If your folks need sorting out and it doesn't concern the rest of the ship, I don't need to know about it. If it does, I want to hear the story before anything reaches the first officer's ears, let alone the captain's."

Haataja nodded. "Like we do within the regiment."

"You have any hard cases that might come to my attention?"

"One or two like any other unit. They're mostly under control, and their platoon leaders will keep a closer eye on them while we adapt to this new lifestyle."

"Good. Make sure the bosun doesn't end up frog-marching any of yours to the brig. Speaking of platoon leaders, they're enlisted, right?"

"Yep. Command sergeants one and all. The CO and Lieutenant Puro are the only officers left. Not that we had many before the attack."

"I'll want to have a little group chat with your command sergeants in the next few days, maybe around a beer, since they'll be messing here as well."

"Consider it arranged."

Guthren grinned again. "I like a man who doesn't dick around. Last thing, booze when off duty is fine. Getting shit-arsed isn't. Going on watch still soused or with a hangover will have any crew member doing the hatless quick march in front of the captain, including our household infantry."

"I wouldn't have it any other way, Kurt."

The cox'n raised his beer in salute. "Welcome aboard." Then he drained the bottle in one mighty gulp and sighed with contentment. "It may not be a late vintage Shrehari ale, but at least it's not Pacifican horse piss."

— Thirteen —

"How are they shaping up?"

Dunmoore turned her head and gave Holt a smile. She was standing in the hangar bay's control room, arms crossed, watching Company Group 31 go through endless repetitions of boarding party drills under the direction of the bosun and her mates.

"About as well as we might expect from soldiers still grieving for their slaughtered comrades and who have never served aboard a starship."

The one-eyed first officer joined her by the armored window and watched the fast-paced activity on the depressurized deck. "Keeping busy is the best way to get over shock and grief, especially if it's mind-numbingly repetitive, something Chief Dwyn is expert at inflicting on the unwary."

Dunmoore chuckled. "That she is. However, as long as we don't have to use them within the next day or two, they should be okay on their first boarding action. Tatiana Salminen strikes me as being hard-nosed enough to keep them at it until she knows they're ready, never mind Chief Dwyn's tender mercies."

"It's amazing what a thirst for vengeance will do, Captain, provided it's well controlled and directed." A brief grin flashed across his face. "As you know."

"Please." She rolled her eyes in an exaggerated fashion, to Holt's amusement. "Haven't you heard that in taking revenge, a man is but even with his enemy; but in passing it over, he is superior?"

"Indeed. Attributed to Francis Bacon if I recall correctly."

"You do. I take his words to heart, Zeke, and merely carry out my duty as prescribed by the Navy and by Commonwealth law."

Holt snorted. "If you're going to tell me you don't derive immense satisfaction from sending the baddies to their just reward, I will call bullshit."

"Would I lie to you? Yes, I enjoy seeing bastards who desperately need a dose of justice receive their due in full, but I don't make it an obsession. My name isn't Ahab. Knowing I've done my duty is enough."

Even as the words left her mouth, she recalled telling him about the unexpected eruption of fury towards Andrew Devine and his cronies two days earlier in Anton Gerber's office and realized that Holt had deliberately struck a nerve. The knowing twinkle in his eye confirmed it.

"If I start seeing white whales in space, you have permission to relieve me of command, Zeke."

"No worries." He nodded at the armored soldiers, now reforming into ranks opposite the mock-ups *Iolanthe*'s crew used to keep boarding parties fresh and on edge. "Are you staying for another round?"

"Unless you tell me I have more pressing business elsewhere, I'll stick around for a while. I prefer to form my own opinion of their readiness before we commit them to action."

"You don't trust Chief Dwyn all of a sudden?"

"Dwyn's not the one making the hard calls. I am."

He dipped his head in acknowledgment. "Fair enough. If you don't mind, I'll keep you company."

"I never mind your company, Zeke, even when you're baiting me." She nudged him with her elbow.

"How about adding sound to the show?"

"Be my guest. There was too much chatter earlier, so I turned it off."

He reached for the control panel and linked them to CG31's company net.

"... but you didn't look like a complete clusterfuck this time," Dwyn's hectoring voice erupted from the speakers, "only a partial one, so I guess that's progress. Now, which one of you was the boarding party idiot this time?"

"Saari here. That would be Corporal Vallin, Chief."

"May I assume Vallin received no tight quarters combat training during his career?"

"He has, just like the rest of them, but figures he can improve on tried and true protocols."

"I suppose from the enemy's point of view, a dead soldier is an improvement," Dwyn replied. "Take this as a lesson; never rush aboard a hostile starship. Smart marauders will see you coming and prepare accordingly. You are most vulnerable once the airlock opens and you will not have a viable foothold until you've seized control of the first passage beyond the airlock. Any comments you'd like to make, Major?"

"Vallin trying to play Space-Viking aside, I agree with the bosun. You're improving. Keep at it and remember that the captain may call on us to do this for real once we catch up with the scum who murdered half of ours. Sergeant Saari, you may stand your platoon down and play spectator. Sergeant Alekseev, you're up."

Holt and Dunmoore witnessed number two platoon's battle run in silence, both wincing from time to time at some of the radio chatter and the occasional stumble.

"No Space-Viking stumbling over his own shadow in this lot," Holt said once Dwyn waved them back into three ranks for the after-action review. "Nice to see troops learning from the mistakes of others instead of needing to pee on the electric fence for themselves."

"Is that something you've experienced?" Dunmoore asked with a mischievous smile.

"No. I learned when I saw my cousin Harry do it on a dare when we were both fourteen. He joined the Marines the same year I entered the Academy and likely drove his basic training instructors around the bend."

"Is he still in the Corps?"

"I hope so. He was with the 11th Regiment on Cimmeria when it fell to the Shrehari. We've had no news since then, though it wouldn't surprise me that he's still fighting them in the hills as a ragged partisan."

They fell silent again, listening to Chief Dwyn tear second platoon's performance apart, though she grudgingly admitted that they had improved again this time around. Eight chimes of the bell rang softly through the ship, and Dunmoore's stomach growled in response.

"I think I've just been told it's lunchtime." She nodded towards the door. "Their third platoon should perform even better at this rate, so I'll let the bosun give me her evaluation. Shall we?"

*

When Holt and Dunmoore entered the wardroom, a visibly excited Sirico waved them over, while hastily swallowing a bite of his sandwich.

"Chief Yens figures some or all of them might still be in the system, sir," he said once they were within earshot. "The ion trail goes well past the hyperlimit for ships of that size, and it's marauder SOP to jump the moment they can do so without tearing themselves apart. Plus, it seems to lead us towards Rocinante, the largest of the gas giants. That beauty has enough moons to make a whole new set of planets, which means plenty of hiding places.

Then there's the added advantage of Rocinante's wild magnetic field messing with our sensors."

Dunmoore glanced at her first officer with a raised eyebrow. "Are you thinking what I'm thinking, Zeke?"

"If you're thinking the buggers went to ground because they're waiting for us to leave, then yes."

A light came on in Sirico's eyes. "Of course. They saw *Iolanthe* entering the system. Not knowing whether we were Navy or a harmless civilian ship, they decided to avoid tempting fate and risk detection by going FTL right in front of our sensors. We dropped out of hyperspace around the time of the attack. If that's the case, they'll be running silent."

"I mean we'll just have to flush them out, won't we?" Dunmoore replied. "If they're lying doggo, they won't be talking to their friends on Toboso. That means their first reaction when they see us will be wondering why a big honking bulk freighter is playing hide and seek in Rocinante orbit."

A wicked grin tugged at Holt's lips. "That should stun 'em long enough to let us hit hard, then board in the smoke, or rather escaping gasses."

"Or we could run out of trail well short of Rocinante and still be beyond a sloop's hyperlimit," Dunmoore said. "Let's not get too excited."

"True." The first officer looked at the buffet. "Lunch won't get me excited either."

Dunmoore was mopping up the last of the salad dressing with her bun when Tatiana Salminen entered the wardroom, minus her battle armor. The short dark hair plastered against her skull with sweat bore witness to the hard training laid on by Chief Dwyn.

"Major," Siobhan raised a hand to attract her attention, "join us once you've picked up your lunch."

"Yes, sir."

The quantity of food Salminen piled on her tray could have fed a squad of Marines. But after witnessing the morning's evolutions, Dunmoore knew the same scene would be repeated in the other messes as ravenous soldiers refueled after hours spent cycling through the same drills over and over again. An equally sweat-slicked Lieutenant Puro showed up soon after, proving that no one in CG31 was exempt from the bosun's continuing education on the life of a Marine in a man-of-war.

"You had an enjoyable morning?" Holt asked Salminen after she put her tray down and sat.

She winced. "It was a timely reminder that garrison duty makes you soft, notwithstanding regular field training exercises. By now, my troops will be discovering a newfound respect for our Marine Corps brethren. I know I am. We'll be instituting regular physical training while wearing full battle armor once Chief Dwyn and her crew are done torturing us, to reinforce the point. We have a two-hour break, then it's back into the suits for another bout. This time, she'll deploy us a platoon at a time off the ship and bring us in as if *Iolanthe* was the target rather than use the mock-ups on the hangar deck."

"How confident are you about your people's ability if I have to call on them soon?" Dunmoore asked, giving the soldier a thoughtful gaze.

An apologetic grimace twisted her face. "Truth is, our first time will be more of a clusterfuck than either of us wants. However, there's no getting around the fact we're new to this game, and all the training in the galaxy can't replace first-hand experience. However, unless we're going up against hardened professional troops, casualties should be limited to the opposition. We're new at the whole fighting in space thing, not at fighting in general. If you could have your best boarding party noncom backing up the platoon leader who'll be leading the boarding party, it would help."

"Agreed." Dunmoore nodded. "Please mention it to the second officer at the next daily update. She'll assign someone well before I order you out on a mission so your platoon leaders can get used to the idea."

"Did I hear you say soon, sir?" Salminen asked.

"According to my sensor chief, who has a touch of the second sight, some, perhaps all the attackers may still be in this system, preferring to hide until we leave. Faced with multiple ships, I may have to toss your folks in at the deep end within the next few days."

"Oh." A thoughtful expression replaced Salminen's frown. "We'll certainly do our best once you give the word, Captain. Until then, we'll train as if we're about to liberate Cimmeria single-handed."

Holt drained his cup, climbed to his feet, and said, "The doc will let us interview the wounded now, so if you'll excuse me, I have to track down the cox'n."

— Fourteen —

"Chief Petty Officer Third Class Marko Trane, I presume." Guthren pulled a chair up to the bed where a bald, middle-aged man with a boxer's face sat, staring absently at a tablet in his lap. One of the sick bay attendants drew the privacy curtain shut, isolating both men from the rest of the compartment. "I'm Kurt Guthren, *Iolanthe*'s cox'n."

Trane studied Guthren with deep-set, blue eyes radiating suspicion. "That would be my name, Chief. You'll have to forgive me for not snapping to attention. A chunk of rock took me down during the attack. What can I do for you?"

"First of all, if no one's told you yet, what's left of Sigma Noctae's naval personnel have been entered in *Iolanthe*'s books until Fleet HQ reassigns you, so welcome to the crew."

"Yeah, I heard. Can't pretend I'm overjoyed to serve on an armed freighter, but as they say, if you don't have a sense of humor, you shouldn't have joined."

"We're really a Q-ship, and that means plenty of action and plenty of bad guys breathing vacuum when we get 'em." When Trane did not react, Guthren shrugged. "Happy or not, here you are. What's your occupational specialty?"

"Bosun by trade, operations chief by training."

"Is that what you were doing at the depot, running the operations center?"

Trane nodded. "Sure. The officer figured he was running it, but we all know how it goes. Shame he was vaporized along with the rest of the crew."

"Lieutenant Commander Cullop, our second officer, will be glad for an extra chief as watch stander for the deck department once the doc releases you."

"Whatever you say, Cox'n."

"Second item, we're trying to put together a timeline of the attack, to help us track the bastards down and give 'em hell. What's left of Company Group 31 saw nothing more than the attacking ships lift off, so we're interviewing everyone who was at the depot when it happened."

"Okay. Ask away."

"Why don't you tell me about that morning? Take whatever time you need."

Trane seemed to collect his thoughts, eyes on the foot of the bed, and then shrugged.

"What's to tell? It started like any boring old day on Toboso. Wasn't a ship due anytime soon, or a delivery from the co-op, so we were on the low end of the cycle, taking care of maintenance, individual training, that kind of crap. Then everything went to shit without warning."

"You mean no one picked up any of the raiders as they approached the planet?"

"That's the job of civilian traffic control, not us. Buggers must have been spoofed because they never said boo. Usually, when something shows up that doesn't seem right, we get 'em screaming in our ears. The last mistake they ever made. Traffic control operated from the colonial administration complex in Doniphon. Someone said it's as gone as the depot."

"Where were you when the kinetic strikes came in?"

"Halfway to the damned ground station. When the commo system alerted us that we were no longer talking to the platform in orbit, let alone the subspace relay, the lieutenant sent me to check if something was wrong with our transmitter array. The AI said everything was fine, but it's been wrong before, so out I went. It saved my life. One strike took out the HQ building and the operations center, another took out the array, and a couple more turned everything else to dust. I was mowed down by a piece of something hard bouncing off the ground. Couldn't get up again and passed out. A few hours later, the soldiers found me and took me into the warehouse which was the only place not punched into a crater, although they tell me the bastards emptied it. If the lieutenant had been a minute or so slower in reacting to the outage, you and I wouldn't be talking, Chief."

"So you never saw them land."

Trane shook his head. "Nope. I was unconscious until the Army medic started working on my legs. The pain yanked me back into the land of the living. Could have been worse. Thankfully I was hit low, so there's no spinal damage." He pointed at the regeneration sleeves covering his lower limbs. "Doc says I'll be walking on them again within a few days. Makes me luckier than most."

"Anything else come to mind that might help finger the bad guys?"

"Nope." Trane shook his head without looking up. "Can't think of a single thing, Chief, but if you get 'em, give the fuckers my everlasting love."

"You mean when *we* get them."

"Sure. If I'm out of sickbay by then."

*

"I didn't get much of anything from the four Navy guys in sickbay," Guthren said, settling into one of the chairs facing Dunmoore's day cabin desk, next to the first officer. "At least not when it comes to the identity of the attackers. The three ratings were caught out in the open and knocked into next week by the concussion of the kinetic penetrators. They're no more useful than the ten who were working the warehouse and went to ground in dark corners, pissing their pants, the moment it started. All of 'em are about as useful as left-handed spanners. Chief Trane on the other hand, though he was taken down almost in the same way as the other three, is a little more interesting. Turns out he was Sigma Noctae's operations chief."

Dunmoore's eyebrows shot up. "That gave him the access needed to screw with anything plugged into the depot."

"Aye." Guthren nodded. "That was my thought as well. Yet the way he tells it, he survived because his officer sent him out to check the ground station a minute or so before the strike hammered home. That left him halfway between two targets. Kind of hard to time."

"But an easy enough story," Holt said. "Trane wouldn't be the first Chief to lie."

"True, Commander, but he gave me the impression of being a man with a heavy heart. A man who escaped death by mere chance while everyone around him died, someone who figures he almost bought it. Not someone who got away with it."

"Good actor?"

The coxswain shrugged. "That's always a possibility, but Trane reminds me of guys I've known who have seen unexpected death and can't quite believe what happened. If he's the inside man, he'd have made sure to be as far away as he could from ground zero, not end up in the middle of it. If that chunk of debris had hit him any higher, he'd be in a regen tank for months while they fix his spine instead of an easy week in leg sleeves."

"Pay a man enough," Holt replied, "and he'll take six months in a tank."

"I'm not sure of that," Dunmoore said. "A few people don't take to regen, and there's no way of knowing until you're stuck trying. Besides, how would you organize specific injuries during a bombardment from orbit to cover your own malfeasance? Sounds to me as if Trane has a case of survivor's guilt."

Neither Holt nor Guthren had an answer to that.

"What about the soldiers in sickbay?" She asked.

"Sarn't Major Haataja interviewed them. We figured that between us, they'd be more at ease with him," Guthren said. "Four of them were training for the annual Doniphon to Stoddard marathon. Apparently, the two settlements are exactly forty-two kilometers apart, town center to town center. Their story is pretty much the same as Trane's. They were jogging around Sigma Noctae's perimeter and were caught between the strikes that took out two of the defensive domes. Flying debris knocked them down. The other six were helping in the warehouse and found themselves in a firefight with the raiders once they landed. Since they weren't expecting an attack, they had side arms only and no armor. Whoever did it wasn't wearing armor either, but carried heavier weapons. It turned into a one-sided fight that ended with the soldiers out of action and left for dead. All they could say is that the bastards are human and speak Anglic, but didn't sound like they were military."

"You know," Holt said after a moment of silence. "If we hadn't shown up when we did, the raiders would have gotten away with what was obviously a well-planned operation."

"And if Major Salminen hadn't taken the infantry component of Company Group 31 out into the hills for some fun and games, it would also have ceased to exist, leaving next to no witnesses."

"Let's hope that for the people who did this, those two little things turn into the horseshoe nail that lost a kingdom."

Guthren gave the first officer a puzzled look. "What's that now, Mister Holt?"

"There's an old proverb that goes,
For want of a nail, the shoe was lost;
For want of a shoe, the horse was lost;
For want of a horse, the battle was lost;
For the failure of battle, the kingdom was lost
All for want of a horseshoe nail."

The coxswain gave Holt a knowing smile. "Seen. We're a mighty big nail they didn't expect. Too bad for them."

"Let's not count our prize money just yet, gentlemen," Dunmoore warned. "We still have to run the marauders to ground and seize them. So far Yens has nothing more than a feeling based on the fact we're well past a sloop's hyperlimit without losing the ion trail."

The intercom chimed, and then Lieutenant Commander Sirico's voice called out. "CIC to the captain."

"Speak of the devil," Guthren said.

"Dunmoore."

"Chief Yens has determined that the trail we've been following vanishes somewhere near Rocinante's orbit, no doubt dissipated by the planet's magnetic field. Considering we've not picked up any transitions to FTL since arriving in-system and the trail is fresher than that..." Sirico sounded distinctly enthused by the news.

"As I just told the first officer and cox'n, let's not divvy up the prize money yet. We've sixty odd moons to scan in a less than sensor-friendly environment. They could bolt on us and jump out pretty quickly, in spite of Rocinante's gravity well, while we need to be much further away thanks to our being an order of magnitude more massive than four sloops put together, never mind just one."

Holt made a face at his captain and muttered, "Party pooper," earning himself a hard stare in return.

"However," Dunmoore continued, "once we're within gun range of the nearest moon, call the ship to battle stations but don't unmask."

"Can we give the sensors full military power now?" Sirico asked.

"I suggest we do," Holt said. "If a hard ping flushes them out while we're still far enough from Rocinante to go FTL, so much the better."

"Very well. Make it so, Mister Sirico. Ping the hell out of Rocinante's moons."

— Fifteen —

Holt picked up his bishop and moved it to threaten Dunmoore's queen, but her faint smile as he glanced up before releasing the piece made him hesitate. Chess was not his game of choice. He preferred the more sophisticated Go and had been trying to introduce her to it. However, this was not the time to try again. Not while they waited for Chief Yens and the sensor crew to get a hit on starships trying their best to stay hidden. Unlike Gregor Pushkin, Holt's skill at chess barely rose above Siobhan's level, if that, and she had been winning three games to his two. Moreover, after months of playing, he still could not decide whether her little tells were intentional to mess with his head or unconscious. He let go of the bishop. Sure enough, he realized a fraction of a second later that he had just exposed himself to defeat in three moves, four at most, something she had seen. Holt sighed.

"You want to play it through, or can I resign now?"

"I'll take your resignation without gloating, Zeke. It's obvious part of your mind is elsewhere."

He nodded. "I'm still trying to tease something useful from what we know so far about the attack, find a pattern of sorts." He chuckled. "You can put the counter-intelligence officer back on a ship of the line, but you can't erase his habit of analyzing everything all the time."

"Thank God for that. You can carry the weight for both of us in such matters. My mind refuses to twist itself into a pretzel contemplating the possibilities, which is probably why Go doesn't appeal to me."

"More's the pity. Should I set up the board for another game?"

She waved his offer aside. "No. Even I'm losing my ability to concentrate after five bouts. Never mind that I keep expecting a call from the CIC telling me Yens has locked on to our quarry."

"We'll be going to battle stations in less than half an hour, anyway."

Dunmoore grunted. "Then I can do my fretting in full view of the CIC crew."

"Watching you act like a normal human from time to time is endearing to most of us."

She made an obscene gesture at him. "Show some respect, Commander."

"Oh?" He grinned at her. "Was that respectful towards me, Captain?"

Holt packed away the chess and then slumped back in his chair. "I'm still puzzled by what the end game was supposed to be if we hadn't shown up when we did. Their wiping out the colonial administration seems gratuitous if what you're after is booty. It's not as if a replacement regime will last long after declaring independence from the Commonwealth. In war time that sort of behavior smacks of treason."

"Perhaps not full independence. Though it isn't beyond the realm of possibility that home rule is part of the goal, although I shudder to think about the people who'd be running the place."

"Hah." Holt barked a derisive laugh. "Killing the governor and her staff will make sure that Toboso stays under the Colonial Office's thumb for the next hundred years. It still makes no sense, and that's what's bothering me the most."

"Does anything related to greed have to make sense?"

The first officer considered her question for a few heartbeats, then shook his head. "No. History's proved that greed for power is the human failing that makes the least sense."

"Unless it's the gateway to wealth, I suppose. You and I have been to the same lectures at the Academy, Zeke, so I'll not offer any arguments against the notion. But as you said, events on Toboso make little sense to us. At least for now."

The chimes of a ship-wide warning cut off whatever Holt may have wanted to say in reply. It was followed by the voice of the officer of the watch. "Now hear this. Battle stations in five minutes, I repeat, battle stations in five minutes. That is all."

"I suppose we should grab our protective gear and take our stations." The first officer jumped to his feet with a spryness that belied his still not fully stabilized leg. "As they say in the junior ranks' mess, shit's about to get real."

"Or so we hope."

*

Although the soldiers of Company Group 31 had practiced going to battle stations many times between endless rounds of boarding party drills and the somewhat less intense but still exhaustive training to repel boarders, the barracks armory, where they kept their battle suits and weapons, was a barely contained hive of chaos. They had yet to master the economy of movement that was second nature to their Marine Corps counterparts and were bumping into each other like excited rubber balls.

When Salminen dropped a piece of armor for the second time in a row, Sergeant Major Haataja, already dressed, grinned at her. "Nervous in the service, Major?"

"No," she growled, visibly annoyed with herself. She picked up the gauntlet again. This time it clicked into place. "Do me a favor, will you? Within company lines, it's still captain. We'll use Navy protocols when there's one of them around to hear us. Or I'll start calling you chief. There, done." Salminen picked up her helmet.

"Let me check you over, Captain, before you head up to the splendors of the CIC while we peons play heavily armed security guards."

"Which was what we were doing at Sigma Noctae if you'll remember. We might actually earn our keep around here."

Haataja nodded. "True and true, though I'd rather the Navy doesn't point us at the enemy just yet. The boys and girls could use more training, judging by how much of a fuck-up this preparation for battle stations is turning out to be."

"That's what happens when you train 'em platoon by platoon. Everyone is in here at once for the first time. Things were bound to turn ugly," Lieutenant Puro pointed out. "We need to find a better way to organize ourselves, that's all."

The frantic hoot of the battle stations siren cut through the armory's din with a heart-stopped suddenness.

Salminen waved a mock salute at her second in command. "That's my signal to go. Enjoy the TAC."

Their barracks had, besides squad bays, cabins, and the armory, several additional compartments, one of them outfitted as a rudimentary tactical command post, or TAC in Army parlance. It would allow Puro and the sergeant major to control the deployment of individual platoons and sections within the ship.

She met few of *Iolanthe*'s crew on her way to the CIC. Most had already taken their stations before the actual siren went off, thanks to the five minutes warning. The CIC itself, when she entered, seemed like an oasis of calm utterly at odds with the chaos of the armory. The combat systems officers and noncoms spoke with each other in subdued tones instead of shouts, and each gesture appeared deliberate and unhurried. As she took her assigned console after nodding at the captain by way of greeting, Salminen could not suppress a rueful smile. Dunmoore noticed the expression and, catching her eye, raised a questioning eyebrow.

"Just noting the contrast, sir. My armory was still a charlie foxtrot when I left it while this place has the calm of a Zen monastery. As my deputy said, we'll have to figure out a better way to organize ourselves."

"I know you will, Major, and don't censor yourself on my account. I've been known to call a clusterfuck a clusterfuck. Besides, Fleet folklore has taught us that our esteemed ground forces use a saltier language than we do and I'd be disappointed to discover the contrary."

A message flashed on her screen, Puro advising that First Platoon had finally pulled its thumbs out and was headed for the hangar deck. As the ones who had shown the most improvement, they would wait by the shuttles as the designated boarding party backup.

"Lieutenant Puro reports that my valiant troops have overcome the chaos and are moving out."

Dunmoore smiled encouragingly. "It's not yet been five minutes since we called battle stations, so well done."

"A good thing we had five minutes warning, otherwise I'd still be trying to figure out which end of this battle suit fits where, sir."

"If it makes you feel any better, the crew, including myself, also have to adapt. Most of us don't have much of experience when it comes to working with an integral

Marine company. Any suggestions or ideas on how to improve things are always welcome."

"Yes, sir. Or am I expected to say aye, aye, sir?"

"Yes will do fine."

A raised hand from the sensor section caught Dunmoore's attention.

"You have something, Chief?"

"Aye, Captain. A whole lot of nothing. The moon designated as Rocinante Twelve is clean, so far as the sensors can tell. Rocinante Eleven is coming up next."

"Sir," Sirico said, "I can't help thinking that if we pop out a flight of probes, this might go faster."

"Perhaps," Dunmoore nodded in agreement. "However, probes could also confirm to anyone looking, such as our quarry, that *Iolanthe* isn't quite what she pretends to be. Armed naval transports, let alone civilian freighters, don't carry recon drones and I'm loath to give up my most potent weapon, surprise. If there are indeed four or more marauders, and they receive warning to scatter, the chances are that a few might escape and I want all of them."

"Agreed, sir, but since we're already pinging this area with full military power…"

"Which we would if we were the armed transport we've been pretending to be, or at least, so it'll seem to them." She winked at him. "Patience, Mister Sirico, patience. I doubt they'll have landed on one of the moons. It would make them too vulnerable while they lift off. If the buggers are hiding near Rocinante, they'll be orbiting something in a way that lets them light up and punch out as fast as possible. That means we'll eventually find them, even if they're running as silent as civilian ships possibly can. We merely have to get close enough."

Turning to Salminen, Siobhan said, "I'm sure you've heard the expression that war is long stretches of boredom punctuated by moments of sheer terror, Major.

Well, this is our version of it. Long stretches of boredom searching for our quarry followed by what we hope will be moments of sheer terror for him. If things go on too long without an enemy contact, we'll cycle the crew down to a lower alert status, one watch at a time, so they can eat, use the heads and rest. That would include your troops as well."

"Coming within gun range of Rocinante Eleven," Yens announced. "Beginning in-depth scan."

— Sixteen —

"Mister Dulce?" The mercenary sensor tech turned to get his first officer's attention.

"What's up, Jess?"

"The passive receiver just picked up a sensor ping, and it has a definite Navy vibe."

"Has to be the damned freighter that dropped in on us unannounced. I knew it was an armed naval transport coming in for a pickup or a delivery."

"Most likely," Jess replied, "unless someone else showed up and we didn't register the drop out of FTL. Considering how well Rocinante's magnetic field fucks with our gear…"

The duty officer shrugged. "Does it matter? Someone's decided to scan Rocinante's moons, and that can only mean they figure we might be hiding here."

"What can an armed transport do? We can both outrun it and outshoot it, depending on the boss' mood."

"Speaking of which." The duty officer touched the nearest intercom. "Bridge to the captain."

"Yes, Mike?" An irascible voice answered a moment later.

"Someone's scanning in our vicinity. Jess figures it's the Navy."

"That transport? Ridiculous. Who in his right mind would chase putative raiders with a glorified bulk freighter?"

"We should find out soon enough," Mike Dulce replied, staring at the tactical screen. "Whatever it is, it'll come into visual range within the hour."

"Are we still linked with *Sigrun* via laser?"

"Aye. Shall I inform them of the contact?"

"No. Let's wait until they wake up over there, Mike. No need to cause undue alarm." *Skögul*'s crew had long ago become inured to their captain's proclivity for sarcasm, and Mike merely smiled at his mock exasperation. "Of course I want you to tell them. Then make sure both of us are ready to go up systems at a moment's notice, preferably to run. We've already left too many clues behind as is. This contract was supposed to be untraceable. Fighting will only make it worse."

"What about *Skalmold*, *Sanngrior*, and *Herja*?" Mike asked, naming the other three ships that had taken part in the Toboso raid, the latter a transport carrying most of the booty. He immediately regretted opening his mouth.

"Can we contact them without giving ourselves away? Of course not. They're living it large around Rocinante Nine, beyond our line of sight, because some bloody genius decided to split us up. As if that would reduce the chances of being found." Though Captain Vanger did not name the flotilla commander by name, everyone within earshot knew he was referring to Captain Tarkon, *Skalmold*'s master, a man Vanger thoroughly disliked.

The communications tech raised his hand, "Sir, *Sigrun* just reported the contact. They're calling it a Navy vibe as well."

"Glad to see they're on the ball," Mike replied in a sour tone.

*

"Where are you, my pretty?" Chief Yens murmured, loud enough for Dunmoore to hear.

"You have a contact?" Dunmoore was just about ready to abandon Rocinante Eleven after almost an hour's worth of fruitless scanning.

"More of a sensor ghost, but a ship running silent and Rocinante's interference would account for that." She paused, then, "We must have hit a radiation eddy. I call a contact. One sloop-sized starship in orbit around Rocinante Eleven. Excellent emissions control, but not good enough at this range. Now to find the others."

"Let's try to make like we didn't discover them, folks," Dunmoore told the CIC at large, her words repeated to the bridge via an open video link. "At least not until we know where the remaining ships are hiding. Remember, we're looking for four, perhaps five of the scum."

"Are we going to try the old surrender or die approach?" Holt asked.

She smiled down at the small, three-dimensional image of her first officer hovering over the command chair's arm. "Of course. It may be an oldie, but it never gets old."

"Especially after we turn into an infernal ship of doom," Sirico added, a bloodthirsty grin distorting his elegantly trimmed beard.

"Doom, yes." Dunmoore smiled at him. "But I've never considered us infernal."

The minutes ticked by while tension in the CIC rose as they waited for Yens to find the other ships. Dunmoore had to suppress dancing fingers more than once, forcing herself to stay silent and let her people work their magic. Then, a second starship icon joined the first one on the tactical projection, both orbiting Rocinante Eleven.

"That's it, Captain," Yens said. "Two sloops. If there are more in the raiding force, either they've buggered off without us noticing, or they're hiding around another moon. I guarantee they're not here."

"Good enough for me. Keep a light touch on them so we can lock targeting sensors the moment we're up systems. Mister Holt, maintain current heading. We'll unmask when we're point-blank."

"Maintain current heading, aye," the first officer replied. "All systems are ready to go to full military power."

"I have a visual lock, Captain." Yens pointed at a side screen. "Their hull configuration is consistent with the ships seen by Company Group 31 and the communications platform."

Dunmoore raised a clenched fist. "Got you."

*

"I think they might have made us, Captain."

Skögul's master, who had been pacing across the small bridge, unable to sit still with a massive naval transport slowly coming into gun range, stopped to peer over the technician's shoulder. He grunted. "No sensor lock let alone a targeting ping. What makes you say they made us?"

"The last sensor sweep lingered a second or two longer on us than the earlier ones. It tells me their techs have picked up something they figure is not supposed to be there, such as a starship or two running under full emissions control."

Vanger grunted again, the vaguely dismissive sound masking a sudden surge of anxiety. His instincts began screaming at him to light up and use *Skögul*'s superior rate of acceleration to escape. On the other hand, how much of a threat did that lumbering giant present? He looked up at one of the side screens, where a video feed displayed the approaching vessel's boxy shape. Then he glanced back at the main tactical display where his gunnery officer had traced the transport's projected course, which, if it held, would take the ship away from Rocinante Eleven towards Rocinante Ten. In another fifteen minutes, *Skögul*'s orbital period would place the moon between both vessels, with *Sigrun* following shortly after that. Vanger, giving in to his fears, resolved to light up and run for the hyperlimit once they were in Rocinante Eleven's shadow, Tarkon be damned. He could find his own way home. On the other hand, if he was using his brains to think tactically for once, he might figure out it was time to go when he saw *Skögul* and *Sigrun* high tail it away from Rocinante. If all five ships lit up at the same time, the Navy would have too many targets at once.

"Umm, Captain?" Jess turned to look up at him. "I was wrong a moment ago. Their last sensor sweep didn't linger for a second or two longer. It's still on us. A light touch, but I'm almost sure they have a lock."

Vanger swore with unusual vehemence. They would not be able to brazen it out after all. Fortunately, the sloops could out-accelerate anything that large, transport or warship. Once out of weapons range, they would be free to jump. So much for an untraceable contract, but the universe does not care about the desires of sentient beings. Nor does it care whether they live or die. Vanger preferred to live.

"Signal *Sigrun*, prepare to go up systems, then get us ready to light ours, Mister Dulce. We're leaving. Helm, prepare to break out of orbit." He touched the navigation screen and traced the course he wanted, something that would aim them towards the outer fringes of the system and away from the intruder, using the moon as a shield against direct fire as much as possible. "Transmit that course to *Sigrun*."

A tense minute ticked by, then Dulce said, "We're ready," moments before the communications technician announced that *Sigrun* had reported ready as well.

"Up systems. Helm, maximum acceleration."

*

"Power surge on both contacts," Yens called out. "They've raised shields and have begun accelerating. I'm designating them Tango One and Tango Two." The pair of orange icons in the three-dimensional tactical projection at the center of the CIC turned red, now that the Chief had tagged them as a hostile threat. "The contacts are powering weapons."

"Unmask," Dunmoore ordered, "then give me an open frequency."

In mere moments, *Iolanthe* turned from a sluggish, nonthreatening bulk carrier into every pirate's nightmare. Her energy emissions spiked as dampened systems came to full military power and shields snapped into place. Vibrations rumbled through the Q-ship, signaling that the massive hull plates hiding her true nature were sliding aside. Gun turrets rose from their recesses, the barrels of those able to bear on either of the Tangos orienting themselves in preparation to fire. Midship, on either beam, missile launcher tubes opened to expose row upon row of gaping menace. Then, targeting sensors locked onto the fleeing ships, making *Iolanthe* ready to mete out a lethal dose of retribution.

"You're on all channels, Captain," the signals petty officer said.

"To the unidentified vessels in Rocinante Eleven orbit, this is the Commonwealth Starship *Iolanthe*. You will cease accelerating, drop shields, and prepare to be boarded for inspection. I am detaining you on suspicion of having taken part in unlawful activities on and around

Toboso. Failure to comply will result in my opening fire, which can lead to the loss of life. Yours." Dunmoore made a cutting gesture, and when the petty officer nodded, she said, "put that on a loop and let's hope they show enough sense to surrender. If we haven't given them a heart attack yet, they'll soon understand that resisting is futile."

*

Stunned silence enveloped *Skögul*'s bridge, the crew too shaken by *Iolanthe*'s transformation for words.

"What the fuck is that?" Mike Dulce's voice rose by two octaves when it finally dawned on him that something akin to a battle cruiser had them in its sights.

"Q-ship," Vanger said in a low growl, snapping out of his surprise-induced stupor. "We've been conned by a fucking Q-ship."

"Sir, there's a looped message on the emergency channel," the radio operator said in a voice turned raspy by fear.

"Play it."

Dunmoore's voice erupted from the bridge's hidden speakers, causing the already alarmed crew to blanch even further.

"To the unidentified vessels in Rocinante Eleven orbit, this is the Commonwealth Starship *Iolanthe*. You will cease accelerating, drop shields, and prepare to be boarded for inspection. I am detaining you on suspicion of having taken part in unlawful activities on and around Toboso. Failure to comply will result in my opening fire, which can lead to the loss of life. Yours."

A hint of panic appeared in Dulce's eyes. "If they can pin Toboso on us, we're dead. The Navy doesn't screw around when it comes to anyone who raids colonies, especially not during a war."

Vanger, nervously chewing on his lower lip, raised a hand, palm outward to still the first officer. "Let me think, damn it." His eyes went from the tactical display to the video feed and back. "We should have run as planned right after the operation and to hell with leaving tracks."

"Captain, I'm getting an active missile lock," Jess said, his voice trembling.

"At this range, our calliopes don't stand a chance," Dulce replied.

"*Sigrun*'s calling. Captain Nilla says she will not surrender."

Vanger whirled around to face the technician. "What?"

"I think she means to fight it out," Dulce said in an awed whisper, pointing at the video feed. The other mercenary sloop had begun to pump out missile after missile at the Q-ship, guns blazing bright with long plasma streams. *Iolanthe*'s close-in defense calliopes answered almost immediately, taking out the missiles in short order while the plasma splashed harmlessly against her shields, giving birth to a dancing blue-green aurora as energies clashed.

"Fool!" Vanger shouted.

"Perhaps." Dulce dropped into a vacant chair. "But if we're condemned to die, it's better we do so fighting than in front of a firing squad."

The Q-ship was swift to return fire, and *Skögul*'s aghast crew witnessed a vicious barrage that would have crippled a cruiser. Their sister ship swiftly lost her shields and then her hull integrity. Blackened holes appeared on her armored skin, some venting gasses that immediately crystallized while secondary explosions erupted from failing gun capacitors. Then, a bright flash of light blinded the video pickups. When the bloom subsided, nothing but torn wreckage remained. The sloop's antimatter containment unit had ruptured before anyone could eject it. The resulting explosion had doomed *Sigrun*'s entire complement.

From the time *Sigrun* opened fire to her fiery death, mere minutes had elapsed, testimony to *Iolanthe*'s overwhelming power.

"It wasn't supposed to end like this," Dulce murmured. "It was just a job."

"A job where we killed a few hundred people," Vanger reminded him. "Not the kind you put on an application to join the Merchant Guild." A sly smile tugged at his lips. "However it's the kind the Navy will want to hear more about. Where I come from that's known as a bargaining chip."

"You're surrendering?" Dulce asked, a dangerous edge in his voice. He made as if to stand, but Vanger pulled his blaster from its hip holster, keeping its muzzle pointed downward, the gesture a clear warning.

"I intend to negotiate our surrender, Mike, and if I can, I want to give Tarkon payback for having pulled us into this mess. A can't fail, he said. Easy money."

Something on the sensor display caught the first officer's attention. "He seems to have been paying attention after all, Captain. If I'm not mistaken, *Skalmold*, *Sanngrior,* and *Herja* just broke cover and are making a run for it." He paused. "The Navy noticed. They just launched missiles."

"Good luck to them. I hope the bastards choke on it." Vanger pointed at the communications tech. "Get me a link with that damned Q-ship."

— Seventeen —

Lieutenant Commander Sirico let loose an appreciative whistle at the sight of the wrecked mercenary vessel. "Wow. That never gets old." He patted the weapons systems console. "Our girl does carry a heck of a kick."

"Bugger should have known better than to pick on something ten times its size." Yens shook her head at the folly of *Sigrun*'s now dead captain.

"The fact that we transformed from a harmless transport into his worst nightmare probably didn't register," Dunmoore replied. "The bugger thought he could escape. What's the other one doing?"

"He still has his shields up, but I'm not seeing him prepare to fire." A pause. "He stopped accelerating." Then Yens swore in a language Dunmoore could not identify. "Flushed out three more of the bastards around Rocinante Nine. They're accelerating like all the demons of hell are nipping at their heels. I make two sloops similar to the one beneath us, and a fast freighter."

"Launch missiles, Mister Sirico, four per. Let's see if we get lucky before they hit the hyperlimit and jump."

"May I remind you that our missile stocks are at half and the enemy has our reloads?"

"Two per, if it'll make you happy, Thorin."

Sirico nodded, his fingers on the controls. "Firing starboard tubes."

The signals petty officer raised his hand. "We're being hailed by the survivor, Captain. He wishes to discuss terms."

"Does he now? Put him through."

A holographic virtual screen materialized in front of the command chair, showing a red-faced, choleric looking man in his fifties. Calculating eyes examined her for a few moments, and then he spoke.

"I'm Gar Vanger, captain of the freelance sloop *Skögul*."

Dunmoore cocked a skeptical eyebrow at him. "Freelance? Is that new euphemism for pirate? I understand you want to discuss terms. You appear to be under the mistaken impression that the Navy negotiates with those it detains on suspicion of piracy."

"We can sit here all day trading witticisms, captain whatever your name is, but we both know you also want the three that just lit up. You won't catch them in your Q-ship. They can out-accelerate you all day long, even *Herja*, though she looks like a garbage scow. By the time you can jump, it'll be too late to pick up their bubble and trail them. You can see my crew and me hang, but you'll never retrieve your naval stores. Nor will you see justice done to the one who set up the Toboso operation."

Dunmoore sat back in her chair and studied Vanger through half-closed eyes.

"What do you propose?" She asked.

A crafty smile tugged at the mercenary's lips. "Treat us as combatants. I'll surrender my ship, my crew and I will allow ourselves to be interned in your brig. Instead of prosecuting us, you drop us off on a planet other than Toboso, free to find our own way home. Do that, and I'll tell you what I can, including where you might find the others."

"If I refuse?"

"Come now," Vanger replied, "you wouldn't reject a chance to bag the rest of them. I'm sure your superiors will agree that it makes sense to come to a mutually beneficial agreement. What else would you do? Destroy us? Let us self-destruct? That wouldn't be especially useful to your mission."

Dunmoore's eyes shifted to the tactical display. The chances of *Iolanthe*'s missiles intercepting the fleeing ships appeared to be decreasing by the second.

"I could always accept your terms, squeeze you dry of information, then hang you anyway," she said, watching for Vanger's reaction to her words.

The man chuckled. "You don't strike me as being dishonorable, Captain, and the Navy's sense of fair play is well known, even in the mercenary community. If you accept my surrender on negotiated terms, you'll keep your word. To do otherwise would violate your own rules."

"What's the size of your crew?"

Vanger's smile broadened. He knew he had won.

"Twenty-eight, including me."

Dunmoore nodded. "We can accommodate you and your crew in our brig."

"What about the terms?"

"These are the terms I offer, and I am formally logging them for review by the Admiralty. You will drop your shields and power down all of your systems. You will receive a boarding party that will take you into custody. I will have you brought aboard *Iolanthe* and placed in the brig. You may bring a single bag of personal effects, but no personal weapons, not even knives. We will search you upon arrival, and anyone discovered carrying a weapon will spend his or her first two weeks aboard in solitary confinement on water and ration bars. You will turn your ship over to us in the exact condition it is now. It becomes my prize."

Vanger made a dismissive hand gesture. "You can have it with my compliments. *Skögul* doesn't belong to me."

"You and every member of your crew will, at all times, obey every lawful order given by myself or a member of my crew. Also, you will answer every question to the best of your abilities. You will remain my prisoners until we've caught the rest of your friends. If we do not catch them, I will hand you over to the proper authorities for investigation and prosecution. If we catch them, I will set your entire crew free on a human-occupied planet of my choosing, not including Toboso. Any deviation from these terms once you've accepted them will result in immediate punishment, up to and including execution. For example, booby-trapping your ship to kill the boarding party will see you pushed through an open airlock without a pressure suit."

"I can live with those terms, Captain. By the way, if we're to shake on a deal, I'd like to know your name."

"Siobhan Dunmoore."

"We have ourselves mutually agreeable terms, Captain Dunmoore. Send your boarding party over. I'm dropping the shields now."

Yens raised a fist with an outstretched thumb, confirming Vanger had done so.

"I can assure you of our complete cooperation," the mercenary continued. "We value our lives more than Diane Nilla did."

"Nilla was the captain of the ship that foolishly opened fire on us?"

"Aye. *Sigrun*. I look forward to meeting you in person, Captain Dunmoore. If there's nothing else, I'll prepare my crew for our upcoming internment."

"Be ready in half an hour. *Iolanthe*, out."

The holographic display vanished, and for the first time, Dunmoore realized most of the CIC crew were staring at her.

"What?" She asked.

"We're wondering whether you intend to keep the prize for the duration of this mission and if so, who will take her," Sirico said, grinning.

"Yes, and you're not on the list, Thorin. A sloop's a lieutenant's command."

Dunmoore glanced at holographic Holt. "Any recommendations, Number One?"

"Astrid. She has the seniority and the experience, and she won't get lost if we have to send the prize out on its own. Besides, it'll look good on her next performance evaluation. Her file is due to appear in front of the lieutenant commander's promotion board next year."

"Make it so. Lieutenant Drost may choose her prize crew, up to a maximum of twenty-five. We'll send her and the first half dozen over with the boarding party. The rest will transfer to the prize once we've taken off our prisoners."

"Bosun to lead the boarding party?" Holt asked.

"Yes. I'd like her to take First Platoon and give the soldiers a taste of the real thing." Dunmoore turned to Major Salminen. "I trust your people have had training in how to handle POWs?"

The soldier nodded. "We have. If you don't need me here anymore, Captain, I'll go down prepare my people. I would need a few of the second officer's folks to guide us regarding the brig, just this once."

"Consider it done, Major," Holt said. "Either Lieutenant Commander Cullop herself or one of the senior deck department petty officers will meet you in the hangar."

"All right, folks, unless I've forgotten something, let's seize our prize and receive our involuntary guests."

"If I may ask one more question, sir," Salminen said. "What if they're playing along hoping to pull a nasty trick on us?"

"They'll pay for any treachery, and they know it. If Vanger and his crew truly are mercenaries, then the urge to die needlessly or for a noble cause isn't part of their makeup. Mercs aren't in it for self-sacrifice, unlike us regulars, because death doesn't pay at the end of a job. As long as they think we'll release them once we're done, they should be cooperative to a fault."

"Let's hope they are as familiar with mercenary psychology as you are, Captain," Holt replied with a chuckle. "That little sloop might come in handy for going places *Iolanthe* can't, and I'd hate to lose it."

"You and me both. Okay, folks." She clapped her hands. "Let's move. The sooner we can return to the hunt, the better. To quote our esteemed combat systems officer, they have our reloads."

*

Chief Dwyn noticed Command Sergeant Saari fidgeting with his scattergun and grinned at him. "Nervous in the service, Karlo?"

The soldier looked up and across the shuttle's passenger compartment at the bosun. "Easy for you to be calm, Anita. You squids breathe vacuum for fun. Us, not so much. What happens if the bastards decided to self-immolate the moment we're locked onto their docking ring?"

"That's an easy one to answer. I looked it up, and *Skögul* was one of the Valkyries, meaning we would have our next drink in Valhalla."

"I prefer to have mine in the chiefs' mess. From what I heard, the only booze on offer in Valhalla is mead and I prefer vodka, like any good Suomalainen."

"Like any good what now?" The bosun asked.

Saari chuckled. "You ought to get out more. In Anglic, you would call a Suomalainen a Finn. I'm the proud descendant of one of the people who colonized Scandia, the coldest inhabited planet in the Commonwealth. So are many of the soldiers in Company Group 31."

"Then the cold of space shouldn't be a new experience."

Saari opened his mouth to reply when the pilot's voice interrupted their banter.

"We're on final approach to the target. Zip up your suits."

"Right." Dwyn nodded. "Close her up, folks, check integrity, and raise your hand to confirm."

As one, twenty visors slammed shut and then, ten seconds later, twenty hands shot into the air.

"Lock and load."

The bosun's shuttle was one of the two preparing to dock with *Skögul*. Lieutenant Drost and her advanced party, as well as the rest of the boarders were aboard the other, approaching the starboard airlock, while Dwyn's was creeping up on the port side. *Iolanthe* had closed most of the distance between the two ships, putting them within unaided visual distance of each other. It further emphasized that any foul play would find a swift and deadly response. Somehow, knowing she loomed over the sloop reassured the boarding party even though they understood that *Skögul* self-destructing now would take all of them with it. The soldiers, who had not yet become inured to the swiftness of death in space, felt it most of all.

An unexpected thud resonated through the craft causing the soldiers to look around with alarm. The pilot's voice said, "We've latched on." He paused, then announced, "The other shuttle's also latched on. Lieutenant Drost has given the go-ahead to board."

At Dwyn's orders, four of the ratings assumed firing positions facing the aft hatch. A fifth stepped forward to open it, revealing the blackened and pitted metal of *Skögul*'s airlock. He pounded on it with his armored fist and then stepped aside to clear his mates' line of sight. Saari's troops stood further back, weapons at the ready.

Clunking sounds emanated from the sloop before its hatch swung inward. A spacer wearing nothing more than battledress stood on the other side. He raised his hands and placed them on the top of his head in the universal sign of surrender. Dwyn patted two of the ratings on the shoulder, sending them over the coaming and into the mercenary vessel. The spacer backed out into the corridor to free up the airlock for the armored men, stopping when he was hard against the opposite bulkhead. One of the ratings scanned the immediate surroundings, then raised his hand to signal that nothing untoward waited nearby. Both followed the crew member into the passage, the first turning forward and the second aft to secure the approaches to the airlock.

"Sergeant Saari, you and your troops are with me," Dwyn said stepping aboard *Skögul*. "Lieutenant Drost, this is Dwyn, we've boarded. No resistance and no funny business so far."

"Same here," the sailing master and soon to be prize captain replied. "Gar Vanger met us at the airlock and has now turned the ship over to the Navy. We're headed for the bridge."

"Acknowledged. We'll have the engineering compartment secured in a moment."

As they headed aft, they left a boarding party member at each corridor intersection and staircase. The mercenary crew members they met along the way acted exactly like the first one had, placing their hands on their heads and their backs against the bulkhead. Saari expected dirty looks, a bit of truculence if not outright hatred, but saw nothing more than the blank expressions of men and women resigned to their fate. He found the experience rather unnerving, but with the bosun busy securing her assigned part of the ship, he did not dare ask if this was normal. The prisoners remained equally inscrutable as they patiently filed off the ship, each carrying a duffel bag, after being scanned for any hidden weapons.

Once the twenty-eight mercenaries had been secured to their seats aboard Dwyn's shuttle, she ordered a deck-by-deck and compartment by compartment scan of the ship, to make sure that no additional crew members had stayed behind, hiding in the hope of retaking the sloop.

"*Iolanthe*, Lieutenant Drost, this is Dwyn. The prize appears clear," she reported half an hour later.

"Concur," Chief Yens immediately replied. "We haven't picked up anything either, but the lieutenant should still carry out a full visual inspection of the ship once the rest of the prize crew is aboard. There are ways of fooling sensors."

"We will, have no fear," Drost said. "Chief Dwyn, you may leave with the prisoners."

"Aye, aye, Captain." The bosun nudged Saari. "You and your lot are on your own until the shuttle returns with the rest of the prize crew, Karlo. Try not to touch any unfamiliar controls and keep your pongos out of the booze locker. And please, please try to remember that it's Captain Drost while she's in command of this tub. Officers are touchy if you forget protocol."

Saari gave her thumbs up. "Don't I know it? Now get off this ship, swabbie. The longer you take to send the prisoners back, the longer I have to wait for an ice cold vodka."

— Eighteen —

"Do you intend to greet Vanger personally?" Holt asked, handing Dunmoore a full coffee mug. With *Skögul* secure, she had retreated to her day cabin for a breather while her officers sorted out the details.

"No. Major Salminen will be the highest ranking officer he'll see until his first round of interrogation, but I'll be watching the show." She nodded at the large screen covering one of the bulkheads. "We have to give Astrid a few hours to survey our prize and get organized. Speaking of which, since I seem to have forgotten that we need a naval transponder for *Skögul*, how long until Renny makes us one?"

"Already done." Holt winked at her. "Your first officer was awake and sober for once. It's going across with the rest of the prize crew and instructions to use it only if needed. As far as the balance of the universe is concerned, *Skögul* remains a dastardly mercenary vessel of uncertain parentage and for now, of unknown ownership."

She gave him a warm smile. "What would I do without you?"

"Wear yourself out on details instead of planning our campaign of revenge and retribution."

The ship-wide intercom chimed, then Emma Cullop's voice rang out. "All hands, now hear this, prepare to recover shuttles and receive prisoners, I repeat, prepare to recover shuttles and receive prisoners. That is all."

Dunmoore touched a control and the star map dissolved, replaced by a panoramic view of the hangar deck. Armored and armed soldiers, the better part of Salminen's company, were formed up on three sides, with the rapidly opening space doors on the fourth. Moments later, a large shuttlecraft crossed the force field that prevented the compartment's air from escaping into space, towed in backward by a gravitic tractor. As soon as it settled on the deck, the space doors closed again. The shuttle's aft ramp dropped, and Chief Petty Officer Dwyn appeared in the opening, recognizable by her size and the chief's starburst rank insignia on the chest. Her helmeted head pivoted from left to right, then stopped to acknowledge Major Salminen with a nod, which the latter returned. Satisfied with the eighty-strong reception committee, the bosun waved a hand over her shoulder.

*

Major Salminen, the only one not wearing a helmet, called her company to attention as the first of the prisoners, Gar Vanger, walked down the ramp, duffel bag in hand. He looked around him, surprised at the size of the reception committee evident in his expression, then he noticed her pointing at a spot on the deck.

"You will form three ranks here."

Vanger nodded and stopped at the indicated spot while the rest of his crew filed out of the shuttle in silence. Most showed the same reaction to the number of soldiers waiting for them, with more than a few visibly surprised at *Iolanthe* carrying an Army unit rather than Marines. When Dwyn gave her the signal that all had disembarked, Salminen let her eyes roam over the prisoner formation. She met each captive's gaze with a stony face that masked the hatred she felt. Dunmoore expected her and her troops to behave with utmost professionalism upholding the honor of the Scandia Regiment in full. Her talk to the company group earlier would see to that, as would Sergeant Major Haataja's firm disciplinarian's eye.

"I am Major Tatiana Salminen, Commanding Officer, Company Group 31, Scandia Regiment, assigned to the Commonwealth Starship *Iolanthe*. We were on Toboso when you and your accomplices attacked. You killed half of my command in that strike. I'm telling you this so you'll understand that my troops won't take any crap. We will treat you as POWs under the Armed Services Code of Discipline and the Law Governing the Use of Military Forces, more commonly known as the Rules of War. We will also correct anyone who steps out of line instantly and without gentleness, using the leeway afforded to us by the Code to impose order and obedience. Attempts to escape will be met with deadly force. Keep in mind that if it were up to me, I'd gladly shove you personally through the nearest airlock. But Captain Dunmoore has given you terms, and we will honor them. Make sure you keep to your part of the deal. If anyone has left unpleasant surprises aboard *Skögul* for the crew that had taken over your ship, now is the time to confess. Punishment for things they find later on will be all the worse." She let her words sink in before continuing. "You will be individually searched and processed, then taken to the brig. Prisoner interviews will start shortly after that. You will stay silent throughout, speaking only when spoken to."

Salminen speared the mercenary captain with blank eyes. "Ser Vanger, Captain Dunmoore holds you responsible for the behavior of your crew. I trust you understand what that means under the provisions of the rules applicable to prisoners of war."

Vanger nodded solemnly. "I do. You can rest assured that we will cooperate to the utmost, and if I may have a brief word with my crew?"

"Go ahead."

He turned to face his crew. "Folks, always keep what the major has said foremost in your minds. We will be released once the Navy has accomplished its objectives and can go back to our lives though we shall be forced to find another employer. That being said, if anyone of you has done something aboard *Skögul* before leaving, in contravention of my orders, speak now. If we find out later, the culprit will never work as a freelancer again. I will make sure of that personally. That is if the Navy doesn't decide on a drumhead court-martial, followed by immediate execution."

None of the mercenaries made as if to speak up though one of them refused to meet Vanger's eyes.

"Out with it, Klassen. You have that guilty look again. What have you done?"

The man fidgeted for a moment before shrugging. "Nothing terrible, Captain, a little prank is all. It's just that they might get the runs from our food."

Vanger glared at Klassen and asked, "Anyone else inspired to do a little pranking?"

Another member of his crew raised her hand. "The starboard heads might have a reverse flow pressure problem." When Vanger turned his glare on her, she said, "Come on, Captain, you didn't expect us to just hand her over to the Navy without getting a bit of our own back. At least it's not as if I reversed the plasma flow to the sublight drives. That wouldn't have been a prank."

The spacer beside her guffawed. "No, but you still did a shitty thing, Caroline."

The joke drew grins and chuckles from the rest of the crew. Even Chief Dwyn, who had removed her helmet, allowed herself a tiny smile.

"Okay," Vanger said, "that makes two jokers, who apparently coordinated their pranks. Anyone want to make it three? Going in three, two, one…"

He turned back to face Salminen. "Please give Captain Dunmoore my apologies. I'll take whatever punishment she sees fit."

*

"Food that gives the runs and sabotaged heads." Holt grimaced. "Evil buggers."

"As pranks go," Dunmoore replied with a sly smile, "I've seen worse. In fact, as a middie, long before I became respectable, I've done worse. Let's hope one of them didn't do something that could actually cause damage."

"Aye." Holt climbed to his feet. "If you'll excuse me, I'll let Astrid know and ask Joelle for rations to go across with the rest of the prize crew."

"Thanks, and tell Astrid to take the time she needs to survey *Skögul*, just in case the prank confessions are a smokescreen to cover more serious sabotage. We're not haring off after the rest of them until I've interrogated Vanger."

"Glad to see a touch of the old paranoia return, Captain. I was worried you were entirely too trusting of someone who surrendered without firing a shot."

"I trust Vanger's self-interest, Zeke, not the man himself, or his crew. He wants to live and is obviously smart enough to figure out pissing me off isn't the way to go about it. His crew wouldn't be much different. Mercs don't sign up with commanding officers who'll get them killed."

"Again, let's hope they know about this aspect of freelancer psychology."

The intercom interrupted her reply.

"Captain, officer of the watch here. Lieutenant Drost is hailing us. She wishes to speak with you."

"Pipe her to my day cabin."

The view of the hangar deck dissolved, replaced by Drost's angular, severe face.

"How are things over there, Astrid?"

"Cleaner than I expected, but they wiped their log and most of the ship's database, including the navigation data. Unless there's a backup of the log hidden away somewhere in their system, it's a complete loss. Not even the smartest specialist will pull it back from the dead. I'll need a dump from *Iolanthe*'s computer core and time to rebuild before we can go anywhere."

A burst of grim laughter erupted from Holt's throat. "There we go, Captain. Serious sabotage. So much for Vanger keeping to the terms of surrender."

"Perhaps, but I should have expected them to do something like that. Leaving us with the ability to analyze their sailing history would cost Vanger his bargaining chip. The man's no dummy. Thankfully, it's easy to remedy. Theo will transmit a dump forthwith. While you're on the link, two jokers apparently left you two surprises. Throw out whatever food you find and check the starboard heads. In fact, check all the heads. You were supposed to suffer a case of the runs, then find yourself with reverse flow pressure problems."

Drost's eyes widened in revulsion. "Ugh. That's nasty."

"That's what they've confessed to so far, but there might be a few more surprises, so take your time with the survey. We won't catch up with the others in stern chase anyhow, so we might as well prepare ourselves properly if we're to hunt them down with any hopes of success.

You'll be receiving new rations, of course, along with a naval transponder, to be used only on my orders."

"Of course, sir. If the prize is to be a stalking horse, it won't do to advertise that it's crewed by the good guys. Are we keeping the name?"

"I don't see why not."

The sailing master smiled. "Excellent. As a distant descendant of the Vikings, I'm chuffed at commanding a starship named after one of the Valkyries."

"Valkyries?" Holt's eyebrows shot up. "A bit dramatic for a mercenary ship to be named after something from Norse mythology, no?"

Dunmoore had to repress a pained smile at the memory of another Valkyrie. This one had been an operation cooked up deep within the Navy to overthrow a Commonwealth government unable to manage the war effort with any degree of success. She might have pruned one of its branches at Arietis, but the roots remained deep and viable.

"*Iolanthe* is named after the main character in a nineteenth-century operetta, Zeke. Is that any less dramatic?"

"A fiery fairy with a sword, if our ship's crest is any reflection of that *Iolanthe*, Captain? Touché." Holt inclined his head. He turned his head to face the screen again. "I wish you joy of your Valkyrie, Astrid. Just make sure they didn't tamper with anything that could be worse than the heads, crappy as that prank may be."

"No shit, Commander," Drost replied, deadpan.

"All right, people." Dunmoore raised a hand. "If we're done with the pungent jokes, let's return to work. We have a pile of stuff to shovel through before we can leave."

Holt snapped to attention. "With your permission, I will go sort things out for Astrid."

"And I'll run another, more in-depth survey of the prize," Drost said.

"You're both dismissed."

*

"Bridge to the captain."

Dunmoore reached for her communicator. "Yes?"

"Major Salminen reports all prisoners processed and brought to the brig. She raised no issues for your attention."

"Excellent. That was quick work. Ask her to have Captain Vanger brought to the conference room. I'd like to speak with him now."

"Aye, aye, sir."

"And pass the word for the cox'n. I'd need to see him in my day cabin."

Guthren showed up a few minutes before they heard a knock on the door leading to the conference room. It was barely enough time for Dunmoore to tell him what she wanted. She stood, gave herself one last glance in the mirror, and took a deep breath, then she touched the controls. The door vanished into the bulkhead, and she stepped through.

Vanger stood beside the rectangular table, an armed but no longer armored soldier on each side. He wore the same guarded if sly expression she had seen over the video link. Clearly a man who thought he had made a reasonable deal under the circumstances. The soldiers snapped to attention, one of them nudging Vanger to follow suit.

"Corporal Lehto reporting with the prisoner as ordered, sir," the other barked out, saluting.

"At ease." Dunmoore took her seat at the head of the table, then indicated that Vanger should sit. "You can wait out in the corridor, Corporal."

"Sir. Major Salminen ordered us to stick to the prisoner like a drunk to his vodka."

"I'm sure Captain Vanger presents no threat, Corporal, and I want to speak with him in private. Please wait in the corridor."

"Sir." Lehto snapped off another precise salute, and both soldiers marched out of the conference room.

"Seeing an Army unit aboard your ship surprised me, Captain Dunmoore," Vanger said in a conversational tone. "Not as surprised as when I discovered this was a Q-ship and not a harmless armed transport, but still…"

"It's rare, but not especially unusual. There are more ships than available Marines, and more Army regiments than available enemies, so we make do. Besides, as you heard Major Salminen announce earlier, her company group was among the victims of your raid. She and the rest of her troops have a vested interest in accompanying us on this mission."

Vanger inclined his head by way of showing that he grasped her meaning. "I'm happy to report they've been entirely correct with us so far, Captain."

"I should hope so. We are professionals."

"And we mercenaries aren't. Understood. I presume you've had me brought here for more than mere persiflage. Please go ahead and ask your questions."

"Why did you attack Toboso?"

The mercenary shrugged. "It was a contract. We were to raid the Fleet depot and remove the colonial administration."

"Ordered by whom?"

"I have no idea." When he saw the expression of disbelief on her face, he raised a placating hand. "I honestly don't, Captain. Nils Tarkon handled the contract. He's the senior captain in our group and commands *Skalmold*, one of *Skögul*'s sister ships. The rest of us were merely given our targets and the stricture that the origin of the raid had to be untraceable. It would have been so, had you not appeared as we were leaving Toboso. I urged that idiot Tarkon to go FTL as soon as we could and to hell with the traceability clause. The idiot instead decided to hide and wait for you to leave. Much good that did Diane Nilla her crew. We weren't expecting you to be a damned Q-ship."

A cruel smile twisted Dunmoore's lips. "No one ever expects a Q-ship. That's the whole point of the design."

"Quite effective."

"What is this group you belong to?"

"It's a private military corporation. The owners provide the ships. We crew them on individual contracts. That's why I didn't suffer too much heartache surrendering *Skögul*. Before you ask, it's the sort of private military corporation that's owned by a series of shell companies, so I have no idea who the real backers are. We specialize in contracts beyond the Commonwealth sphere where the Rules of War don't apply. As you can imagine, it's pretty lucrative."

"This time, someone ordered you on an illegal operation within the Commonwealth. Your ultimate owners must be quite sure we'll never trace them. Whoever's behind the Toboso raid faces the death penalty if convicted. As you might if we don't track down Tarkon and the others."

Vanger smiled. "I'm sure our mysterious owners know how to cover their tracks. The group has been in operation since well before the war, well before I joined. So far, no government has ever raised an eyebrow at what we do."

"Until now."

"Until now, for sure. You weren't supposed to show up, Captain. That was a huge stroke of misfortune."

"For you. Not for justice. Now, the Commonwealth government will not only raise an eyebrow at your group's operations, but it will also terminate them. I will terminate them."

"Believe me, that factored heavily into my decision to surrender and spill everything I know. They pay well, but not enough to ensure my loyalty to the grave. I'll find another job somewhere else once this is over."

"So you know nothing about them?"

Vanger shook his head. "An agent hired me."

"Does this group have a name?"

"It has had several names over the years. Right now, we go by Orion Outcomes. After this little fiasco, it'll probably change again."

"Let's talk about the attack on Toboso. How did you arrange for the communications and surveillance satellites to go down? What happened to the subspace relay?"

"Tarkon's ship destroyed the subspace relay. As for the rest, I don't know. We were told things would be arranged so the Fleet garrison had no warning; that Toboso would be unable to call for help and that nothing and no one would be able to track or trace us. As a matter of fact, it was a condition of our taking the contract. I assume whoever hired us took care of those things, just as they told us exactly how it had to go down."

Vanger sounded so matter of fact about a callous act of piracy that cost hundreds of lives that Dunmoore felt a surge of anger nearly overwhelm her determination to stay calm and detached.

"You had no qualms about attacking a Commonwealth colony, killing innocent civilians and, massacring a Fleet garrison, thereby turning yourselves into capital criminals?"

"Captain, you have to understand that people hired by Orion Outcomes, myself included, are the kind who crave action but would never be allowed into any regular military service if you understand what I mean." His casual tone did nothing to help defuse her growing rage. "After a few years with the organization, what little scruples we had in the first place vanish. You do not understand what goes on outside the Commonwealth. It's enough to turn a feeling man into an automaton. Plus, the money offered for the Toboso raid was too good to refuse. As I've said several times before, you weren't supposed to show up and turn things pear-shaped. From our point of view, it wasn't a big deal, or wouldn't have been if we'd all made it out of here."

Dunmoore struggled to keep an impassive expression though she seethed inside. Something in Vanger's eyes told her he had sensed the repressed fury, and he had the grace to look away.

"It's a good thing you surrendered under terms, Ser Vanger," she said through clenched teeth. "In the interests of full disclosure, what was your role in the raid?"

He looked up at her again. "I fired the kinetic strikes on the Fleet depot's defensive arrays, nothing more. After that, our job was to provide top cover while the rest landed."

Dunmoore held his gaze for what seemed like an eternity, convinced he was whitewashing his role by claiming the part that took the least amount of lives, none of them civilian. The anger dissipated, replaced by revulsion.

"Now explain how and where I can find this Tarkon and the rest of them, or so help me, I'll hang you myself."

— Nineteen —

"So?" Dunmoore asked Guthren when he entered the conference room moments after the soldiers had removed Vanger. She was massaging the bridge of her nose with a thumb and forefinger.

"A migraine coming on?" The coxswain asked, dropping into the chair recently vacated by the mercenary. He had watched the interview live from her day cabin, his attention focused entirely on Vanger.

"A stress migraine, the kind that happens when your mind overrides your body's intense desire to strangle a sonofabitch who desperately needs killing."

Guthren nodded. "I know how those feel. There were a few folks that triggered mine aboard *Stingray* in the early days when we first took her."

"Aye. I'm almost sorry I accepted the cold-blooded bastard's surrender, but without him, we'd have had no chance in hell. Since I formally logged the terms, shoving him out of the nearest airlock wouldn't fly with the Admiralty. They'd remind me in no uncertain terms we'd never again convince rats to turn on their fellow vermin. Of course, if he lied, all bets are off."

The coxswain shrugged. "He mostly told the truth, or what he believes to be the truth. It's sometimes hard to tell with sociopathic buggers like him. They can fake human emotions. Did he tell us where to find Tarkon?

I'm pretty sure he did. We'll see soon enough if he hasn't, and he knows it would void the terms if he lied. I'm also sure he had a bigger role in the attack. The tells were there when he discussed it. As to the mysterious owners behind his mercenary mob, and whoever hired them, I'd wager he doesn't know for sure but suspects something or other."

"So all in all, he hasn't given me cause to shoot him?"

Guthren shook his head. "Sorry, Captain. Perhaps another time." He paused for a few heartbeats, then asked, "Do you intend to go through with it after hearing his story? The Admiralty might take violent exception to your actions this time. Or the government will and force the Admiralty to come down on you. There's plenty of senators that hate Navy captains who go sticking their guns where the profits are high, and rules don't exist."

"I don't see that I have much of a choice. If we leave this unpunished, we'll see more of it. Besides, we have to find out why the attack happened and at whose behest, so that we choke off any more treason. I'll take my lumps after the fact if the Admiralty is in the mood to hand them out. You remember what they say about success, right? It's the key to forgiveness."

"You may have that one backward, Captain. As I remember it, forgiveness is the key to success."

"I think my version's much better."

The coxswain smiled. "If you say so. I wouldn't dare contradict my captain, not after being on my third tour as her cox'n."

"You would dare if it was for a good cause."

"Of course. That clause is in the cox'n union rules, sir." Guthren gave her a broad grin.

"Why did I just picture Gregor Pushkin?"

"Because he'd tell you to tread with caution."

"Commander Holt won't?"

"You and he are too much alike in some ways," the coxswain replied. "There's nothing wrong with daring on a pretend pirate ship like *Iolanthe*, and he even looks the part. Another saying comes to mind, however. There are old captains and bold captains, but there aren't many old, bold captains. Mister Pushkin was enough of an anchor to keep you going at the right speed. Mister Holt, well, he likes high speed. He's an excellent officer, but you two together?" He shook his head in mock despair. "Try to remember those of us running as fast as we can to keep up."

Dunmoore gave him a warm smile. "Always, Chief. You should know that by now."

"You did bring *Stingray* home for decommissioning in good order, I'll grant you that."

"*Don Quixote* as well."

"Barely, sir. We were lucky our antimatter containment unit hit the Shrehari command ship at just the right angle to avoid a massive dose of feedback."

"But it worked."

"Only too well." Guthren sighed. "God looked kindly upon us on that day. Of course, it's said that he takes care of fools and drunks, and most of the old Don's crew qualified."

"Dare I ask what category applied to me back then?"

"No, you don't, Captain."

*

"Comments?" Dunmoore asked, surveying her assembled department heads, including Astrid Drost who had joined by in video, after briefing them on Vanger's revelations. She sat back in her chair, elbows on the arms, and the fingertips of both hands touching each other.

"You're proposing a trip into the heart of darkness," Renny Halfen commented, his face a mask of uncertainty. "We're not exactly full-up on parts, ammo, and supplies, though if we catch up with the bastards, we'll have our replenishment."

"There's also the matter of General Order Fifty-Three," Emma Cullop said. "Last I checked, permission to pursue anything other than Shrehari beyond the Commonwealth sphere requires the authorization of a four-star admiral. Since the one who runs Special Operations Command is on Earth, it'll not only take time for a message to get there and back without a subspace relay buoy to boost the signal but also time to make it through ten thousand layers of desperately slow bureaucracy. We could be sitting here for a week or two waiting while they and the stuff they stole are scattered to all corners of the Orion arm."

"Presuming I'd actually be daft enough to ask for permission," Dunmoore replied, smiling. "Better to ask for forgiveness after presenting HQ with a victory, no?"

Cullop grimaced. "If this mercenary group's owners are in any way connected to those in positions of power on Earth, forgiveness might be long in coming if we go in without top cover, sir."

"It's a risk I'll have to take. I'm more than happy to log anyone's objections or reservations as a hedge against official disavowal later on. But since I'm solely responsible for the decision, I'll be the only one to suffer adverse consequences should Command decide I overstepped my authority."

The second officer raised a hand, palm outward, a hard smile tugging at her thin lips. "I appreciate the offer, sir, but that won't be necessary. I don't disagree with your intentions, but we need to keep in mind the risks beyond the immediate pursuit and destruction of the enemy."

"Those risks are manageable," Holt replied. "The captain no doubt intends to have us change into our privateer duds, meaning we won't sail into the Badlands as a Navy ship. Once beyond the Commonwealth sphere, we don't have to raise our colors before attacking anyone other than the Shrehari. That'll give Command the ability to deny Fleet involvement with a straight face."

"If we're successful," Thorin Sirico added. "Otherwise, logged objection or not, we might wait a long time for our next promotion. Then again, what's life without a bit of risk? For my part, giddy-up. Let's do this."

"We will indeed change into our privateer duds, as the first officer put it," Dunmoore said, "starting the moment we're done here. I intend to conduct this operation under a false flag from now until we return to Toboso, not only because of plausible deniability but because it'll be our way into Renny's heart of darkness." She winked at her chief engineer before turning to Salminen. "Major, you've been rather quiet. Any thoughts? Have you decided on a mercenary cover identity for Company Group 31?"

"We go where you go, Captain," the soldier replied, "and if that allows us to avenge our comrades, then any political risk is worth taking. As to a mercenary identity? I'll confess that though a small matter, it hasn't been easy to find consensus." She smiled. "You should have seen some of the names the troops came up with. In the end, we agreed on a historic name associated with the ancestors of the people who colonized Scandia. I'd like to propose we be known as the Varangian Company if that meets with your approval."

"Of course it does, and I'm sure the logistics department can produce suitable insignia. We can't have you engaging the enemy while wearing Commonwealth Army rank and unit badges if you're to pass as dodgy mercenaries."

"We can do that," Lieutenant Biros confirmed. "Just give your designs to Chief Simms. He'll take care of the rest."

"Are there any other comments, suggestions, objections, or lewd jokes you folks need to get off your chests?"

"One last question, Captain," Holt said. "Do you intend to tell the acting governor that we'll be away for a few weeks, perhaps longer?"

"No. The less anyone else knows the better."

"Agreed."

"Anything else?" After receiving headshakes in return, she concluded, "I intend to spend the next few hours coming up with an operations plan that'll inevitably fall apart the moment someone opens fire. Expect me to pick your brains now and then. We'll reconvene once I've decided on a course of action. For now, I'll need Lieutenant Commander Sirico and Sub-Lieutenant Pashar with me in the CIC to kick off the planning process."

Both the combat systems officer and the junior navigator, now acting sailing master with Lieutenant Drost in command of *Skögul*, nodded.

"As of six bells," Dunmoore said, rising, "*Iolanthe* will no longer be a vessel of the Commonwealth Navy, but full naval discipline will stay in force. Please make sure your people don't go overboard with buccaneer fashion statements."

*

"Hey, Cox'n!" Chief Petty Officer Third Class Marko Trane waved Guthren over when the latter entered the Chiefs' and Petty Officers' mess to grab a cup of coffee. "What's this about the ship turning privateer?"

"Look who's out of sick bay already," Guthren replied, smiling at the man.

"Doc's put me on light duties and kicked me out. I'm waiting for a moment of the bosun's time to find out what she wants me to do."

"Anita will be by within the hour. It'll be her afternoon tea time soon, and yeah, we're turning privateer, which is one of our better cover identities, particularly where we're headed. You probably heard we captured one of the ships that attacked Toboso and destroyed another. The captain of the one that surrendered spilled his guts and told us where to find the rest of them in return for his and the crew's lives. We'll have the bastards rolled up and torched soon enough. A bit of revenge for you folks who were on the ground when they hit."

"You took prisoners?"

Guthren nodded.

"We have prisoners. Twenty-eight of them to be precise. Snug and secure in the brig until we find their buddies and the assholes who paid them to attack Toboso. Matter of fact, running the brig might just be the job she'll give you, with that many guests, you being on light duties and all. I expect it'll be a while before you're fit to run a damage control party in battle." Trane stared wordlessly at the coxswain with eyes that reflected a whole mess of unvoiced emotions. After a moment, Guthren said, "We interned them as genuine prisoners of war, Marko, and we'll treat them as such. If you're thinking about opportunities for revenge, don't. We'll get that when we catch up with the remaining three ships and find the scum behind the deaths of your comrades."

When Trane did not reply, he asked, "You read me, Chief Petty Officer Trane?"

"Loud and clear, Cox'n. Loud and clear."

*

"All hands, now hear this," Commander Holt's voice echoed from hidden speakers, "*Iolanthe* will assume the privateer identity at six bells. Crew and Marines are to don appropriate non-Fleet attire. Full naval discipline will remain in force. Department chiefs will make sure that no one goes overboard with privateer accouterments. That is all."

Salminen smiled at her command group, crowded into the compartment set aside as Company Group 31's TAC.

"That was the other thing I wanted to brief you on, folks. Captain Dunmoore has approved the name Varangian Company, and it's what we'll become at six bells. Sarn't Major, if you'd be so kind as to track down a Chief Simms from the logistics department, he'll arrange mercenary badges for us. Based on the captain's final words before the briefing ended, I inferred that the crew might become inventive with its accouterments. I want none of that in my unit. The only change for us will be different insignia. Otherwise, it's battledress while on duty, with no modifications or fashion statements. Make sure your troops don't have any ideas after seeing our naval colleagues."

"I'll make bloody sure," Haataja growled.

"It does mean we won't go into combat under our own colors," she continued.

"As long as we can use the regimental battle cry I'm happy, sir," Command Sergeant Saari said. "Why give up one of our best weapons to scare the enemy?"

"I'd be taking my life into my own hands if I forbade the *Hakkaa päälle*, Karlo," Salminen replied with a grin.

Saari nodded once. "Good. As long as we have that, as far as I'm concerned, we can wear any damn thing the Navy wants when we cut the bastards down, up to and including a fucking tutu."

Approving nods from the other platoon leaders greeted his statement, though Jon Puro said, "Let's stick to wearing armor. A tutu leaves things a bit too exposed."

"Fine, a tutu over the armor then," Saari replied.

Salminen raised a hand. "People, let's not get sidetracked. Next item of business, planning. Since we might have to seize a moon base deep in the Badlands, I want each of you and your section leaders to start thinking about how we might do this. The ship's library probably has a ton of manuals and historical accounts on the subject, so read, digest and discuss. The day after tomorrow, I want to hold the first of several planning sessions where we'll discuss the issue. I don't want to get there and tell Dunmoore we need a week to organize. The first session will involve this command group only. Later ones will include the section leaders and maybe even the squad leaders. The Navy taught us how to board a starship. We'll have to teach ourselves how to take something a heck of a lot bigger, because no one aboard has ever done it, not even Chief Guthren, and he spent time with the special ops teams."

"Why not stay a few thousand klicks away and shoot until it blows up?" Command Sergeant Alekseev asked.

"Because we want to find out who hired the mercs, Courtlyn," Salminen replied, "and the answer might be on the base or someone living there might know."

"Oh." Alekseev's pale cheeks reddened with embarrassment. "I should have known. Sorry, sir."

The company commander gave Alekseev a tired smile. "We've all been through a lot in the last week. I'm surprised we're still able to think clearly."

"That's a fact," Haataja said, nodding once. "Any other items, Major?"

Before she could answer, a soft chime rang out six times. When the last peal faded away, she reached up to her collar, unpinning her Commonwealth Army rank insignia and then removed the Scandia Regiment crest from her sleeve.

"Welcome to the Varangian Company, my fellow mercenaries."

*

"What's with the Navy's non-standard uniforms? They don't look too military all of a sudden." Mike Dulce asked Vanger in a low whisper when both were taken to the hangar deck for ten minutes of exercise. "Is it related to your chat with their captain, perhaps?"

Vanger shrugged. "How should I know? This is a Q-ship. Maybe playing silly bugger is part of the job."

"Mind telling me just what you discussed with the bitch?"

"I discussed ideas on how to make sure you, me, and the rest of the crew won't face execution for piracy, Mike. I'm not about to join Diane Nilla on the roster of stupid starship captains. You ought to be thankful for that."

"Turning on our superiors will get us killed just the same," Dulce hissed. "Except without a trial and in whatever way makes the most of them laugh the hardest. Not an improvement, I'd say. Fighting it out would still have been better."

"No talking among the prisoners," one of the soldiers assigned to guard them snarled.

Vanger raised a placating hand to signal he understood before giving Dulce a meaningful glance. "Where there's life, there's hope, Mike," he whispered.

— Twenty —

"Come." Dunmoore looked up from her tablet as the door to her day cabin opened.

Holt poked his head in. "I just checked in on the bridge watch standers and thought you might like to know that according to the navigation plot, we've left the Commonwealth sphere and are now in direct violation of General Order Fifty-Three."

"Alea iacta est."

"Beg pardon?" The first officer entered the cabin and stared at her with a raised eyebrow.

"The die is cast. It's Latin, a phrase Julius Caesar apparently uttered when, in defiance of the Roman Senate, he took his Army across the river Rubicon, triggering a civil war. The expression has come to mean that one has crossed the point of no return."

"I remember it now." Holt made a face. "Let's hope that our defiance of the Commonwealth Senate won't trigger a civil war."

"Caesar was eventually murdered by his close associates. That part concerns me even more," she replied in a dry tone.

"Ah yes, beware the Ides of March or something like that. No needn't cower in fear, it's mid-June on Earth right now, and your current associates prefer to see you alive and well."

"Five years elapsed between crossing the Rubicon and his murder, so there's plenty of time."

A frown creased Holt's forehead, and he stepped over to the coffee urn to pour himself a mug before sitting across from her. "You sound gloomy today, Captain. What gives?"

Dunmoore sighed. "Unlike you in your carefree first officer's lifestyle, I experience mood swings, especially when remembering that every time I've taken a ship beyond the Commonwealth sphere, things have gone pear-shaped and people died."

"Considering we're in the Navy and have been at war for over eight years now, that's hardly a reason to brood. If any of us had wanted a safe job, we'd have stayed on the farm, and I object to my lifestyle being called carefree. As the first mate of the scummiest privateer in the galaxy, it's all I can do to keep the crew from displaying tasteless fashion statements."

Holt's quip brought a quick smile to her lips. She touched the gaudily elaborate piece of jewelry dangling from her left ear. "I gather this isn't tasteless enough to attract your attention?"

He grinned. "Nothing you'll ever wear could be considered tasteless, Captain."

"That's because I haven't tried yet. Spooking the crew would be bad for morale."

"Perhaps we should hold a costume contest — the one that's most overdone wins."

Dunmoore snorted. "Wins what? An all expenses paid trip into the Badlands? That would make everyone a winner, including the losers we took prisoner."

"Prisoners who have so far been cooperative to a fault. The bosun's put the chief we rescued from Sigma Noctae, Marko Trane, in charge of the brig. No love lost there. Between Trane and the soldiers who make up the guard detail, Vanger and his crew have every reason to stay meek."

"Aye." Dunmoore nodded. "I suppose they do, though I'm still bothered by the fact that we're no nearer to figuring out who blinded the garrison before the attack. The paranoid in me wonders whether it's the one among the survivors who we've put in charge of guarding the very same raiders they let in."

"If Guthren couldn't figure it out, then I doubt anyone else will, short of putting the survivors to the question and that'll be bad for morale. Anyway, if there's a traitor aboard, he or she will do well to stay quiet and do nothing that might attract attention, especially since Vanger has no idea who let his gang of pirates in through the front door."

"At least not until we get closer to the truth at the end of this voyage of retribution." She glanced at her screen. "I see it's time for the dailies."

As if on cue, chimes softly echoed throughout the ship, ringing four bells in the afternoon watch. Holt sprang to his feet. "With your permission, Captain, I'll go make sure our favorite miscreants have assembled before you make your grand entrance."

He stuck his head through the connecting door, then gave Dunmoore thumbs up. When she stood, he entered the conference room and called out, "Ladies and Gents, the captain."

Iolanthe's department heads rose to attention, the military gesture at odds with their appearance. Though everyone aboard save for the soldiers wore black, merchant-style tunic and trousers of various styles, complete with merchant rank insignia on the collar, the uniformity stopped there. Both men and women wore enough jewelry to give the Fleet Coxswain fits of apoplexy, while footwear ranged from shoes to knee-high or even taller boots, depending on the wearer's mood.

They wore their tunics without regard to sameness, some preferring them half or even fully open rather than done up to the collar. The soberest among her officers was Renny Halfen, who had long ago decreed that civilian wear for the engineering department would be coveralls, safety boots, and nothing that could constitute a hazard for crew or machinery. The other department head that had placed severe limitations on the freelancer chic was Salminen. Her Army battledress now sported a standard mercenary major's insignia — a silver lozenge above a silver bar. She had put it up under protest, preferring the three smaller lozenges of a captain — until Dunmoore pointed out she might as well wear a disguise that reduces confusion, since, by naval tradition, she was addressed as major anyway. They were FTL, meaning Drost could not join in, but she would no doubt look as stylishly seedy as her comrades.

"As you were," she said, taking her seat at the head of the table. "If you haven't heard yet, *Iolanthe* and *Skögul* are now officially in violation of General Order Fifty-Three."

"Or as the captain said to me a few minutes ago," Holt interjected, "the die is cast. I won't try to repeat it in the original Latin."

"Alea iacta est," Renny Halfen intoned with mock somberness. "Though where we'd find a Rubicon in interstellar space is open to question."

"Glad to see I'm not the only one conversant with the history of ancient Rome," Dunmoore said, giving her first officer a sweet smile. Then, turning her attention on Emma Cullop, she asked, "Anything from our second officer?"

"Aye. The prisoners have requested access to exercise equipment. Chief Trane figures we can use the empty storage compartment next to the brig and cycle them through four at a time, under armed guard."

"Major? Any comments?"

"As long as we're not talking about free weights or other implements they could turn into weapons, then I'm okay with the idea, Captain."

"My thoughts exactly," Cullop said, "so no fears on that account. I have nothing else, sir."

Dunmoore went around the table until she reached the second to last before the first officer's turn.

"Anything from our Varangian Company?"

"Yes, sir. As you know, we've been war gaming ways of seizing a station or at least getting enough of a foothold to let Lieutenant Commander Cullop's people do their part. Since we don't know much about anything, I'd like to practice a few maneuvers the next time we drop out of FTL, using *Iolanthe* as a station stand-in and the shuttles for transport. That way we face fewer chances of falling flat on our faces when it comes to the real thing."

"Agreed. How much time would you like per session?"

"Six hours ought to be enough. More and we'll be stumbling over our own shadows."

"Done. Mister Pashar, take note for your navigation planning. Let's make the window eight hours to give the major and her troops more time if they find the energy."

Drost's replacement as sailing master nodded. "Will do. I'm sure Mister Halfen will be glad for added time to retune the drives."

"Aye." The chief engineer nodded. "Heading into the Badlands, I'd rather take longer than usual. It'll be a hard way home if something breaks. I wouldn't want to try what you did with *Stingray* a few years ago, Captain. *Iolanthe* is too massive for those sorts of shenanigans." Unvoiced but clear to Dunmoore's ears was Halfen's desire to not share the fate of the late Lieutenant Commander Tiner, *Stingray*'s chief engineer at the time.

"Caution is my middle name, Renny." She tried on a reassuring smile, but the amused glint in Holt's eye showed that no one believed her, not even their newest department head, Major Salminen.

Pashar caught Salminen's eye and said, "Major, we're due to drop out of FTL tomorrow during the morning watch for a navigation check. Do you want to begin then?"

"Absolutely. Thank you."

"Was there anything else?" Dunmoore asked her.

"No, other than to say the last two weeks have been quite the learning experience for my troops, but they're getting comfortable in our new surroundings. A few are even speculating about a transfer to the Marine Corps when this is over."

Guthren chuckled. "They'd be mightily disappointed, Major. Most of the Corps spends its life planetside, and not on the nice ones either these days. There's maybe a regiment's worth aboard starships in the entire Fleet, no more, and the Marines themselves are carefully selected by their parent units."

A knowing smile pulled at the corner of her pale lips. "I figured as much after reading a fair chunk of the literature on Marines in the ship's library, trying to find useful nuggets to help us adapt. However, I have a few dreamers who won't let facts interfere with a perfectly good fantasy."

Cullop snorted. "Don't we all."

Dunmoore turned to Holt. "First officer?"

"May I suggest the various messes hold a 'Crossing the Rubicon' party or whatever we choose to call it, to mark the event? It'll be good for morale."

"Sure. Why not? Let's celebrate our going rogue. The mess presidents may name it as they wish as long as decorum is maintained."

"Decorum?" Guthren, the president of the Chiefs' and Petty Officers' mess, asked in a stage whisper. "Here I was thinking to call ours the Fuck the Senate's Corrupt Rules party."

"Chief..." Dunmoore glared at him.

The coxswain put on an air of false contriteness. "Sorry, sir."

She turned back to her first officer. "Mister Holt?"

"I'm glad you agree because as president of the wardroom, I intend to organize an event before the day is out." He smiled with piratical glee, giving her a seated bow. "Captain, the wardroom will host a Crossing the Rubicon celebration tonight. I'd like to extend an invitation on behalf of your officers for you to join us, considering your orders inspired the occasion."

Dunmoore inclined her head in thanks. "Gladly. If there's no other business for today's daily, thank you all."

*

"All hands, this is the bridge. Transition to normal space in one minute, I repeat transition to normal space in one minute. That is all."

Thirty seconds later, a warning klaxon blared from the speakers. The crew braced for the inevitable disorientation and nausea once *Iolanthe*'s hyperspace bubble collapsed, shoving her back into Newtonian space.

With the ship at battle stations in preparation for emergence into unpatrolled and potentially hostile space, Dunmoore sat, fully suited up, in the CIC's command chair. Company Group 31 had already boarded their shuttles to prepare for the first of many attempts at refining tactics as unfamiliar to them as tolerance to a zealot.

The universe twisted into a figure eight with a suddenness that left Dunmoore both giddy and disoriented. She swallowed a stomach determined to escape and blinked a few times until her surroundings swam back into focus.

"Is *Skögul* still keeping station?" She asked in a raspy voice that owed much to her parched throat, a common affliction of transition to and from hyperspace.

"Aye," Chief Yens replied, sounding just as thirsty, "and no further off our port beam than when we jumped."

"*Skögul*'s captain is a sailing master. I expect precise navigation from our prize. Anything else?"

"Nothing visible to our sensors within immediate range."

Dunmoore let a good five minutes elapse, allowing their detection signals to spread well beyond *Iolanthe*'s defensive envelope and return if they met a solid target lurking in the cold of interstellar space. When nothing lit up Yens' screen, she glanced at Holt's holographic image hovering over the command chair's arm. "Secure from battle stations. Pass the word that Major Salminen can begin her battle drills and open a link with Captain Drost. I'll take it in my day cabin."

She barely had time to make it down the passage to her private sanctuary before Drost's face replaced the star map on the cabin's screen. Stripping off her protective gear, Dunmoore asked, "Good passage, Astrid?"

"Fine as these things go, Captain, but it felt peculiar nonetheless, just twenty-six of us in a strange ship, cut off from *Iolanthe* and headed for parts unknown. I'll not hide that flagrantly violating General Order Fifty-Three hasn't filled everyone aboard with glee."

"The various messes held their own version of Rubicon Day last night, to banish the spirits of stupid regulations and celebrate our defiance. You might want to consider something similar."

"Rubicon Day? As in Julius Caesar and casting the die?" Her pale features lit up with a wicked smile. "I like it. Thank you for the idea."

"Any issues aboard *Skögul*?"

"Nothing that can't be explained away by stupidity rather than malice, such as the still we found in a corner of the engine room once the rotting mash stank up the place. Sabotaging the heads seems to have been the worst of it. We took advantage of the boredom over the last few days to dismantle and examine virtually everything that sucks power from the antimatter reaction chamber. It was all in proper working condition. I intend to tackle the remaining systems during our next spell in hyperspace, even though Chief Larson assures me he'd have detected any sabotage by now."

"Our esteemed engineering chief petty officer would, I've no doubt of that, but it'll be good practice for your crew to become even better acquainted with their ship."

"That's what I thought, sir." Something out of the video pickup's range attracted Drost's attention. "You've launched shuttles?"

"Major Salminen and her company are trying to figure out how to seize a space station when there's no one with experience to guide the way. *Iolanthe* will serve as the target every time we drop out of FTL to tack and retune the drives."

"If the major needs *Skögul*'s assistance, sir, just let me know. We'll be thrilled to help if only to break the monotony."

Dunmoore smiled at Drost's pleading expression. "Tiny ship, long voyage syndrome, eh?"

Drost nodded. "Aye. I don't think many of my crew ever spent much time aboard anything smaller than a frigate."

"We can always offer to exchange individual crew members."

"No." Drost shook her head. "That would just make things worse. Going from hand-picked volunteer to quitter isn't something any of them is prepared to swallow."

"I need your crew ready and able when we reach the target."

"It will be, Captain. That, I promise you."

"On the premise that pride conquers all?" Dunmoore smiled at her. "Don't let it get away from you. We've barely started."

— Twenty-One —

"Hey, Karlo, how are they hanging?" Gus Purdy, the petty officer piloting First Platoon's shuttle grinned at Command Sergeant Saari when he stuck his head into the cockpit. "Recovered from the cox'n's Fuck the Senate party yet?"

The soldier let loose a derisive bark of laughter. "Remember that I'm from Scandia. We use vodka as anti-freeze in our veins."

"The way you pongos were slamming the stuff down last night, I believe it. Are all of your chicks on board?"

"Yep. Button her up, buddy. Time to see how badly practice differs from theory."

"In my experience, the first few rounds will be FUBAR to the max which is always entertaining to watch." Gus chuckled.

"Glad we can give you fun times, but keep in mind it won't be entertaining if we can't climb up from FUBAR to reasonably competent before the shit gets real."

"Ain't that the truth? What's the program for today?"

"A shake-out to help build the old muscle memory. Our CO figures the only way we can take a damned station is by surprise, so we want to make sure everyone can work through a boarding party drill without hiccups. That'll be a platoon at a time. Once she's happy, we'll try several platoons at a time through several ingress points to sort out the coordination problems. After that, we'll be running amok inside *Iolanthe* practicing close quarters combat, clearing out one compartment at a time. I figure your lot will have a ball playing opfor when the time comes."

"We sure will." Gus glanced at his control panel. "Grab on to something and standby for departure. Flight control just gave the thirty seconds signal. They're depressurizing the hangar deck."

Saari stepped back into the passenger compartment and took one of the jump seats facing aft, his eyes scanning the seated soldiers of First Platoon, looking for anything Sergeant First Class Mattis, his platoon sergeant, might have overlooked during the pre-boarding inspection. He saw nothing amiss and did not expect to find anything. Mattis was no slouch. If she had been a less than effective noncom, Saari would have sorted her out long ago.

The shuttle lurched forward, expelled into the cold, hard vacuum of space by *Iolanthe*'s gravitic catapult system, essentially a reverse gravitic tractor. Three more of its siblings followed in quick succession, each carrying one of Company Group 31's rifle platoons. The four craft arced away from their mothership, circled *Skögul* and came back at a shallow angle until they were fifty kilometers out, at which point the pilots put them on a parallel course and matched velocities.

Saari's helmet speakers came to life with Major Salminen's voice. "One, this is Niner, your target is the starboard cargo hold. It'll stand in for the enemy's shuttle hangar. This will be a non-forced entry. The enemy expects no foul play. You will seize the target and hold it until follow-on forces land."

None of the company's soldiers had so much as seen either of *Iolanthe*'s cargo holds, which made them ideal for training to board an unknown space habitat, and since Salminen's transmission came over a dedicated tight-beam push from the ship, the other command sergeants would not know until they received their own assignments. Slick.

"Ack," he replied. "Starboard cargo hold, non-forced entry. Seize and hold for follow-on. Stand by."

He switched to his platoon frequency.

"Folks, attention to orders…" Saari spent the next five minutes explaining what he wanted done and assigning jobs to each section. He gave the section leaders ten minutes to sort out their squads. It was no different in concept and planning than executing a hasty attack dirtside, something that had become second nature by the time a corporal was ready for his sergeant's stripes. The execution, however…

When all three section sergeants reported ready, Saari switched back to the tight-beam push. "Niner, this is One. We are go."

"Execute. Niner, out."

He stuck his head back into the cockpit. "You ready, Gus?"

"Yep. Starboard cargo hold. We make like a regular delivery van and mosey on in, Greek-style."

Saari stared at the pilot in puzzlement. "What's Greek-style?"

"You know the story of the Trojan horse, right? Well, we're the Trojan shuttle, so to speak." When the soldier's eyes still shone with incomprehension, Gus smirked. "Look it up when we're done, Karlo. You might find it educational. Oh, and for future reference, you should always confirm with your pilot before telling control you're ready to go. It might save you a red face or two."

Saari's eyebrows shot up. "Indeed. Thanks for pointing that out. It won't happen again."

"All part of the wonderful learning experience, buddy. You'll have more of those little lessons before this is over."

A wry smile twisted the soldier's lips. "No doubt. Try not to enjoy watching me step on my dick over and over again too much."

"You're aware the CIC will record every nanosecond of your attempts, right? It's not me you have to worry about, Karlo. It's everyone else aboard *Iolanthe*. You might want to eat in your barracks mess tonight."

Saari made an obscene gesture at the pilot, but that merely increased the latter's merriment. Then, Gus became serious with a suddenness that brought the soldier up short. "Okay, buddy. I'm on final approach. They're opening the space doors. The hold is not pressurized, I say again, not pressurized, so lock visors down and start breathing canned air. I'll depressurize the passenger compartment the moment you give me an all clear. Now back up so I can seal off the cockpit."

The soldier did as he was told and less than a minute later confirmed First Platoon was ready to operate in a vacuum. A red light began to strobe, and Saari let his eyes roam over his troops once again, watching for anyone who showed signs of trouble as the shuttle's pumps sucked the air away. Operating in space presented a dimension of difficulty ground troops could not understand until they tried it, something Saari was beginning to appreciate. Hopefully, the other twenty-four members of First Platoon had experienced the same epiphany. Then, the strobe died away, and they felt, rather than heard the shuttle's skids touch the deck.

"They're closing the space doors, that means they'll be re-pressurizing the hold," Gus announced over the platoon push. "I suggest we wait until that happens and do the same in here, but you should stay on suit air, anyway."

"Ack. Will do."

The next two minutes dragged by with the speed of a millennial glacier reaching for the open sea, then Gus came back on the push. "They're done, and if I'm not mistaken, they've released the inner doors. Pumping air back into the passenger compartment."

A green strobe began its dance, but after less than twenty seconds, it died away to the pilot's warning.

"Dropping aft ramp now. Go get 'em, tigers."

Moments later, Alpha squad burst through the opening, carbines at the ready, ran for a few meters, then stopped to spread out so they could cover the others. Saari loped down the ramp on the file closer's heels and tried to take his bearings while the rest of the platoon disembarked. They had to seize the points of entry into the ship proper before someone with good reflexes could bar them and turn the hold into a shooting gallery. Speed and surprise.

"Bravo squad," he pointed at the main doors directly in front of the shuttle's nose. "Over there. Charlie squad, to our right, the secondary doors. Alpha, the secondary doors on the left."

Armored soles pounded the metallic deck, but when charlie squad reached the main doors, they slammed shut, followed by both secondaries. Too slow. A red strobe began pulsing in the hold, and by now, all of them knew what that meant.

Saari wanted to curse, but before he could articulate the first in a long string of Suomi invective, the platoon push came to life.

"Niner here. Stand down. The drill is over. This was meant to be an introduction to the difficulties of taking a ship or a station by surprise rather than brute force. As you can appreciate, it takes high speed and luck to seize the points of entry leading from a hangar deck, and that's only if they re-pressurize it, or keep it pressurized in the first place. One of the challenges is that we'll not know what conditions to expect until we're there, so the leaders at all levels have to be mentally agile as never before, and that might include deciding to abort the operation the moment it becomes clear there's no chance of success. You're going around for another try while the next victims live through their introduction. Expect the unexpected, even this early in your training, folks. Niner, out."

"You heard the boss," Saari said. "Mount up. Time to get out of here. We'll do the hotwash while we're waiting for our next turn."

*

"I wouldn't worry too much right now, Major." Thorin Sirico gave Salminen a reassuring smile after they had watched the four platoons cycle through the first two rounds on the CIC's multiple screens. "You don't know what you don't know. Frankly, I expected more stumbling around after witnessing how difficult Emma Cullop's folks found their first training runs at storming a ship once they'd done a non-forced entry. And we're talking about trained spacers with years of experience. A lot of the success depends on luck. More so than speed, I'd say."

Salminen inclined her head. "I appreciate the encouragement, sir, but I'm aware we have a lot of work ahead of us and not much time. Today, we will be able to run a third round of practice, but that will be it." She pointed at the countdown to FTL clock in the bottom right corner of the main screen.

"At least you can work on the part after you've breached the inner doors while we're in hyperspace."

"True, but that part is comparatively easier. We are infantry. This is part and parcel of what we do. Aboard a starship, it just means we work in tighter quarters with control delegated to the lowest level. Getting to that point is my problem." Salminen shrugged. "You mentioned luck. I say luck comes to the side that prepared best."

"So I've heard," Dunmoore said from the CIC's door. Salminen made as if to stand, but she waved her down. "At ease, Major. If you haven't noticed yet, the bridge and CIC are chickenshit-free zones, to quote my crew. How are the boarding drills going?" *Iolanthe*'s captain slid into her command chair.

"So-so." Salminen held up a hand, palm down, and wiggled it from side to side. "My people are struggling with the idea they have to favor speed over our deeply ingrained battle drills. What we call hasty attack drills dirtside are as slow as molasses in this environment, and equally ineffective."

"No one has yet developed a fool-proof way to capture a habitat in space," Dunmoore replied. "Every time someone attempts to do so, it turns into improvisation from start to finish. Speed is necessary, true, but so is mental agility."

"A point I've made to my platoon leaders, one after the other, Captain." Salminen gave her a tired smile. "They're good troops. They'll learn, given time. If I were a religious person, that's what I'd pray for — time."

"Unlike Napoleon, who apparently said, 'ask me for anything but time,' I can increase the number of intervals by shortening our hyperspace legs, but only up to a point."

"That would help, sir."

Dunmoore saw the pleading look in Salminen's eyes and nodded. "Consider it done. I'll have a chat with the sailing master before we go FTL again."

"Thank you." Salminen glanced at her station's readout and said, "they're about to come around for the final round, sir, if you'd care to critique. Perhaps you might see things I'm missing and offer advice."

"If you wish." Dunmoore settled back into her command chair and turned it to face the bank of screens showing various aspects of the oncoming shuttles and both cargo holds. "But as Thorin — Lieutenant Commander Sirico — can tell you, I'm a harsh critic."

"No harsher than I can be, I'm sure."

"I wouldn't be surprised. Good commanding officers invariably live and breathe the notion that the more you sweat in training, the less you bleed in battle."

*

When Command Sergeant Saari emerged from his shuttle, the last of the four to land, the first person his eyes lit on was Sergeant Major Talo Haataja, standing by the inner doors, arms crossed, and a derisive smile on his face.

"Welcome back, mighty space warrior."

"How are they hanging, Top?"

"Better than yours, Karlo."

"You watched?"

"You bet. Watching your face the first time around was priceless. Remember the look a Scandian werefox gets when you shine a light into its burrow? That was your face, right down to the oh shit gleam in the eyes. You forgot to blank your visor."

"*Voi vittu.*" Saari shook his head in disgust. "At least we improved the second and third time."

"Marginally. The only one in your platoon who didn't seem to have a thumb up his ass was Vallin. Maybe you should think about reorganizing things, so you let him and his squad loose first. He might just take one of the entry points for you before it slams shut."

"I'll think about it."

"Actually, we will discuss it. The boss has called a hotwash for the command group in an hour. Go climb out of your tin suit and take a shower."

The ship's public address system came to life with its usual lack of warning.

"Now hear this, prepare for transition to hyperspace in one minute, I repeat, prepare for transition to hyperspace in one minute. That is all."

Both soldiers grimaced.

"Good thing I haven't eaten in eight hours." Saari took a sidestep to brace himself on the nearest bulkhead, imitated by the sergeant major while the soldiers of First Platoon variously scattered to do the same or simply dropped to the deck.

Exactly sixty seconds later, the universe shifted to one side, their stomachs to the other and nausea seized all but the few aboard with the inexplicable immunity that affected one in a hundred or less. Saari thought he heard at least one of his soldiers retch. When his vision cleared and his internal organs settled in their usual positions, he scanned the hangar deck to see if someone had puked, but mercifully, whoever made the sound seemed to have retained what little food remained in his stomach after over seven hours of hard physical work.

Haataja slapped him on the shoulder. "One hour, Karlo, in the TAC. Bring your brain because the boss wants to discuss every insane idea that might help us improve. Captain Dunmoore will arrange for shorter FTL jumps to give us more off-ship training time."

Sergeant First Class Mattis resumed chivying the tired, grumpy platoon off the hangar deck and aft to the barracks, and Saari, helmet tucked under one arm, carbine slung over a shoulder, followed them. Once in the armory, he realized that the usual banter and horseplay had gone AWOL, the soldiers stripping off armor and securing weapons in silence or conversing in low tones.

"Some days it sucks being a Marine, doesn't it?" Command Sergeant Courtlyn Alekseev remarked when Saari sat on the bench in front of the platoon leaders' lockers with a weary sigh. She had already stripped off her armor and was in the process of unfastening her battledress tunic.

Saari snorted. "Some days? The top-kick just compared me to a stunned werefox."

"Really? Apparently, I looked like a spastic ice lemur trying to decide which way to jump."

"Serving aboard a starship seems to agree with Talo," a voice behind them remarked. Saari turned to see Command Sergeant Arik Ritland, Third Platoon's leader, emerge from the showers with the fourth and final rifle platoon leader, Command Sergeant Aase Jennsen hard on his heels, both naked as the day they were born. "His insults are becoming more inventive and have a more refined flavor of home. He compared me to a retarded glacier louse, unable to find my ass with both hands."

"The hotwash should be a thing of beauty," Jennsen said, toweling off her short, damp hair.

"What did our beloved sergeant major compare you to?" Saari asked.

"A snowy eagle," she replied with a sly smile.

"Bullshit."

"With a broken wing, capable only of stumbling around in ever tightening circles until it vanishes up its own ass."

"Yep," Saari nodded. "Talo's upped his game all right. It'll be one to remember."

*

"How did our Army contingent do today?" Holt asked, handing Dunmoore a cup of black coffee before settling into one of the day cabin's visitors chairs with his own mug.

"About as you might expect, but no worse than a boarding party learning how to do it for the first time. I didn't witness the first run, but Tatiana tells me it had the effect she wanted." When Holt cocked a questioning eyebrow, Dunmoore smiled. "It opened their eyes to the degree of difficulty involved. Apparently, the Army has a training technique where they administer the test before giving the lesson, so that the lesson really sinks in. Their second and third attempts showed incremental improvement, but we'll have to give them more time than planned."

"Hence the shorter jumps you've had navigation plot." Holt nodded. "We need to keep in mind that our food stocks are limited. The longer we go without replenishing, the closer we get to living off the hydroponics and protein vats only, which won't help morale. Of course, the Army folks don't know how we keep them going so they might not think of it as recycled shit like the crew does."

Dunmoore wrinkled her nose. "I'm sure they'll find out soon enough if someone hasn't already told them. The alternative is to stop off at one of the unregistered colonies littering this sector in the hope they stock provender that humans can digest and will part with it at a price that won't deplete our precious metal reserves. That being said, I'd rather not advertise our presence, in case word gets back to our quarry that a large unmarked bulk freighter accompanied by an equally unmarked sloop are headed in their general direction, and they connect it to the recent incident around Rocinante."

"Indeed. If luck is with us, we might be able to plunder that damned pirate lair Tarkon and his merry bunch of mercenaries use as their home port."

"Plunder, Zeke?" She snorted. "Let's not take the privateer theme too far, but it is an option if time and circumstances allow."

Seven bells chimed overhead, and Siobhan glanced at her desk's display. "Have you ever witnessed an Army hotwash?"

"No. Why?"

"Tatiana invited me to listen in on hers, in case I had suggestions to pass along afterward."

Holt shrugged. "I have nothing better to do for the next half hour. Or at least I have nothing I really want to do. How does this work? We head for the barracks and sit in a corner?"

"No." She touched the controls and the star map that had filled the day cabin's main screen dissolved into a view of Company Group 31's TAC. "Having either of us in the room will most assuredly inhibit the conversation."

"They don't look particularly pleased with their day," Holt remarked after examining the platoon leaders' faces, "although Sergeant Major Haataja appears to be enjoying himself."

Then, CG31's command group stood as one and snapped to attention.

*

"At ease." Major Salminen waved them back into their chairs. "It's been an interesting day, hasn't it? I want to start by hearing what each of you thinks impaired your platoon's performance. We'll discuss possible remedies afterward." She turned to Command Sergeant Saari. "How about we start with you, Karlo? Don't hold back."

A pained expression twisted Saari's face. "What do I think, sir? We stink, on ice. It's obvious we're not used to starships and because of that, we lose precious time orienting ourselves after we step aboard. Since no one knows what the target will be like until the moment we enter whatever passes for a shuttle hangar, we have to develop much faster reflexes and tighten the old OODA loop, so it's no bigger than a gnat's asshole. I had no problems deciding and acting, but the observing and orienting beforehand? Too slow. Much too slow. I'll get us killed during the real thing at that rate."

The other three platoon leaders nodded in agreement. Salminen turned to Alekseev. "Courtlyn?"

"Same as Karlo, sir. Sloppy OODA loop that wasted too much time. We're not used to attacking with so little knowledge about a target. Unless we can make decisions instantaneously when we finally see what we're up against, we'll be too slow."

Salminen pointed at Command Sergeant Ritland. "Arik?"

"Nothing to add, sir. We're too slow on the uptake once we're on the target."

"Agreed," Aase Jennsen said.

"Okay." Salminen nodded. "We have a consensus. The sergeant major, Lieutenant Puro and I came to the same conclusion independently of each other after watching your performances. Now to find solutions we can work into our drills so that the next battle runs go better. The floor is open."

Saari raised a hand. "Sir, the sergeant major said something when I came back aboard, to the effect that Corporal Vallin and his squad almost took one of the entry points on the last battle run and that I should consider letting him loose first." He glanced at Haataja, who nodded.

"What do you deduce from that observation, Karlo?"

"If we platoon leaders are the weak point because of the time we take to observe and orient, before dispatching our sections, time during which the enemy can figure out what's happening and take defensive measures, we need to step out of the loop. At least for the part of the battle between exiting our shuttles and securing the beachhead, and delegate the decision-making."

Jennsen tapped Saari on the shoulder. "Exactly. But not to the section sergeants. We have to push the initiative and decision-making down to the squad leaders."

"How would that work in practice?" Salminen asked, a faint smile of pleasure creasing her lips.

"Appoint two or three squads per platoon as door kickers, preferably three," Ritland said. "Each one goes in a different direction the moment they exit the shuttle to take whatever ingress point they see or might have seen during landing. Say one goes left, the other right, and the third goes straight. No need for us to make on-the-spot decisions after taking in the lay of the land. Let the squad leaders rush whatever target they see, the moment they see it. Shock and awe, sir. This isn't a hasty attack in the way we know them."

Saari nodded with enthusiasm. "Assign the corporals with the sharpest and quickest wit to lead these door kicker squads. Say what you want about Vallin, but he has the wits to go with that mouth of his. Once the squads are on their way, we can afford to take a minute to orient and lead the rest of the platoon wherever it needs to go to reinforce the beachhead."

"Shock and awe, eh? No doubt shouting the regimental battle cry along the way?" Salminen's smile broadened.

"Of course, sir. We couldn't awe the bastards without it."

Lieutenant Puro raised his hand.

"Yes, Jon?"

"Sir, we can practice the proposed drill while we're FTL. I'll ask the second officer to shift things around so we can use *Iolanthe*'s hangar deck. Maybe set up mock ingress points that won't be visible until the shuttle's aft ramp drops, to introduce the random factor we're bound to meet when it gets real. If nothing else, trying the proposed technique will give us an idea of whether it's workable and identify problems we haven't thought about yet."

"Perfect. Let's aim for tomorrow morning, then. Karlo, since you came up with the root of the idea, and you have a squad leader who's already shown promise in this new environment, you'll be up first."

"Gee, thanks, Major. I'm always ready for another chance to make an ass of myself."

— Twenty-Two —

"Shuttles are ready to launch," Lieutenant Commander Sirico announced when Dunmoore entered the CIC shortly after *Iolanthe* dropped out of a three-day FTL jump. Company Group 31 had used the time to practice on the hangar deck for hours on end, eventually choosing the door kicker squads for each platoon after a series of competitions to identify the ones with the quickest wit, Corporal Vallin among them. "The video feeds are on the port screens."

"Thank you." Dunmoore took the command chair and swiveled it left to face the displays.

Behind her, Major Salminen, still dressed for battle stations even though Dunmoore had stood the ship down ten minutes earlier, said, "I hope we will present you with a better spectacle today than the last time, sir."

"Your folks certainly worked hard over the last few days, but it's a given we'll witness mistakes, if only because the adrenaline level is a few notches higher now. Besides, they'll soon find out the bosun reconfigured both holds overnight so your troops will face brand new tactical problems."

"I wouldn't want it any other way. Train hard, fight easy."

"And live to tell the tale." Dunmoore nodded with approval. She pointed at the display. "They're launching."

In rapid succession, *Iolanthe*'s hangar bay spat out four shuttles whose drives lit up the moment they cleared the ship, headed out into the void before turning back more than five hundred kilometers out. They split into two flights of two, one aimed at the port cargo hold, the other at the starboard one.

"All call signs, this is Niner," Salminen spoke into her microphone. "Begin operation."

Two hours later, with the shuttles back on an approach course, Dunmoore turned her command chair around to face the soldier and said, "That was better than three days ago, by a few orders of magnitude, although from where I sit, the mad rush for the entry points seemed chaotic. However, I can't argue with the results. Each of your platoons managed to seize at least one, in a few cases more of the inner doors before they slammed shut, which suffices to gain a foothold. I do have a question, however, what in heaven's name were they shouting?"

One corner of Salminen's mouth pulled up in a half smile. "*Hakkaa päälle*. It's the Scandia Regiment's battle cry. Roughly translated from old Suomi into Anglic it means cut them down. Our battalion war song, the Hakkapeliittain Marssi, is derived from it."

Dunmoore chuckled. "If I were facing an onrush of armored and heavily armed berserkers shouting at the top of their lungs, I'd probably think hard about the wisdom of turning tail. *Hakkaa päälle*, eh? You don't get that kind of historical character from the Marines."

"There's a lot more history if you ever want to experience utter boredom, Captain. Tales of a glorious past are one of the things that help us through our years-long winters on Scandia."

The signals petty officer raised his hand. "Shuttle flight reports ready."

"Excuse me, Captain." Salminen switched on the company push. "One, Two, this is Niner, you may proceed."

The lead shuttles accelerated and arced outward on a shallow path before aiming their snouts at the cargo holds, the pilots carefully adjusting velocities to allow for a gentle landing aboard a starship traveling at over a hundred thousand kilometers per hour through interstellar space. Dunmoore, Salminen, and Sirico watched the training run unfold with such intensity that Chief Petty Officer Yens' muffled curse caught them by surprise.

"Emergence signatures, three of them. One million kilometers aft and on a converging course." A pause. "Small, approximately *Skögul*'s size."

Dunmoore repressed a string of cuss words that would have made Sergeant Major Haataja blush. Chance encounters in interstellar space were rare occurrences. Rarer even when they happened while *Iolanthe* was at her most vulnerable. "Abort training exercise and recover shuttles."

"Based on the configuration and emissions signature, I make the ships as Pradyni," Yens continued, naming a humanoid reptilian species that acquired FTL technology via unscrupulous traders at a time when their civilization was still mired in its equivalent of Earth's dark ages. Despite the sudden jump in technological ability, Pradyn society had made little progress since, other than discovering the joys of deep space piracy. "They definitely have that baroque on steroids decorative enhancement thing on display."

"Wonderful." Dunmoore took a deep breath and slowly released it. "I suppose there's no avoiding this. They must have detected our hyperspace bubble and figured it was big enough to carry a juicy prize. Signals make to *Skögul* — they're to go silent."

"Aye, aye, sir."

With any luck, the Pradyni had not detected the sloop yet thanks to inferior sensors. Although their ships were not of the same quality as those built by humans, it would be foolish to underestimate the damage they could cause to something their own size before going down. Or even to something larger.

"Bridge, call us back to battle stations," she continued, "but maintain current velocity. We'll let them believe we're a fat, dumb freighter who can't see a thing until they reach point-blank range. We'll lure them in close and use guns only, to spare our missile stocks, unless one or more breaks off and tries to run when we unmask. Once the battle is joined, none of the Pradyni can make it out alive, lest they spread word of a Q-ship in the sector."

"Acknowledged." Holt's voice rang out from the CIC speakers. "Calling battle stations now."

The urgent klaxon burst forth almost at once, and Dunmoore climbed to her feet. "I'll go fetch my protective gear. Perhaps next time, I'll imitate the major and keep it on during training runs."

Once Siobhan had left the CIC, Salminen turned to Sirico and asked, "I'm curious, sir, why is the captain assuming we must fight these Pradyni?"

"Because chance encounters in interstellar space are rare, indicating that they probably hunted us. Because Pradyn isn't close by, which generally means sloop-sized ships aren't engaged in honest trade, and last but most important, the lizards have built up a thriving piracy business condoned, if not outright encouraged by their government. If they're honest and merely want to satisfy their curiosity about us, we'll stay outwardly inoffensive and let them go."

Yens laughed. It sounded harsh and bitter to Salminen's ears. "Honest Pradyni? That'll be the day."

"The chief has had a few encounters with that species in her long and colorful career," Sirico explained. "As you can see, she's not a fan."

"I'm a fan of dead Pradyni, sir. Here's hoping they will do something stupid and earn themselves a few well-deserved broadsides." Yens paused. "That was fast. *Skögul* dropped off the sensors. If I didn't know where she was, I wouldn't be able to find her. The scaly buggers won't know we're not alone."

"They don't actually have scales, Chief," Sirico said. "More like a leathery skin."

"Whatever, sir." Yens shrugged off the correction. "Doesn't make 'em any nicer."

The CIC's doors opened, readmitting Dunmoore with her personal protective equipment. "Anything new?"

"The ship's at battle stations," Sirico replied, "the first two shuttles are on final approach, the others are almost there and, *Skögul*'s vanished from the sensors. How about the Pradyni, Chief?"

"They're coming on like the hounds of hell. At this rate, they'll need to decelerate hard by the time they halve the distance between us. They're increasing separation as well, probably to try to box us in. I ran a compare with the database, and these buggers seem to be a new and improved version of the Pradyni pirates we love to hate. Cleaner power signatures, newer hulls and once they charge weapons, I wouldn't be surprised to find they've modernized those as well. However, they still look like a space monster barfed precious metals over them."

"Different species, different aesthetics, Chief." Dunmoore winked at Sirico. "Be tolerant."

"That'll be the day, sir. With all due respect, you know I've spent too many years chasing non-human scum who enjoy preying on my species to show any tolerance. But thanks for yanking my chain."

"Don't worry, Major," Sirico said when he saw Salminen's puzzled expression. "Chief Yens' bite is much worse than her bark."

"Shuttles one and two secure," another voice from the bridge announced. "Shuttles three and four on final approach."

"The Pradyni have begun active scanning, but aren't targeting us yet."

Several minutes passed in silence before the bridge announced the shuttles had been retrieved and the hangar deck secured. *Iolanthe* was in all respects ready for battle once she unmasked.

"Now," Sirico said to no one in particular, "we wait in abject boredom for the next fifteen or twenty minutes."

"I don't think so, sir," Yens replied, drawing out each word. "Three starships just dropped out of FTL ahead of us, at a distance of two million kilometers, on the same heading as we are. They're decelerating hard and spreading out. Ship type and configuration conforms with the others, right down to similar space monster puke aesthetics."

"Someone's been teaching the Pradyni new tricks, Captain." Sirico's eyes turned to the three-dimensional tactical projection where the number of red enemy icons had doubled. "This is the first time anyone's seen them using wolf pack techniques."

"That we know of," Dunmoore said. "Previous sightings of a Pradyni wolf pack might have ended with the target destroyed before it could broadcast a warning. This changes the math, however. Prepare the aft missile launchers. We'll fire down our pursuers' throats when we come within gun range of the newcomers."

"May I ask a question, sir? For my education as an aspiring Marine?"

"You may, Major." Dunmoore turned to face the soldier. "There's time before we enter combat range."

"Why don't we simply jump out and avoid a fight?"

"Three issues. First, we have to give engineering time to retune the drives between jumps; otherwise, we might come out of FTL somewhere other than intended. Lieutenant Commander Halfen still needs another hour or so to complete that work. Carrying out an emergency jump is always a possibility, but the risks in an area that isn't nearly as well charted as the Commonwealth are higher, as is the risk of damaging the drives. Second, for *Skögul* to go FTL, she would have to unmask, meaning word might reach enemy ears that the big freighter has a smaller and nastier companion. Finally, they're within close enough range to launch an FTL stern chase and stick to us even if they're not equipped to torpedo us out of hyperspace. When we inevitably drop out of FTL, we'll be no further ahead than we are now."

Salminen nodded. "Understood."

"Besides," a cruel grin tugged at Dunmoore's lips, "my job is to remove every form of sentient garbage from this universe, and a Pradyni wolf pack deserves special attention, lest they become bold enough to raid within Commonwealth space."

"Since the captain won't say it, I will. We also take great pleasure in combat," Sirico added. "Otherwise, we'd have joined the Merchant Guild for real instead of merely pretending to be members."

"Speak for yourself, Guns," Holt replied from the bridge. "Some of us prefer to do the job without fighting. You should read Sun Tzu's Art of War one of these days."

"To subdue the enemy without fighting is the acme of skill. I'm well up on my Sun Tzu, Commander, thank you. I also heed the old saying that in war, the enemy has a vote, and he often votes to fight it out."

"Signals here, I hate to interrupt a witty repartee as much as the next man," Lieutenant Kremm interjected, "but right now the enemy wants to speak. We're being hailed."

"Voice or data?" Dunmoore asked.

"Data. It's in Anglic but the translation program that produced it has a strange accent. I've piped the message to the CIC comms screen, sir."

"I see what you mean by strange accent, Theo," Dunmoore said after skimming the short text. "Human ship trespasses the domain of his Imperial Majesty, the Glorious Ruler and Guardian of the First Egg, Bvaniss the Sublime. Human ship will permit soldiers of his Imperial Majesty to enter and collect tax. If human ship not cooperate, humans die. Humans cooperate, ship go home after paying tax. Here I thought surrender or die was my line."

Sirico guffawed. "The domain of his Imperial Majesty? These guys are suffering from serious delusions of adequacy. I can see them claiming their star system, but out here, light years from Pradyn?"

Dunmoore waved her hand in a dismissive gesture. "They're just trying to seize us without having to fight. Heck, they may actually let a ship go after plundering it for all we know."

"In that case, shall we invite them aboard, sir?" Holt asked facetiously.

"Not quite aboard, no, but we'll ask them to come closer."

"Ah. The old step into my parlor said the spider to the fly gambit."

"Six at once?" Sirico sounded dubious. "*Iolanthe* is powerful, but that might be risky if a few of them coordinate and start pounding at the same part of our shields in unison."

"Then our shock and awe will have to be faster than their ability to figure it out. We don't have a choice."

"Just pointing out the risks, Captain. Shock and awe, we can deliver to order."

"Good. Theo, reply with a message stating that we will cooperate and await their arrival. Then, let *Skögul* know our intentions. Tell them if one of the Pradyni tries to make a run for it once we unmask, she's free to go up systems so she can pursue and destroy."

"Will do, sir." Then, "Done. *Skögul* acknowledges."

Dunmoore sat back in her command chair, eyes on the tactical display and waited for the Pradyni to make their next move. She did not have to be patient for long.

Yens raised her hand. "They've powered up weapons and have gone to active targeting. Power curve seems consistent with known Pradyni technology, so no upgrades there. No change in the rate of acceleration and deceleration. Looks like they're bringing all six ships in close. Scratch that. One from ahead has just fired additional braking thrusters."

"I guess we have the winner of our 'get all the plasma you can eat' prize," Sirico remarked.

"Make that two winners, sir. One of the buggers aft just poured on a little more acceleration. Both are now on direct intercept vectors. Assigning designations Tango One and Two." The notations T1 and T2 winked into existence above the closest enemy ship icons in the tactical display, then further notations appeared above the rest. "Assigning designations Tango Three and Four to the ships aft and Tango Five and Six to the ships ahead."

"Transmit the Tango designations to *Skögul*. Then, prepare to launch missiles on Tangos Three to Six the moment we unmask. The initial priority for the guns is the two closing in."

Dunmoore's fingers began dancing on the command chair's arm. When she noticed her display of impatience, she dropped the offending hand into her lap. The Pradyni would come into point-blank range soon enough.

"They sent another message," the signals officer announced, breaking the tense silence of both bridge and CIC. "We're to prepare for their shuttles and open our hangar deck doors."

"If we do that, they'll see our squadron and smell a rat," Holt said.

"Agreed." Dunmoore nodded at his holographic image. "Open both the port and starboard cargo hold space doors instead. We've been using them as mock shuttle decks for the soldiers. The Pradyni wouldn't know the difference."

"I hope you're not planning on letting their shuttles land, are you?"

"Don't tempt me, Number One." She thought about it for a moment while a cruel smile replaced the impassive expression she had worn so far. "Actually, we'll let them launch and allow their craft to approach. The close-in calliopes will turn them to wreckage with a few bursts."

"Now you're just mean, Captain." Holt grinned at her. "Opening port and starboard cargo hold space doors."

"They chose to intercept us, not the other way around."

"What a mistake to make, eh?" Sirico seemed positively filled with glee.

"They did indeed choose poorly," Dunmoore replied in a dry tone.

"Tango One and Two have entered optimum gun range," Yens announced. "The rest have entered extreme gun range. One and Two are opening hangar deck doors."

"They're launching while still on approach? Impatient critters, aren't they?" The combat systems officer turned to his console and scrolled through the targeting assignments, making a few last minute adjustments.

"Aye, and they've launched. Tango One has started braking.   Tango Two is adjusting his rate of deceleration."

"Are we ready, Mister Sirico?" Dunmoore asked.

"As ready as we can be, Captain."

"Then I believe it's time we show these fine subjects of Bvaniss the Sublime the error of their ways. All systems to full military power, shields up, weapons active. You may open fire when ready."

— Twenty-Three —

The rumbling of hull plates moving aside and gun turrets rising from their recesses had barely faded by the time Sirico sent the first brace of missiles streaming at the four outlying Pradyni pirate ships. Seconds later, the two shuttles, now mid-way between their motherships and *Iolanthe*, came under sustained fire from the calliopes while the main guns began hammering the ships themselves. History would never record the reactions of the Pradyni captains when an easy prey turned into a thing from the deepest, darkest recesses of their terror-filled nightmares. Nevertheless, Dunmoore fancied she could sense their confusion, and the primal surge of fear when they finally understood they had been hoodwinked.

Iolanthe's calliopes shredded the shuttles in less than a minute, leaving little more than debris clouds composed of metal, plastics, and plenty of organic matter. Though Tango One and Two had their shields up, at close range, they proved to be no match for the Q-ship's main guns. The onslaught of plasma on a single spot quickly created an energy feedback loop powerful enough to stress and finally burn out shield generators, opening gaps in the protective bubble. Subsequent salvos, now unimpeded, splashed on gray hulls, eating through metal, until a few rounds punched through releasing columns of rapidly freezing gasses. One of the captains seemed to have regained his senses faster than the other. Tango Two turned on its axis so that an intact shield now faced *Iolanthe*. The other reacted too slowly. *Iolanthe*'s salvo likely struck a power conduit or weapon capacitor on Tango One because secondary explosions erupted. With five of its six shield generators still working, the force of the onboard explosions was turned back against the ship, adding to the mayhem.

While the starboard guns kept hammering Tango Two, hoping to burn out the generator of the shield now facing *Iolanthe*, Sirico ordered the port guns to swivel and join the belly guns in targeting their pursuers. He recognized a ship in its death throes when he saw it, and the crew of Tango One had minutes left to live. The secondary explosions dotting its hull put it beyond any attempt at damage control. A brief flare of light obscured its stern as the crew vented antimatter fuel before the magnetic containment units failed, but it proved to be in vain. Tango One began to break apart.

A second shield generator failed on Tango Two, and *Iolanthe*'s gunners resumed punishing its hull. Moments later, the crew of doomed Pradyni sloop joined its Tango One comrades in whatever heaven or hell their belief system prescribed.

Major Salminen stared at the video displays with awe, stunned by the violence and by the speed at which Dunmoore's gunners had dispatched two starships. When she glanced at Siobhan, she saw her watching the tactical schematic, lips slightly parted, exuding an intensity the soldier found fascinating.

"Our missiles are coming under defensive fire, Captain," Sirico said over his shoulder. "So far ineffective."

"Not anymore," Yens chimed in. "One down."

A blue icon vanished from the schematic as if swallowed by the holographic projection. Then a second one faded. Salminen suddenly realized that every muscle in her body had become so taut that she had difficulty breathing. Life aboard a man-of-war really was weeks of boredom followed by minutes of almost unbearable tension.

"Hit. We have a hit. Tango Three. Engaging with the guns."

Salminen had time to see a bright bloom blot out the image of a Pradyni ship before a brief, but intense blue-green aurora sprang to life as the shields fought off the intense radiation released by the missile's nuclear warhead. Then a concentrated stream of plasma struck, the first few round splashing off, the next salvos punching through to the hull. That ship lasted no longer than its companions, but it died in a more spectacular fashion with its antimatter containment units ruptured.

"Three down, three to go." Sirico raised a hand with the appropriate number of digits showing.

"One of the buggers ahead of us, designation Tango Five, just lit his drives. Looks as if he's figured it out."

"So has Lieutenant Drost," Dunmoore said when the icon representing *Skögul* shone with greater intensity. "She's gone up systems. That leaves us two targets."

"One, actually," Sirico replied. "Two missiles struck Tango Four. He's as good as gone."

"We might want to kill him quickly," Yens said. "The last lizard woke up as well. Tango Six is lighting his drives."

"He'll be for us, then." Dunmoore glanced at Holt's image. "We will pursue Tango Six. Come to full acceleration."

"Full acceleration, aye."

"How long until we've cycled the hyperdrives?"

"Another hour," Holt replied.

"Which means they should need even longer. Let's hope they won't try an emergency jump. Pradyni don't enjoy a sterling reputation for maintenance and are probably skating on the edge of jump drive instability as it is. There's no knowing where they might take us."

"Will we pursue?" Sirico asked. "I mean if they go FTL before we're ready?"

Dunmoore grimaced. "No choice. They've seen us unmasked." She glanced at the tactical schematic. "How is Tango Four?"

"About to…" He broke off when the icon winked out of existence. "He's gone. Four out of six."

"Can the two remaining Tangos outrun the missiles?" Salminen asked.

"No." Dunmoore shook her head without taking eyes off the tactical schematic. "But they'll have more time to destroy them. Tangos Three and Four faced birds coming at them while they were still on an approach vector, which means the distance between them was shrinking at almost twice the missiles' speed. They had little time to react. Five and Six will have plenty of time to adjust their fire. The chances are excellent that we're facing a stern chase which invariably ends up being a long chase."

"Unless they do a Crazy Ivan, albeit on drives that haven't properly cycled," Sirico interjected.

"Sorry, sir, I will sound ignorant again," Salminen said, "but what is a Crazy Ivan?"

"It's what we call a set of unpredictable FTL jumps. The ship carrying it out simply changes headings at random between emergency jumps," the combat systems officer replied. "The Crazy Ivan maneuver is the best way to shake a tail in interstellar space, and it's also the most dangerous. Ships have torn themselves apart. Please don't ask me for the origin of the term. It's been part of

Navy lingo for longer than anyone's been alive. The term may even hearken back to pre-spaceflight days."

"Oh." Salminen's eyes darted from Sirico to the captain when she noticed the latter smiling.

"Of course," Dunmoore said, "history has recorded precious few verified instances of successful Crazy Ivans. Less than, say the number of ships that vanished without a trace over the years. The ones we know about, meaning either the pursuing ship or the quarry survived, invariably involved humans or Shrehari. I doubt the Pradyni could make it beyond two random emergency jumps before suffering a severe breakdown."

"Let's hope they know that," Holt said. "I would strenuously recommend against us following a Crazy Ivan."

"We would have a better chance of surviving, though," Siobhan replied with an evil grin.

"A better chance than the Pradyni? I hope so. A better chance than a starship not carrying out a series of random emergency FTL jumps? Never."

"You have no sense of adventure, Zeke."

"Perhaps not, but my survival instinct is excellent. It's one of a first officer's more defining qualities. Union rules, you know."

Dunmoore snorted. "You're just as bad as Gregor — always thwarting my tactical creativity."

"Rules, Captain, rules."

*

When Lieutenant Drost saw a bright orange glow fill the nozzles of Tango Five's sublight drives, she swallowed a choice curse word, then said, "Oh no you don't. Mister Protti, up systems. Helm come to full acceleration. We're not letting him escape."

"Up systems, aye," Sub-Lieutenant Magnus Protti, one of *Iolanthe*'s junior combat systems officers, now Drost's acting first officer, replied. The sloop *Skögul* came to life with a suddenness that took many of her prize crew by surprise. "Do you think they'll attempt an emergency jump, Captain?"

"I bloody well hope not. They've not finished cycling drives yet." She glanced at her command chair's display. "Heck, we're not done and we've been sublight for longer."

"Who knows with the damn lizards," the petty officer operating *Skögul*'s helm muttered. "Stone age critters who don't know about indoor plumbing yet won't give a flying fuck about the laws of multiverse physics."

"Unfortunately, we do," Drost said, "and equally unfortunate is the fact that we can't allow them to live, so this might become a hairy ride."

"Chief Larson won't be happy," Protti warned. "He's taken quite a shine to *Skögul*. Perhaps a warning…"

"Good idea." Drost tapped her communicator. "Bridge to engineering."

"Larson here, Captain," the sloop's acting chief engineer replied moments later. "I gather we went up systems because one of the bastards is making a run for it and you're warning me we might have to go FTL before I'm done with drives."

"You got it, Chief."

"You're looking at an hour before we're ready, sir. *Skögul*'s an elegant little lady, but without a proper survey done at a Fleet shipyard, I can't tell you how she might react if we stress her too much." He let his words hang between them for a few seconds. "That being said, odds are one or two emergency jumps won't do us fatal harm, but the more time we give our drives to cycle through now, the better."

"Understood, but this is one of those situations where the enemy gets a vote on what happens next."

"Aye, ain't it always that way? I'll see what I can do to shorten the cycle."

"If anyone can, it would be you, Chief. Bridge, out."

Drost looked up at the tactical schematic again, and a grim smile appeared on her narrow face. "Looks like *Iolanthe*'s about to face the same questions as we are. Tango Six is trying to run as well."

"If we're lucky, the missiles will take care of preventing them from going FTL before we get our licks in," Protti said.

"If." Drost gave him a skeptical grimace. "It's a stern chase, and that gives their defensive systems time to engage. Captain Dunmoore would have to let loose enough missiles to saturate them, and *Iolanthe*'s stocks are getting low." A change in the schematic attracted her attention. "Case in point. Tango Five just destroyed the last of the birds aimed at it. Unless *Iolanthe* fires another volley, it's on us to make the kill, and what missiles we carry won't cut it, not like this. Let's hope we have a better rate of acceleration than the Pradyni do."

*

"That's the last of the missiles gone," Sirico reported when the last blue icon tracking the red of the Tangos disappeared from the tactical display. "Another volley, sir?"

Dunmoore shook her head. "There's no point. Separation and relative velocities being what they are, even Pradyni gunners have a chance at knocking all of them down short of a saturation volley. We'll likely need our remaining stock against more formidable adversaries anyway. No, we'll run them to ground and finish this the old-fashioned way, broadside to broadside."

"Aye." Sirico nodded. "As long as they've reached the limit of their capacity to accelerate, because we're almost there, and we're a lot bigger."

"What's the estimate to intercept? If they don't go FTL within the next hour that is?"

"At this rate, fifty minutes, a little more maybe."

She glanced at Holt's image. "Take us to fifty percent battle stations crewing. Everyone gets twenty minutes to relieve themselves, eat, and grab something to drink. I want us back at one hundred percent in forty-five minutes."

"Fifty percent crewing, aye." Holt nodded. The announcement echoed through *Iolanthe* moments later, and Dunmoore stood, suddenly overcome by a craving for coffee. "I'll be in my day cabin, Mister Sirico."

She had just finished pouring herself a cup when the door opened, and Holt poked his head through the opening. "I figured you'd be here, Captain. Mind if I raid your urn as well? There's likely to be a lineup in the wardroom."

"Who has the bridge?"

"Kremm and Pashar are relaying each other."

"Good. The youngsters need as much time as they can get in the command chair while we're in a running battle." Dunmoore handed Holt the full mug and poured herself another.

Holt chuckled. "Youngsters? I seem to recall not too many years ago that you were one of the youngest captains in the Fleet."

Dunmoore brushed her hair with one hand. "Yet I now have the silver strands of an elder stateswoman."

"They give you added gravitas, elder stateswoman who isn't quite forty years old yet."

"Silver-tongued rogue." She raised her mug in salute.

"Charm is my middle name." He took a sip. "Ah, that's good stuff. I wish we could convince the steward to let Vincenzo make the wardroom coffee besides brewing yours."

"Sorry. Rank has its privileges." She gave the day cabin's main screen, now showing a two-dimensional feed from the CIC's tactical schematic, a pointed glare. "This tangent is irritating."

"We're doing the galaxy a favor by removing that bunch permanently. Who knows how competent they might have become in time with their wolf pack tactics, and how many true civilian ships might suffer but for our intervention. Consider this our good deed of the week, or the month, even."

Dunmoore smirked at her first officer. "Thanks for pointing that out, Mister Boy Scout. It wouldn't have occurred to me that we were performing an interstellar civic service."

Holt gave her an abbreviated bow. "All in a day's work, *mon Capitaine*."

"How about we take a break from the day's work." She nodded at the chairs. "I'm sure the ship will run fine without our involvement for at least forty minutes, don't you?"

"Of course, but we should take care to make sure our officers don't know that. It might give them ideas."

"Can I interest you in a game of chess?"

*

"Captain," the gunnery petty officer sitting at a console to Drost's left raised her hand. "I'm getting an energy spike from Tango Five. It looks like he's about to go FTL."

"Damn." Drost glanced at the countdown timer in the lower right corner of the main screen. Only fifteen minutes to go until *Skögul* completed its tuning cycle. She touched her communicator. "Engineering, this is the captain. The target is powering up hyperdrives. I intend to pursue."

"Aye," Larson replied. "I'm not surprised. Most engineers, the lizards likely among them, consider two-thirds of a cycle to be a sufficient margin for an emergency jump, and he's almost there. As long as he doesn't do a Crazy Ivan, we should meet again in another part of the sector soon enough. Drives ready at your command, Captain. Please try not to strain them overmuch."

"No promises, Chief. Bridge, out." Drost called up the navigation display and confirmed one more time that *Skögul*'s heading matched the Pradyni's down to three decimals. The precision was vital to keep some sort of contact once both ships were enveloped in their own hyperspace bubbles. "Helm, the moment that bastard jumps, rev up the drives."

"Aye, sir. Preparing to rev up the drives." The helmsman could not help but smile at the captain's casual terminology.

"Mister Protti, call the ship to jump stations if you please."

A minute ticked by, then another before the gunnery petty officer said, "I'm losing contact with Tango Five. He's going FTL."

The image of the Pradyni ship on the main screen wavered and became indistinct, then it vanished altogether.

Skögul dropped off *Iolanthe*'s own video feed two point three seconds later, the time it took the helmsman's finger to tap his controls. With Tango Five gone, Tango Six skipped the full hyperdrive cycling period as well. He jumped shortly after that with the Q-ship hard on its trail, despite the chief engineer's reservations.

— Twenty-Four —

"You've apparently heard," Holt said dropping into a chair across from Dunmoore in the otherwise empty wardroom. The ship's bell had just chimed twice, marking the first hour of the morning watch, or as the soldiers called it, oh-five-hundred. "You wouldn't be eating your favorite calorie bomb to get you through until lunch if you hadn't."

She took another bite of her thick breakfast sandwich and nodded. The CIC officer of the watch had woken her ten minutes earlier because the sensors had finally, after almost eighteen hours of pursuit, picked up Tango Six's hyperspace bubble. Siobhan had begun to fear they had missed it altogether due to a navigational quirk or the Pradyni captain's cunning.

After swallowing the mixture of meat, egg, cheese, and bread, she said, "I'm glad we caught up, though right now, it serves to point out *Iolanthe*'s most glaring flaw."

"Lack of hyperspace torpedoes." Holt shrugged. "Q-ship's aren't designed for pursuit. We're supposed to let the enemy come to us."

"I know, but I'm still peeved at the shipwrights." She made a face at him.

"Consider that we would have had to give up half of the missile launchers and the adjoining magazines for something we might use every so often. Missiles, we use in every engagement."

She made a wry face. "Try not to be right all the time, Zeke, and let me grumble once in a while, especially this early."

"As long as you grumble only at me and not your loyal, hardworking crew, go nuts." He watched her take another bite and chew, her eyes on the sandwich. "Any intuition about when he might decide to drop out?"

Dunmoore shook her head without looking up at her first officer. He decided to let her finish the hasty meal in peace and walked over to the covered self-serve buffet. The wardroom steward kept it stocked around the clock for officers who had missed the regular meals or needed a snack at odd hours. Holt might as well imitate his captain and eat. She may deny having any gut feeling about the enemy's intent, but her subconscious expected action if it had her eat enough to sate a fully-grown Marine. After building a sandwich to rival Siobhan's he sat down again. However, before he could take his first bite, the universe lurched sideways, and his inner organs attempted to escape through his throat. The sensation of sickness vanished within a second or two, and his blurred vision returned to normal. Then, the howl of the battle stations siren killed all thoughts of finishing his breakfast.

Holt looked at his sandwich with dismay, took as big a bite as he could, then dropped the rest on his plate Dunmoore gave him a mordant smile and, shrugging, she shoved the rest of hers into her mouth. Still chewing, they left the wardroom, one headed for the bridge, the other for the CIC, both dodging crew members rushing to their stations.

Sirico looked up the moment he spied his captain entering the CIC.

"We're six hundred thousand kilometers in front of Tango Six," he said. "So far, he's not changed course."

"Only six hundred thousand? Impressive. Who was at the helm?"

"I can answer that, Captain," Holt's voice echoed from the CIC speakers. "The cox'n took his turn and relieved the quartermaster. We can thank him for a quick reaction when Tango Six vanished from the sensors."

"In that case, blessed be the cox'n. Guns, a full brace of missiles on Tango Six if you please. This ends now." She took the command chair from Sirico and studied the tactical display. "No sign of Tango Five and *Skögul*, I take it."

"Negative," Chief Yens replied. "Not even the faintest trace of a hyperspace bubble passing at the outer edge of our sensor range."

"Salvo away," Sirico reported. Half a dozen blue icons materialized at the center of the tactical schematic, headed for the red icon bearing the designation T6.

"Tango Six veering to port, forty degrees, zee minus fifteen. I'm reading a power surge."

"Puta." Sirico slammed a fist against his console. "He's doing a Crazy Ivan."

"Guns, open fire with everything that bears on target, maximum rate," Dunmoore ordered. "Bridge, change course to match the enemy's, stand by for emergency jump."

"Sir, I strongly counsel against another jump in such short succession," Holt replied. "In my opinion, the risks it entails outweigh the risk of having Tango Six carry word of a Q-ship in the sector."

Dunmoore glared at the Holt hologram, her lips compressed into a thin line. "Sometimes, I hate it when you're right. Let's see how this goes. Even with the best engineers in the galaxy, our Pradyni friends can't form a proper hyperspace bubble for several more minutes."

"Someone needs to tell 'em that," Yens interjected, pointing at the video feed showing Tango Six's image shimmering in and out of view. "They're trying real hard to beat the laws of physics."

"In the meantime, they're forgetting to fire on our birds," Sirico said, smiling with glee.

"No one ever accused the damned lizards of being smart, sir," Yens replied. "Looks like they stopped trying to jump."

Tango Six's image solidified once more. Less than a minute later, streams of plasma from its close-in defense guns reached out to intercept *Iolanthe*'s missiles, crossing streams with incoming rounds from the Q-ship's main guns. One missile icon went dark, followed by a second, then a third. The fourth, however, exploded hard against Tango Six's shields. The onslaught of radiation from the nuclear blast on top of the energy unleashed by the splashing plasma proved too much. A massive blue-green aurora enveloped the sloop before popping out of existence. The next salvo ate through hull plating while the one after that sheared off the Pradyni's starboard hyperdrive nacelle.

"And it's over." Dunmoore nodded with satisfaction. "Finish them, Mister Sirico. Bridge, get us back on course. We'll jump once our chief engineer's happy."

"Let's hope *Skögul* meets with equal success and rejoins us at the next waypoint," Holt said. "In the meantime, perhaps Major Salminen and her troops could resume the training so rudely interrupted by the Pradyni. I'm sure Renny will appreciate the extra time to make sure we broke nothing by going FTL too early."

"Absolutely." She turned her head to see the Army officer give her thumbs up. "Let's make it so folks. Eight hours until the next jump, and let's hope that bunch was the only pirate wolf pack of any kind within light years. At this rate, we'll be firing rocks through our missile tubes by the time we sight the bastards who attacked Toboso."

*

"Hey, Chief," Vanger called out from his cell when Marko Trane entered the brig. "What's with all the commotion?"

Trane eyed the mercenary with suspicion, lids half closed. "What's it to you?"

"If bad shit happens while we're stuck in our cells, we might die. It seems fair that someone tells us what's going on with your ship, right? Besides, the entertainment is pretty minimal, so any bit of excitement helps keep the old spirits up."

As far as Trane figured, none of the prisoners knew he had been on the receiving end of their bombardment. The former Sigma Noctae operations noncom preferred to keep it that way. It meant avoiding casual conversation, lest something slipped out that might identify him as a survivor. Bad enough he had to see their faces several times a day during his mandated inspections of the brig.

"We had trouble with a Pradyni pirate wolf pack," Trane replied. "They won't be troubling anyone else ever again."

Vanger gave him a knowing nod. "Of course. I probably should have discussed them with your captain, but it never occurred to me we might run across the buggers."

"You knew they operated in this sector?" Trane asked in an accusatory tone.

"Sure. To you, they're pirates. As far as the Pradyni government is concerned, they're privateers. Those of us operating in the area don't bother them, and they don't bother us. The worst that usually happens to ships they intercept is losing most of their valuable cargo. However,

I can see why paying so-called taxes wouldn't work in your case." Vanger winked at Trane. "Thanks for the update, Chief. If your captain has questions about pirates or privateers active around here, I'm more than happy to visit her for a chat."

Trane's grunt could have meant assent just as much as it could have been a sound of dismissal. He pulled a tablet from his coveralls and said, "Let's get the daily checklist sorted. Prisoner Vanger, do you have any complaints?"

"None."

"Prisoner Dulce, do you have any complaints?"

*

"That, folks, is how it's done." Command Sergeant Saari took an ironic bow after Major Salminen finished commenting on the video of First Platoon's final assault drill before *Iolanthe* went FTL.

"Yeah, yeah." Command Sergeant Alekseev dismissed him with a wave of the hand. "We know everyone in your platoon wants to become a Marine when they grow up. Let the major review the rest of us before putting on airs, Karlo. You might be surprised at how well we did."

"Let Karlo have his little moment of glory, Courtlyn," Command Sergeant Ritland said, chuckling. "After all, he had a lot more handicaps to overcome than we did."

"Oh?" Saari raised a skeptical eyebrow. "Such as?"

Knowing the banter would keep flowing until everyone had contributed, Salminen held up a restraining hand. "All right, people. You can throw darts at each other when we're done. For the record, every one of you performed at a comparable level. It's still far from perfection, but a lot better than before."

When Salminen finished reviewing the performance of the other three platoons, Sergeant Major Haataja grunted. "Far from perfection is the right term, but at least I no longer have reason to be embarrassed when Chief Petty Officer Guthren asks me how it's going."

"Does that mean vodka for everyone?" Saari grinned at Haataja.

"Not for you, sunshine. Your platoon has the sixteen hundred hours to midnight watch today, meaning you're on the moment we're done here, and not for Courtlyn either. Second Platoon has the midnight to oh-eight-hundred. The rest of you, go nuts. Just make sure you're sober, bright-eyed and ready at oh-eight-hundred tomorrow. I plan to provide you with quality time practicing your skills in seizing vital points inside a confined space designed primarily to confuse soldiers. It should be interesting since most of your folks are already confused enough."

"In that case, it'll taste all the more glorious when we come off watch at midnight. Now if you'll excuse me, I apparently have to go post the guard for the evening."

"Give the scumbags in the brig my love," Alekseev said. "It's a shame they won't let us use them as sparring dummies. That might go a long way towards relieving my frustration."

"There are other ways than beating up prisoners to release frustration." Ritland gave her his best leer. "Feel free to call me if you need any help."

Alekseev blew him a kiss. "You're not my type."

"Of course." He slapped his forehead. "I keep forgetting. Never mind then. I'll offer my assistance to someone who will appreciate it."

Salminen and Haataja exchanged exasperated looks, the former shaking her head. "Some days, I feel as if I was running a high school rather than an infantry company."

"A heavily armed high school, sir," Saari replied, "one whose pupils have learned how to board and seize just about anything."

*

"Check." Holt released his bishop and sat back with a sly smile on his lips. "And mate."

Dunmoore scanned the board and then nodded, tipping her king over on its side. "Well done."

"Your mind was elsewhere, Captain. I could tell."

She sighed. "You're correct. At some point, I must decide how long we wait for *Skögul* at each waypoint, in particular the last one, on the edge of the target system. Astrid doesn't have the advantage of a massive broadside like *Iolanthe*'s to bring her quarry down."

"You're worried something may happen to her and figure it'll be your fault." Holt opened the chess set's velvet-lined wooden box and stowed the chessmen in their respective niches. "Astrid is a highly competent officer, that's why you gave her command of the prize. If anyone will find her way home from the far end of the galaxy, it's a sailing master with a knack for precise FTL jumps. So she doesn't show up by the time we reach the target. We were only ever going to use *Skögul* as a Trojan horse to carry Major Salminen and her folks to the surface. No sloop, no problems. The soldiers have been training with shuttles. We use shuttles. A ship the size of *Iolanthe* can reasonably be expected to carry a whole squadron of them, especially if she claims to visit places without orbital stations as a matter of routine."

"True." She nodded. "But I'll still feel better when *Skögul*'s back to sailing on our port beam."

"Naturally. If you didn't care about your crew, you wouldn't be the wonderful captain we all love and trust."

She gave him a wry smile. "Do you ever tire of spouting blarney?"

Holt put on a mock hurt face and clutched his chest with his right hand. "Blarney? You wound me."

"Yet you keep proving my point." A thoughtful look erased her mischievous expression. "I never got around to asking, Zeke, but since you used to work on the dark side of the street, perhaps you'll know. Why is it the Fleet has no record of a free port deep inside the Shield sector that calls itself by the colorful name of Barataria and hosts unlicensed mercenary outfits, among others? If not for Vanger tipping us off, we'd still be none the wiser."

"That's a question better answered by my former colleagues on the offensive side of the aisle. Remember, I used to work counter-intelligence, and they kept us well segregated in our silo of excellence. I'd venture the Fleet has knowledge of the place, and perhaps an agent or two in place, but it's far enough from the Commonwealth sphere that it presents no immediate security concern. Remember, the system itself is of little interest, other than to xenobiologists."

"Aye. One high-gravity planet in the Goldilocks zone with an atmospheric mix inimical to most humanoid life," she recited, almost verbatim from the navigational database, "populated by life forms radically different from our own, five gas giants and three atmosphere-less rocks in orbits so close to the primary they're tidally locked. A charming place to spend one's furlough."

"Yet it's a good one to set up a free port. There are a dozen systems inhabited by oxygen-breathing humanoids surrounding it, including the home world of our late Pradyni friends."

The old clock with the figure of a gaunt knight on its face chimed four times, and Dunmoore smiled.

"I forgot to mention this, but the other day, I was leafing through my copy of Don Quixote and came across a passage concerning the Insula Barataria, or Barataria Island, which appears as a fictional territory supposedly governed by Sancho Panza, the old Don's faithful sidekick. Do you think the founders of the free port read the story?"

Holt raised one shoulder in a half-shrug. "I doubt it. According to the database, Barataria Bay on Earth's Gulf of Mexico was used in the early nineteenth century as a hideout for the pirates, privateers, and smugglers led by a chap called Jean Lafitte. That's probably what recommended the name to whoever established the place. It does tell us we're dealing with humans rather than any of the other species endemic in the vicinity, or at least principally dealing with humans."

"That would make it easier for us. At least we can figure out how they might think and thus anticipate their reactions."

"To a point."

She inclined her head in acknowledgment. "To a point. Nonetheless, it'll be easier to bluff humans than inscrutable lizard people, although beating the tar out of them doesn't seem so difficult."

"True." Holt stood and nodded towards the door. "Buy you supper in the wardroom?"

— Twenty-Five —

"Nothing on sensors, Captain," Chief Yens announced five minutes after *Iolanthe* had dropped out of FTL on the edge of the Shamash system, home to the free port of Barataria. "Not even *Skögul*, though I suppose she could be running silent a few thousand kilometers off the starboard bow, Lieutenant Drost getting a laugh at our expense."

"Do we have a line of sight to Barataria yet?"

"Negative. The moon supposedly home to Barataria is on the far side of the planet." A hologram of the colorful, ringed gas giant Ashur appeared at the center of the tactical display. One of its many satellites pulsed with a red glow, identifying it as the target. "That's the best the AI can figure from the navigational database. Since its orbital period is supposed to be in the vicinity of ninety-one hours, we'll have our first sighting in under thirty hours, give or take."

"All right. Until we get a glimpse of what to expect and meet up with *Skögul*, we will maintain our present course. Let's make sure we do nothing that might give an observer the impression we're more than just a big, ugly bulk carrier."

"Aye, aye, Captain. Maintaining present course and the pretense we're harmless," Holt replied from the bridge.

"We can secure from battle stations." Dunmoore climbed out of her command chair. "I'll be in my day cabin. Alert me when Barataria comes into sight or *Skögul* gives us a sign of life."

"Will do, sir," Sirico replied. "I'll have the video feed linked in for you if you'd like."

"Please do." It would make a change from the ever-present image of the surrounding star fields.

Ashur loomed large in the day cabin's display when she entered, its bands of green and orange seeming almost gaudy against the brightly speckled black of space. Dunmoore gave up counting the planet's moons after she reached twenty and turned instead to the coffee urn hoping a hot cup would help ease her worry about Astrid Drost and *Skögul*. The prize ship had failed to appear at any of the preceding waypoints. Now, time had almost run out.

*

"It doesn't seem particularly impressive for a free port that's supposed to be home to all manner of dread pirates, mercenaries and other assorted riff-raff," Holt said once *Iolanthe*'s video feed had stabilized. "A few boxes, a runway, and artificial mounds that have to contain gun emplacements."

"Perhaps a large part of it is underground." She pointed at an oblong shape in the wall of the crater cradling Barataria. "That looks a lot like the entrance to Sigma Noctae's warehouse."

"Aye, it does. Hard to tell how big without a frame of reference, but I'd say fairly large." The first officer shook his head in disbelief. "How could anyone finance that sort of construction, or rather excavation and turn it into a money-making proposition?"

"A played out mining operation?" Sirico suggested. "Re-purpose the shafts, seal them and voila, instant underground city."

"It seems like a rather random spot for a mine."

The combat systems officer thought about Holt's statement for a moment and then nodded. "True, seeing as how the one and only recorded survey of the Shamash system has the native species on Enki at a level that barely exhibits sentience. The species inhabiting most star systems around here are still stripping their own backyard for minerals."

"Maybe we should have another chat with Ser Vanger," the first officer suggested. "It appears to me as if he held back a few details germane to our intended course of action."

"Oh, I intend to do so, Number One. I've long suspected he kept a few trump cards up his sleeve to make sure I wouldn't space him and his crew, a detailed description of Barataria among them. Since I was operating under the mistaken belief our sensors would provide more reliable data, I didn't press him on the matter. We'll correct that mistake shortly." A mischievous smile tugged at her lips. "Does anyone notice something else striking about Barataria, per chance?"

"Other than it's on an airless moon nearly the size of Sol's Mars, sits at the bottom of a crater, and appears to have defensive weaponry?" Sirico shrugged. "Can't say I do, Captain."

Holt chuckled. "I think she's talking about something that isn't there, Thorin. Three somethings as a matter of fact."

"Oh." A faint blush of embarrassment crept up Sirico's swarthy cheeks. "Of course. The two mercenary sloops and their freighter. Sorry. I guess I'm the Doctor Watson in the old Sherlock Holmes camping joke."

"In all fairness to Thorin," Dunmoore said, "perhaps the thing that reminds me of Sigma Noctae's warehouse entrance leads to an underground hangar large enough for a few small starships such as the ones we're trying to find."

"It would need to be huge, Captain," Holt replied, "and that's a lot of air to waste, even if Barataria's sitting on several million cubic meters of subterranean ice to manufacture a breathable atmosphere. If they're not pressurizing the hangar, they might as well leave visiting ships out in the open, unless the moon suffers from a major meteorite problem."

"The only way we find out in advance is via Vanger. Please have him brought to the conference room."

*

The mercenary's face lit up with a smile when he entered the conference room, escorted as before by two of Salminen's soldiers.

"Captain! A pleasure to see you again."

Dunmoore nodded once. "Ser Vanger. Please sit."

One of the guards, a corporal, pointed at himself and then back at the corridor, wordlessly asking whether they should leave. She shook her head, so the two men took up positions behind Vanger, not so close as to crowd him, but within arm's reach.

"As you may have surmised, we've reached Shamash and obtained our first glimpse of Barataria. You were holding out on me, weren't you?"

"I'm not sure what you mean, Captain. I gave you the free port's location, and it appears that you found it as indicated."

"You didn't mention it's underground."

Vanger shrugged. "Most outposts on airless worlds are underground. I didn't think it unique enough to warrant a mention."

"I'd like to hear more now."

"What's to tell? The story is that Barataria's founders, while examining the moons of Ashur for any valuable ores, discovered a large opening in the side of a large crater, apparently made by something sentient. They landed near it and noticed that beneath the dust outside the opening was a smooth, even surface several square kilometers in size, also created by something sentient that had excavated a large part of the crater wall to establish an outpost. Nothing remained to identify those beings, save for perfectly smooth, perfectly angled corridors, rooms, stairs and the like. Further investigation proved that the entire complex could be pressurized and oxygen extracted from an immense reservoir of ice beneath the surface. The rest, as they say, is history. Barataria has been around for decades, so there's no one left of the original crew that established it. Nowadays, the place has all the comforts of home, entertainment facilities for visiting crews, plenty of ordnance for defense and the best market for dozens of light years when it comes to tech, weaponry, AIs and such."

"Lovely story. It still doesn't tell me much." She touched a control, and the image of Barataria appeared on the conference room's primary display. "Describe its configuration."

When Vanger seemed to hesitate, a cruel gleam appeared in Dunmoore's eyes. "You've already compromised yourself with your former employers by leading us here, and if you think by denying me further information or by attempting to mislead me, you might find a way back into Orion Outcomes' good graces, don't.

Nor do you have a chance of escape if I'm heading into a trap. We can space the brig in less than a minute."

The mercenary held up a placating hand.

"Nothing of the sort, Captain. Believe me. I wish to uphold the terms as much as you do and walk free on a habitable world once you've done what must. My hesitation stems from the fact I know little of the interior. Visiting crews are confined to the recreational facilities near the surface, and my former employer's offices are next to them. I'll draw what I can, which isn't much." When he saw her face harden, he added, "it's no different from docking at any orbital station, Captain. Transients aren't allowed to gad about at will on any I've visited back home. It may be different from the naval ones, but I wouldn't know, of course."

"Very well," she said, after holding his eyes long enough to decide he was telling the truth. "Those domes around the rim of the crater, gun emplacements, I presume?"

"Yes, and missile launchers, I'm told. I have no idea who made them or what weight of ordnance they can throw at a starship. Heck, I don't even know if they work. All I know is what we've been told. They've never been deployed in our presence."

Dunmoore walked over to the display and tapped it with a fingertip. "That dark oblong is the entrance the founders discovered."

"Yes. It leads to a large cavern. There must have been doors at one time because they found the rock around the opening was cut to accept them, so they put up their own, along with a force field to keep the cavern pressurized when the doors are open. You can access the habitable sections from there."

"Is it big enough for starships?"

Vanger nodded. "Pretty much anything small enough to land on the average inhabited planet can get inside."

"Such as *Skögul* and the rest of your bunch?"

"Aye. Not that we ever have, except for *Herja* and she's not one of ours, strictly speaking. It costs money to use the inner docks. Only ships with freight to unload or take on enter, or if the ship is too big to land, its shuttles will. The rest of us stay on the tarmac and go ashore via gangways that deploy from those blocks bordering the landing strip. They lead into the port via underground tunnels."

"Meaning if there are no ships in that crater, Tarkon and the others aren't there."

"*Herja* might be in the cavern, but I'd be stunned if *Skalmold* and *Sanngrior* were. Mind you, there would be enough room. Just no reason."

"You said they'd be sailing straight here. Any idea where they are instead?"

"No." He shook his head. "Tarkon may have changed his mind after you intercepted me, or he may have had orders for another destination he wasn't going to share with us until we'd made good on our escape."

"Did he often do that?"

"Do what?"

"Share information with the other captains drop by drop?"

Vanger grimaced. "More often than any of us liked, though hardly unusual in this business, especially when you're sailing close to the dark edge of the law."

"You did more than sail close, Ser Vanger, you went right over the edge, but fine, I take your meaning. Any guesses where he might have gone?"

"If it wasn't here, then no."

"Where did Tarkon intend to dispose of the stolen naval stores?"

"I assumed it would be here. As I said, it has the reputation of being the best market for purloined merchandise around here."

Dunmoore pointed at the screen. "Please draw what you remember about Barataria's innards and over the next few days, try to remember as many details as you can. A few of my officers will likely want to question you on them."

"You intend to attack?"

"I intend to recover the Navy's property and punish all those involved in the piracy on Toboso, including whoever hired your outfit to execute the raid. If that means I leave Barataria a smoking, radioactive hole, then so be it."

Vanger's eyes narrowed as he studied her. "I don't doubt you're ruthless enough to do so, Captain, but the people there like to make money. If you offer them the sort of reasonable terms you've offered me, you'll not need to sow destruction."

"Maybe it needs to be rooted out on general principles."

"I thought taking the Commonwealth's anti-piracy efforts to such an extent was against government policy. We're far from the Navy's carefully circumscribed sphere of authority."

A cruel smile lit up her face. "Do you see the Navy around here? As far as anyone is concerned, *Iolanthe* is a privateer, unfettered by rules made on Earth to benefit the friends of the regime. She'll turn back into a Commonwealth Star Ship once we're home again."

"Point taken." Vanger inclined his head. He stood and joined her by the display where he drew a schematic of those parts he had visited, all the while watched closely by Dunmoore. "There," he said, stepping back. "That's as much as I remember."

"Thank you." Dunmoore gestured at the soldiers. "Take him back to the brig, please."

*

"A ready-made outpost cut into that moon with utmost precision, ready to pressurize and turn into a pirate market?" Holt sounded incredulous. "Seems hard to believe."

Several of the department heads nodded in agreement, but Renny Halfen said, "It wouldn't be the first artifact of an unknown elder civilization that's cropped up in this part of the galaxy."

A secret smile twisted Dunmoore's lips as she remembered the buried treasure trove on Arietis, left there a hundred thousand years earlier by the long vanished proto-Shrehari race known only through legend as the L'Taung. The trove, plaything of an admiral who had lost his grip on reality, had been destroyed by a kinetic strike at the height of the battle of Arietis, courtesy of an unknown attacker.

"It certainly wouldn't," she said, "but this new information changes things. Unless our quarries are tucked away out of sight in the hanger, a raid won't help, especially with no reconnaissance beforehand. Remember, we want our stuff back, we want information, and then we want to remove Orion Outcomes from the face of the universe. Wiping out a piratical viper's nest, satisfying as that might be, wouldn't do a damn thing unless we've achieved those three because right now our best lead is the people in Barataria."

"What do you propose?" Emma Cullop asked.

"I propose to follow Vanger's advice and tread gently by presenting myself as a privateer looking for supplies and for work. It'll be the best way of carrying out a reconnaissance. Once we have the lay of the land, I intend to negotiate with the folks running Barataria to further our three goals."

"You propose to carry out the reconnaissance yourself, Captain?" Holt's voice held an edge of disapproval.

Dunmoore raised a hand. "Peace, Mister Holt. We'll discuss who gets to visit Barataria as one of their fellow lowlifes another time. First, we have to get there and scan that place to the nth degree when we're at close range. Then, we will open a comm link with them and take it from there. Of course, if the freighter *Herja* is tucked away inside, all bets are off."

"And *Skögul*?" Holt asked.

"We'll go ahead without her. I don't want to wait any longer, in case we've been detected, and our reluctance to head inward sets off alarm bells. Besides, with what we know now, she wouldn't do us much good as a means to ferry Major Salminen's troops down. You heard Vanger. It'll be shuttles if it's anything at all, and with none of our targets sitting in the hangar, there's no point in landing troops."

"That's just as well, sir," Salminen said with an approving nod. "My people have developed enough muscle memory using shuttles that switching over to a starship might cut into our reaction speed when we disembark."

"A good point." She let her eyes roam around the table, "any comments or questions?" When Dunmoore received nothing more than brief shakes of the head in reply, she rose and caught the sailing master's eye. "Mister Pashar, put us on a course towards Barataria. I'd like to go FTL for the final jump within the hour."

"False flag transponder on, Captain?" Holt asked.

"No. I doubt a real privateer would bother broadcasting his identity so far from patrolled star lanes."

"Agreed and having gone well beyond our authority by now I suppose we're as close to a real privateer as we can come," he replied with a wicked smile. "The only thing missing is a letter of marque."

"If the Baratarians ask to see it, we'll draw one up ourselves. Dismissed, folks."

— Twenty-Six —

"Sorry, Captain, but unless I switch the sensors to full military power, we'll not see much more," Chief Yens said over her shoulder. "Most of the place is under a thick enough layer of rock to block civilian strength signals."

Iolanthe had entered into orbit around the ringed gas giant Ashur little over an hour earlier and was gradually creeping up on the moon Barataria called home. It gave Yens and her crew time to carry out as full a survey of their target as possible but to little practical effect. However, Dunmoore had to assume that the Baratarians operated sensors of their own able to detect someone scanning the free port. It meant switching to full military power would almost certainly make them wonder about that big, lumbering starship on final approach.

"So be it. Bridge, take us into a geosynchronous orbit above Barataria. It's time to say hello."

"Geosynchronous orbit above Barataria, aye." Holt paused, then said, "It looks like they're trying to say hello first. We're receiving a transmission. Do you want me to take it, or will you shift to the bridge?"

"I'll come up. If they become impatient, accept the link and tell them your captain's on her way. Chief, keep scanning."

When Dunmoore reached the bridge, which, unlike the CIC, had nothing to betray it as a Q-ship, Holt had already vacated the command chair and taken the first officer's station.

"They do not sound aggrieved yet. We're unlikely to be the first ship taking its own sweet time responding."

"Probably." She slipped into the still warm seat and nodded at Lieutenant Kremm. "Put them on."

A swarthy, seamed face sporting a fringe of salt-and-pepper beard around the jawline and topped with black hair pulled back into a queue materialized on the main screen. Deep-set black eyes examined Dunmoore with evident suspicion.

"Who the hell are you?" The man asked in accented Anglic. "And why are you scanning us?"

Dunmoore inclined her head by way of salutation and said, "Captain Shannon O'Donnell, merchant vessel *Persephone*. We're freelancers who like to know as much as possible about a new port of call before we reach it."

"Never heard of you or your ship before now. Who told you about this place?"

"We're new to this sector. Due to some unforeseen circumstances involving — well, let's just say we had to relocate for a while until things calm down. A friend who's been here before recommended we visit Barataria."

"Oh yeah? Who would that be?"

An ironic smile pulled up the corners of her mouth. "Now that would be telling. He's a fellow freelancer, the sort of friend who prefers to keep a low profile for business reasons."

The man's eyes narrowed for a second, then to Dunmoore's relief, he nodded. "Fair enough. What are you looking for?"

"Supplies and maybe a few leads on potential contracts."

"How would you be paying for anything you purchase?"

"With precious metals." Dunmoore's tone implied an unspoken 'of course.' "My friend mentioned it's the only currency you accept aside from barter."

"Captain Shannon O'Donnell of the merchant vessel *Persephone*, eh?" He stroked his beard with a calloused hand examining her once more with a cold, calculating stare. "I'm Eddard Ragetti, operations manager here. On behalf of Barataria, welcome. You'll find us good friends but also deadly enemies. As your scans will have shown, Barataria is as well protected as they come. Now, what sort of stores are on your list, Captain?"

"Fresh food and ammunition principally, and raw materials for my engineering section's maker machines."

Ragetti's thick eyebrows crept up towards his hairline. "Ammunition? Your guns see a lot of use, then?"

"It depends on the contract. We're somewhat more heavily armed than your average freighter. A lot of our jobs take us into sectors where you'd better be able to outshoot what you can't outrun, and considering *Persephone*'s size, we can't outrun much."

The man nodded. "It's not an uncommon story. We can offer pretty much everything you need, including leads on potential contracts, for a finder's fee, of course."

"Of course."

"It goes without saying that we would have to know more about your ship, so we can steer you in the right direction."

"Naturally. I'll provide you with our specifications. Now, if you wish. We have a standard file for clients." She glanced at Holt over her shoulder. "Please transmit the specs, Mister Larkin."

"Done," the first officer replied moments later.

Ragetti's eyes dropped at an unseen and unheard signal. When he looked up at her again, a spark of interest had replaced the calculation in his gaze. "You have an impressive ship, Captain. I'm sure we can help you find a client or two. Tell me, are you the owner?"

"Every member of my crew is an owner, Ser Ragetti. I just happen to hold fifty-one percent of *Persephone*'s common stock."

"No outside investors?"

She nodded. "There are, but as bond and preferred stockholders, they have no voting rights."

A brief smile appeared on Ragetti's face for the first time, though Dunmoore suspected it held a large dollop of irony. "How very business-like of you. Few freelancers are as well organized."

"I'm sure you see all kinds passing through." She glanced at the navigation plot. "We're about to enter orbit. Do you have any objections if I and a few of my crew land for a face-to-face meeting with you and the folks with whom we'll be dealing? If we're going to make Barataria our base of operations while we're in this sector, I'd appreciate getting to know the right people and perhaps look over your wares with a view to making a few purchases."

"By all means, Captain O'Donnell. Shall I expect you within the hour?"

"Within the hour, Ser Ragetti."

He nodded once, then his face dissolved as he cut the link.

"Not a man I'd cross lightly," Holt said in the ensuing silence. "And no, I won't argue about your heading for the surface. It's too late for that. Who do you want in your party? I mean other than Vincenzo?"

"I'd like to keep it as small as possible. The fewer tongues, the less slips thereof. Vincenzo, of course, and Chief Guthren — he can frame the tactical picture if we end up having to carry out a raid." Dunmoore's eyes narrowed in thought. "A pilot for the shuttle this time, Petty Officer Purdy would do nicely. I'd rather take in the surroundings than concentrate on the controls. Keep in mind that while we may pass as privateers, General Order Eighty-One is in force. If Ser Ragetti's a double-dealer, we become expendable."

"I'm not ready to take command of *Iolanthe* just yet, Captain. Try to find your way back aboard, for both our sakes."

*

The hours spent observing Barataria from a distance did not do the sheer scale of its setting justice. Nestled at the foot of a crater wall hundreds of meters high, the outer spaceport facilities were impressive. They could accommodate a dozen ships at once on a tarmac large enough for several *Iolanthe*-sized freighters, if ships that large could actually brave the moon's gravity well.

A massive space door dominated everything while portholes dotting the cliff side twinkled in the wan Ashur-light. As they swooped in, lining up with the cavern's gaping maw, the door split into two leaves, spilling brilliant light onto the dusty runway through a gap just large enough to admit the shuttle. Petty Officer Purdy slowed his craft to a walking pace and gingerly threaded it through the narrow opening.

"We've just gone through a force field," he said, "so you'll have to wait until they bleed off the static charge before disembarking, Captain."

Though it was something she, as a pilot in her own right, knew from long experience and training, Dunmoore nodded. Purdy was merely doing his job with the reminder.

A cylindrical ground control droid with a display panel instead of a head flashed the universally recognized 'follow me' signal in bright red to attract their attention, then led them to a marked spot inside the immense cavern. Purdy settled on the exact center, then shifted his gaze to the droid. Several moments elapsed before its display turned a glowing green. He consulted the shuttle's control panel and gave a satisfied nod.

"Static charge bled off, Captain. You're good to go."

"Button her up once we're off and let no one aboard. Also, refrain from using your sensors in the active mode. We don't know who might detect the signal and wonder what an innocuous civilian shuttle might be doing. Call me if there are problems."

"Will do, sir."

Dunmoore climbed out of the copilot's seat and headed aft, where Guthren and Vincenzo waited patiently. Though wearing civilian spacer clothes and armed with only well-worn blasters in open hip holsters, both men nonetheless exuded an aura of controlled, disciplined violence, a warning for anyone who might think of doing their captain harm.

"Are you gentlemen privateers ready?"

"Aye, Captain. Our eyes are open, and our mouths will be shut," Guthren replied. "Did you see if anything we're looking for is sharing this hangar with us?"

"There's at least one ship in the hangar, and a few shuttles, but my brief glimpse didn't tell me much." She turned back towards the cockpit. "We're good. You can open now."

The portside hatch unlocked with a loud clank, then slid out of the way. Vincenzo, followed by the coxswain, stepped out of the shuttle. After examining their immediate surroundings, Guthren gave Dunmoore the okay to disembark. The imposing hangar, cut into the moon's solid crust long before humanity reached for the stars, might have been pressurized, but the air was cold enough to let them see their breath. She set foot on the stone floor, expecting to feel a moon's lighter gravity but it was no different from the artificial gravity setting aboard *Iolanthe*, meaning they had embedded a generator somewhere beneath Barataria, a not inconsiderable expense.

Guthren nodded towards the gray-skinned freighter looming over them. "Look familiar, Captain?"

Dunmoore examined the pitted and scarred hull, blackened from many atmospheric re-entries, for anything resembling a registration number or name, but it was as anonymous as *Iolanthe* and just as generic, if not as massive. However, the freighter's shape and configuration appeared to be a close match to the image Chief Yens had captured of *Herja* during its escape in the company of the two missing mercenary sloops. She could see no activity around it although the belly ramp common among its breed had been dropped, making its cargo hold readily accessible.

"Could well be. I'll simply have to ask."

The droid rolled up to them, and a message appeared on this display, instructing them to follow it. With one last glance at the silent freighter, they complied. The cylindrical machine led them to an open inner airlock where a muscular, well-armed human male greeted them with a polite nod.

"Captain O'Donnell and party, on behalf of Manager Ragetti, welcome to Barataria." Dark-haired and olive skinned, he had the same accent as his boss, though his voice was easily two octaves lower and rumbled like the innards of a volcano. It matched his solid bulk and somber mien. "My name is Gerrard, and I've been assigned to escort you to the manager's office."

Without waiting for a reply, he turned and headed deeper into Barataria, leading them through a warren of passages and up stone stairs cut with the exacting precision Dunmoore had seen before, on Arietis. They met few beings along the way, but the ones that crossed their path were invariably human, a few appearing more villainous than others. Gerrard was a man of few words and Dunmoore did not try to engage him in conversation. He eventually ushered them into a room that looked like nothing so much as the antechamber to an admiral's office. After knocking at a door marked 'Manager' and receiving a muffled command to enter, he pushed it open and ushered them in.

Ragetti's domain would have been the envy of every senior officer she had met and overlooked the impressive hangar thanks to a thick porthole that almost took up that entire wall. The man himself, seated behind an imposing wooden desk that might have come from the Arietis stash, with its intricate carvings, raised a bejeweled hand in greeting and motioned towards the chairs arrayed across from him.

"Captain O'Donnell, welcome. Who are your companions?"

"Kurt Guthren, my business manager and Vince Vincenzo, his assistant. Thank you for seeing us so quickly, Ser Ragetti."

He waved away her thanks. "I'm always happy to receive newcomers calling at our free port for the first time, especially when they command such a leviathan of the star lanes as *Persephone*."

"You manage an impressive installation yourself." She nodded towards the porthole. "I've not seen any other ground-based port with an inner dock capable of accommodating several starships."

"It makes loading and off-loading a much more pleasant experience for my stevedores, and as you can imagine, the added convenience brings in healthy docking fees."

"No doubt." Dunmoore nodded. "Though I should think ships such as the one in you hangar must carry high-value cargo to offset the added cost."

Ragetti chuckled. "You think correctly, Captain O'Donnell. In fact, right now she holds the sort of merchandise for which you've expressed an interest."

"I'll guess it's not food." She gave him a warm smile.

"Indeed not. Barataria has extensive hydroponic greenhouses and protein vats. No, *Herja* — that's her name, by the way, and I'm one of the owners — arrived no more than forty standard hours ago, carrying ordnance as well as parts. My stevedores haven't begun unloading yet. Since she pays no docking fees, there's no hurry. We usually broadcast the arrival of new merchandise via subspace radio and often receive offers for the whole consignment. If you're not overly concerned about sourcing, then perhaps we might talk business."

"I'm merely concerned about price and quality, Ser Ragetti. The provenance of consumables is easily hidden if necessary."

"Did you perchance bring a list?"

Dunmoore glanced at Guthren. "Please give Ser Ragetti our requirements, Kurt."

The coxswain nodded. Then he wordlessly pulled a small data wafer from his tunic's breast pocket and leaned over to place it in the center of Ragetti's desk.

"Not very talkative, your business manager, Captain," the latter said. He reached down to collect the chip and placed it on a tablet lying by his left elbow.

"Kurt rarely wastes a word, but there's none better for sniffing out opportunities and seizing them."

"Yet he'll use every word he knows to tell you when you're on the verge of doing something he considers unprofitable," Ragetti replied with a knowing grin that did not quite reach his watchful eyes. After reading through the list, he looked up at Dunmoore again. "We can accommodate your needs for everything, including the munitions. May I assume you've been in a fight recently?"

"You may. A few Pradyni with more greed than sense tried us on for size. They won't ever get smarter if you understand my meaning."

A transient expression crossed Ragetti's face, gone as soon as it appeared, but not before Dunmoore noticed.

"They can be a pain at times, Captain." He tapped his tablet. "My business manager, Hinrika Schelts will be here shortly to take you to inspect *Herja*'s cargo. Once you're satisfied with the merchandise, we'll negotiate a price."

"Much obliged."

"You understand," he continued, "that you take delivery under ex-works terms, meaning we'll offload from *Herja*, but the moment it touches the hangar floor, it's yours. That goes for the food as well. We'll deliver it to the hangar but no further."

"Of course," Dunmoore replied. "I have enough shuttles to carry all we need in one flight. When you sail a ship of *Persephone*'s size, you're used to making most of the dirtside pickups."

The door behind them opened, and she turned to see a tall, lean woman with a lived-in face beneath short black hair enter. She wore the sort of severe business suit that would not seem out of place in the Commonwealth's more prosperous financial centers, though the traders on Earth or Pacifica would not openly carry a weapon that powerful in an open holster.

"Captain, this is Hinrika Schelts. Hinrika, Captain Shannon O'Donnell, her business manager Kurt Guthren and Kurt's assistant Vince Vincenzo."

Schelts inclined her head. "A pleasure. Welcome to Barataria. I hope we will have a mutually profitable business relationship, Captain."

She examined them with intense eyes, visibly dismissing Vincenzo as unimportant but unsure about Guthren. Dunmoore guessed the woman did not recognize him as her opposite number aboard *Persephone*.

"As do I."

"Please take our new friends on a tour of the merchandise *Herja* brought back," Ragetti said. "Let them examine whatever they wish at leisure, then show them our food production facilities. If Captain O'Donnell and her business management team are satisfied, you may begin the sales negotiations." He smiled at Siobhan. "Hinrika will take good care of you, Captain. I look forward to our concluding the first in what I hope will be many deals."

Schelts led them back the way they had come under the taciturn Gerrard's guidance, but the man himself was nowhere to be seen. She, however, proved to be the opposite of tongue-tied.

"It's always interesting when new people show up unannounced," Schelts said the moment they had left Ragetti's office. "This place, while well known to the cognoscenti, isn't exactly on any major trade routes. The one inhabited planet in this system can't support our kind of life. Ser Ragetti tells me one of our regulars directed you here after a spot of trouble in your usual area of operations?"

"That's what I told your boss," Dunmoore replied, trying to keep her tone light.

"Do you offer transport services only, or is there added value you can provide to potential customers?"

"As I told Ser Ragetti, we're well-armed for a freighter, on the principle that we have to outgun what we can't outrun, so we accept higher risk contracts."

"Such as?" Schelts glanced at Dunmoore over her shoulder before taking the stairs.

"Forced entries, for instance. Not against anything defended by the Commonwealth military or the Empire, mind you."

"I see. We have a resident private military corporation in Barataria who often contract out for augmentation on a particular operation or set of operations. They most emphatically avoid working within the Commonwealth sphere, let alone the Empire's. You might interest them. I can put you in touch."

"For a finder's fee, of course?"

"Of course, Captain, but payable by Orion Outcomes if they decide to hire *Persephone*, not by yourself."

"Good. I can't afford pay-to-play scenarios, Sera Schelts. Especially not after topping up my ship's stores. I'm sure that the premium wares you're about to offer me command a premium price."

They walked through the same airlock and out into the docking cavern's cold air, headed for *Herja*'s belly ramp.

"Do you accept high-risk contracts for anything besides forced entries, by which I assume you mean blockade running, Captain O'Donnell?"

"*Persephone* can transport troops. They won't be comfortable, and I wouldn't recommend it for long voyages, but if you need a battalion's worth shifted from one system to another, we can handle that, as long as they bring their own rations. I prefer humans, but any oxygen-breathing species will do."

"Have you ever done so? Transporting troops, I mean?"

"A few times. Freelancers looking for a quick shift from one contract to another. Those weren't blockade running scenarios, so the risk was minimal."

"I suppose asking for references would be futile?" Schelts asked with a touch of irony in her voice.

"I'm chagrined that someone with your apparent experience even asked," Dunmoore replied in a tone that conveyed amusement. "As the old saying goes, no names, no pack drill, right?"

They stopped at the foot of the ramp and Schelts made an expansive 'after you' gesture with her arm, inviting Dunmoore to take the lead.

It did not take long to determine *Herja* was heavily laden with naval stores taken from Sigma Noctae. Many of the containers still bore the telltale tags that identified their provenance, markers the Barataria fencing operation had not yet spotted but which were more than obvious to someone such as Dunmoore, one of the depot's former executive officers. She felt pleased by her ability to stay impassive and ask the questions any normal, if shady customer would, down to demanding they open random crates so she and Guthren could inspect their contents, in the interest of quality control.

"I won't ask where you got these Commonwealth Fleet missile reload packs," Dunmoore said, slamming the last container shut, "and that means you won't have to lie." She turned to face Schelts. "I'm interested in purchasing all of it."

"Even the spare parts?"

"My chief engineer can take whatever piece doesn't precisely fit *Persephone* and mill it to slip right into place. The savings in time, material, and effort can be worth our while, provided the price is right."

Schelts gave Dunmoore a smile that was probably meant to be encouragingly warm though it struck Siobhan as being more predatory than friendly. "Why don't we visit the food production plant, where you'll see our greenhouses and protein vats before heading up to my office for a hot cup of coffee, or tea if you prefer, to talk numbers?"

— Twenty-Seven —

Schelts' office, while not as opulent as Ragetti's, also overlooked the docking cavern. She invited them to sit around a small conference table and busied herself with drinks on a sideboard.

"What did you think about our food production facilities, Captain?" Schelts asked over her shoulder.

"Impressive. You must have one heck of a power plant to run those on top of the rest."

"A lot of our electricity comes from geothermal sources. This moon has a molten core and enough ice beneath the crust to last us for millennia. The first inhabitants chose well when they excavated this site." She handed Dunmoore a steaming cup, then sat with one in her own hand, Guthren and Vincenzo having declined the offer. "Since you're new to us, I won't do my usual and ask you to make me an offer. Instead, I'll tell you what we think your shopping list is worth. Fair enough?"

"Fair enough."

Schelts then named an eye-watering sum that would deplete *Iolanthe*'s precious metal stocks, but Dunmoore and her companions were thankfully able to keep straight faces. Of course, she had no intention of paying. The stores aboard *Herja* belonged to the Fleet, and her food needs were not dire enough to justify paying the asking price. However, Schelts clearly expected to haggle, and so she countered with an offer that was not small enough to be insulting but close. After fifteen minutes of back and forth, they agreed on a price that was less than the first proposal, but still high enough to give her logistics officer, Joelle Biros, a bad case of heartburn, if she actually intended to go through with it.

"Congratulations, Captain, it's a deal." Schelts reached over the table to shake Dunmoore's hand. "We can execute the purchase at once if you wish. Just call down your shuttles and have someone aboard deliver the payment."

"I'm afraid that I must return to my ship for that. We keep our stock of precious metals in a vault programmed to open only if my first officer and I simultaneously enter our authorization codes." It was not quite the truth, but close enough to pass muster.

"Really?" The woman raised one eyebrow. "You certainly take commendable precautions. What if either or both of you become incapacitated?"

"We have a formal protocol transferring authority." Dunmoore felt the sudden urge to rejoin *Iolanthe* as quickly as possible. There were planning and preparation to be done and little time in which to do it without raising suspicions. "But since I'm not incapacitated, I must play my part, and the sooner I'm back aboard *Persephone*, the faster we can consummate our transaction."

"Consummate?" A faint smile appeared on Schelts' lips. "You do have a way with words, Captain O'Donnell. I like that in a business partner. Let me walk you back to your shuttle. Will you be coming down again?"

"That would be the plan, Sera Schelts." Dunmoore stood, imitated by Guthren and Vincenzo, who had remained silent and expressionless throughout, though she could see a gleam of amusement in the coxswain's eyes. "A payment that large is a captain's personal responsibility."

"Perhaps I can show you some of our amenities, should you decide to give your crew a taste of shore leave."

*

The moment Dunmoore's shuttle broke free of Barataria, she opened an encrypted link with *Iolanthe*. Holt's face appeared on the cockpit screen within moments.

"And?" He asked.

"The freighter *Herja* with the naval stores stolen from Sigma Noctae is there all right. They haven't unloaded yet, in case a buyer shows up for the whole consignment."

"Such as you."

Dunmoore nodded once. "Such as me. I did not delve into the Orion Outcomes matter, but I saw the doorway to their corporate offices during our tour of the port."

"What do they want for a shipload of ill-gotten loot?" When she told him, Holt's eyes widened. "That's almost as much as the government paid for it, including the contractor backscratching premium. Nice profit margin."

"Aye, and Ser Ragetti is one of *Herja*'s owners to boot."

"Nothing on the other two mercenary sloops?"

"No, but they can wait right now. We have to move fast." She recounted her conversation with Schelts almost verbatim. "Alert Major Salminen and her troops for action. I'm sending you the extensive visuals Petty Officer Purdy took of the docking cavern while we schmoozed with the local pirate grandees. The cox'n, Vincenzo, and I will confer on the way up to flesh out the interior layout and transmit as we're going along. That should be enough to start the planning process. My intent is to seize a chunk of Barataria's vital ground, including the docks, airlocks, and the immediate innards, then convince Ragetti that resistance would be unprofitable. Capturing *Herja* as a prize and putting the Orion Outcomes folks in port to the question are the objectives. Select a prize crew and get them ready. A dozen should suffice. *Herja* can carry a platoon of soldiers during the extraction to give them some added muscle power."

"You intend to unmask?"

"Once the operation is under way, meaning when Company Group 31 begins its assault, we'll drop part of the pretense but without fully unmasking as Fleet. Barataria is solid, but one well-placed nuclear strike by a naval grade warhead can take them out of business. I'm sure they're smart enough to know it. The goal is surrender, not destruction, hence intimidation through superior firepower. If we can extract in good order and keep them wondering which competing organization hired a privateer Q-ship for a hit, so much the better. "

"Meaning it's your favorite surrender or die kind of operation." He grinned. "Concur. Confusion to the enemy has always been my favorite unofficial principle of war. Anything else, sir? If not, I'll set things in motion while you consolidate the target intel."

"Go."

"*Persephone*, out."

Dunmoore climbed out of the copilot's seat to join the others aft.

*

"Play time is over, folks." Major Salminen flicked on the company TAC's primary display once the last of the platoon leaders took his seat. "Captain Dunmoore has given us her intent so what follows is my concept of operations." She indicated the image of the freighter dominating the screen. "This is one of the ships that touched down at Sigma Noctae during the raid. It carries the stolen naval stores. The thing's name is *Herja*, and the Captain wants to take it as a prize with its cargo intact. Commander Holt has assigned Lieutenant Kremm as prize master along with a dozen crew. One of our platoons will help seize it and ride it out of there. That would be Sergeant Saari's since his folks have shown a talent for rushing into situations without regard for their own security. And because First Platoon helped secure *Skögul*, proving they know the front end of a starship from its rear."

"No rest for the wicked," Saari replied with a pleased grin.

"The rest will take the docks and the three airlocks." She pointed at the composite image created from Petty Officer Purdy's pictures that had replaced *Herja*. "Second Platoon, here; Third Platoon here and Fourth Platoon here. HQ Platoon will guard the shuttles. Once we've secured the docks, Captain Dunmoore wants us to seize two areas." A schematic augmented by individual stills replaced the panoramic view of the cavern. "Sergeant Alekseev, your job is to take Barataria's executive offices here and keep them suitably cowed. Captain Dunmoore will be speaking with them from the ship. Sergeant Jennsen, you will secure the Orion Outcomes offices here. Chief Petty Officer Guthren will go with you and question whoever you find there. Sergeant Ritland will stay in the docking area and secure the space door controls. The control room is here. Our aim is to convince the Baratarians that surrender is better than risking destruction, or at the very least, enough damage to make their free port unprofitable. *Iolanthe* will unmask as a Q-ship the moment we seize *Herja* and the airlocks, but we will keep the fiction of being privateers and not Fleet. Once *Herja* has lifted, and Captain Dunmoore has obtained whatever information she needs, we're withdrawing aboard the shuttles, except for First Platoon. The idea is to avoid fighting, but if they start shooting, we will respond with maximum violence. Any questions on the concept of operations?"

"Can we still do the *Hakkaa päälle* if we're to avoid fighting?" Command Sergeant Saari asked.

A wicked smile lit up Salminen's face. "Of course. Anything that'll scare the enemy into a quick surrender should always be used, and I can't think of anything more frightening than your troops screaming like mountain trolls gone amok. If there are no other questions, let's move on to the finer details, so we avoid misunderstandings. This has to be a shock and awe operation, which means no do over if we fuck it up the first time around."

*

"That looks rather impressive," Petty Officer Purdy remarked, nodding towards the rapidly forming ranks of Company Group 31 as he landed Dunmoore's shuttle in its usual spot on the hangar deck. Armored and armed, the one hundred and twenty soldiers exuded an aura of controlled violence palpable even inside the craft's cockpit.

"I hope the Baratarians will share your sentiments," Dunmoore replied, "and surrender the moment they see them dismount."

"If the pongos scream that battle cry of theirs, sir, I figure Barataria's laundry service will have plenty of customers once it's over. I know they scared the shit out of me the first time they did it during training." He glanced at his control screen. "Looks like I'll be going down again. I have orders to take Lieutenant Kremm and the prize crew. The static charge has bled off. You can exit now, sir."

"That would explain why Lieutenant Kremm and Petty Officer Lukas are heading this way." After climbing out of her seat, Dunmoore pointed at a pair of armored men, helmets under their arms, approaching the shuttle.

"You'll forgive me if I break protocol," Guthren said from the passenger compartment, "and get off first, Captain. I need to retrieve my own tin suit."

"We have it," a voice called through the open hatch. Kremm stuck his head into the shuttle. "The bosun was kind enough to raid your quarters on our behalf, Chief."

He backed away again to let Dunmoore, the coxswain, and Vincenzo exit. "Any words of advice, Captain?"

She shook her head. "None that come to mind, Theo. You know what you're up against."

"That I do." He grinned at her. "Can't let Astrid have all the fun."

Dunmoore clapped him on the shoulder. "I won't wish you luck. Instead, I'll wish you success. Bring *Herja* up, Lieutenant."

"Aye, aye, sir!" Kremm raised his arm and waved at the cluster of spacers waiting patiently by the inner doors. "Climb aboard, folks. We have a prize to take."

She spotted Major Salminen issuing last minute instructions to her command group and walked over to where they stood, behind the row of waiting shuttles. Before she reached them, they snapped to attention as one, pivoted on their heels and marched off to their respective platoons.

"Ready to go?" Dunmoore asked.

Salminen gave her a shy smile. "Not just ready, sir, but eager to mete out some much-needed retribution. After the training runs we've been through, my soldiers are happy they'll finally do it for real and prove to the Navy that they're just as capable as Marines."

"Good. Just remember, the fewer bodies we pile up, the better our chances of obtaining voluntary cooperation. The people down there aren't the ones we need to remove from this universe permanently, but they can help us track down those who do require termination with extreme prejudice. Better to win this one without fighting, right?"

"Absolutely, sir. My troops understand it as well. Sun Tzu is on the mandatory reading list for anyone wanting to become a noncommissioned officer in the Army."

"I wish I could come with you, just to see the expression on Ragetti's face when he first realizes a profitable sale just turned into a repossession by the lawful owner, along with penalties in the shape of a starship. But Commander Holt would likely place me under arrest if I tried. What I will do, however, is monitor every moment from the CIC. Without interfering, of course," she added, seeing the glint of alarm in Salminen's eyes. "Second-guessing the commander on the ground is a bad habit the Marine Corps successfully beat out of the Navy during the last Migration War."

"Glad to hear it, Captain." The shy smile returned.

"It also means you have tactical control of the prize crew and Lieutenant Kremm until he's taken *Herja* out of the Barataria docking cavern."

The soldier nodded. "Commander Holt explained it to both of us."

"Any last minute questions or concerns, Major?"

"Plenty, sir, but none you can answer right now. I must tackle them myself when we touch down."

"Understood." Dunmoore gave her knowing half grin. "I'd worry if my ground commander was sinning through overconfidence."

"I've been accused of doing many sinful things, Captain, but overconfidence is not one of them. Company Group

31, Scandia Regiment, will do its duty to the utmost, that's what I promise. That's all I can promise."

"That's the only thing I or anyone else can expect."

"Now hear this," Ezekiel Holt's voice boomed throughout the ship, "Operation Repo launch in five minutes, I repeat, Operation Repo launch in five minutes. That is all."

Operation Repo? Dunmoore mouthed, eyebrows raised in question. Salminen shrugged. "Commander Holt came up with the name when I asked him what we would call the raid. I guess we'd better load the shuttles. With your permission, sir?"

"Godspeed, Major."

Salminen snapped off a salute, pulled her helmet on and turned to her troops. She raised her right arm in the air and made a twirling motion with her hand. "Company Group 31," she shouted, "mount up."

Five minutes later, while Dunmoore watched from the control room, the bosun's mate responsible for hangar deck depressurized it. Then the space doors opened to reveal Ashur's colorful cloud bands and the gravitic launcher sent the shuttles into space one after the other. They peeled off to one side and quickly disappeared from view.

"Time to go fret in the CIC," she muttered to herself.

"Pardon me, sir?" The bosun's mate asked.

She gave him a crooked smile. "Nothing, Petty Officer Harkon. I sometimes speak to myself."

"You and me both, sir. As long as you don't answer yourself, it's all good."

"Thankfully, I haven't quite reached that point yet."

— Twenty-Eight —

Major Salminen, sitting up front with the pilot of the shuttle carrying Lieutenant Puro and headquarters platoon, knew the butterflies in her stomach did not come from the launch, nor the plunge towards Barataria. She had seen combat in the opening months of the war when the Scandia Regiment had fought off an attempt by the Shrehari to establish a foothold on her icy homeworld. However, it had been as a mere lieutenant, the senior platoon leader of Alpha Company, Second Battalion. Like everyone else in her current command, this raid from space would be a novel experience.

"Repo Niner, this is Repo Mother," Holt's voice sounded over the cockpit's speakers. "We've advised the target you've launched. They're expecting a friendly bunch of spacers geared up to load naval stores. Try not to enjoy their disappointment too much."

Salminen could not help but smile at the first officer's light-hearted tone. "No promises, Repo Mother. We Scandians have a reputation to maintain."

"So I understand. Something about being berserkers with a predilection for cutting them down, right? I've been told that you terrified your pilots during training."

"The tale has grown with the telling, Repo Mother, but we'll try to leave a mark."

"Something tells me you'll leave a mark for sure. We'll be monitoring you all the way through, but unless something comes up, you won't hear my charming voice again. It's your show, Repo Niner. Bring us back good war stories along with everything the bastards stole. Repo Mother, out."

It took Salminen a few moments to realize the butterflies in her stomach had settled. No one saw the fierce smile that slowly spread across her face, resembling nothing so much as the toothy snarl of the loping timber wolf at the center of the Scandia Regiment's crest. However, if any of her troops had, they would have matched it with their own. For some, it would have been more bravado than confidence, perhaps for many even. The younger soldiers had not experienced the terror and elation of forcing the Shrehari to withdraw almost a decade earlier, but the noncoms, from Corporal Vallin on up the chain of command, were veterans of that desperate fight. Those experiences might not necessarily help them face what was coming next with complete equanimity, but having survived and won back then, they knew it was possible now. However, like soldiers throughout the ages, when heading into battle, they each prepared in their own way.

The most phlegmatic snoozed, the jokers shared gallows humor with all who would listen, the obsessives checked their weapons over and over again. Most simply stared down at the deck beneath their feet, mentally rehearsing what they would be called on to do the moment that rear ramp dropped, as a way to deal with the enforced wait while their shuttles brought them to the target. Whatever each soldier's way of coping, none of them would even think of discussing their fears and hopes with the others. Not now. They were trained to be stoics, none more so than those recruited in the towns and settlements scraping a living from the desperately thin soil in the shadows of the continent-sized glaciers on Scandia.

More than one might have been surprised to find out that thousands of kilometers above them, ensconced in the command chair at the heart of *Iolanthe*'s CIC, Captain Siobhan Dunmoore, a veteran of all too many savage battles, was equally unsettled. Ever since the shuttles disappeared from sight, her mind had parsed every worst-case scenario imaginable, knowing she would have little influence if things went wrong. Little beyond offering the threat of the Q-ship's devastating broadside, that is, though such a threat might well turn into a broken arrow fire mission, seeing as how her ground troops would soon be deep inside the enemy's lair.

*

"We're on final, Major." The pilot's words snapped Salminen from her meditative trance, and her eyes snapped open.

One by one, the six shuttles dropped below the crater's spiky, broken rim, shedding speed and altitude until they flew a bare two meters above the dusty tarmac, aimed at the dark oblong of Barataria's space door. When they were a little over one kilometer away, it split in two, spilling a rectangle of bright light onto the crater floor. Salminen could see the faint shimmer of a force field across the opening, proof the cavern was still pressurized. The two leaves pulled open wider than they had for Dunmoore's shuttle and soon she saw six ground handling droids with flashing screens, three on each side of *Herja*.

At a terse command from Petty Officer First Class Purdy, the flight's senior pilot, the shuttles lined up horizontally in two packets of three. Then, they slowed to a walking pace and crossed the energy barrier simultaneously, each aimed at a droid. After a brief hover over marked spots, the shuttles touched down, their pilots waiting for the static charge to bleed off before dropping ramps.

"Shit." Salminen's heartfelt curse distracted the petty officer beside her.

"What?"

She nodded at the cockpit window. Armed men were streaming from the inner airlocks, scatterguns held at the high port.

"An escort for the precious metals we're supposed to be carrying?" He asked.

"Six is an escort. Three dozen with weapons locked and loaded means they didn't intend to honor the deal."

"To be fair, Major, neither did we." He glanced at his control screen. "Static charge bled off. You're clear to dismount."

She climbed out of the copilot's seat and headed aft into the passenger compartment where HQ Platoon, already standing and lined up to exit, waited for the word to be given.

"To all Repo call signs, this is Repo Niner. You may have noticed that the reception committee is larger than expected and I figure we were supposed to fall into a trap. That means all bets are off. If they're dumb enough to open fire on us, shoot to kill. Shuttles, drop ramps." When hers touched the deck, she yelled, "*Hakkaa päälle!*"

The battle cry drove one hundred and twenty armed and armored infantry soldiers out of their shuttles and into the docking cavern, shouting at the top of their lungs, "*Hakkaa päälle!*"

Stunned, as much by the soldiers' utterly unexpected appearance as they were by the roar of their war shout, the Baratarians seemed rooted to the spot. Salminen's troops engulfed and disarmed many of them. Others, with better reflexes, turned and ran, staying a few paces ahead of the shouting attackers, while a handful opened fire, their scattergun pellets useless against the battle suits. The latter died a second or two after pulling their triggers. In a matter of moments, Company Group 31 had seized the docking cavern and all three inner airlocks. Shortly after that, Third Platoon took the control room without firing another shot, the duty watch fleeing deeper inside Barataria.

"Repo Niner, this is Repo Two, ready to hit the executive offices."

"Repo Four, here, ready to hit Orion Outcomes."

"Two, Four, this is Repo Niner, go, go, go," Salminen replied, eager to keep the momentum and prevent the enemy from regrouping. "Repo One, Repo Prize Crew, *Herja*'s yours."

Command Sergeant Saari, with Lieutenant Kremm, Petty Officer First Class Lukas and the rest of the spacers hard on their heels streamed by her and thumped up the freighter's belly ramp. A belated alarm siren began to howl, and airlock doors attempted to slam shut, only to be countered by Command Sergeant Ritland at the dock controls. Salminen allowed herself a satisfied smile. So far, so good.

"Bastards never knew what hit 'em," a voice said behind her. "Our folks have done good, and it was nice to hear the old regimental battle cry in something other than a training exercise. Downright sent shivers up my spine. They'll remember us for sure."

"Ain't it the truth, Sarn't Major," she replied. "But things still have time to go sideways."

"They always do in one way or another."

*

"Ser Ragetti."

When Barataria's operations manager, appalled by the reversal of fortunes to the point of paralysis, did not look up from the jarring scenes on his video display, his aide stepped into the office and touched his shoulder. "Ser Ragetti."

Startled, he glared up at him. "What?"

"*Persephone*'s captain is calling us from orbit, and some of those mercenaries are outside, keeping everyone penned in their offices."

Ragetti cursed. "Order our defenses activated and get ready to target that damned pirate ship and then connect me with O'Donnell. The guns are not to open fire until I personally give the order."

When Dunmoore's face replaced the feed from the docking cavern, he snarled, "What the hell is the meaning of this? How dare you? This is sheer piracy."

Siobhan laughed. "That's rich coming from someone who thought he'd simply take my payment and my shuttles and then shoo me away. Throwing stones in glass houses and all that. I only intended to take the stolen naval stores, which you gained because of an act of piracy, but since you tried to cheat me, I'll take *Herja* as well. Consider it a warning that you should never underestimate the people you intend to screw over. I won't bother collecting the food I bargained for since I never expected to pay for anything."

Ragetti snorted with derision. "We'll see about that, O'Donnell. Look at Barataria. You'll see my weapons unmask. Try to fly *Herja* out of here, and I'll bring her down. Your prize crew will die. Try to fly your damned shuttles out of here, and I'll shoot them down too. Your mercenaries will die. I hold the high ground here. In fact, it would be easy for me to reach up seventeen thousand kilometers and touch your ship."

A sweet smile tugged at Dunmoore's lips, something her crew had long ago recognized as one of the danger signs. "Observe the weapons emplacement directly across from Barataria, on the top of the crater's rim."

"What are you on about?"

"Observe, Ser Ragetti. Then we can discuss matters involving the high ground."

He turned on a secondary display and zoomed in on the now open gun dome. No sooner had the image come into focus that it vanished in the bright flash of a nuclear detonation. Ragetti jumped back, startled.

"I have more missiles than you have defenses, Ser Ragetti, and after a few strikes on the same spot, I'll be able to punch through all that rock protecting Barataria and detonate the last one where you sit." Her face hardened again. "Do. Not. Fuck. With. Me."

"Striking ground targets with nuclear weapons has been a capital crime for almost a hundred years, O'Donnell. You'll not get away with this."

"Under whose law would that be a capital crime? Barataria's? Good luck enforcing it."

"Commonwealth law," he replied through clenched teeth, "as well you know."

"Ser Ragetti." She shook her head in mock disappointment. "Are you so astrographically challenged as to forget we're well beyond the Commonwealth sphere? Laws decreed by Earth stopped applying many light years ago, and from where I sit, the only legislation that applies is the one I can enforce by the grace of my superior firepower."

"Who the hell are you?" He asked after a moment of silence.

"Who are we?" She gave him a dismissive shrug. "We're privateers hired to recover stolen goods, and as you can see, *Persephone* isn't your average freighter. She has the firepower necessary to be a success at privateering. It comes in handy when we have to deal with actual pirates such as yourself. Be happy that Commonwealth laws don't apply. Otherwise, my letter of marque would require that I arrest everyone in Barataria and pound your precious free port into rubble. As it is, if you cooperate and let both *Herja* and my shuttles leave unmolested, I will leave Barataria unmolested."

A vicious surge of anger gleamed in his narrowed eyes. "You do not understand who you're fucking with, Shannon O'Donnell. If that's even your real name."

"What's in a name? I'm sure a cultured man such as yourself knows the famous Shakespearian line to that effect. Why don't you tell me who I'm fucking with, Ser Ragetti? Better yet, why don't you tell me what possessed you to renege on our agreement? You couldn't possibly have known I intended to repossess stolen goods." When he did not reply, she said, "Should I ask one of my mercenaries to come in and twist a limb or two, see how flexible you are? If I have no compunction about nuking Barataria into radioactive rubble, I won't balk at torture."

As if on cue, Command Sergeant Alekseev pushed the aide aside and took one step into Ragetti's office. Her blank helmet visor met his eyes, and with deliberate slowness, she placed her right fist into the palm of her left hand, leaving no doubt as to the meaning of the gesture.

"All right," Ragetti growled. "The folks who escorted *Herja* here told us to beware if an unknown bulk freighter appeared over Barataria, showing interest in *Herja*'s cargo."

"That would be Captain Tarkon of the pirate ship *Skalmold*, correct?"

Ragetti's expression showed visible surprise at her words, but he said, "Nils Tarkon is a mercenary, not a pirate. He works for Orion Outcomes, one of the larger PMCs in the sector."

"He, his crew and that of the pirate ship *Sanngrior* have condemned themselves to hang for piracy after carrying out a raid on a Commonwealth colony and stealing naval stores, should they be so stupid as to place themselves within reach of the Fleet. Fortunately for everyone concerned, I'm interested only in the stolen items. Now to my other question. Who exactly am I fucking with? It can't be Orion Outcomes. PMCs know they won't find profit in vengeance."

A sick smile twisted Ragetti's lips. "Sorry, Captain. Some lines I simply can't cross. This is one of them. Your tin soldier here can do her best, but if I cross that line, I won't just forfeit my own life, but those of the people closest to me. Take *Herja* and get your mercenary scum away from here. Never come back. In fact, leave this part of the galaxy for good, because you've just painted a big, glowing target on your hull. I expect the bounty for your capture or destruction to be profitable indeed."

"I'll take your suggestion under advisement," Dunmoore replied, mulling over what he had told her. After holding his eyes for over a minute in silence, she said, "I suppose I can guess what your situation might be, Ser Ragetti. You have backers, wealthy and powerful, well-connected in the Commonwealth and part of the arrangement leaving you in charge here to make money through means both fair and foul, has them holding a gun to your family's head."

He did not react, and she continued, "You're obviously hoping that when word gets to those backers, they'll be motivated to find a privateer by the name of *Persephone*, Captain Shannon O'Donnell, commanding, and teach us a lesson. I suppose that's a risk I must take." Her eyes shifted to one side. "A moment please, Ser Ragetti."

"By all means," he muttered back. "It's not like I don't have a gun to my head."

"*Herja*'s preparing to lift," Dunmoore said, looking at him again. "Remember what I said. Open fire on her, and I wipe out Barataria."

Ragetti waved a dismissive hand in front of the video pickup. "You've made your point, Captain. Just leave and be damned. I won't stand in anyone's way."

"Wise choice." The display went dark, and it took Ragetti a few seconds to realize she had severed the link. When he looked up, the armored soldier had gone.

*

The three men in the Orion Outcomes office drew their sidearms in unison when Command Sergeant Jennsen's troops burst through the door. Guthren pushed his way past them and raised a hand, wagging his index finger.

"Bad idea, gentlemen. We're not here to kill you, although I figure you've all done something to call for a shot in the back of the skull. Cooperate, and you'll live until you run into someone who's not as nice as I am." When they hesitated, he barked out in his best coxswain's voice, "Drop those weapons now, assholes."

With evident reluctance, they bent over and placed their blasters on the ground.

"Good choice," the cox'n said, raising his helmet visor so they could see his unfriendly grin. "I'm here to play twenty questions. Give me the right answers, and you can go on with the rest of your day."

The one who seemed to be the oldest of the trio gave Guthren a wry smile. "Twenty questions, is it? What if I tell you to fuck off, tin man?"

"Then I'll shoot you and ask your buddy. I figure by the time there's only one of you left, whoever that is will be downright chirpy."

"Speaking of doing something that warrants a shot in the back of the skull." The mercenary snorted.

"Ironic, isn't it? That's the golden rule for you. He who has the biggest guns makes the rules. So here's the deal. I want to know who hired your lot to raid Toboso. That's all I need. Oh, and I'll be taking your database. Not a copy, but the entire thing, hardware, backups and all." He waved over his shoulder at Jennsen, then pointed at what looked to be the office's central computer. "Go ahead, Aase. Cyber-rape the bastards to your heart's content."

When he saw the older man's face harden, his grin broadened. "You lot are pirates trying to pass as a PMC, so be happy I don't have Aase collect your testicles as well. She has a thing for castrating your kind of subhuman scum. That's before she cuts through your ribs and pulls your lungs out. Now, who put out the contract to raid Toboso?"

The mercenary cocked an ironic eyebrow. "Fuck off."

Guthren pulled out his blaster in one fluid movement and snapped off a shot that grazed the man's upper arm, leaving a black, smoking crease in his skin before drilling a hole in the far wall.

"Missed," he replied through clenched teeth, clearly trying not to scream in pain.

The coxswain shot again, grazing him exactly two centimeters lower. "You think? Shall we go for three? Beautiful permanent sergeant's stripes on that arm, maybe? I can add rockers and promote you all the way to master sergeant. Now, let's try this again. Someone contracted Orion Outcomes to raid Toboso. I want to know who that someone is, so we can pay them a visit and have a chat about the evils of aiding and abetting piracy."

"Even if we wanted to tell you," the man on the left said, "it wouldn't do much good. The contract and down payment came through several layers of anonymity."

"Care to speculate from where?" Guthren asked.

"Not really, but it wouldn't surprise me to find those channels lead right back into the Commonwealth. The most convoluted ones usually do. Out here, potential employers need not hide behind triple and quadruple blinds."

"What about the second half of your fee?"

He shrugged. "Probably through another set of anonymizing layers. Look, we do jobs that guys like you wouldn't touch — they pay really well. But we rarely, if ever, deal directly with a client, for reasons that should be obvious enough even to a pistol-packing thug such as you."

"Want to become a noncom like your buddy?"

"I can't tell you what I don't know."

"Where's the guy who led the Toboso raid, the one called Tarkon?"

The man's eyes slid to one side, and his lower lip twitched. "Off on a fresh contract."

"Bullshit. Promotion to lance corporal coming right up."

"Wait." He raised both hands in surrender. "Tarkon saw some asshole take *Skögul* on his last contract and figures said asshole is fixing to come after him. So he backtracked for a little interception."

Guthren examined them for a few moments, then said, "That interception wouldn't include using half a dozen Pradyni with delusions of adequacy, now would it?"

Comprehension dawned on the faces of all three men, even the one nursing his injuries.

"It's you," the latter said. "You're the people who blew up *Sigrun* and took *Skögul*."

"Sure." The coxswain gave them a dismissive half-shrug. "We enjoy doing our civic duty by keeping the star lanes clean of your kind. When is Tarkon due back?"

"Whenever he figures. Our senior captain is a law unto himself, and just so you understand what kind of crap pile you stepped into, he holds a grudge forever, so don't think you can find anywhere safe. Now that he knows you've got teeth, he'll figure out a way to track you down and get his own back."

"Good. My captain would hate to waste time crisscrossing the sector, trying to pick up the fecal stench of his exhausts." He glanced at Aase Jennsen. "You about done?"

"I'm done," she replied, climbing to her feet with a small black box in her left hand. She pulled her carbine up with the other hand and sprayed the terminal, the console it sat on and the case containing Orion Outcome's computer core. "Whether it'll be of any use, someone smarter than me will have to make that call. You want us to mess this place up a little more?"

Guthren winked at her. "Fill your armored boots, pongo. If you find hooch, it becomes the property of the ship, and the captain will divide it among the messes as per privateer custom."

When he saw one of the men's face tighten, he laughed. "There's bound to be good stuff around here. Thieves can afford the best they can steal."

*

Major Salminen felt a weight lift from her shoulders when *Herja* slipped through the force field protecting the docks and arced upward at an alarming angle, her thrusters glowing bright orange. The shuttle that had carried the prize crew followed in her wake moments later.

She watched as Command Sergeant Alekseev's platoon finished loading, and the moment the shuttle's ramp was sealed, it lifted, pivoted one hundred and eighty degrees, then followed *Herja* out of Barataria. That left Aase Jennsen's platoon and the coxswain, plus those in the cavern. She knew from bitter experience that a controlled withdrawal could turn into an utter clusterfuck if the enemy timed the moment at which Company Group 31 was at its most vulnerable. Command Sergeant Ritland must have had the same thoughts because he walked over to where she stood by HQ Platoon's shuttle.

"If I remember doctrine, boss," he said in a low voice, "with half of the company gone, it's time for the CO to pull back. Aase and I will extract our butts fine without you playing mother hen."

She glanced at Sergeant Major Haataja, who shrugged. "Once in a while, Arik gets things right. I'd say this is one of those rare occasions."

Before Salminen could reply, Jennsen's platoon emerged from the right-hand airlock, Chief Petty Officer Guthren at their head. He made the mount up signal. "I have what I came for."

"Go," Ritland said. "We'll make sure no one slams the door shut in our faces."

"Right." She turned to Lieutenant Puro. "This would be us."

He nodded and recalled HQ Platoon. Salminen made a point of being last aboard the shuttle, riding a rising ramp. As she strapped into her seat, the pilot pivoted his craft, and then a giant hand pushed her back while the gas giant Ashur filled her field of vision. After a few minutes, during which their course took them on a path almost perpendicular to the surface, the pilot tapped one of the cockpit screens to attract her attention. The last two shuttles had cleared Barataria's space door.

"Repo Mother, this is Repo Niner. Keep the barn doors open. The last of the chicks are coming home." Suddenly, an immense wave of weariness came over her. The adrenaline spike was finally subsiding, but she smiled to herself, nonetheless. Company Group 31 had done its duty as she promised it would.

— Twenty-Nine —

"That actually went better than I expected," Dunmoore said, rising from the CIC's command chair. "I'll head down to the hangar deck and greet the returning heroes."

"Considering the gall of those bastards to try double-crossing our double-cross," Holt's tiny hologram replied, "I'm surprised there weren't more casualties on their side. Ser Ragetti can be happy at the light punishment he received in return, rather than us burning out his pirate's nest

"As he so aptly pointed out, Zeke, out here, he and his ilk aren't pirates. They're entrepreneurs, and right now they've been found guilty of nothing more than possession of stolen goods, hardly a hanging offense. The two remaining mercenary ships on the other hand... I hope the cox'n squeezed useful information from the Orion Outcomes shore office."

"If it was there to squeeze, Chief Guthren will have done it. The day they beach him, he'll easily find a home with my old bunch in counter-intelligence."

She tugged her tunic down and said, "The day they beach him, he'll open a spaceport dive on an out-of-the-way planet with a large Marine garrison. Make sure *Herja* takes station as close as possible to us. Lieutenant Kremm had better accustom himself to sailing under

Iolanthe's maternal wing until we're back inside Commonwealth space."

"Are you expecting further trouble?"

"Always, Number One, especially since we've yet to hear from *Skögul*. This part of the Orion arm isn't a safe place for small ships."

"Nor is it safe for those who mistakenly believe we're a helpless, honking big ship. Give Major Salminen and her folks a Bravo Zulu from me, Captain. They've earned it."

"I will after I explain to them it's Navy lingo for a hearty 'well done' and not an obscure insult. Company Group 31's performance today might meet Marine Corps standards, but they're still pongos lost in a strange land. After-action review in the conference room in one hour. Lieutenant Kremm to patch through via tight-beam. CIC, out." She waved at Lieutenant Commander Sirico. "The chair's yours, Thorin. If Ragetti looks like he's about to fire off a few shots because he's feeling a deep sense of regret at folding his cards, take out the next defensive dome. But I think he's impatient to see the last of us and will stay quiet."

She made her way to the hangar deck's control room, arriving just in time to watch Salminen's shuttle cross the force field, followed in short order by the last two. Once Petty Officer Harkon had shut the space doors and unsealed the inner airlocks, soldiers spilled out of the boxy craft and formed up by platoons in their now accustomed spot along the aft bulkhead. The bosun's mate nodded at Dunmoore. "You're cleared, Captain."

Salminen saw Siobhan entering and checked her step. She turned to face *Iolanthe*'s captain.

"Congratulations on your first Marine-style raid being a smashing success, Major."

"Thank you, sir." The soldier's habitual shy smile made a brief appearance. "Train hard, fight easy is an old saying that's always proved correct when one faces the real thing, especially with a bunch of stubborn Scandians like my troops."

"Your stubborn Scandian troops can be proud of themselves. That was nicely done."

"Maybe they'd enjoy hearing it from you, sir."

"Would now be an appropriate time?" Dunmoore asked, glancing at the assembled company, waiting patiently for their commanding officer to dismiss them.

"Now would be good, yes."

*

"It wouldn't surprise me if the contract came from within our own sphere, perhaps even all the way back to Earth," Holt said with a thoughtful expression on his face once Chief Guthren finished recounting his part of the raid to the assembled department heads. "I've come across things you'd find hard to credit during my shore posting with counter-intelligence — maybe not you, Captain, after your earlier experiences aboard *Stingray* — and they mostly stemmed from good old-fashioned greed."

Dunmoore turned to Chief Petty Officer Third Class Day, acting as department head for information systems in Lieutenant Kremm's absence. "Any initial comments about the Orion Outcomes data repository the landing party retrieved?"

Day grimaced. "I inspected it before coming to the after-action review, and while we were able to make out the structure, the contents are thoroughly encrypted. My folks have instructions to call the moment they find something, but so far, nada."

"What manner of encryption?" Holt asked.

"The kind you'd have recognized in your old job, sir."

Dunmoore's right eyebrow crept up. This sounded all too familiar for reasons she could not discuss with anyone else, except perhaps Ezekiel Holt. "Naval grade, Chief?"

"Not exactly, but my gut tells me it's from the same general family of algorithms. My folks are trying variations of the ones we have to see if they can force a crack into its shell."

The first officer raised a finger. "So we don't get too excited, keep in mind that private entities in the Commonwealth legally use encryption methods similar to the ones developed by the Fleet. It's a matter of imitating the best in the business to obtain the best results. That being said, if what we're facing proves to be derived from one of ours, then my former colleagues face a whole new world of hurt trying to find whoever sold top secret material."

"You think they'd be used to it by now," Dunmoore replied with a mischievous half-smile.

"Common peculation, sure, but once you start talking about crypto material going walkabout, it's an entirely new game."

She inclined her head towards Holt. "Granted, Number One. All right then, this means that unless Chief Day and his wizards dig up answers, we're one for three so far, although recovering most of the stolen naval stores is worth nearly as much as our other two objectives. In any case, Operation Repo was as sweet a raid as anyone could have wanted. Well done."

"Our Army contingent was thoroughly terrifying when that war cry erupted from a hundred and twenty throats," Holt said. "Remind me to never annoy you or any of yours, Major."

Salminen bowed her head in acknowledgment, a smile of undisguised pleasure lighting up her lean face.

"If there are no last minute points up for discussion, let's segue into what I intend next." She looked around the table but received nothing more than brief shakes of the head. "First, the givens. Take it as a given I won't head back to Toboso without trying everything I can to terminate the operations of the last two mercenary ships. It's also a given we can't send *Herja* back without an escort, so we'll be operating with a little duckling following us around, and that has to factor into any decisions I make when it comes to fighting. It's a given we have to marry up with *Skögul* before heading home. What's less of a given and more of a hope is tracking down whoever financed the raid on Toboso, but this Tarkon, who's supposedly looking for us might know more than the Orion Outcomes shore office did. That's pretty much the last straw we can grasp at. If we're no wiser after sending Tarkon and his crews to join their ancestors, we'll have to hand the matter over to counter-intelligence once we're in range of a Fleet subspace relay station. Did I miss any givens?"

Dunmoore looked around the table but saw nothing more than silent head shakes.

"I guess not," she said when no one spoke up. "On to my intentions. I plan to stay in this system after giving Barataria the impression we've left, and hide out somewhere in Ashur orbit running silent, hidden from Ragetti's sensors by one of the moons. When Tarkon and his ships show up, as they inevitably will, I intend to end their depredations — preferably after determining whether or not Orion Outcomes' senior captain knows something of value, but if need be whenever the occasion presents itself. Then, we will return to Toboso. Questions or comments?"

"Aye, Captain, about logistics. There's a hard limit on the time we can spend here," Holt said. "Our food stocks being the most important factor. Lieutenant Biros and I will confirm the state of our inventory after this meeting, and then we'll run the numbers so we can give you the date on which we have to leave. I assume you'll be transferring stocks over from *Herja* at some point?"

"Once we're hidden from Barataria, yes, along with Sergeant Saari's platoon."

"That should take care of munitions, parts, and raw materials for engineering's maker machines. Finally, fuel. We have enough to see us comfortably back to the antimatter cracking station in the Cervantes system, but not enough to cover a lot of light years crisscrossing the sector."

"That's why I want to let the enemy come to us."

"Of course." Holt nodded. "I've no further comments, sir."

"Anyone else?" She went around the table. "I'd like Lieutenant Pashar to stay behind so we can plot our course to somewhere hidden from Barataria while giving the idea we've buggered out. Thanks, folks."

*

"You had a bit of a reaction when Chief Day mentioned the crypto matter," Holt, coffee cup in hand, said taking a seat across from Dunmoore in the latter's cabin. "Would there be issues of interest to your loyal and hardworking first officer?"

She stared at him for a good while, debating what, if anything she could share. Then, coming to a decision, she asked, "Are you familiar with Rear-Admiral Lucius Corwin?"

To her surprise, a knowing smile crept across his lips. "Mad Lucius. Died while running a hush-hush operation out in the Badlands."

"I was there when he died. Let's say I was largely part responsible for his death, even if I didn't pull the trigger."

"Oh?" Holt's expression invited her to continue.

"There's a method for disposing of disgraced officers — I seem to recall it goes all the way back to the days of the Prussian Army when cavalry still rode horses. One gun, one round, one last chance to redeem one's honor."

A light went on in Holt's eye. "Meaning you gave Corwin a gun with one round in it because he'd disgraced himself and the Service. Fascinating. The official story had Corwin die in battle against a massive reiver assault on the secret base he commanded. From the dossier I saw, a combat death didn't fit with the man's history."

She tapped the side of her nose with her index finger. "Of course, after I presented my report to Rear-Admiral Ryn, a lot of important details vanished into the memory hole, where they'll stay until the end of time. However, that's not why I bring his sad story up, Zeke. It's the crypto angle. *Stingray* ended up attached to Corwin's command for a while, and at one point, he had us raid a reiver base in a nearby star system. Except it wasn't a real reiver base. Once on the ground, we sifted through the ruins and found data wafers encrypted with an algorithm that closely aligned with those in use by the Fleet and other government agencies. An older SSB algorithm, to be precise."

"Ah." Holt nodded. "You figure our friendly enemies of the Special Security Bureau might be involved here as well?"

"The target of our raid back then, as best we could tell, was a money-making operation run by the SSB. We seized a ship on the ground we had encountered before, and we knew had been connected to the SecGen's secret police in the past. I wouldn't be at all shocked to find them backing Orion Outcomes for some nefarious schemes of their own. Or involved with Barataria itself, for that matter."

"Why would their puppets, if that's what those mercenaries are, carry out a deadly raid on a

Commonwealth colony, one that wiped out a Fleet supply depot and almost the entire colonial administration? Cui bono, as our JAG friends like to ask."

Dunmoore gave him a wan smile. "That's the ten million cred question, isn't it? Someone tried to raid the Sigma Noctae Depot before though at the time I saw no connection to the SSB. I still believe Andrew Devine and his clique were behind that one, motivated by profit more than anything else, and maybe a desire to kick radioactive sand in the Fleet's face. This time around, if it's supposed to be a money-making operation, why wipe out the colonial administration?"

"To obtain an even greater measure of independence from the Colonial Office?"

"Yet, Anton Gerber and a dozen or so from the late governor's office remain to fly the Commonwealth flag on Toboso."

"At least they did when we left. We've been gone for a couple of weeks, Captain."

She made a face at him. "Thanks for adding that to my list of worries, Zeke."

He grinned at her. "Always happy to oblige. Being a pessimist is one of those obligations specified by the first officers' union rulebook."

"You just earned yourself a drubbing at chess, Mister Holt. Pull out the set. I'll give you white if you like, though your opening moves aren't up to the standards of a former first officer fond of quoting some of those same so-called union rules."

Holt made as if to stand. "I believe duty calls, Captain."

"Sit. The watch standers are perfectly capable of shifting *Iolanthe* to her designated hiding spot without us, and I'm sure everything else aboard is under control. Enjoy this moment of peace and relaxation."

He sighed. "You're the only person I've met who thinks of chess as a blood sport. I'll take white and may you choke on black, Captain."

*

"Now hear this, prepare to rig for silent running in five minutes," the bridge officer of the watch announced via *Iolanthe*'s public address system, "I repeat, prepare to rig for silent running in five minutes. That is all."

Holt studied the chessboard in silence for another thirty seconds before he tipped his king over, conceding defeat. That made it two for Dunmoore and one for him.

"I guess we're about to vanish from Barataria's line of sight, meaning we'd better head for the bridge." He scooped up the chessmen and stowed them in their box.

"Aye. By the way, you'd have still been able to escape my trap."

"Oh?" Holt snapped the box shut.

"Your queen's knight."

He thought for a moment, then a pained expression creased his face. "Damn. I missed that. I guess my mind went elsewhere after the OOW's announcement."

Dunmoore chuckled. "And they say I'm easy to distract."

She led the way forward to the bridge and took her command chair, eyes on the status readout. "I have the bridge, Mister Pashar."

"I stand relieved, Captain." The acting sailing master, currently bridge officer of the watch, gave her a formal nod before taking his usual station beside the helm console.

"Staying hidden will be an interesting problem in orbital mechanics," the first officer remarked, studying the navigation display, "considering how often these moons pass each other. We must stay on our toes lest some sharp-eyed sensor techs see a speck in the heavens that shouldn't be there, or God forbid sees us silhouetted against our hiding place."

Dunmoore nodded, eyes also on the holographic projection. "It'll need a light touch on the thrusters for sure." She paused before saying, "Does it strike anyone else as somewhat ironic that we're now the ones hiding behind a gas giant's moon?"

"Not really, Captain," the coxswain answered from his accustomed spot at the helm. "We're not sitting in the dark praying the enemy goes away without finding us. On the contrary. What's the expression Mister Holt used when the Pradyni tried us on for size? Step into my parlor, said the spider to the fly?"

A crooked smile tugged at her lips. "It is, and you're right."

"Ashur has cut us off from Barataria's direct line of sight, sir," Sub-Lieutenant Pashar reported. "Adjusting course to enter the outer moon's orbit."

"Now we settle in for the wait," Holt said, "while hoping the buggers show up before we're forced to head home." He checked the countdown timer on his screen and activated the public address system. "Now hear this, silent running in sixty, six zero seconds. That is all."

The outer moon, ice-covered and even larger than the one Barataria called home was not an ideal choice. Light in surface color, it could easily betray *Iolanthe*'s boxy shape if someone spotted her transit. Yet it was the only one available to both give Barataria the impression they had left for good and preserve the Q-ship's maneuvering room for when the rest of the mercenary ships returned.

"Now hear this, go to silent running, I repeat go to silent running. That is all."

Nothing perceptible changed on the bridge. It was well shielded against emission leaks. Nevertheless, Dunmoore knew the CIC would be half-blind, its sensing, and targeting capacity limited to optical and passive reception, while all weapons would be powered down. The reactors feeding the ship's systems would by now be dampened, their output minimized by shutting down secondary functions such as the entertainment facilities and cutting off power to unused compartments. With her matte black hull capable of absorbing and redirecting any active scans short of those done at point-blank range, *Iolanthe* had, for all intents and purposes, become an electronic hole in space.

"Ship rigged for silent running, Captain," Holt confirmed a moment later. "Chief Day wonders whether we have time to pay him a visit."

"He has something?"

"It appears so."

"Mister Pashar, you have the bridge." Dunmoore sprang to her feet and followed Holt down the passage to the most heavily shielded part of the ship, other than the reactors, the compartment home to *Iolanthe*'s computer core where Chief Petty Officer Day usually held court.

"You summoned us, Chief?" Dunmoore called out by way of greeting the moment she stepped into his domain.

Day turned in his seat and nodded. "We've broken the encryption, but I'm not sure I can make heads or tails of a fair chunk. This might take a while." He waved towards the empty chairs beside his station.

"What sort of algorithm did it turn out to be?" Holt asked once they were seated.

"A purely civilian one, but definitely derived from government crypto, probably SSB. Whether it's a legal derivative or not, I can't tell, but it has no signature, and that usually means it isn't."

Dunmoore made a face. "SSB? Buggers get around, don't they?"

"I said possibly, sir. It also has commonalities with the crypto used by the Colonial Office and a few of the more obscure government agencies reporting to the SecGen."

"What about the contents?"

"Most of it is commercial — accounts receivable, accounts payable, spare parts management, and purchases, pretty much anything related to logistics, human resources, and the like. The interesting stuff is under contracting and banking. Some of it isn't merely encrypted; it's also in gibberish as far as I can tell, which likely means another, unique code giving that data an extra layer of security."

"Let me see," Holt said.

Day called up the relevant data on the primary display and scrolled through it slowly.

"Stop." The first officer raised a restraining hand. "Go back to the previous packet."

He stared at it for a full minute and nodded. "I've seen this before. It's not gibberish but commercial backchannel instructions. We ran across a lot of these during counter-intelligence investigations. They disguise the parties from each other and anyone who wants to snoop on their business. Organized criminals are prime users. These sorts of backchannels are technically illegal, but there's so much money involved that enforcement is spotty. Keep scrolling, Chief."

"These too," Holt pointed at a fresh set of instructions under banking. "They're similar to the commercial backchannel routing instructions but optimized for payments. Definitely illegal and used mainly where said payments can't be laundered via other means."

"So what does that mean?" Dunmoore asked.

Holt rubbed his chin, lips tightened in a grimace. "What does it mean? That the mercs are doing business with folks in the Commonwealth who'd rather keep their identities hidden. Chief, show me the stuff in the contracting database that doesn't look like gibberish."

"That seems clear enough," Dunmoore said once the relevant data appeared.

"All related to contracts originating outside the Commonwealth." Holt nodded. "No need for backchannels. I'll bet we won't find any banking data related to these."

"We didn't," Chief Day confirmed, "but we found precious metal acquisitions instead of creds associated with these."

"You found nothing related to Toboso, right?"

"Nothing we could read, sir. If it's there, it'll be hidden in your backchannel instructions."

"I guess we have our first real clue, Captain," Holt said turning his head to glance at Dunmoore. "The contract to hire Orion Outcomes must have originated somewhere within the Commonwealth, and I'll bet the down payment is sitting somewhere there in an untraceable bank account."

"Any chance of deciphering those backchannel instructions?" Dunmoore asked.

"Without the computing power and comprehensive historical database available at HQ? Unlikely. These instructions are often onetime use so standard analysis techniques won't work. What works is finding similarities between sets and from that, tracking down one of the parties. Most people become sloppy and don't vary their backchannels much over time. I'll work my way through them when I have the chance, in the hopes of something jogging my memory, but don't hold your breath, Captain. We'll have to hand this one over to my old gang when we return home. Anything else, Chief?"

Day nodded. "Their operations log. Makes for interesting reading, even if names and locations are in some sort of substitution code they probably cooked up over a couple of drinks. I figure we have enough evidence to hang the bastards ten times over. There's an entry corresponding to the approximate time of the attack on Toboso. Again, no names or coordinates in clear, but there are two sets of instructions on communicating with assets on Toboso, one identified as being inside the target whose job was to take the communications and surveillance capabilities offline. Let me pull that data packet up."

"Putting a sleeper agent inside a target or corrupting someone already in place isn't unusual," Holt said.

"They seem to do that frequently from what I read, sir, but this one has a twist. If you'll look at the display..."

Dunmoore exhaled audibly. "That's a Fleet frequency and generic address. If it's indeed related to the Toboso raid, then as we suspected, they had help from someone inside Sigma Noctae, someone with high-level access."

"The message they sent to that address is innocuous in the extreme," Holt pointed out, "proving that the operation this log entry describes was prepared well in advance and the asset briefed ahead of time. I doubt Orion Outcomes could take on two complex operations within the same period. That's Toboso all right, Captain, and whoever contracted for it made sure to either plant or develop an asset inside Sigma Noctae. Considering that only properly vetted naval personnel would have access to the satellite constellation, I'd say we're looking at someone relatively senior who was either coerced, corrupted or blackmailed. I've seen that sort of story all too often."

Dunmoore and Holt locked eyes, both seized by the same thought. Chief Petty Officer Third Class Trane, former Sigma Noctae operations chief and the only survivor who would have had the necessary access. When she glanced at Day, she could see he had come to the same conclusion.

"What about the other set of instructions?"

"Similar to the first, except for a civilian frequency and a generic colonial government address."

— Thirty —

"Chief Petty Officer Third Class Marko Trane reporting to the cox'n as ordered."

Guthren pointed at a chair on the other side of the conference room table. "Sit, Marko."

"What's this about, Cox'n?"

"Remember that chat you and me had when you were still in sickbay, recovering from the mess on Toboso? When I asked you about the raid on Sigma Noctae?"

"Sure." Trane nodded.

"I have follow-up questions, now that we have a little quiet time. When we raided Barataria, I came across new intelligence that might point us at the stupid fucks who killed most of your crew. Since you're the senior survivor outside of the pongos, I wanted to run a few things by you and hear your take. See if we're on the right track and all."

Trane shrugged though he had a guarded expression in his eyes. "Whatever you want, Cox'n."

"Folks there ever use the naval communications system for personal messages?"

"Sure. Shore billet on the ass-end of nowhere, anything that'll help morale, right? Why are you asking?"

"Is it possible the bad guys sent a message on a carrier wave spoofing Fleet channels that would mean something to only one member of the garrison, something telling him or her to screw with the satellite constellation?"

Trane hesitated before giving Guthren a non-committal grimace. "Anything's possible, Cox'n. You know how it is."

Guthren shook his head. "Actually, I don't. Why don't you spell it out for me, Marko?"

A distinct aura of unease enveloped Trane. "Personal subspace messages aren't cheap. Often, a friend of a friend will hook a buddy up to piggyback a message on a Fleet carrier wave and send a hello to some place out in the back of beyond, like Toboso, for free. A lot of stations have a generic Fleet address that's supposed to be used for general business, but if you're friendly with the signals guy, it can be the local catch-all for personal stuff. Because some COs don't like it, anonymity is the rule. Whoever the message is addressed to will know."

"You had that on Toboso, then?"

"Sure."

"You ever receive any of those personal messages on the Fleet's cred?"

Trane's eyes hardened. "What's this about, Cox'n?"

Guthren slid a tablet with the relevant section from the Orion Outcomes operations log displayed on its screen. "Someone inside Sigma Noctae let the bad guys in through the front door. This much proves it. I figure it involved blackmail or something like that. Navy folks with the access it takes to shut down a satellite constellation are high up the food chain, meaning they've been around for a while. Scum don't have the patience it takes to feed their own assets through the system starting with boot camp."

"So?" Trane asked with an edge of defiance in his tone.

"Anyone come to mind, Marko? A senior petty officer or an officer with something a blackmailer can pull on?"

"They're all dead now, so who cares?"

"We want to find out who paid for the raid. Someone set this up, financed it, corrupted one of your crewmates, and watched them die. I figure that someone deserves to hang. Don't you?"

"How the fuck would I know anything about that?"

"A chief always knows what's happening around him, right Marko? That's why guys like you and me are chiefs. Think back and try to remember anything that struck you as strange in the days or weeks before the attack. Anyone acting strangely. Perhaps someone in the operations center who liked to gamble, hang out with entertainers or play with folks who are legally married. The kind of thing that a blackmailer might use. It could be something that didn't seem like much at the time, but in light of events?"

Trane's eyes slid to one side. "It's bad luck to speak ill of the dead, Cox'n."

"Maybe where you're from, Marko. Where I'm from, it's bad luck to let a traitorous bastard get away with murder, or in this case, mass murder." When Trane looked up at Guthren again, the coxswain said, "Spit it out, buddy. Your face is telling me you made a connection. As they say, confession is good for the soul."

"My officer, Lieutenant Duff, he liked to go nuts in town. Well, as nuts as you can in places like Doniphon, Valance and the rest of the shit holes around Sigma Noctae. Thought he was a wizard at the card tables and hot with the ladies. The truth is, both fleeced him blind every payday. Could be he got in over his head, and someone offered to cancel his debts in return for unlocking Toboso's front door, so to speak."

"So you're saying someone might have corrupted or blackmailed him?"

Trane made a face. "Duff wasn't on Toboso because of his excellent track record. He was a blowhard who figured the promotion boards had been fucking him over for a long time. The truth is, he couldn't find his ass with both hands."

"Meaning you were actually running the operations center."

"Exactly. Duff was all talk no walk. I figure it wouldn't have been hard to put the squeeze on him. It's not like he was a virgin when he showed up at the depot. Guys like him were weak fucks to begin with."

Guthren nodded. "Ran across a few like that myself. Way too many commanding officers in the Fleet who don't want to do the dirty work to separate bad officers from the service. It's easier to keep posting them to worse and worse duty stations until they figure it out."

"That would have been Lieutenant D.P. Duff all right, Cox'n."

And you? Guthren wondered, knowing the same could be said of chief petty officers, although in their case, it was usually because the Navy promoted them beyond their abilities, unlike officers who went downhill because the Navy denied them the promotions they craved.

"So you figure Duff could have been dirty enough to betray everyone?"

"More like stupid enough," Trane replied, grimacing. "There's a few sharp operators on Toboso, folks who figure anyone in uniform is ripe for picking. Duff was riper than most. Buggers try to screw the Fleet over on contracts too, from what I was told. Purchasing wasn't my area, so I don't know for sure."

"You must have gone to town yourself regularly, right? Play a little, take in some entertainment? Did you see who Duff liked to hang out with? Perhaps with a few of those operators sharp enough to be the pirates' insiders on Toboso?"

Trane chuckled. "The lieutenant and I didn't move in the same social circles, Cox'n. I like my fun more rough and ready. He liked to stick his nose up wealthy and powerful bums."

"Such as?"

"Folks on the governor's staff, the guys who own the big co-op that did business with the depot, town councilors, the kind of rich and powerful that run Toboso."

"Remember any names?"

"Like I said, Duff and I didn't move in the same circles. Anyway, the governor's staff are all dead, from what I heard, right?"

"A couple survived. They weren't working in the colonial administration complex when it was hit. One of the late governor's aides, a guy by the name of Anton Gerber is now the acting governor."

Trane snapped his fingers and pointed at Guthren. "Gerber. Right. Duff liked to tell us about how the man was well-connected in the Colonial Office and how he would arrange a plum job for Duff when his hitch was up. So he survived, eh? Lucky bastard. Governor to boot. Talk about coming out smelling of roses. Too bad Duff's not around anymore to hitch a ride on Gerber's coattails, now that it's really worth sucking up to him."

"Any other names you can remember?"

"Sure. Devine, the co-op guy, was one of the regulars at the same card tables as Duff in the Doniphon saloon. Him and a woman, Kila something or other. Meanest eyes I've ever seen. Vanclef — that's her name. Kila Vanclef. I think Duff had the hots for her. No accounting for taste, I suppose." Trane's eyes took on that faraway look Guthren had seen during the first interview in *Iolanthe*'s sickbay. He shook his head. "If it was Duff that betrayed us, he sure didn't look like a man who figured he was about to die when I saw him for the last time."

"They probably told him the raid wasn't going to come anywhere near Sigma Noctae or the colonial administration complex. He might not have agreed to go along if he'd known the real targets."

"That might have been it," Trane nodded. "As much as he was a useless sack of rocks, I don't think he was bent enough to put all of our lives on the line."

"The fact that he's dead is a good sign. Anything else come to mind, Marko?"

Trane thought about it for a moment. "Nope. If something does, I'll be sure to tell you right away."

"That's what I figure. See you at supper."

*

"So our best bet is that the screw-up lieutenant running operations did it?" Holt asked after Guthren had finished briefing Dunmoore and the first officer. "Kind of convenient that he's dead."

"That had occurred to me as well, sir. Trane could have been speaking about himself for all we know."

"What I find interesting," Dunmoore said, "is hearing Gerber's name. Our esteemed acting governor was conveniently away from the office that morning, supposedly bird watching in the mountains. As for Devine and Vanclef, they already figured high on my list of suspects after my prior run-ins with them and their cronies."

"Too bad birds can't give Gerber an alibi," Holt replied. "Any idea whether Trane was lying about it being this Duff character, Cox'n?"

"I figure the story itself is true, sir, and Duff being one of the Navy's bad bargains is probably just as true. He was speaking from the heart there. But I'm undecided about who the story's real main character was. He could have been telling his story and hanging the lieutenant's name on it. As you said, Duff's death is mighty convenient,"

"The bad bargain tag might apply to Trane as well," Dunmoore said. "You can find them in the Chiefs' and Petty Officers' mess too, not just the wardroom. When I was Sigma Noctae's XO, most of the senior noncoms were as useful as teats on a boar hog."

"True, but I've seen no signs of it yet," Guthren replied, "and the bosun hasn't passed on any complaints about Trane's performance."

Holt gave a dismissive shrug. "He would be on his best behavior if his conscience isn't clean."

"Equally true. At least he gave us a lead to follow when we're back on Toboso. I'll gladly rattle a few cages when we're back if you'd like."

"Interrogating an acting governor will be delicate," Dunmoore warned. "We can't just walk into his office and ask him whether he corrupted a Navy officer into taking down the satellite constellation. All we have is the word of a chief petty officer that Duff displayed questionable behavior and frequented known, but unindicted criminals and the man propelled into the governor's chair by the attack."

"Yet I'm sure you'll find a way to do it, Captain."

She smiled at her first officer. "Probably, and I'll enjoy watching Devine and the rest of the rotten bunch twist in the wind. They still owe me a few lives. More now, if they were involved this time."

"Here's to hoping we'll figure out the motive once we finger the guilty party," Guthren said. "I still can't make heads or tails of this whole business and you know I like my explanations clear and straightforward."

"I'm not sure about finding a clear and straightforward motive, Cox'n," Dunmoore said. "Something so well planned must have taken into account the possibility of a Navy ship showing up for supplies. I'm sure if we check, we'll find that the patrol plot for the sector shows no scheduled visit during the time of the attack. But we're free-runners, not on anyone's sailing schedule, top secret or otherwise. That means there could well be a Navy angle as well as a Colonial Office angle. Of course, my old friends on Toboso will most certainly be working their own angle."

"A real triangle, then," Holt quipped. "Which we turned into a polygon by showing up unannounced, throwing everything askew." When both Dunmoore and Guthren stared at him as if he had just passed gas during a fleet admiral's inspection, he threw up his hands in disgust. "You two don't possess a sense of humor well-developed enough to understand mine."

"Oh we do, sir," the coxswain replied, deadpan. "We just don't know why you figured that was supposed to be amusing."

"Philistines."

"I prefer to think of us as connoisseurs, Zeke," Dunmoore said, a sardonic grin pulling up the corners of her mouth.

"Sure. Take his side. I know the two of you go further back than we do."

"Third time as the captain's cox'n, sir. I believe this is only your second time as her first officer."

"That's no excuse to gang up on me, Mister Guthren." Holt's wounded look was enough to make Dunmoore laugh.

"Enough," she said, raising her hands in surrender. "Perhaps we should return to the matter at hand. Do we trust Trane?"

"No," Guthren and Holt replied in unison.

"At least not when it comes to the culprit on the Navy side," the first officer added. "We're now reasonably confident that someone in the colony's involved, someone either within the former administration or with access to its communications node. That means his fingering a few prominent names without prompting has a higher degree of reliability."

"Anton Gerber? He practically begged me to take over."

"Smokescreen, Captain. Gerber figured you wouldn't want any part of it, especially if he's in cahoots with Devine and company, who would have gleefully poured out all of their venom at the mention of your name. He did obtain an accelerated promotion to acting governor. These days, it's an even bet the Colonial Office will make it permanent, especially on an out-of-the-way colony like Toboso. That's a potent drug for a minor functionary."

"Gunning for a chance at a governorship on the backs of so many corpses?" Dunmoore made a skeptical face. "That's ice cold, and Gerber didn't strike me as being a psychopath. He's not charming enough, for one thing, besides, the psychos I've had the misfortune to meet didn't come across as nervous, twitchy types."

"He wouldn't be the first or the last to sacrifice others on the altar of ambition, but I get your meaning. There has to be more to the Toboso raid than wiping out the government and stealing tons of naval stores that, admittedly, would fetch a pretty price on the black market. I'm sure Orion Outcomes charged a premium to commit such a flagrant act of piracy within the Commonwealth sphere, knowing death awaits anyone caught by the Navy. That premium had to have been financed by someone for a reason, one that goes beyond mere theft."

"Greed is always a good reason, Zeke."

"Power is an even better one, Captain. Wealth comes a lot easier with power. Why do you think so many in the Senate and the Executive Branch are filthy rich?"

"Rigged military contracts?" Guthren suggested.

"Give the ex-special forces man with a chief's starbursts on his sleeves a big fat prize. The war has made a lot of fortunes, which is why it's been dragging on for so long."

"Cynic," Dunmoore said.

"I prefer the term realist. Some things I've seen can never be unseen, and there's sweet fuck all the Fleet can do about most of them. Don't be surprised if we can't do anything about the Toboso affair either, beyond blowing the Orion Outcomes bastards to kingdom come that is. If Tarkon doesn't show up with his remaining two ships before we reach our time limit for staying here, we won't even have the pleasure of doing so."

"Then I'll take what I can, but it isn't over, not even close. This time, the bastards back on Toboso won't slip out of my grasp if I have anything to say about it."

"Your optimism is an inspiration to all of us," he replied with a roguish grin, "as is your fearsome air of ruthlessness."

"Flattery will get you nowhere, Zeke."

Just as Holt opened his mouth to reply, the intercom chimed.

"CIC to the captain. Sirico, here."

Dunmoore touched her communicator. "Go ahead, Thorin."

"Sir, we detected three emergence signatures at the hyperlimit. Preliminary data shows them to be sloop-sized and of very similar configuration. Their course appears to aim them at Ashur. We should have a visual lock shortly."

Holt's eyebrows shot up. "Three?"

"Maybe Tarkon had a fifth ship off on another mission, or those aren't the sloops we're looking for," Dunmoore replied.

"Actually, sir," Sirico responded, "Chief Yens just flashed up the visual as well as their power curve signatures. She's almost ninety percent sure that two of the ships are the ones that escaped, *Skalmold* and *Sanngrior*."

"And the third?"

"You won't like this, Captain, but the chief thinks it's probably *Skögul*."

— Thirty-One —

A string of curses in at least five different languages escaped Dunmoore's lips, causing both Holt and Guthren to stare at her with astonishment.

"I wasn't aware you had such a colorful vocabulary," the first officer said when she finally fell silent.

Sirico emitted a low whistle. "That was impressive."

"You can blame it on a misspent youth. Dammit, I figured something had gone wrong. I could feel it in my bones."

"Perhaps Astrid captured the rest of the bunch and is bringing them home to show mother," Holt suggested in a half-hearted tone.

Dunmoore gave him an exasperated glare. "Please, Zeke. You know as well as I do she wouldn't try a stunt like that."

"You would."

"Which is why I spent most of my junior years as a gunnery officer and not a navigator. After witnessing my astrogation skills, no captain in his right mind would let me plot a complicated course for fear I'd take a few risky shortcuts to reduce transit time or see if an ion storm actually can collapse a hyperspace bubble. Astrid is much more careful and cautious than I was. She'll have been captured somehow, and it means we'll have to intercept them before they reach Barataria, although until we can determine what happened to our people, we can't open fire."

"General Order Eighty-One applies, Captain. Astrid and her crew know full well the Navy doesn't negotiate with pirates who've taken hostages."

She made an obscene gesture. "Bugger General Order Eight-One. We're already operating beyond our mandate so one more violation of the rules won't make a difference if HQ decides to get pissy. Besides, the last violation of that damned order saved my life and those of two others, one of them being Vincenzo."

"Aye," Guthren nodded. "Mister Pushkin wasn't going to let rules interfere that time either."

"I sense a story for another time," Holt replied, "but my statement was merely the sort of reminder I'm duty bound to give you as first officer. Ezekiel Holt, intrepid commander in the finest Navy ever seen, will support whatever you decide when it comes to recovering our people."

"If they're still alive." Dunmoore gave him a bleak look.

"If they're not, then the Orion Outcomes folks will die that much faster." The coxswain slapped a meaty fist against his other hand's open palm.

"Thorin, I need an intercept plot that'll allow us to stay hidden as long as possible and still cut them off from Barataria."

"On it, sir. Considering the orbital mechanics involved, it'll be interesting."

*

"Ten minutes until we light up, Captain," Sirico said, breaking through Dunmoore's absent-minded contemplation of the tactical plot. She could not do anything other than worry about the fate of Astrid Drost and her crew. However, studying the three-dimensional projection of Ashur, its moons, and the three mercenary ships beat the alternative which was pacing around the CIC like a trapped she-wolf, something that would irritate everyone, herself included.

Dunmoore glanced up at him. "Thank you, Thorin. Please have the bridge call battle stations."

The insistent whoop of the siren sounded moments later, warning her crew to prepare for — what? Battle? Withdrawal if they held a figurative or literal knife at Drost's throat? Not knowing the fate of her sailing master and the prize crew gnawed at Dunmoore's gut like a metastasizing cancer, one that fired shots of self-doubt and recrimination up her spine and into the deepest parts of her consciousness. She checked her personal protective equipment, as much to keep her fingers busy as to give the CIC watch a good example, then settled back into the command chair and stared at the plot once more, only partly hearing Holt confirm her ship was at battle stations.

"Now hear this," the first officer's voice rang out a few minutes later, "up systems in sixty seconds, I repeat, six zero seconds. That is all."

Dunmoore watched with fascination as the icon representing *Iolanthe* cleared the moon's shadow, coming into view of her quarry, a view still impeded by silent running, but that last bit of camouflage evaporated one minute after Holt's announcement. Chief Guthren, at the helm, lit up her drives, breaking them out of orbit on a course to place the Q-ship between Barataria and the sloops. For now, she seemed nothing more than a large, if spry bulk freighter, her emissions signature that of a lumbering giant and not a man-of-war. Coming out of hiding allowed Chief Yens and her crew full access to the high-grade naval sensor suite, and she quickly confirmed the identities of all three vessels, cementing the sick knot in Siobhan's gut.

"We're being pinged in return," Yens said.

"I doubt our appearance comes as a surprise. Barataria must have informed them of our little raid the moment they dropped out of FTL."

"Enemy has raised shields and is powering weapons."

Sirico frowned. "Did they not get a good look at us the last time we crossed paths? If I were them, I'd try to run. We're outmatched when it comes to acceleration, and they're not pinned against Ashur yet."

Dunmoore's head tilted to one side, narrowed eyes once more focused on the red icons moving through the holographic tactical plot. "I'm sure they had a good enough look to understand we're dangerous, Thorin. Otherwise, they wouldn't have bothered using those Pradyni privateers to stop us coming here."

"A fat lot of good it did them."

A cruel smile twisted her lips. "They know we're dangerous, but perhaps not how dangerous. Since they're pinging us, why don't we go to full military power but without unmasking and see what that does."

"Full military power, aye," Holt replied from the bridge. "You have it, Captain." Moments later, he added, "So does the enemy. Incoming transmission. A Senior Captain Tarkon wishes to speak with you."

"Really? Put him through."

The usual holographic virtual screen materialized in front of her command chair, displaying the image of a swarthy, heavily bearded man of indeterminate age. Small, close-set black eyes beneath equally black brows studied her in silence for a few moments.

"So you're the infamous Captain Shannon O'Donnell, of the privateer *Persephone*. You have a lot of nerve stealing two of our ships. As you can see, I've recovered part of our property already. I'm Nils Tarkon, by the way, and I'd like *Herja* back with all of its cargo intact."

She choked back questions about Drost and her crew before they could escape her mouth and gave him a scornful smile. "Just like that?"

Tarkon grinned, revealing large, yellowing teeth. "Just like that."

"You saw what we did to *Sigrun* and perhaps heard from your Pradyni hirelings about their unfortunate encounter with *Persephone*?"

"Sure." The grin widened. "You've done us a favor in sending the lizards to join their ancestors. They were beginning to show signs of wanting a bigger piece of the freelance pie."

"Then in what demented universe do you expect me to release *Herja*?"

"The universe in which I don't space the crew you put aboard *Skögul*." Something must have shown in her eyes because he chuckled. "Yes, Captain O'Donnell, they're alive and unharmed — for now. I figured you would end up here and thought they might be useful as barter and if not, I can always sell them. However, if you're willing to cooperate, I will find myself ready to release them and no hard feelings between us."

"Perhaps I can space Gar Vanger and his crew instead of cooperating."

Tarkon's hand rose in a dismissive wave. "You may do so at your leisure. I have no use for them anymore. A captain and crew who would surrender without firing a shot? Useless."

"You're a hard man to work for."

"And you're a danger to our continued operations. Here's the deal, Captain O'Donnell. It's non-negotiable, and a one-time only offer. You turn *Herja* and her cargo over to us, and we will turn your crew members over to you, alive and well."

Dunmoore, aware that all eyes in the CIC and all ears on the bridge were turned in her direction, replied, "If I refuse, you'll shove my people out the airlock one by one, and when that happens I'll destroy all three of your ships. It sounds like we have a stand-off."

Tarkon's earlier chuckle turned into a derisive laugh. "Good luck trying to destroy us with an overweight armed freighter. You might have been able to blast *Sigrun* to bits, but Diane Nilla wasn't one of the smartest captains in the corporation, and you had the element of surprise on your side. Vanger? A coward and a fool. No, Captain O'Donnell, you have no chance against three of us at once, especially not in Barataria's vicinity. It has a bite that's put stronger ships than yours out of business. Now, do we make the exchange, or do I shove bodies through the airlock?"

Instead of replying, Dunmoore turned to Sirico. "Unmask."

Once the rumble of plates moving aside and turrets rising had subsided, she caught Tarkon's dark eyes again and waited for them to widen once his own sensor techs reported.

"Here's my amendment to the deal," she said. "*Herja* for my crew, but you tell me how you recaptured *Skögul*, why you're so insistent on retrieving the freighter, and who hired you to raid Toboso."

Tarkon stared at her in silence, his jaw muscles working. After a long exhalation, he said, "Now I understand why the Pradyni failed so miserably, and why Vanger surrendered so quickly. We didn't notice how well-armed you were when we ran for Cervantes's hyperlimit. You're a damned Q-ship and the biggest I've ever seen. Are you sure you're privateers?"

"Answer my questions, and we can discuss how best to conduct the exchange. If all goes well, we'll part ways in a few hours and as you said, no hard feelings between us."

He nodded once. "Very well. All of our ships have a command override code allowing another of our ships to take remote control and lock out the crew. The last of the Pradyni, panicked out of his lizard brain, ran for our rendezvous point with *Skögul* on its tail. You can ask your prize captain how she felt when she came face-to-face with *Skalmold* and *Sanngrior*. We opened a com link, and when your folks made the mistake of accepting it, we transmitted the command override. That was the end of it. Thankfully, your prize captain was smart enough to surrender, and before you wonder whether you can make Vanger cough up the codes, I've had them all changed the moment we took *Skögul* back. Good enough?"

Dunmoore nodded. "Good enough. Next question."

"Why do I want *Herja* and its cargo back? We were engaged to do a job, and if I let you keep it and what it carries, I won't have fulfilled the contract. We receive the second part of our payment once the cargo is sold and the folks who hired us get their cut. Besides, these are people we would be wise not to cross, you included, for all your size and firepower."

"If you know they're not to be crossed, you know who they are. Third question, Captain Tarkon. Answer it, and we can discuss the nuts and bolts of the exchange."

"I don't have the first clue about their identity, Captain O'Donnell. No one knows who they are, but it's been made clear they can reach out as far as Barataria if they wish to express their disappointment."

"Then I'll ask another question instead of that one. Who were your contacts on Toboso?"

Tarkon shrugged. "Again, no clue. Our employers were careful to keep everything compartmentalized. We were to send two innocuous messages via two different frequencies, the first a day before we entered orbit, the second shortly before triggering the attack. I have no idea what the first one was in aid of, but the second one resulted in Toboso's satellite constellation going dormant. Now, enough with the questions, Captain O'Donnell. Time to arrange the exchange and it'll be on my terms."

"Feel free to state them."

"First, we keep our current separation, meaning you'll decelerate until you match our velocity."

"Done." She glanced at Holt's hologram. "You heard the man."

"Immediately, Captain," he replied.

"Second," Tarkon continued, "you'll take your crew off *Herja*. They'll open a link with my ship before leaving, and we will take remote control. Third, you'll send one of your shuttles, also on remote control, to dock with *Skögul*. There, it'll take on your crew. Recover the shuttle, bugger off and never return to this part of the galaxy again."

Dunmoore shook her head. "Wrong. We'll send a remotely piloted shuttle to take our crew off *Skögul* while *Herja* moves to place itself halfway between us. Once that's done, the shuttle will join with *Herja* to pick up its prize crew after they give you remote control. You may keep your guns on the shuttle until I recover it to make sure I won't double-cross you, and I will keep mine on *Herja*. You can take it, or you can experience what your Captain Nilla felt in the moments before her death. I'm assuming you don't want Vanger and his crew back."

He stared at her again, jaw working, then dipped his head once in acknowledgment. "Fine, we'll do it your way, and you can keep Vanger. I've already appointed a new captain and scrounged up a crew. I expect to see your shuttle dock with *Skögul* in one hour."

The screen went dark and the projection dissolved.

"I hope you don't intend to hand the stolen naval stores back to him," Holt said.

"No, I don't. If we can't have them, they won't either, but the first objective is to extract Lieutenant Drost and her crew. The second objective is to destroy *Herja*. The third is to destroy the rest of Tarkon's ships. I'll be happy to accomplish the first, and I may have an idea how to do the second." She tapped her communicator. "CIC to engineering, captain here."

"Yes, Captain," Lieutenant Commander Halfen replied a second or two later.

"We're about to pull the prize crew off *Herja* and return her to the enemy in exchange for Lieutenant Drost and her people, but I'd rather not let them have it. Is PO Lukas capable of rigging the missiles *Herja*'s carrying to explode when the ship attempts some sort of maneuver such as going FTL? Do it so that a civilian or a mercenary wouldn't be able to tell and do it in the space of an hour?"

A grim chuckle sounded over the link with engineering. "You're not asking for much, are you, Captain? Lukas is no armorer, even if he's a damn fine engineer. Chief Henkman's the one you want to be talking to. Perhaps he can guide Lukas through it if that sort of booby-trap is even possible."

Sirico held up a finger, then spoke into his communicator, presumably to Henkman down in the missile bay. After listening to the reply, he said, "It can't be done. Henkman suggests it might be possible to bypass a warhead's fail-safes, arm it while still in the transport pack, and activate a delayed fuse to blow in an hour or two. He can try to talk Lukas through the process."

"In that case, if he can make it so that we're able to disarm the warhead remotely so much the better. Mister Holt, pass the word to Lieutenant Kremm and prepare the shuttle. Mister Sirico, keep active targeting on all three of Tarkon's ships. The moment he tries to screw us over, I'll be gifting them a full salvo, and I'd like him to remain aware of that fact."

"Won't you be gifting him a full salvo anyway?"

"Of course, once we've recovered everyone, but he doesn't need to know."

"Shame we can't find a way to keep *Herja*," Holt said. "I think we'll end up expending a lot of our remaining ammo shortly."

"We can always let them go," Dunmoore suggested with a hint of mischief in her tone.

"In that case, I doubt we'll be able to beg the Admiralty for mercy if they take issue with our violating General Order Fifty-Three, even though we've disguised ourselves as privateers."

"You didn't think I'd let a cold-blooded bastard like Tarkon get away with mass murder, did you? Speaking of murderers, have Vanger brought up to the conference room. It's time I canceled my arrangement with him. He conveniently forgot to tell us about the command override."

*

"Good day, Captain." Vanger stopped on the threshold and gave Dunmoore an abbreviated bow. "To what do I owe an interview during battle stations, and in restraints to boot?" He held up his shackled hands. When Vanger made as if to sit, she shook her head, and the soldiers of his escort seized him by the upper arms.

"Would you care to tell me," Dunmoore asked in that sweet and reasonable tone her crew had identified as a harbinger of peril, "why you so conveniently forgot to mention the command override system on Orion Outcomes ships? Could it be because you hoped that Tarkon would find a way to retake *Skögul* and exchange my prize crew for yours?"

The mercenary tried to shrug, an embarrassed smile briefly crossing his face. "Would you believe forgetfulness?" When her stare didn't waver, he said, "I guess not."

"Tarkon has retaken *Skögul* and now holds my prize crew prisoner. He's proposed an exchange."

"Oh?" Vanger's face lit up with hope.

"Indeed. My people for *Herja*, which we cut out from Barataria the other day. He has no interest in you or yours. In fact, he told me I was free to space the lot of you if I wanted. Would you like to hear what he said?" Before Vanger could answer, Dunmoore played the relevant part of the transmission and took a measure of joy at seeing his face blanch. When the playback stopped, she said, "If we had known about the command override, *Skögul* would still be ours, as would *Herja* and I would honor my part in the terms under which you surrendered. However, you tried to play it both ways, didn't you? If Tarkon retook your former ship, he'd exchange prisoners, and you'd be back where you started. If Tarkon didn't, we'd eventually let you go. Too bad your former boss seized *Skögul* but doesn't want you back. I can understand why."

"What happens to us now?" Vanger asked in a voice barely above a whisper.

"Do I really need to spell it out? You've lost your prisoner of war status, and I will hand you to the authorities on charges of piracy. It goes without saying that there will no longer be any exercise periods, entertainment or other amenities. Since we'll soon find ourselves low on fresh food, you'll be eating ration bars starting today. I don't intend to see you enjoy the same standard of catering as my crew and Marines. You gambled and lost. I'd recommend you take the lesson to heart, but once a court finds you guilty…"

"That's hardly fair, Captain." Vanger seemed to recover some of his bravado. "I upheld my part of the deal. You found Barataria and the rest of the ships that raided Toboso. It's not my fault if your prize captain was stupid enough to accept an incoming transmission. Or that you're sentimental enough to exchange something as valuable as *Herja*'s cargo for a few lives."

Dunmoore stared at Vanger with eyes cold enough to make him shiver, and when the mercenary looked away, she said, "Take him back to the brig, Corporal."

Holt found her a few minutes later, alone in the conference room, fists clenched hard enough to distend the leather of her gloves.

"How did Vanger take his change of status?"

Dunmoore glanced up at her first officer. "As you'd expect."

"Then why are you quivering with anger?"

"Because I almost reached across the table to tear his throat out."

The first officer gave her a wan smile. "Since there's no blood on the bulkheads, I assume the bastard's still alive. More's the pity, I suppose, but he will get what's coming soon enough, and without you having to sully yourself. I've come to tell you the shuttle has left, *Herja* is on her way, and Chief Henkman seems to think he and Lukas have a good booby-trap going."

"In that case, I had better return to the CIC and you to the bridge." She extended her fingers and waggled them. "Perhaps venting my spleen on Tarkon will make up for letting Vanger live."

— Thirty-Two —

The rattle of the cargo hold's inner door yanked Lieutenant Astrid Drost out of a trance that was part self-recrimination, part misery, and part hopelessness. Though her prize crew, beaten and battered by the mercenaries during their recapture of *Skögul* was still alive, she figured it would not last. Her sole consolation was the knowledge that *Iolanthe*'s cover identity remained intact. Once it became apparent that escape would not be an option, her crew had destroyed everything that could link them back to the Navy and wiped the transponder. As far as the mercenaries knew, they came from a privateer named *Persephone* under the command of Captain Shannon O'Donnell. Perhaps it was the only reason they had been allowed to keep their lives up to now. If the mercenaries had identified them as Fleet personnel, death would have come more swiftly. As it was, they had been kept in the hold, legs shackled and fed nothing other than ration bars for the last week.

The door swung aside, admitting a pair of armed men who aimed their scatterguns at the prisoners sitting against the far bulkhead. A third mercenary entered on their heels, this one with his weapon slung over his shoulder.

"This is your lucky day, folks," he said. "Your captain and mine have come to an agreement, and part of that agreement has us turning the lot of you over to her."

When neither Drost nor her crew reacted, he shook his head. "Can't please anyone around here, can I? We're taking you to the port airlock where one of your shuttles is about to dock."

"Are we really being exchanged?" Drost asked, her mind whirling with questions, not least about how Dunmoore had won their freedom. If the mercenary was telling the truth. "Or will you shove us out an airlock minus our pressure suits and this is just an easy way to get us there without resistance?"

He stared at her for a few moments, hands on his hips. "Not a trusting lot, are you? Get up. We're going to shackle your hands, so no one has any funny ideas, then put you aboard that shuttle. I'll be happy to see you gone without leaving a bunch of flash-frozen bodies in my wake. You've stunk up the hold long enough."

Drost climbed to her feet and held out her hands, wrists together, quickly imitated by the others. The mercenary slapped restraints over them with practiced ease, then led the way to the port airlock. All the while, Drost tried not to get her hopes up. Lying to prisoners facing execution was a time-honored practice. But when she saw the interior of one of *Iolanthe*'s shuttles through the open hatch, her spirits soared, even though she realized it had no pilot on board.

The mercenaries shoved them into seats and fastened their manacles to the frames. When they had secured her crew, a pair of men carried a large metallic box through the airlock and bolted it to the shuttle's deck by the cockpit.

"A little something to make sure your captain doesn't think about chasing us after we've done the exchange," one of the said. "If she takes this shuttle aboard without disarming the device, it'll blow out your hangar deck the moment you try to go FTL. This little beauty has an active anti-tampering device so I would recommend no one touch it until Captain Tarkon shuts the detonator down once we're clear. Then, all you have to worry about is setting it off because none of your lot knows his ass from a hole in the ground." He winked at Drost. "Have fun."

The mercenaries stepped through the airlock again, and it slammed shut behind them. As the shuttle broke free of *Skögul*, a new voice came on, startling Drost.

"Hi folks, it's your friendly remote pilot, Gus Purdy, speaking. Just to let you know a few things as I take you home. One, we've been listening in, and the captain knows about the explosive device. Two, we're stopping off at the freighter *Herja* along the way to pick up its prize crew. As you may recall, *Herja*'s carrying most, if not all of the naval stores stolen on Toboso."

"The price of our freedom, I would imagine," Drost said in a bitter tone. "Wouldn't it be smarter to send another shuttle for *Herja*'s prize crew rather than have them sit on a bomb with the rest of us?"

"No can do at this point. Sit tight and try to enjoy the ride as much as possible. Top explosives experts are pondering the problem as we speak."

"Shit," Chief Larson said, "if he's talking about Henkman, we're in trouble."

"Why?" Sub-Lieutenant Protti asked.

"Because Henkman likes to make things go boom, not stop them from doing so."

"Right now, Chief Henkman is otherwise occupied," Purdy said.

"Like that's supposed to help," Larson grumbled. "Fly the damn thing, Gus, and stop trying to make us feel better."

*

"You really think it'll work?" Petty Officer First Class Vladimir Lukas, *Herja*'s chief engineer for what little time the prize crew had left aboard, glanced up at the portable projection screen showing Chief Henkman and the warhead mock-up the latter had put together for Lukas' benefit.

"Like a charm, Vlad. Like a charm. You did good for a newbie. I'll buy you a beer in the mess tonight to wet your new status as a guy who makes things go boom."

"As long as the warhead doesn't go off while we're still anywhere near, I suppose." Lukas sounded dubious.

"It won't. Time to seal the warhead again and repackage the bird, so no one's the wiser. I'm told the shuttle's left *Skögul* already."

Lieutenant Kremm stuck his head into the cargo hold just as Lukas finished stowing the last of the ammo containers back atop the missile packs. "Time, PO. Our ride's here."

"Good thing I'm done, sir. Shame to blow all of this up, but better that than the ordnance coming back at us with a vengeance. There." He stepped out of the stevedore exoskeleton, now that it was once more secured against the bulkhead. "Chief Henkman doesn't think it'll go off prematurely, but why take chances?"

They joined the remaining three members of *Herja*'s prize crew in the airlock moments before the remotely piloted shuttle docked with a loud thunk. When its hatch slid aside, Kremm climbed aboard only to freeze when he saw twenty-five of his shipmates shackled to their seats.

"Glad to see you guys are alive," he said, recovering from his surprise.

"It's not quite over yet," Drost replied, jerking her chin at the metallic box containing the explosive device. "That's a bomb, designed to keep us busy while the bastards make their getaway. The thing supposedly has an anti-tamper device so please don't touch it."

"I guess we're not the only ones getting sneaky," Kremm replied, waving his crew into the remaining seats.

"What do you mean?"

"Hang on. Let's make sure they're not listening to us." He pulled out a handheld sensor and ran it over the device. "The buggers weren't lying. That reads like something designed to go boom, but no transmitter. Only a receiver."

"They won't get far with *Herja*. PO Lukas received a crash course in IED construction from Chief Henkman."

"Good." Drost nodded once. "If we can't have the supplies, then no one should. Now could someone please figure out how to remove these damned restraints?"

*

"Sneaky bastard." Sirico shook his head after hearing the mercenary describe the device placed aboard *Iolanthe*'s shuttle. "You can't trust anyone nowadays."

"In all fairness," Dunmoore gave him a wry half-smile, "we've done the same to him. I hope he doesn't also intend to set his IED off."

"Tarkon knows if he does, we'll chase him round perdition's flames before we give him up."

She tilted her head in a gesture of admiration. "Quoting from Melville's Moby Dick? Well done, Thorin. I hadn't figured you were one for the classics."

Sirico's swarthy face darkened a shade more. "That would be your influence, sir. It's hard to hold up your side of the conversation at the captain's table without a thicker veneer of classical education than what the Academy forced down our throats."

Holt's hologram chuckled. "He's got you there."

"Tarkon will not become my white whale, Number One. I can assure you of that. Prepare another shuttle to take our people off the booby-trapped one, but let's try to place *Iolanthe* between the murderous bastards and both shuttles so they can't see what we're up to and trigger the IED."

"Then, once we've recovered our crew, we can chase them to our heart's content." Sirico nodded. "Will we be abandoning the shuttle?"

"Only until we've taken care of our piratical friends over there. Then Chief Henkman can see whether it's removable or not. If it isn't, your folks can enjoy a round of gunnery practice."

"The shuttle has left *Herja*," Yens reported. "It's heading for us now."

Dunmoore settled back into the command chair and tried to keep her impatience from showing, but had to stop her dancing fingers more than once.

"We're launching recovery craft now," Holt said from the bridge.

"Nudge *Iolanthe* to port so we can mask the incoming shuttle as soon as possible."

"Captain," Yens raised her hand, "the enemy ships appear to be breaking out of orbit instead of heading for Barataria."

*

"Folks, it's your friendly remote pilot again." Purdy's voice momentarily stilled the low rumble of nervous conversation in the shuttle's passenger compartment. "One of my mates is flying out another craft to meet you. She'll dock belly to top and take you off. Don't worry about the enemy seeing it, big momma will mask us. Make sure you take your belongings because we'll be abandoning this one, at least until we've dealt with the scum."

"Good." Relief flooded Drost's face. "I don't trust the lying bastards one bit."

"Neither does the captain." Kremm patted her shoulder. "She wants us back safe and sound."

"Speaking of which," Drost replied in a whisper so only her colleague could hear, "I don't look forward to standing in front of her and explain how I gave away *Skögul*, forcing her to give away the freighter with the loot."

"You didn't force the captain to do anything, Astrid. She knows shit happens. There's no way she would ever abandon any of us if there was even the glimmer of a chance, general orders to the contrary be damned."

"It's still bloody embarrassing to have lost my first and only command."

"Yet you didn't lose a single crew member, and I think that's what Dunmoore will remember when she writes up your annual efficiency report. You know how many ships she's lost to enemy action over the years, right? She even faced a court-martial over one of them."

Drost raised a hand in surrender. "If that's you trying to make me feel better, please stop. I don't need thoughts of a court-martial dancing through my head right now."

"Hello, there." A new voice, this one female, sounded over the speakers. "Eve Knowles here, with your connecting flight. You're about to experience a bit of a bump as I dock with your top side. Once I give you the go, open her up and climb on. Last one off shuts your shuttle's hatch."

"I'll do it, PO," Kremm replied.

Moments later, true to her word, Petty Officer Third Class Knowles mated the two craft with a muffled thud. "All's good. Climb aboard."

Chief Larson reached up to unlock the hatch and pulled it aside, revealing the pilot's smiling face. A Jacob's ladder dropped from the ceiling, and Kremm ushered the others up and out. When Drost, second last to leave, had pulled her legs up and out of the way, he climbed up the ladder, hauling himself into the rescue craft. Once aboard, he dropped to the deck, reached through the opening, and pulled up the heavy hatch with a grunt.

When Kremm heard it locking into place, he said, "You can close up and kick us free, PO Knowles."

"Closing up and kicking free, aye," she replied from the cockpit. The hatch in the middle of the deck pivoted and dropped into place, then, after a brief pause, followed by another loud mechanical noise, Knowles spoke again. "We're clear."

"Not a moment too soon," Drost muttered, her shoulders drooping as the anxiety and fear of the past days bled off.

*

"Everyone's off," Holt reported. "We're pushing the booby-trapped shuttle away now."

"As soon as we've recovered our folks, break orbit and follow in Tarkon's wake."

"Considering their rate of acceleration," Holt cautioned, "it might turn into a long stern chase. Since they have our reloads..."

"Our reloads are scheduled to transform into small debris shortly, Number One, perhaps significantly affecting their rate of acceleration, but point taken."

"Shit." Yens' voice cut through the soft murmur of the CIC. "The remotely piloted shuttle just blew up. Thank God we recovered our people in time."

"How's PO Knowles' shuttle?"

"Safe. The bomb was a good one thousand kilometers out before it went."

Dunmoore bit back a surge of anger. "Get me a comlink with Tarkon, Mister Holt."

"That would be in aid of what, Captain?"

"In aid of venting my spleen, unless you'd like to be the target…"

"Comlink coming up," the holographic rendering of the first officer grinned up at her, Holt not put out in the least by his captain's sharp tongue, "and as soon as we've secured the shuttle, we'll pour on the gees."

The minutes passed in relative silence, then just as Dunmoore was about to inquire about the holdup, a voice said, "Shuttle recovered, hangar deck secure."

"Captain," Holt's image looked up at her again, "Tarkon is refusing to answer, but as you heard, we're now clear to pursue."

"In that case, pour on the acceleration and keep pinging the buggers. I want to see Tarkon's face before he dies. Or failing that, his face when *Herja* vanishes in a bright flare once PO Lukas' IED goes off and collapses her antimatter containment units." She glanced at the tactical projection again and decided it would be best to spend the next few hours in private rather than fidgeting in public. "I'll be in my day cabin. Once Lieutenant Drost has had time to freshen up, I'd like her to join me for a coffee."

— Thirty-Three —

"Sailing Master reporting to the captain as ordered." Drost stood on the threshold to Dunmoore's day cabin, fatigue imprinted on her narrow features, eyes glimmering with anxiety.

"Come in, Astrid. Make yourself a coffee and take a seat. I'd like to know what happened after you left us to pursue the last Pradyni." Dunmoore's tone was deliberately soft and welcoming. She knew only too well how the younger woman felt after losing her first command to the enemy.

"Yes, sir. Thank you, sir." Drost stepped over to the urn, her gestures shaky and abrupt, outward signs of inner turmoil.

When she had a cup in hand, Dunmoore pointed at a chair across from her desk. "I'm glad everyone came back alive, and that's commendable."

"But you'll not commend me for losing *Skögul*." Bitterness oozed from every word.

"The fortunes of war, Astrid. Sometimes they blow against us until everything sucks." Dunmoore gave her a sad smile. "Or as they say, shit happens. Vanger forgot to tell us about the command override and for that, the terms of his surrender are void. He and his crew will face justice and if found guilty, they'll either be condemned to death or to such a long sentence in a penal unit they'll beg for summary execution."

"Good." A spark of anger stiffened Drost's spine. She took a sip of her coffee, eyes focused on something only she could see, and sighed. "We ran the Pradyni down within a day and tore him to shreds, not realizing he'd led us into Tarkon's arms. His ships were running silent because we only picked them up after finishing off the lizards. At two to one odds, I tried to run, but we were still cycling the hyperdrives, so it became a sublight stern chase between evenly matched ships. When Tarkon called us, I made the mistake of opening a link. Next thing we knew, he'd taken control of *Skögul* and ordered us to surrender. We barely had time to dispose of anything that might identify us as Navy and wipe the transponder. When his people stepped aboard, they weren't gentle even though we offered no resistance." She touched the purplish bruise beneath her right eye. "They questioned us, but we convinced them that *Iolanthe* was a privateer by the name *Persephone*, Captain Shannon O'Donnell, commanding. After that, they confined us to *Skögul*'s cargo hold, on water and ration bars. At first, we didn't know why they let us live, but after a few days, they hinted we could either sign on with them or they'd sell us off as slaves. Fortunately, before they made anyone face that decision, you came along and bartered for our lives with *Herja*. Sorry about that, sir."

Dunmoore waved away her apology. "It doesn't matter now. The important thing is that you're all alive and back aboard *Iolanthe*. Tarkon will get what's coming to him soon enough, and if we didn't recover the stolen supplies, at least we'll have denied them to the thieves. That'll be good enough for the Admiralty, under the circumstances."

"Does that mean I won't be court-martialed for losing *Skögul*?"

A delighted peal of laughter escaped Dunmoore's throat. "Whatever gave you the idea that anyone might proffer charges? Losing a prize is hardly in the same league as losing a Commonwealth starship. *Skögul* fits in the easy come, easy go column. As for *Herja*, your lives are more important to the Fleet than naval stores."

"That's a relief." Drost's smile, although tentative, wiped away much of the weariness that had lined her face. She took another gulp of coffee, her body visibly relaxing. "I'm ready to return to my usual duties now, sir. I'd like to be the one who navigates *Iolanthe* into a position where we can deal with those scum once and for all."

"Glad to hear it, Astrid. I'm sure the first officer will be happy to put you back on the OOW rotation. With both you and Theo gone, he's been picking up the odd watch himself."

"I'm not surprised, sir. He'll probably be mad at me if he finds out I've told you, but Mister Holt often relieves us, especially during the night watches when he's feeling restless, so we can take a breather, have something to eat and the like."

Dunmoore snorted. "That would explain why I've so often found him on the bridge when he's supposed to be off duty. He always functioned with less sleep than most people. No worries, your secret's safe with me."

A soft chime sounded, and Holt's face appeared on the day cabin's primary display.

"Speak of the devil," Dunmoore grinned at him. "We were discussing your virtuous habits, Zeke."

"That would have been a very brief conversation. Tarkon's condescended to speak with you."

"Put him on." Holt glanced at Drost, then back at Dunmoore who nodded. "Let's let him see that his IED didn't kill the intended target, shall we?"

"Indeed."

Holt's face faded out, replaced moments later by Tarkon, whose piggish eyes immediately widened when he noticed Drost. "Your people survived, Captain. The speed with which you recovered them is commendable."

"So you intended to kill them all along, is that it?"

"Not particularly. I intended to let you disarm my present, then trigger a second detonator on a ten-minute timer once it entered your shuttle hangar, said detonator connected to another device hidden within the main IED. The little maneuver you pulled changed my timetable. Once we lost sight of your shuttle..." he shrugged. "It seems that I didn't cause you any damage. Too bad, but I don't see how you can catch up with us nonetheless. We have you beat on the acceleration front, and if you told Ragetti the truth about getting low on ammo, you won't lob shots at extreme range hoping to make me decelerate. You have your people back, I have my ships back. Shall we let bygones be bygones and go our separate ways now? There's no profit in continuing to feud."

"I was hired to retrieve the items you stole on Toboso and put you out of business, Tarkon. That's where my profit lies. I'm willing to let you go if you turn *Herja* back over to me. She'll get me most of my payment. Failing that, I'll keep on your ass until I'm within optimum firing range. Once that happens, I'll wipe you off the face of the galaxy and take *Herja* anyway. Make no mistake, I will catch you. Your remote control trick won't work in hyperspace, and we haven't seen you send a crew over yet, so even if you are approaching the hyperlimit, you're not going FTL anytime soon."

Tarkon's attempt at derisive laughter sounded forced to Dunmoore's ears, and that meant he was far from convinced that he could outrun her forever. "As a famous man once said, *molon labe*."

"An educated pirate, I'm impressed, but you're not King Leonidas, I'm not Xerxes, and this isn't Thermopylae. I'll give you high marks for defiance, but low marks for realism. Sure, my rate of acceleration isn't as impressive as yours, but that'll serve you only for so long. Better you accept a partial defeat now instead of facing total disaster later."

"I see you're equally well up on your Plutarch, Captain O'Donnell, but I'll decline your offer. As I mentioned, a fair chunk of my profit lies in delivering what *Herja* carries, so I'll have to risk your wrath. As long as I can keep a comfortable distance from your ship, I don't fear its firepower."

"It'll be your funeral, Tarkon." She glanced at the time display. "I already hear the Grim Reaper sharpening his scythe."

Something in her tone must have given him pause. His eyebrows knitted, and he asked, "What do you mean?"

"Do you think you're the only devious, lying scoundrel with explosives experts among his crew?"

Tarkon stared at her without speaking for a few moments. "You—"

"Yes, we booby-trapped one, or perhaps even both of your ships while they were under our control. At any moment now, you could find yourself buffered by massive explosions. It'll be the end of Orion Outcomes. Sailing in such a tight formation is suitable for mutual protection against a big predator like me, but not so useful for surviving an antimatter containment failure, augmented by any number of nuclear explosions. It'll be enough to keep you from going FTL. After that, we'll catch up and give you the final blow."

"Bluff, pure bluff. Destroying *Herja* won't earn you payment for services rendered."

She shrugged. "Destroying *Skögul* and the rest of your ships will earn me enough to make it worthwhile, even if I don't bring home your ill-gotten loot. You can believe what you wish. It won't change the reality that's about to kick your pirate ass into the afterlife. Give me *Herja,* and you might escape. Stay obstinate, and you won't even have that faint hope."

Text scrolled on the secondary display, informing Dunmoore that the mercenaries were spreading their formation further apart.

"If you think I'm bluffing," she said, "why are you increasing the separation between your ships?"

"Taking a few precautions hurts no one while underestimating your opponent often does."

"Educated and wise." She glanced at the time again. "The Grim Reaper's almost here, Tarkon, but you're just about able to go FTL. Time to choose. Drop *Herja,* and you can try to make your getaway while I recover her."

A new text message from the bridge showed that one of the sloops had launched a passenger pod at the freighter.

"I'll have crew aboard *Herja* shortly," Tarkon replied. "Then all four of my ships will kiss you goodbye, O'Donnell. You won't come near enough to stop us now."

"In that case, we shall hunt you through hyperspace, and when you next emerge to cycle your drives, we'll be right there, except even closer and your chances of surviving will decrease accordingly. If not during that tack, then during the next one, and with any luck, you'll lead me to many exotic ports of call, places that need a good cleansing via nuclear fire. That should make Orion Outcomes popular in this sector. Speaking of popular, I hope you gave the poor sods in that passenger pod a good send-off. Your putting them aboard *Herja* is a guaranteed death sentence, which should do wonders for morale aboard your own garbage scow. I wonder what it would be like if she exploded while FTL... Do you think we'd ever find her wreckage?" Dunmoore gave him a predatory grin. "I don't believe that you can send her into hyperspace before the end, so the point is rather moot. However, we might witness *Skögul* attempting the experience. Wouldn't that be interesting? You drop out of FTL at the end of your jump and no *Skögul*. In fact, you never see her again."

Another message appeared on the secondary display. The passenger pod had returned to the sloop without reaching *Herja*. Dunmoore knew she had won this round, provided they could disarm the booby-trapped missile warhead before it blew. She looked up at the primary display again, only to watch Tarkon's expression twist into a grimace of distaste.

"It's been interesting, Captain O'Donnell, but I'll be saying my goodbyes now. *Herja*'s all yours and may you choke on her."

"You're leaving me with the loot? How generous of you."

"I've already lost one ship, and it's been made clear to me that losing more would be counter-productive."

The screen went dark. Shortly after that, *Iolanthe*'s first officer announced that the mercenaries had recovered their passenger pod and gone FTL.

"Have that warhead disarmed, Mister Holt," she said upon hearing the news.

"Already done. Chief Henkman's modification to the warhead has accepted the signal and stopped its countdown, but he wants to go aboard alone and dismantle it, in case it's a false return. Considering how much is left on the timer, it should be low risk. If the detonator hasn't shut off, it'll blow well before he reaches *Herja*."

"Go, and have Lieutenant Kremm stand by with his prize crew at a safe distance. The moment Henkman gives the all clear, they're to board. First order of business will be to find and disable the remote control function. If they can't disable it, they're not to accept communications from any ship other than this one. We still have a chase on our hands, and *Herja* needs to follow along."

Drost stood. "With your permission, sir, I'll head for the bridge and work on the pursuit course. If we can go FTL within the next two hours, we should be able to catch up and make contact."

"You heard that, Zeke?"

"Aye. Two hours. We'll make it, Captain. Astrid, your navigation plot awaits."

With a quick wave instead of a salute, Drost left Dunmoore to contemplate the image of the freighter that had replaced Tarkon's choleric face.

"I guess he figured you weren't bluffing," Holt said. "At least about *Herja*, knowing what she carried and how much time we had to prepare her."

"Probably, and he didn't believe me concerning *Skögul*, but I'll take one out of two right now. However, it's more likely that he ran the odds and decided his chances of survival were better if he tossed us a juicy bone as a distraction while making his getaway, booby-trap or not. He doesn't know we have Navy-grade sensors that can track ships in hyperspace better than anything he's carrying."

"It's a good thing you're into chess and not poker, Captain."

"Why? Because I'm good at bluffing or because I'm terrible at it?"

There was a moment of silence, then Holt replied, deadpan, "If you'll excuse me, sir, duty calls."

Dunmoore chuckled. "Coward."

"I prefer to call it a well-developed sense of self-preservation."

*

"The bastards wiped *Herja*'s navigation database, Captain," Kremm reported. "It has to be an Orion Outcomes SOP. We're having a copy transmitted from *Iolanthe*, but it'll take time. I'm still checking the rest of the computer core to make sure they didn't erase something vital. However, as far as I can tell, it has the standard safeguards preventing unauthorized modifications. Unfortunately, I haven't come across anything hinting at the remote control capability yet."

Dunmoore bit back a few choice words. The extra delay might just buy Tarkon a clean escape. "All right. Thanks for the update. Keep plowing through it. We'll leave when you're ready and if that's too late to catch their spoor, as I told Astrid earlier, the fortunes of war sometimes suck."

"Yep. Shit happens, but don't worry, there are still a few more tricks up my sleeve. I'd better get back to it."

"Thanks, Theo."

Kremm gave her a quick wave, and his image faded from the display. If only she could play a round of chess to help contain her growing impatience, but Holt was busy with his first officer duties, and none of the others had shown much interest in the game so far, or if they had, they kept it well hidden. Perhaps she should ask Major Salminen the next time she had a chance.

Dunmoore stood, walked across the day cabin to the bookshelf where she kept the few mementos that had followed her from ship to ship throughout this long war. She picked up a thick, centuries old book, gifted to her by *Stingray*'s wardroom the night before the frigate's decommissioning ceremony, Carl von Clausewitz's On

War. Unlike so many of his adherents, she did not take the old Prussian general's ideas as gospel, accepting them instead as the dialectic discussions on the nature and conduct of warfare they were intended to be. Heavy reading under any circumstances, but Clausewitz would quell her impatience for the next hour or so. She opened the book at random, falling on the chapter titled 'Perseverance' and smiled. It was the one that came after 'Boldness' and seemed entirely too apt for her present circumstances. Settling back into her chair, she read words printed four centuries earlier and written over two centuries before that, at a time when war on an interstellar dimension would have seemed the phantasm of a deranged mind. Yet Dunmoore fancied that given enough time to adapt, Clausewitz would have been able to perceive and point out the mistakes of a human general staff overwhelmed by campaigns spanning inconceivable distances. She preferred the simplicity of Sun Tzu's precepts, but understood the meaning behind a gift no doubt carefully selected by Gregor Pushkin, now captain of the frigate *Jan Sobieski*, and honored it accordingly.

*

"Captain, this is the bridge. *Herja* reports ready and is linked to our navigation plot. We can go FTL at your command."

Holt's voice jarred Dunmoore from her contemplation of Clausewitz. She glanced at the time display, and a predatory smile crept across her lips. Somehow, Kremm had managed to make it a mere minute under two hours.

"Sound jump stations."

"Sound jump stations, aye," Holt replied. A few seconds later, the public address system chimed. "All hands, now hear this, jump stations in sixty, that's six zero seconds. We will run the buggers to ground. That is all."

Exactly a minute later, the universe went sideways, and Dunmoore swallowed convulsively, fearing her last meal would escape with predictable results. When her stomach had returned to its usual spot, she stood, tugged her tunic into place, and gave her reflection in the day cabin mirror a wink. It was time to pretend calm and patience in the CIC, until that is, *Iolanthe*'s hyperspace bubble touched one belonging to a mercenary ship. Once that happened, Orion Outcomes' end would no longer be in doubt, at least as far as Dunmoore was concerned.

— Thirty-Four —

Emergence nausea yanked Dunmoore from a light sleep, leaving her half-disoriented. Before she could even roll out of her cot, the battle stations klaxon filled the ship with its mournful beat. Adrenaline shot through her body, making her nerves vibrate with anticipation. Like everyone on board, she had slept fully dressed, ready for action at a moment's notice. Dunmoore grabbed her personal protective gear and joined the stream of crew members rushing to their posts, though she tried to keep a statelier pace.

Iolanthe's sensors had touched the hyperspace bubble of at least one starship going FTL a little over twelve hours earlier. She must have lost it moments ago, indicating that her quarry had dropped to sublight velocity. If Guthren was at the helm, they would have followed a fraction of a second later, placing them almost within missile range. Upon entering the CIC, she glanced at the duty roster displayed on a side screen and noted that the coxswain had indeed taken a turn steering the Q-ship.

Sirico surrendered the command chair to her, saying, "Three contacts, five hundred and seventy thousand kilometers aft, moving at a constant speed. Helm has initiated deceleration meaning we will enter missile range shortly. *Herja*'s keeping station off our starboard beam."

"Thanks." She settled in and studied the tactical projection. Guthren's deft hand had placed them in an excellent position to intercept Tarkon's ships.

"Identity confirmed," Chief Yens said. "Those ships are *Skögul, Skalmold,* and *Sanngrior.* They've noticed us. We're being pinged." Then, "They're veering away to port."

"Got that," Holt said from the bridge. "Ceasing deceleration and changing course to conform. I'd have paid good money to see the bastard's face when he realized we followed him after all."

"So would I. Make sure we stay between them and *Herja* at all times," Dunmoore replied, "in case Tarkon decides that if he can't have her, nobody will."

"They're accelerating," Yens reported.

"They want to escape a meeting engagement and turn this back into a stern chase." Sirico nodded. "Not a bad tactic under the circumstances."

Dunmoore nodded towards the minimum time to jump counter in the bottom right corner of the main display.

"He still has a while to wait before he can go FTL again, even if he does a Crazy Ivan, and that gives us a chance to cut him off. Mister Holt, increase acceleration to maximum. We will attempt an intercept." She traced a course on her command chair's screen. It immediately appeared on the tactical projection and its bridge repeater. "I know it doesn't place us well to pursue if he jumps again, but even if we don't converge, it should open their flanks to our broadsides."

"Shall we unmask?" Sirico asked. "Since he already knows what we are, even if he still thinks we're privateers, we might as well bare our teeth."

"By all means. Turn *Iolanthe* into the avenging faerie of death we all love so much," with apologies to Messrs.

Gilbert and Sullivan, she mentally added. "And put a full-power targeting lock on them, so they have something more to worry about. We know they're still out of optimum range, but they don't necessarily understand that."

When the rumble of hull plates shifting and turrets rising ceased, Dunmoore sat back in her chair, knowing the time for showing infinite patience had come again. She turned to Major Salminen, sitting quietly at her now customary CIC station.

"We're in for another one of those stretches of boredom before we can unleash a fresh wave of terror. I've been meaning to ask, do you perchance play chess?"

Dunmoore did not see Sirico make frantic 'no' gestures at the soldier behind her back, but Salminen either ignored him or did not understand his meaning. She gave Dunmoore a shy smile and said, "Of course I do. It's a game almost everyone on Scandia plays."

"Good. For some reason, Commander Holt is the only one among my officers who plays, or is willing to admit an affinity for chess." She turned her head towards Sirico who had pasted an ingratiating smile on his face, one that did not fool her in the least. "Right, Thorin."

"Not my cup of tea, sir."

"Don't I know it." She chuckled. "Once this is over, I'll invite you to my day cabin for a match or two, Major. I find it helps me develop patience."

"Take this as a friendly warning." Sirico's tone tried to come across as innocent, with the same degree of success as his earlier smile. "The first officer has occasionally mentioned our captain considers chess a blood sport."

Salminen's smile broadened. "So do we Scandians. It'll be a pleasure, sir."

"Thank you, Major," Holt said. "Finally someone willing to help me shoulder the burden of keeping the skipper amused."

"If you two keep talking, the skipper will not be amused, follow which, neither will you," Dunmoore gave Sirico and Holt a mock scowl.

"Yes, sir. Shutting up now, sir." The combat systems officer turned back to his console but not before Salminen saw his smile. She shook her head at the way Holt and Sirico teased their captain while sailing into battle.

When Dunmoore noticed the amused gleam in her eyes, she winked. "Nothing beats the boredom leading up to those proverbial moments of sheer terror like a bit of banter, right?"

"If you say so, sir."

*

"Incoming transmission from Tarkon," Holt said, jolting Dunmoore from her contemplation of the tactical projection. *Iolanthe* was gaining ground on the mercenary sloops, something that had not escaped their senior captain's attention. The Q-ship had already entered effective missile range, but with stocks almost depleted, Dunmoore wanted to move into optimum range before opening fire.

"Put him on."

"Main or private?"

"At this point, does it matter?" She relented. "I suppose private would be better."

When Tarkon's bearded features materialized on her virtual screen, she asked, "What is this? Your version of ave Caesar, morituri te salutant?"

The man's laugh sounded especially forced. "Excellent, Captain O'Donnell. Splendid. Your classical education must have been excruciatingly complete."

"What do you want?" She asked in a bored tone.

"A return to the status quo ante. I give you *Skögul*, no harm, no foul, and we part ways for good. She's a good ship and worth a lot of money."

"So you're trying to buy your way out of a visit from the Grim Reaper? What makes you think I'd even glance at your offer, considering our recent history?"

"Profits, Captain. In our line of business, that's what counts. *Herja*'s already yours. I'll give you *Skögul*. You'll have everything to please your employers."

"You won't."

Tarkon shrugged. "Losses are inevitable. Living to profit another day is preferable to the alternative."

"Of course, *Skögul* will be thoroughly rigged to blow up in my face. No deal. Surrender all three ships. We will hand you over to Commonwealth authorities to be tried for your crimes on Toboso, and may the hangman enjoy his target-rich environment."

"What if I'd rather not face that fate?"

"Then I'll do the hangman's job here and now."

"You're not offering me any incentives, O'Donnell. An educated woman like you must understand Sun Tzu's precepts on leaving an enemy a way of escape, so he does not fight to the last like a cornered rat, taking much of his attacker's strength with him."

"I've studied Sun Tzu, thank you. The only truth you've spoken is characterizing yourself as a rat, and I'm not the Pied Piper, I'm the exterminator. You had the chance to surrender before using my crew as hostages before you tried to blow a hole in my hangar deck. I'm here to kill the lot of you and rid the galaxy of vicious parasites who think nothing of killing hundreds of innocents with kinetic strikes from orbit for mere profit. Since you can't tell me who hired Orion Outcomes, I see no further reason to keep any of you alive."

She spied Lieutenant Commander Sirico hoisting an upraised thumb out the corner of her eye, the signal that

Iolanthe had finally entered optimum engagement range. The timer on the main display still had not reached the minimum before they could do an emergency jump. Dunmoore nodded at her combat systems officer, authorizing him to launch the first volley of missiles. Moments later, she felt the vibration of the launchers through the soles of her boots.

"Perhaps I can tell you more…" Tarkon's voice died away as his eyes slid to one side. When he looked up at her again, his face had lost color. "Those are Commonwealth Navy anti-ship missiles. Who the hell are you?"

Another volley erupted from the missile bay's tubes, then another.

"Your worst nightmare, Tarkon."

"Fleet," he hissed, "you're a damned Navy Q-ship, not a privateer. No freelancer could carry so many naval issue missiles. The black market simply can't move them in more than ones and twos."

A cruel smile twisted her lips.

"Fortunes of war, old chap. You should have run the moment we entered the Cervantes system instead of trying to be clever by hiding out around Rocinante's moons. We would have never caught up with you if you had." One last brace of missiles left its launchers. "Sure, I'd have liked to take *Skögul* home as a prize. The Admiralty would more than likely have bought her into Service, earning my crew a pretty bonus, but I'll be happy with *Herja*. Of course, I'll be replenishing my own ammunition bunkers with what she carries, but then those were my reloads all along."

Tarkon's face lost its mask of disdain as his eyes went to one side again. Dunmoore could see him do the math in his head. So many missiles, so little time, and so much firepower waiting to be unleashed.

"I surrender, O'Donnell, damn you, name your terms," he growled in a belligerent tone. "I'll take my chances with a court of law. Call off your attack. My three ships are your prizes. You'll be earning a year's pay in the space of an hour."

She studied him in silence for a few seconds, then glanced at her readout. When she saw no sign of his ships dropping shields in the time-honored gesture of capitulation, she knew he was attempting to play for time, that his offer was a lie.

Dunmoore looked at him again and shrugged. "Since your shields are still up, it doesn't matter, does it? I hope you have a coin handy for the ferryman because you're about to cross the Styx."

Then, she made a cutting motion with her hand, and the signals petty officer severed the link. *Sanngrior*'s close-in defense calliopes opened fire moments later, followed by those of *Skalmold*. *Skögul*, bringing up the mercenary formation's rear, remained silent, however. The guns engaged *Iolanthe*'s first volley, and then the second. By the time the third came within range, the rapid-fire weapons showed signs of being overwhelmed. The fourth and final volley struck home, turning the two leading sloops' shields into ovoid auroras of blue and green as massive energy surges fought each other. Then, the first salvo from *Iolanthe*'s main guns struck *Sanngrior,* and its shields collapsed in a spectacular display of light. Black divots erupted from the ship's pristine hull as the first plasma shots hammered it hard. A lucky streak sliced through the pylon securing its port hyperdrive nacelle, sending it into a spin that inevitably intersected with the ship itself. The results were as spectacular as they were deadly. *Sanngrior* broke up, its atmosphere leaking through more holes than any damage control party could contain.

"Captain," Holt's voice broke through her intense concentration, "*Skögul* is signaling unconditional surrender. She's dropped her shields and powered down all of her systems. We have no choice but to accept this one."

"Unfortunately," Dunmoore said. "Mister Sirico, concentrate fire on *Skalmold*. *Skögul* is no longer a target."

"Acknowledged," the combat systems officer replied over his shoulder. "All fire on *Skalmold*."

Subjected to the entirety of *Iolanthe*'s firepower, Tarkon's own ship lasted little longer than its sister *Sanngrior*. Orion Outcomes' senior captain died in a bright flash of light, still cursing Dunmoore, or as he knew her, O'Donnell, and the fates that had them meet with such a deadly result.

Silence fell over the CIC once the flare of *Skalmold*'s demise faded.

"Two out of three's not bad," Sirico said with a touch of awe in his tone. "By the way, Captain, we've expended our entire missile stocks."

"All in a good cause, Thorin, all in a good cause. We'll transfer what *Herja*'s carrying before we go FTL again. Mister Holt, please have the second officer prepare a boarding party to retake *Skögul*. Same prize crew as before. Its current complement can join Vanger and company in our brig and, in due course, stand with them before a tribunal. If anyone is dumb enough to resist, let them know I don't really give a damn whether or not I take the sloop or its soon to be former crew home. I'm sure Mister Sirico's gunners and Major Salminen's troops won't mind a bit of practice."

An intense feeling of weariness engulfed Dunmoore, and she sat back in the command chair, eyes half-closed, taking deep, cleansing breaths.

"All right, folks, let's get this mess sorted out so we can return to Toboso and tie up loose ends. I would like one last full scan of *Sanngrior*'s wreckage, in case there are survivors we need to recover. I don't think there's enough left of *Skalmold* to worry."

— Thirty-Five —

"*Herja* and *Skögul* are in their appointed positions on either beam. Both report all clear," Lieutenant Commander Sirico announced shortly after *Iolanthe* and her prizes dropped out of FTL on the outer edge of the Cervantes system.

"Nothing on sensors within engagement range," Chief Yens added. "Probing out to five light minutes."

Their return to Commonwealth space had been mercifully devoid of dangerous encounters or other unwelcome events. The dozen mercenaries taken off *Skögul* had joined Vanger and his crew in the brig, facing an uncertain future. At least they were alive for now, unlike most of their comrades. *Iolanthe* had shed her privateer disguise a few hyperspace jumps ago and was now nothing more than the armed transport that had left Toboso several weeks earlier.

"Still no subspace relay buoy in the system," Lieutenant Kremm said a few minutes later, "but the automated fueling facility around Benengeli is broadcasting, and I've linked up with the Toboso orbital subspace station. It reports that all is well. Did you want me to advise the colonial government we're back?"

"No. Let's leave that until we're in orbit."

"I assume you want to avoid giving the traitor, whoever he or she might be, warning of our victorious return?" Holt asked.

"Exactly." She saw Yens give the all clear signal out of the corner of her eye and said, "you can place the ship at cruising stations, Number One. As soon as the drives have cycled, we'll make the final jump inward."

"May I suggest we stop at Benengeli before we make the final sublight tack to Toboso? Our fuel reserves have become a bit meager after our wild hunt into the Badlands, and since Benengeli and Toboso are almost in alignment, it wouldn't add much to our last leg in."

"Excellent idea, Mister Holt. Which one of our officers is next in line to handle the maneuver?"

"That would be Lieutenant Drost, who can top up *Skögul* at the same time as we fuel *Iolanthe*. With neither of us to jump in if she goes off track, she'll remember this one for sure. It means Sub-Lieutenant Pashar will take your command chair this time, and he doesn't look overly thrilled by the idea." Dunmoore could hear a hint of amusement in his tone. "But he understands that suffering is good for the soul. While we're at it, perhaps Lieutenant Kremm could refuel *Herja*. He would have taken his turn at proving his ability to execute the maneuver after Mister Pashar in any case."

"Sounds like a plan, Number One. Let's make it so." She climbed to her feet. "That being said, I'll be in my day cabin."

"Sorry I can't join you," Holt replied. "First officer business to take care of. Perhaps the Army can take this shift."

Dunmoore glanced at Salminen who nodded. "The Army will take this shift, Zeke. Don't complain if I find playing chess with you to have become utterly pedestrian."

*

"I would say that Astrid just erased her personal shame at losing *Skögul* the first time around," Holt whispered in a voice only Dunmoore could hear. The entire bridge and CIC crew had just witnessed Lieutenant Drost carry out a precise and error-free refueling maneuver.

"This would be the first time one of my lieutenants did so without me needing the surgeon and his defibrillator. Rin now has a high bar to clear," she murmured back at him.

"In all fairness, *Iolanthe*'s mass is enough to grant him a lot of leeway that Astrid didn't need with her little sloop. Besides, he has nowhere near her experience and seniority."

"Is Doc Polter standing by?"

"Rin will be okay, and so will you, skipper." Holt straightened and directed his gaze on the much-magnified navigation plot, with the Benengeli refueling station at its center.

Dunmoore nodded once, swallowed her response, and stood, stepping aside. "Mister Pashar, you have the chair."

"Aye, Captain."

Guthren gave Dunmoore a quick glance over his shoulder, wordlessly reassuring her he would not let anything spoil *Iolanthe*'s docking with one of the refueling station's buoys. If need be, he would ignore the officer of the watch's instructions in favor of his own experience, knowing she would give Pashar a very brief and very private lesson to explain why the coxswain had acted as he did.

Between them, Pashar and Guthren avoided aggravating Dunmoore's blood pressure issues more than necessary and soon enough, the Q-ship, fully fueled, dropped its mooring, and moved out of the way to allow *Herja* a turn at the spigot. The two prizes would remain Dunmoore's responsibility until the Admiralty decided their future and she preferred to have both prepared for any eventuality, even if the lightly armed freighter would be more of a liability than an asset, should she resume combat patrols. At least *Iolanthe* would stay well supplied in the meantime.

"Bridge, this is CIC."

"Captain here. Go."

"A new arrival dropped out of FTL at the hyperlimit. According to the transponder broadcast, it's the Colonial Office aviso *Leopold*."

"Looks like someone on Earth finally pulled his thumbs out of his backside and sent a fresh set of administrators," Holt said.

"Perhaps." Dunmoore's face took on a doubtful expression. "But avisos are small. Even the civilian versions are little more than a habitat pod stuck atop frigate-sized hyperdrives. It could hardly convey a new government, save for a few people, and not in the sort of comfort Colonial Office bureaucrats expect."

"We can call and ask," Holt suggested.

She shook her head. "No. Whoever that is deserves to be just as surprised by our return as anyone else. Something tells me it isn't the new governor with his or her closest staff. Even those appointed to backward colonies like Toboso prefer to travel in style. Besides," she studied the navigation plot, "we'll be arriving at almost the same time if Theo doesn't drag out *Herja*'s refueling."

"In that case, it's a good thing we kept our own transponders off; otherwise, we might be on the verge of receiving a hail fellow, well met, from *Leopold*."

"More like a who the — expletive deleted — are you and why are you here?" She replied, smirking. "You seem to forget that the Colonial Office and the Fleet aren't best friends. At least not in the corridors of power on Earth."

"No need to delete expletives, Captain. Everyone aboard has become familiar with your ability to curse."

"Only in moments of extreme emotion, Zeke."

Half an hour later, Dunmoore's misfit flotilla, as she thought of it, left the Benengeli refueling station in its wake, the ships aimed at Toboso.

*

"*Leopold* is hailing us," the signals petty officer of the watch reported.

"I was wondering how long it would take them," Dunmoore replied. *Iolanthe* and her companions had turned their naval transponders on just before passing Toboso's inner moon Dulcinea, so as not to spook the colonials. The Colonial Office aviso had entered orbit shortly beforehand. "Put them on."

A narrow, aristocratic face beneath carefully sculpted white hair replaced the dun-colored planet that had been dominating the bridge's main display. Piercing blue eyes met hers, and she felt a jolt of recognition, not of the man himself but of the family traits in his features and haughty expression.

"I am Colonial Office Special Envoy Mikhail Forenza," he said in a nasal, vaguely supercilious tone. "You are?"

"Captain Siobhan Dunmoore, commanding the Commonwealth Starship *Iolanthe*."

Forenza's eyes widened slightly in recognition at hearing her name, which could well indicate that HQ had passed her report to the Colonial Office without providing details about the naval presence in the Cervantes system. It did not seem likely that he knew she was the senior officer present.

"Then you must have known my late sister, Helen," he replied.

"I did." Dunmoore tried to keep from showing any emotion at the mention of Commander Helen Forenza, Dunmoore's Academy classmate and lifelong enemy, who had preceded her in command of the frigate *Stingray*, turning it into a dysfunctional mess that saw her relieved of command. Forenza had died in a traffic accident after a disciplinary board ordered her forcible retirement. "We weren't friends, Ser Forenza."

"I know, Captain. I most certainly know. You were appointed to take over her ship when she was removed from her post, weren't you?" When Siobhan did not reply, he allowed a disdainful expression to play on his lips. "Your career does not seem to have prospered either. Going from command of a frigate to that of an armed transport doesn't look like much of a step up to a civilian like myself, but I confess to insufficient knowledge of naval matters. By the way, what are these ships sailing in consort with yours?"

Dunmoore could almost sense Holt laying a mental restraining hand on her shoulder, lest she lose her temper. Instead, she gave Forenza a pleasant smile and said, "Those are the last two surviving ships of the five responsible for the attack on Toboso a few weeks ago. They're *Iolanthe*'s prizes. We took the freighter with most of the stolen supplies still aboard and have the crew of the sloop in our brig. The other three ships and their crews are nothing more than debris clouds in interstellar space."

The special envoy seemed momentarily taken aback by both her tone and her words, but he recovered just as quickly and inclined his head in an abbreviated bow though his tone held a faint sarcastic edge. "Most impressive, Captain. Shame you couldn't bring all the villains back to face justice."

Stung by his attitude, she replied, "Oh, I haven't finished rooting out those responsible for the deaths of your Colonial Office colleagues and the garrison of the Fleet depot. May I ask what your mission is?"

Forenza's eyes narrowed, and he said, "You may. I'm here to investigate the incident on behalf of the Colonial Secretary and offer recommendations as to the way forward with Toboso's governance. What might your mission be, Captain? Fleet headquarters was its usual opaque self in describing the Navy's involvement in the matter."

"I'm involved in this by pure happenstance. We showed up unannounced shortly after the raid, to take on supplies, and made it our aim to find and destroy the pirates responsible."

"I see. When you say you haven't finished rooting out those responsible, what is it you mean?"

Dunmoore mentally cursed herself for having spoken too much, but it was too late. She might as well use her mistake to good effect. "Someone paid the pirates to raid Toboso and destroy the two centers of Commonwealth government control on the planet with pinpoint accuracy, meaning an inside job of sorts. There's evil to uncover, Ser Forenza, both on Toboso and elsewhere. I intend to find and end it."

"Indeed. A most noble goal, I'm sure, but I wasn't aware that such investigations were in the Fleet's remit, let alone in that of a starship captain."

"Over two hundred of our people died, Ser Forenza, and one of our installations was destroyed. That makes it the Fleet's business, and as senior officer in the Cervantes system that makes it mine."

"I caution you that Toboso is the Colonial Office's jurisdiction. You may deal with military matters only, absent special permission from the governor."

Dunmoore restrained a smile at hearing the opening salvo in the inevitable bureaucratic turf war. He would not be happy to find out that the acting governor had tried to foist the entire colony off on her. And once her history on Toboso surfaced, as it inevitably would, things might turn downright unpleasant. That was without even thinking of the suspicions Chief Petty Officer Trane had raised about Anton Gerber's role in the matter.

"Of course," she replied with a cold smile tugging at her lips. "That goes without saying, Ser Forenza."

"Good. I'm glad to see we're in agreement." He turned his head to one side and nodded. "My captain tells me we're about to prepare for a landing in Doniphon, so I'll have to end this conversation now. I'm sure we'll have occasion to speak again soon. Good day."

The screen went dark with unexpected abruptness.

"Well wasn't that special," Holt said. "Helen Forenza's brother? Are you kidding me? The infernal gods of the galaxy are having a good laugh at your expense, Captain. I suppose we can be thankful our dear HQ gnomes treated the Colonial Office like mushrooms again, so no one on Earth, other than our own command knows what we're up to."

"Perhaps all of my sins are catching up with me at once." Dunmoore realized her muscles had tensed up, and she forced herself to relax. "Mind you, from what I remember there was little love lost among the Forenza siblings. I can't recall Helen ever saying a good word about her brother back during our Academy days."

"It could well have been reciprocated," Holt replied. "I sensed little if any emotion when he mentioned her name."

She sat back, gloved fingers dancing on the command chair's arm. "Now what did he mean by offer recommendations as to the way forward with Toboso's governance, I wonder?"

"If I let my old counter-intelligence paranoia raise its ugly head, I'd say there's more to that statement than meets the eye and it might be related to recent events. After all, he is a Forenza, member of an old and well-connected family that has fallen on hard times. Perhaps the Colonial Office is playing games in a backwater of the war while no one is paying attention."

"Or someone with a lot of pull within the Colonial Office is. I think I'll pay Acting Governor Gerber a visit once we're in orbit. Please have the pinnace prepared. I'll take a pilot this time rather than fly myself."

"Other than Vincenzo, who would you like in your party?"

Dunmoore thought about it for a few seconds and then grinned at her first officer. "How about a squad of Major Salminen's finest? A little reminder that *Iolanthe* can project ground power as well as dominate the high orbitals."

"You're expecting trouble?"

"I don't know what to expect, but I get the feeling this might turn messy before it's over."

"So do I."

"At least seems as if Gerber has moved his administration back to Doniphon and away from Strother Martin's private domain in Valance. Otherwise Forenza's ship wouldn't be landing there."

"Small mercies, I suppose."

"Infinitesimally small."

— Thirty-Six —

Dunmoore's shuttle, with Petty Officer Purdy at the controls, landed in the shadow of the Colonial Office aviso on the edge of the Doniphon spaceport. Though tiny compared to *Iolanthe*, its drive nacelles alone dwarfed her craft.

A rather glum Chief Petty Officer Trane sat beside Vincenzo in the passenger compartment, both surrounded by the better part of Command Sergeant Saari's platoon. She had decided, at the last minute, to bring Trane along under the pretext of wanting to make arrangements for handing their prisoners over to the colonial authorities. What she really wanted to witness was how the former Sigma Noctae operations chief and Anton Gerber would react upon coming face-to-face. It would tell her a lot about Trane's story concerning the late Lieutenant Duff and his involvement with Toboso's notables, including the acting governor.

The Scandia Regiment soldiers, though wearing battledress with the sky blue beret common to all three branches of the Commonwealth Armed Services instead of their more intimidating armor, nonetheless carried their long arms as well as holstered blasters. At Sergeant Saari's signal, they jogged down the aft ramp and formed into ranks. When Dunmoore stepped out into Toboso's wan sunshine, he barked out a word of command, and twenty carbines snapped up in a perfectly executed present arms. She knew they had been under observation since the moment her shuttle appeared unannounced above the colony's capital and hoped the spectacle would keep observers wondering about her purpose.

Once they completed their exchange of salutes, the platoon dispersed into a loose formation, by squads, covering Dunmoore, Trane, and Vincenzo on all sides. For a moment, she wondered whether such a large, armed escort might not seem a tad overwrought, then Saari ordered the formation into motion, and they headed for the temporary Colonial House. Gerber had established it inside the Doniphon spaceport's main administration building, to take advantage of its communications facilities, something her signals chief had determined before she left *Iolanthe*.

Once there, she left the soldiers outside taking only the chief and her bodyguard. Inside, helpful signs pointed them to the governor's office on the second level, where the governor's aide greeted them.

"Captain Dunmoore." He inclined his head politely. "I assume you're here to see Governor Gerber."

"I am."

"You'll have to wait a while. He's conferring with the Colonial Office envoy and the senior leaders of the Toboso governing council."

"Governing council? When we left a few weeks ago, I was under the distinct impression that Ser Gerber opposed the creation of such a body."

The aide held out his hands, palms up. "What can I say? Things change, Captain."

"Who might these senior leaders be?" A dangerous edge crept into Dunmoore's tone.

He hesitated. "The most notable citizens of Toboso, of course. Andrew Devine and Strother Martin."

Dunmoore's lips tightened. All three of her most likely suspects and a Forenza together in one room. "Let me guess. The topic of discussion concerns the recent and tragic events that saw so many of your colleagues die. I'm taken aback by the fact that the senior armed services officer in the Cervantes system wasn't included. I'm here now, so not much harm done."

She spotted a door marked conference room and took a step towards it. The aide made as if to stop her but instead found one of Vincenzo's hands clamped around his upper arm. When he glanced at the stone-faced spacer, Vincenzo wordlessly shook his head.

"Come on, Chief. We're crashing the meeting," Dunmoore waved at Trane over her shoulder.

She yanked the door open and stepped in. Four astonished pairs of eyes turned on her in abject silence. Smiling sweetly at them, she said, "Good day, gentlemen. It appears you forgot to invite the commander, Commonwealth Forces in the Cervantes system to your meeting. Quite the faux pas, considering the military angle of the situation."

Forenza studied her with what almost seemed like a hint of amusement in his expression while Devine and Martin gave her looks of pure loathing. Gerber's eyes, however, after briefly landing on her, switched to Chief Trane, who had entered on Dunmoore's heels and she saw a brief glint of recognition and then fear in them. Dunmoore had to suppress a smile at seeing her improvised stratagem work.

"You may know Chief Petty Officer Third Class Trane. He's Sigma Noctae's former operations chief and now *Iolanthe*'s master-at-arms. As such, he's responsible for the ship's brig, which now holds three dozen of the mercenaries who raided Toboso — the only survivors, I might add. We recovered most of the stolen naval stores and took both the freighter carrying them and one of the attackers' sloops as prizes. Until the Admiralty decides on their disposal, they've joined my ship to form the Navy's new but temporary Cervantes squadron." She took one of the empty chairs, motioning Trane to sit beside her while Gerber seemed to struggle with the situation, clearly unable to form coherent words. "So, what are we discussing?"

"From this point on," Devine replied, "nothing. This is not your place, Dunmoore, and no one cares how many ships you now command. You still have no authority on Toboso, and that means you'd be well advised to leave."

"Are you threatening me, Andrew?" She cocked an eyebrow at him. "Are you that impatient to reacquaint yourself with the inside of a cell?"

"It didn't do you much good last time and won't do you any good this time. Now please leave."

She turned to Gerber. "I thought I had counseled you to stay away from these two and now I find you've made them part of some governing council? In heaven's name, why? Last time we spoke you were adamant you wanted me to take on a greater role in running Toboso until a new administration shows up, precisely because the pressure they were exerting on you."

"He's not answerable to you, Dunmoore," Martin snarled. "Now make like a nice little Navy wanker who knows she's not wanted and fuck off."

"Do you have a cricket bat handy, Strother? I suddenly feel a need to practice my swing." Gerber was becoming visibly alarmed at the venom in her tone but still had difficulties finding his words, so she continued. "You see, I have a problem that needs solving, and I figure someone in this room, perhaps more than one person, has the answer. We uncovered evidence that the raid on Toboso was so well planned that the attackers had people on the inside, one of them at the depot and one or more within the colony, perhaps even within the colonial administration. This wasn't a random attack but had purpose well beyond the wanton destruction of the administrative complex and the naval installation, and the theft of the naval stores. I'm even wondering whether the theft wasn't in part to mislead the Fleet."

"So you think someone in here is part of it?" Devine asked. "You're mad, Dunmoore, even crazier than you were a few years ago. You need your head examined."

"Perhaps." She gave him an icy smile. "But we have evidence and said evidence is already on its way back to headquarters. There will be an investigation."

Gerber's eyes had repeatedly shifted between her and Trane while she spoke.

"Any comments, Governor?" She asked. "You obviously know my master-at-arms."

Devine opened his mouth to speak again, but Forenza raised a restraining hand.

"Enough. For one thing, Captain Dunmoore is correct in seeking a seat at this table, considering the harm inflicted on the Navy and what the future might mean for the devastated depot. For another, I'd like her to pursue this notion of one or more traitors on Toboso." Dunmoore gave Forenza a surprised glance and received a faint smile in return, one that felt strangely encouraging. "Please go ahead, Captain, and please answer her questions, Anton."

"As governor," Gerber stuttered, the first words he had spoken since Dunmoore entered the room, "I don't take orders from anyone on Toboso, Ser Forenza, not even you. I'm answerable only to the Colonial Secretary."

The sudden, if somewhat shaky outburst of defiance almost made her laugh. Instead, she said, "If you've done nothing reprehensible, Ser Gerber, you have nothing to fear from answering my questions."

"The governor is right," Devine interjected, placing a clear emphasis on the title. "He's not answerable to anyone here, and as members of the colonial governing council, we support him fully. You have no jurisdiction when it comes to civilian matters, Captain."

"Perhaps the governor should have her arrested," Martin proposed. "Tossing out scurrilous accusations of treason is a serious offense. Look to your own for the real traitors."

He glared at Trane in an unmistakable gesture of accusation.

"Have you ever heard the expression, Captain," Forenza said in a soft tone, "that enemy fire becomes heavier the closer one gets to the target?"

"Yes. I'm surprised you have."

"Among my many vices, the study of history figures most prominently. Besides, variants of the saying have been common in politics since well before humanity set out for the stars." Forenza gestured at the others. "My sense is that you're approaching dangerous territory. Dangerous for them, that is."

Astonished by the Colonial Office's special envoy, she found herself briefly at a loss for words.

"You know," he continued, "I think I may have a partial answer regarding a motive in removing the colonial administration and the Fleet presence here."

"A forced shift in Toboso's status and governance," she replied. "I'd already figured it might well be something of the kind. It's been tried before, as Messrs. Devine and Martin can attest, having been part of the earlier effort."

"Of course," Forenza nodded. "However, no one expected your arrival in the system shortly after the raid. It allowed you to pursue the attackers and through them, uncover evidence of collusion with the colony's inhabitants. It was to have been one of those unfortunate things that often precipitate change, but alas, even the best-laid plans often go askew due to mere chance."

"I've just about had enough of this." Devine climbed to his feet. "Let's leave them to spin their nonsense, Strother."

Dunmoore jerked her chin towards his chair. "Sit. You're not getting out of here until I say you can leave. There's an angry, armed man just outside the door and a platoon of even more hostile and more heavily armed soldiers surrounding this building."

"Where I'm from, that's called depriving someone of his freedom without cause, a criminal offense in any jurisdiction."

"Do I look like I care, Andrew? Sit, or I'll call my man in and have him make you sit."

"You'll not get away with it, Dunmoore. We have a lot of support around the colony. It won't be the retreads who didn't guard Sigma Noctae properly or your transport ship swabbies who'll help you against us."

Her hand slammed into the table's surface with a crack loud enough to be heard by Sergeant Saari's troops deployed around the building.

"You want to place Toboso in a state of insurrection against the Commonwealth, be my guest. I'll impose martial law faster than you might imagine. Last time, I didn't have that authority. This time, I do." She turned to Trane. "Time to come clean, Chief. You're the one who took the satellite constellation down, not Lieutenant Duff, right?"

"It wasn't me, sir, I swear, but they tried to rope me into some scheme that would wipe away my gambling debts and give me enough to retire on. When I told 'em to pound sand, they went after Duff, pulled him in a bit at a time. A little corruption here, a little there and soon, they owned his ass. Gerber and the other two clowns are nervous because I know what they are." He scowled at the acting governor.

"Why did you, to use your colorful phrase, tell them to pound sand, Mister Trane?" Forenza asked.

"Because I figure that once they had me by the balls, I wouldn't see a damn cred. I saw how they screwed over a couple of the other officers and chiefs so Mister Devine and his bunch could pad their pockets with Fleet money. One of the lieutenants in purchasing offed herself over their blackmail garbage a couple of months ago. I simply stopped going to the saloons, paid off what debts I could and offered to break their tough guys in half if they tried to put the squeeze on me."

"Preposterous!" Devine shouted.

"One more outburst," Forenza gave the man an icy stare, "and I'll ask Captain Dunmoore to send her man in. Now, would you be willing to testify to that, Chief?"

"Sure. Devine, Martin, Gerber and a lot of others had their hands in a lot of tills. I figure one of 'em turned Lieutenant Duff and got damn near every one of my mates killed."

"Let me make sure I understand this correctly, Mister Trane. You're accusing Acting Governor Gerber of corruption, participation in illegal acts and possible connection to the raid that killed his predecessor, Governor LaSalle, almost all of her administration and most of Sigma Noctae's garrison?"

"I am, sir." Trane sneered at the three men he named. "And I'd like to see 'em hang."

Without warning, Devine and Martin each drew a small blaster from shoulder holsters. The former shot at Trane, hitting him in the upper chest, while the latter took aim at Dunmoore, but only singed her hair with a poorly aimed head shot. The chief let out a cry of pain as he collapsed to the floor. It was enough to warn Vincenzo, who burst into the conference room, ready to open fire. Dunmoore drew her own sidearm and aimed it at Devine, who was closest to her.

"Move another muscle, and you die."

A meaty thump, followed by the unmistakable sound of a body hitting the floor caught both their attention. Vincenzo had clubbed Martin into unconsciousness and now pointed his carbine at Devine.

"I can shoot you before your man can react," the latter said.

"No you can't," Vincenzo growled back, pulling his trigger. The blaster in Devine's hand went flying against the far wall, and the man staggered backward, his wrist broken until a chair brought him to his knees. "Next shot takes off your head, asshole."

Gerber rose and tried to run for the door, but the spacer stuck out a foot and sent the acting governor tumbling to the floor at Forenza's feet.

"Congratulations," the special envoy said, "I believe we just carried out a coup d'état against the provisional government of Toboso, Captain." He looked at Gerber. "You're fired, my friend. Once Captain Dunmoore and I have come to an agreement concerning the specifics of your crimes, you will be charged and tried accordingly."

With Devine out of action, Siobhan knelt to check on Trane. The shot had sizzled through his flesh, but based on the amount of blood, it had missed the heart. She pulled out her communicator.

"Sergeant Saari, this is Dunmoore, I need a first aid kit up here now. PO Purdy, warm her up; we have a casevac back to the ship. Warn Doc Polter. Through and through chest shot, but it missed the heart."

"Coming," the soldier replied almost instantly.

Purdy took a few moments longer, then said, "The ship's warned, sir. Warming up the drives and reconfiguring for casevac. Who was hit?"

"Chief Trane."

Saari himself burst through the door, a dun-colored pack dangling from his fist. "Where is he?"

Dunmoore climbed to her feet. "Here, Sergeant. I think nothing vital was hit because he's not bleeding like a fountain and his breathing is reasonably normal."

The soldier knelt at Trane's side. "You're likely right, Captain," he said after examining him. "You'd have made a good candidate for the emergency medical services back home."

"Is that what you were before the war, an EMT?"

"It was my full-time job long ago, but I was in the Scandia Regiment's reserve battalion since well before the boneheads lost their ever-loving minds. I was activated on day two of the war, and I've been at it ever since. I'll probably stay in once we kick the bastards' butts back to Shrehari Prime. He'll be okay. I'll have my people take a door to make an improvised litter and bring him to the shuttle."

"If you don't mind," Trane rasped, "I can walk."

"What you'll do, Chief," Dunmoore replied, "is follow Sergeant Saari's instructions. He knows more about broken bodies than both of us put together." When he didn't answer, she added, smiling, "That's what we call an order in our beloved Navy."

"Aye, aye, sir," he wheezed.

A squad of soldiers appeared soon after and tore the conference room's door off its hinges.

With Trane off to the shuttle, Saari had Devine, Martin and Gerber cuffed at Dunmoore's orders. She turned to Forenza and said, "It seems we no longer have a functioning government on Toboso. Would the Colonial Office take offense if I invoke Article One-Hundred-Forty-Two of the Colonial Administration Act and assume control?"

"Even if it would, Captain, weeks might pass before anyone on Earth bothered to take notice. Will you be imposing martial law as well?"

"I think that's obligatory under the sub-clauses of the article. Otherwise, why would the senior military commander in the system assume the mantle of governor?"

He inclined his head in acknowledgment. "Indeed."

"In that case," she placed her communicator on the table, "let it be logged that on this day, I, Captain Siobhan Alaina Dunmoore, commanding the Commonwealth Starship *Iolanthe*, and de facto senior Commonwealth officer in the Cervantes system, do under Article One-Hundred-Forty-Two of the Colonial Administration Act assume the responsibilities and powers of governor of Toboso, as witnessed by..." She nodded at Forenza.

"As witnessed by Colonial Office Special Envoy Mikhail Forenza, working for the Assistant Secretary, Governance, and Oversight."

"My first act as governor of Toboso is to impose martial law under the provisions of the Act." She picked up the communicator again. "PO Purdy, transmit that to the ship and have Commander Holt send the rest of Company Group 31 down. The new governor needs her household troops."

"You won't get away with it." Devine's voice was a barely coherent growl. "You didn't last time and you won't this time."

Dunmoore ignored him. "Sergeant Saari, have these three men brought to the landing strip. They're headed for our brig on the next shuttle." Then she turned to face her three prisoners. "The one who tells the full truth first will live. The others..." She shrugged. "Treason in time of war is a capital crime, and since I've imposed martial law, I'll put you in front of a military tribunal. Said tribunal will forward its findings to me for confirmation as the highest authority on Toboso. I can assure you that I will sign off on a finding of guilty and see you executed within the following twenty-four hours, unless, of course, you talk. Take them away, Sergeant."

"Which one do you think will spill the beans, so to speak?" Forenza asked once they were alone.

"Gerber. He strikes me as the weak link."

"My impression as well. I pulled his dossier before heading out here, and his performance evaluations over the years show no aptitude for higher office, let alone a spark of administrative genius showing he might be fit to continue as governor."

She considered him for a few heartbeats. "You intrigue me, Ser Forenza. Why did you take my side? Your family has no reason to show me a shred of support."

Forenza made a dismissive gesture with his hand. "My sister was always a disappointment to our parents. I'll not be a hypocrite and tell you I mourned her senseless death after the Fleet forcibly retired her, no doubt for very good reasons, knowing her appetites. Besides, I have no reasons to favor Gerber or his Tobosan friends. They've been filling my ears with cries for greater self-rule since I stepped off *Leopold* earlier today and honestly, it had become tiresome in the extreme. My brief was not to loosen the Colonial Office's leash, but tighten it, something they singularly failed to grasp."

"The Colonial Office doesn't stand behind Gerber?" Dunmoore gave him an ironic smile.

"Anton the useless? Please, Captain." A wry expression twisted his face. "The man's more of an embarrassment than anything else. You saw his ability, or rather inability to function under pressure. A poor showing to be sure. If he's in any way part of a cabal responsible for this lamentable situation, his disavowal will occur without question." Forenza paused before asking, "Now, how can the Colonial Office offer help to Toboso's newly declared military governor?"

— Thirty-Seven —

Dunmoore entered the improvised colonial council room accompanied by Leading Spacer Vincenzo and Major Salminen. Neither of them carried long arms, but the blasters in their open holsters were there for all to see. With Company Group 31 on the ground mere hours after assuming the governor's mantle, she had ordered her bewildered aide to convene the unapproved and as of her assumption of power, illegal assembly. Stunned silence greeted her entrance and more than one face fell when she assumed the governor's chair at the head of the table.

"You may be aware by now that Anton Gerber has been relieved of his duties on suspicion of treason and arrested, as have Councilors Devine and Martin. I have assumed the governorship of Toboso and placed this planet under martial law. Since the governing council convened by Anton Gerber has not been ratified by the Colonial Office, it is hereby declared unlawful and dissolved."

"You can't do that, Dunmoore," a hard-faced, elderly woman, shouted. "This is a democracy, not a dictatorship. You're violating the legal foundations upon which the Commonwealth was built."

"Sera Vanclef, Toboso ceased to be a democracy when you and your friends perverted Commonwealth law in the name of self-enrichment. As a result, I can do whatever I please. Right now, I please to issue a warrant for your arrest on charges of aiding and abetting treason, which I must warn you, is a capital crime. Your case will be heard by a military court in due course." She motioned at Salminen. "Major, have this person removed and take her to the cells."

At an unseen signal, a pair of soldiers entered the council room, shackled a stunned Vanclef and dragged her away.

Dunmoore surveyed the room, remembering many faces from the past, some of them good people led astray, many of them Devine's cronies, willing to sell Navy lives to line their pockets while proclaiming themselves enlightened progressive souls.

"Does anyone else wish to challenge my authority?" When no one replied, an evil smile tugged at the corners of her mouth. "Mind you, I'm not done cleaning up Toboso. A few of you need further examination, and not just for old times' sake. Investigators will take your individual statements on the matter of the perversion of justice in due course. Failure to speak the truth will be severely punished while cooperating will help reduce any sentences a military court might impose." She let her words hang over the assembly before continuing. "This council is dissolved. Any decisions rendered by it are null and void. You will now vacate the premises."

The dirty looks thrown at her by the colony's most influential citizens, ranking just below the ones she had already arrested, evoked a sick sense of glee. Many of them would have gladly seen her bleed to death in the middle of Doniphon's main street a few years ago, as punishment for interfering in their profitable schemes to defraud the Fleet of millions in the midst of a war. People like Kila Vanclef and so many other members of the abortive governing council had become experts at signaling their so-called virtues when it came to colonial self-governance while grabbing what they could and to hell with the hindmost. The surge of satisfaction that flooded through Dunmoore's veins at seeing their discomfiture felt almost obscenely intense.

"You'll not get away with it for long," one of them, a white-haired man with a luxuriant beard whom she remembered all too well, shouted over his shoulder. "I have friends on Earth who will ruin what little career you have left."

Dunmoore, remembering his part in Strother Martin's schemes back in her days as Sigma Noctae's executive officer, pointed the man out to Salminen. Though shouting and protesting, he swiftly joined Vanclef in the improvised detention center set up in one of the spaceport hangars, where Devine, Martin, and Gerber now also waited for their fates to unfold. Though the latter three had been slated for transport to orbit, Salminen, abetted by Forenza, had convinced Dunmoore to keep all prisoners on the surface, pointing out that her troops could quickly build a stockade that met legal requirements. If they were to be prosecuted by the colonial administration, taking them to the ship would prove wasteful. The surviving mercenaries held in *Iolanthe*'s brig would join the Tobosan prisoners within hours anyway.

With the former council chamber empty, save for Dunmoore and her escort, the welcome silence that fell over it allowed her to sit back and relax for a few moments, knowing she would soon find herself in high demand. At least she would not have to worry about *Iolanthe* and her little flotilla. One of her first acts as governor had been to turn temporary command over to Ezekiel Holt.

*

"Can I help you, sir?" Lieutenant Puro, appointed acting provost marshal and thus responsible for the stockade asked Forenza when the latter presented himself at the heavily guarded entrance.

"I'm the Colonial Office's special envoy, Mikhail Forenza. I'd like to speak with Anton Gerber, Lieutenant. Until the Colonial Secretary terminates his employment, he remains our responsibility, and his acts, past, and future will reflect on our office. You may check with Governor Dunmoore, but I'm sure she'll clear my visit."

"That won't be necessary, sir. The governor has put you on the list of approved visitors. If you're able to calm Gerber, it would be a blessing. The man's falling apart, and it's becoming increasingly irritating for everyone."

A few minutes later, a pair of soldiers escorted him to a room set aside for prisoner interrogations, which had yet to begin. Forenza took a chair on one side of the bare metal table and, while waiting for the guards to bring Gerber, he pulled a small device from his pocket, careful to keep it hidden from any video pickups and switched it on. Any surveillance equipment monitoring the room would suddenly experience a series of puzzling malfunctions. Then he composed himself for the interview.

Gerber stumbled through the open doorway a few minutes later, hands and feet shackled, a soldier bearing the single chevron of a lance corporal holding him by the arm. The former acting governor had gone from urbane and polished to maniacally disheveled in less than a day. He stared at Forenza with wild eyes as he dropped into the other chair, leaning forward to place his forearms on the table.

Forenza nodded at the guard. "Thank you. I'll call when I'm done."

The lance corporal hesitated. "I'm not sure we're supposed to leave you alone with the detainee, sir."

"Gerber's no threat to anyone."

"Okay. I'll be just outside the door."

When the door slammed shut, Forenza turned his eyes on Gerber and examined him in silence, then shook his head with an exaggerated air of sadness. "Anton, Anton, Anton, what have you done?"

"I acted as ordered." His words came out as a dry rasp. "Why did you side with Dunmoore, and why aren't you getting me out of here and off this damn shit hole?"

"You failed, Anton, and that means disavowal. As a senior official with the Colonial Office, I had no choice but to back her, under the circumstances. Perhaps if those two idiots, Devine and Martin, hadn't panicked and pulled out their guns, we might still have been able to salvage something, but now? Under the best case scenario, where the Navy can't produce conclusive evidence to connect you, them and their cronies with the attack on Toboso, they'll still be spending years in prison, perhaps even in a penal colony far from here."

"It's not my fault," Gerber hissed. "I did everything right. Dunmoore showing up when she did was sheer bad luck. That's not my fault, nor is Devine and Martin going off the deep end."

Forenza shrugged. "Yet you're still a failure."

"Get me out of this, or I'll tell Dunmoore all she wants to know."

"I don't think so, Anton. My mission here is to survey the damage Dunmoore and her people have done to our interests, and if necessary, end the operation and tie off any loose ends. In my estimation, the entire plan is compromised, and therefore I'm shutting everything down, starting with you, the biggest loose end. Tell me, how much do your Tobosan confederates know?"

"Nothing more than what I was authorized to tell them, of course. I'm loyal. They still think it was their plan all along and that I used my contacts to hire the mercenaries on their behalf."

"Excellent." Forenza reached out and patted Gerber's left hand in a gesture meant to show approval. Gerber barely felt the prick of the needle. "One prison-induced heart attack might escape scrutiny. Three, not so much. Goodbye, Anton."

The special envoy sat back and studied the late Governor LaSalle's former aide, a man whose ambition had always been greater than his ability. True, he was the victim of bad luck, but he had mishandled the aftermath. Forenza's words registered on Gerber almost at the same time as he experienced an intense pain in his chest. His eyes bulged as he tried to take a breath, manacled hands reaching for the special envoy in a final spasm. Satisfied that a fatal cardiac arrest was now inevitable, Forenza shouted for the guard.

*

"I'm afraid the strain was too much for him," Forenza said after reporting Gerber's death to a visibly annoyed Dunmoore. "Intense stress has been known to cause sudden cardiac death in apparently healthy humans. It's a shame that we'll never know what drove him to betray his oath in such a manner. The lust for power, perhaps?"

"Perhaps that could explain Gerber's motivation, but there's more to this than forcing through a larger degree of self-rule under a new governor eager to carve out his own fiefdom. I couldn't figure it out the last time Devine and company tried to pull a nasty one, but I'm damned if I won't this time, seeing as how I now run the place. My coxswain was going to interrogate Gerber, as the easier target, but now he'll have to work on our good friends Andrew and Strother."

"You may find yourself underwhelmed by the answers, Governor. In my experience, there are no such things as grand conspiracies that can't be easily explained away by simple greed."

"What will you be doing now, Ser Forenza?"

"If you'll allow me to use your ship's subspace transmitter, I'd like to send a report to my superiors. They'll either tell me to stay here and monitor the situation until the new civilian governor arrives, or send me on my next assignment."

"*Iolanthe*'s communications facilities are, of course, at your disposal. Prepare your report and pass it to my aide. He'll send it to the ship."

Forenza inclined his head in thanks. "If I can be of any help whatsoever while I'm on Toboso, please consider me at your entire disposal as special adviser on matters pertaining to colonial administration."

"I appreciate your support, Ser Forenza."

"As representatives of the Commonwealth government on this wild frontier, we owe each other mutual support in the face of..." The sound of a meaty knuckle rapping on the door to her office interrupted him.

"Come."

Guthren poked his head through the opening. "Bad moment, sir?"

Dunmoore glanced at Forenza who said, "The governor and I were done, Chief."

He stood and gave her an abbreviated bow. "Governor. I shall leave you to the business of cleaning house. As I said, you may call on my assistance at any time, day or night."

When Dunmoore and Guthren found themselves alone, the latter said, "Butter wouldn't melt in that bastard's mouth, would it?"

"His manners might be more suited to the rarefied atmosphere of our dear government's upper levels of power, but he's been nothing but pleasant and helpful. A very different individual than his late sister."

The coxswain made a dubious face. "He's a Forenza, sir. I wouldn't trust him if he said the sky was blue. Anyway, we received the post-mortem report on Gerber. It was a massive heart attack. The doc says it wasn't survivable even if it had occurred right in an ICU, except he couldn't find an underlying reason. Gerber was healthy. In related news, we don't have a record of his conversation with Forenza right before he died. The interrogation room's monitoring gear malfunctioned from the outset. Perhaps our soldier friends didn't set it up correctly, but they've been pretty sharp with everything else so far. The video keeps fading in and out while the audio is nothing more than white noise. If you want my opinion, it's damn convenient one of the main suspects died just like that, with no record of the events right before his death. Remember what you always say about once being happenstance, twice coincidence and three times, enemy action? This Gerber thing feels like we're at three times, even if I can only see two right now."

"Hopefully you'll obtain something from the others."

"Yep, but even under martial law, there's only so much I can do if they don't want to cooperate." Guthren paused, struck by a thought. "Did you think of seizing Devine and Martin's personal and business computer cores? Maybe Chief Day can dig up some interesting bits."

"No, but I'll ask Major Salminen to do so right away. Not just those two but the records from anyone in the stockade and the colonial administration's database. Chief Day will have plenty with which to entertain himself and his mates."

"In the meantime, I'll try to squeeze something useful out of Mister Devine." Guthren stood. "Oh, by the way, Chief Trane is up and about, but the doc won't let him off the ship. He sends his apologies for having held back. I figure he was embarrassed by his bad habits and didn't want to confess he'd almost gotten himself corrupted by the buggers. If we dig deep enough into his recent past, we'll probably find something that'll be worthy of early retirement." He snapped to attention and saluted. "With your permission, Governor?"

She returned the salute. "Go. Have fun. Find me intel I can use to unravel the whole rotten lot."

*

Dunmoore's aide stuck his head through the open doorway. "Sir, *Iolanthe* is calling. Commander Holt wishes to speak with you."

She looked up and pinched the bridge of her nose in a vain attempt to fight off an oncoming headache. The last three days had been nothing short of hellish. She would have preferred to meet an entire Shrehari battle group head-on than deal with the scheming, whining, posturing nincompoops who seemed to make up Toboso's higher social strata. Between dealing with settlement mayors, unhappy that their municipal police departments had been subordinated to Major Salminen, the families of the detainees, livid at warrant-less, yet under martial law wholly legal searches of their homes and businesses, and major business owners anxious about the effects of her executive orders on their affairs, it was a wonder she did not suffer a permanent migraine.

"Put him on." She pulled her desk display around and waited until Holt's face replaced the Colonial Office logo.

"An excellent afternoon to you, Governor," he said, beaming. Then he noticed her drawn features, and the smile vanished. "You look like someone who's finding out that the only thing worse than defeat is victory."

She sighed. "I wasn't cut out to be a politician. The only redeeming feature of this situation is my ability to throw the weight of Major Salminen's troops around to obtain even the most grudging amount of cooperation from parts of the colony. Sorry, the only two redeeming features are the troops and Mikhail Forenza's help in smoothing over a few of the more ruffled feathers. Guthren isn't making any headway with the detainees. They're blaming Gerber for everything, and since he's conveniently dead, we can't refute the accusations. I don't know if you've ever had those annoying nightmares where you dream you're always on the verge of drowning but it's as if I'm living a wide-awake version, except I'm drowning in liquid manure."

"Then you'll be cheered by my news. We received a message from HQ. A new governor and colonial staff are on their way to Toboso. Estimated time of arrival should be in approximately two weeks. Once he — that being Governor-designate Piotr Alexandrov — arrives, you're to carry out a change of governor ceremony with all due pomp and circumstance and resume your command. Then, we're to sail for Starbase 24 where we'll get a full replenishment and turn over the prizes."

"And our soldiers?"

Holt's infectious grin returned. "Company Group 31 has been redesignated Company E, 3rd Battalion, Scandia Regiment and officially assigned to the Commonwealth Starship *Iolanthe*. We have ourselves a permanent landing party."

"I'm not sure how they'll feel about that."

"The commanding officer of Company E should be happy. Her courtesy title of major has been made substantive. I'll arrange for a set of appropriate rank insignia sent on the next shuttle. Not only that, but there will be new gear for her troops waiting at Starbase

Twenty-Four, so they're equipped to Marine Corps standards."

Dunmoore gave him a tired smile. "All of that is good news. Now I need to survive the next fourteen days fighting off people whose default position is a refusal to cooperate. Has Chief Day made any headway with the databases we sent him?"

"That was my third bit of news. He hasn't flagged anything that might indicate illegal activities. Whatever those folks might be plotting, they appear to have been careful, but he noted a few similarities between individual business records and I ran my analysis last night. As best I can tell, there was a plan afoot, pending government approval, for a joint venture underwritten by the major players. Unfortunately, the tags they used don't give us much to go on."

"There you go dashing my hopes for an easy answer."

"Sorry, Governor. At least you have your two favorite Tobosans dead to rights for attempted murder. That'll put them out of circulation for a long time, and even their buddies on Earth will be hard pressed to mount a rescue operation. Speaking of which, when do you intend to form a military tribunal and deal with those two and the mercenaries?"

"Right now, I'd say on the second day of never. My successor will have to deal with the matter, which shouldn't be a problem with the amount of evidence we've accumulated. I don't see a way to do right in the time I have left at the helm. Command will kick my ass if I mishandle legal matters in a martial law situation when the death penalty is on the table. Besides," she suppressed a yawn, "there's just too much on my plate and not enough time, especially since nature has shortchanged Toboso by almost three hours, compared to the standard day."

Her communicator beeped, and she glanced at it to see Guthren's name on the display. "Hang on for a moment, Zeke." She accepted the call. "What's up, Chief?"

"Devine wants to talk to you. He says he's ready to make a deal, but only with you."

"How did you change his mind? On second thought, it's best I don't know."

"I did nothing, sir. He came up with the request out of the blue."

"I'm on my way. Dunmoore, out." She looked up at the screen again. "Perhaps Devine had an epiphany and realized he would never get away with shooting a Navy chief in front of two credible witnesses."

"Or he thinks we're closing in on him and the others and wants to get while the getting's good. I had no other news. Enjoy your talk."

"Oh, I will. I'll let you know what happened."

— Thirty-Eight —

As Lieutenant Puro led Dunmoore to the interrogation room, she said, "I hope the surveillance gear is working properly this time."

"It worked every time except when Special Envoy Forenza spoke with the late Ser Gerber, Governor. We experienced no other glitches since then. The corporal who installed the gear worked in private security before the war. He knows this stuff inside out and can't figure what the problem might have been. The only thing he figures might have happened is someone used a jammer in the vicinity or something that accidentally jams sensor pickups."

She stopped and turned to the young officer. "Did anyone search Forenza before letting him into the stockade?"

"No." Puro shook his head. "Do you suspect he might have been carrying something capable of jamming military sensors? That's not something one buys at the nearest electronics retailer, or so my corporal says."

"Not a word about this to anyone else, Lieutenant."

"Of course, Governor."

When she entered the interrogation room, Devine already sat in one of the chairs, ankles, and wrists shackled together. She took the other seat and waited until Puro closed the door.

"You wanted to speak with me, Andrew?"

"I want to negotiate a deal, Dunmoore. Since Marko survived my unfortunate moment of panic, I figure that maybe we can talk the charges down, so I don't end up spending the next ten years in a penal colony."

"If it ends up being merely ten years. What happened? Did your lawyer bring you a message from the folks who bailed your ass out last time saying you're on your own?"

His eyes narrowed at her words, confirming she had hit a bulls-eye.

"Let's say I want to be the one taking care of my interests in this instance."

"Why is your lawyer not here?"

"Because this is just you and me, Dunmoore. I know you're a bleeding heart when it comes to truth, honor and all that bullshit so your word will be good. Besides, you're recording this so there will be tangible proof."

"What do you want and what is it you offer in exchange?"

"I'll take a suspended sentence for accidental manslaughter, with exile from Toboso for ten years."

"That's like asking for a full pardon, Devine. Nothing you have can be worth giving you the freedom to roam the galaxy and set up shop elsewhere to start your shenanigans again."

"You desperately want to know what this mess was about. Otherwise you wouldn't have had that cox'n of yours harassing me at all hours of the day and night."

"Confiscation of everything you own, less a few hundred creds to pay for your fare off Toboso, a suspended sentence of attempted murder, and you never return here again. If what you have is enough to unravel everything."

Devine stared at her with calculating eyes before nodding. "Deal. I'd shake on it but..." He raised his manacled hands for a moment, then settled back in the chair and sighed. "Where do I start? Trane wasn't lying the other day. We tried to get him under our thumb, but the man has serious nerves to go along with a gambling problem that was spinning out of control. Ever since you cleaned shop, the Navy has been careful about who they were posting to the depot, and without friends on the inside, business can be hard. Lately, a few people with personal problems showed up, problems that spilled over into town where we could take advantage of them. We eventually put the screws on someone in purchasing and another one in receiving, thanks to their indiscretions. A nice bit of money came from screwing the Fleet on perishables and preserved food items."

"Basically what you were doing last time."

"Why change a winning formula, when friends in high places provide cover? One day about a year ago, Anton Gerber showed up as Governor LaSalle's newest senior aide. Now LaSalle was a hard-ass, a walking cliché of your standard issue by the book bureaucrat with no interest in discussing the kind of increased self-government that would allow us to arrange things on Toboso more to our liking. Gerber starts haunting the entertainment places, and we figured he might be another one we could turn into our man on the inside, this time in the governor's office itself. You're going to love this, Dunmoore. The little fucker turned *us*. Our friends in high places had decided it was time we returned the favor and Gerber was their messenger. He told us we needed a new buddy in Sigma Noctae, this time in operations. Enter Marko Trane. Once it became apparent he wouldn't play, exit Marko Trane and enter Lieutenant Duff, a newcomer to Toboso but not to debauchery. Except Duff doesn't play with tradesmen like myself so Gerber had to cultivate him until he was blackmail material, which didn't take long. Duff was as dumb as a doornail."

"What did Gerber, or rather Gerber's bosses want?"

"Hold on, Dunmoore, I'm getting to that. This is all by way of background, so you understand what happened next. Our friends in high places offered a deal, one which we couldn't refuse because the report you wrote years ago is still floating around with enough evidence to jail the lot of us. They would arrange to have the Colonial Office give us full self-rule in return for a cut of our increased profits and that would include profits from the trade beyond the Commonwealth sphere, the sort that's heavily controlled right now."

"Contraband."

"Controlled items, which would be shipped to Toboso legitimately for use by shell companies purportedly developing the planet, then repacked and shipped from here to parts unknown. Highly profitable, and this is on top of what we calculated to be our increased margins thanks to decreased Colonial Office interference. We're talking tens, if not hundreds of millions. Two obstacles barred the way. One was the current colonial administration and the other the Navy's presence and control over our satellite constellation. Our friends proposed a plan to remove both and fronted us the money. We were told that with the old administration gone, the Colonial Office would send a much smaller replacement with a narrower mandate while the Navy wouldn't bother rebuilding the depot. Gerber arranged the contract with Orion Outcomes. Don't ask me how. He refused to say. The rest you know as well as I do."

"So because of your greed, hundreds of people died that morning."

Devine shrugged. "If you hadn't interfered the first time, we wouldn't be here."

Dunmoore's sudden flare of anger must have shown in her face because he instinctively tried to back away. The memory of suffering her fury remained vivid. "Who are those friends in high places, Andrew?"

"That's the funny part. We don't know their identities."

"Then how did they become friends?"

"Through business contacts. We do a little cross-border trading now and then, strictly off the sensor grid, and mostly on the wrong side of legal. That's how we did a few favors for people looking to make anonymous profits. The communications were through umpteen layers of redirection as were payments in either direction."

"Ironic, isn't it?" Dunmoore smirked at him.

"What is?"

"You and your cronies were turned by those anonymous profit seekers well before I showed up the first time to put a crimp in your lifestyles. Yet now they've cut you loose after their scheme didn't work. No honor among thieves, I suppose."

"So, is that story worth the deal we made?"

Dunmoore nodded once, although she was disappointed that the trail seemed to stop with Gerber, who might well have known Devine's friends in high places or been able to show the way. It seemed too convenient, as the coxswain had pointed out.

"You realize that you'll be looking over your shoulder for those friends in high places for the rest of your life, right?"

Devine shrugged. "I figure my chances of surviving more than a day in a penal colony are even less because I'd be a sitting target. These are not people you betray lightly, and they like to tie up loose ends, such as me. After this, they have no more use for us. I'd make a wager with you that Strother Martin, for example, will repeatedly fall on a knife the moment he enters maximum security. But since you're taking all of my money, I'll leave it at that."

*

A funereal silence filled Dunmoore's office after she recounted Devine's revelations to her first officer, coxswain and major of Marines, who still was not aware she belonged to *Iolanthe* for a full tour of duty.

"Will you share this with the Colonial Office's special envoy?" Holt finally asked, breaking the spell.

"No." She related her conversation with Lieutenant Puro, concluding, "Mister Guthren seems to have sniffed Forenza out well before the rest of us. He's to be kept away from the detainees, Major. In fact, he's to be treated like a mushroom from now on."

"I'll tell you what," the coxswain said with a knowing grimace, "on further thought, I think the bastard has to be a cleaner. None of you saw what little video we recovered from his interview with Gerber, but I recall seeing a fuzzy frame where it looks like he's touching Gerber's hand. It's easy enough to administer a toxin that fakes cardiac arrest and doesn't leave a trace with a touch if you know what you're doing."

"What's a cleaner in this context?" Salminen asked.

"Someone who removes loose ends, in this case an ex-governor who might talk."

"Do we still have the body?" Dunmoore asked.

"The Valance medical center morgue should be keeping it until we hear from the family, so yes."

"Zeke, send Doc Polter down with his diagnostic gear. I want him to examine Gerber's body and see if he can find anything that might indicate the cox'n is right again."

"What if he is?" Holt asked. "What good will that do us? Forenza not only won't allow himself to be arrested, but he's also sure to enjoy the sort of immunity you and I can't begin to understand."

"Is that the former counter-intelligence operative speaking?"

Holt nodded. "Besides, if Forenza is a competent assassin, we won't find anything. And it goes without saying that we must stay mute about Devine. Wait until Forenza's gone before releasing him into the wild."

"And take our lumps in the bargain, Zeke? Very well, never mind about Doc Polter doing an autopsy."

"Good decision, sir. We disrupted something big. Perhaps it would be advisable to enjoy our victory and let it go. Devine's friends in high places are without a doubt well beyond our reach, but at least we gave them a serious setback on Toboso. Governor-designate Alexandrov should thank you for handing him a less corrupt colony than the one you took from Gerber."

"What about the other detainees?"

"Most of them are guilty of something venal enough to merit the full measure of the law. If they fall victim to whatever other cleaners are on the prowl, then justice will have been served without compromising the Fleet. As you said, their fate will be a matter for your successor."

Dunmoore took a deep breath through flared nostrils, then exhaled with slow deliberation. "So be it. The official story is that Devine tried and failed to deal himself out, and thus, with no further evidence, either way, we're concluding the investigation. My report to HQ will be more detailed, but it'll be under the kind of security designation that'll severely limit its circulation. Once Forenza's gone, we let Devine slip away into the night and good luck to him."

"A wise choice," Holt said. "Continuing this fight would bring us nothing more than grief. If it'll cheer you up, I'm pretty sure Devine won't live for very long. Forenza or his masters will deduce he gave us information sufficiently juicy to buy his freedom, as soon as he shows up away from Toboso. And once they figure Devine knew more than he should have, they'll decide Martin's just as much of a liability. Enter the cleaner."

"That was all I wanted to discuss. Major, if you'll stay for a few minutes?"

"Of course."

Holt broke the link from *Iolanthe* and Guthren, after another precise display of military courtesy, left them alone in the governor's office.

"HQ has redesignated Company Group 31 as Company E, 3rd Battalion, Scandia Regiment and assigned it to *Iolanthe* as the embarked ground force."

Salminen's expression at the news was a mixture of surprise and grudging pleasure. "This is now a permanent posting?"

Dunmoore nodded. "It's permanent but will be subject to regular rotation cycles. Also, your promotion has been confirmed." She pointedly looked at the three four-pointed stars of an Army captain's rank insignia pinned to the collar of Salminen's battledress. "I'd say you're out of uniform, Major."

"Are you saying it's no longer a courtesy title aboard ship, sir?" Salminen seemed taken aback.

"The promotion is substantive. Congratulations. If you'd like I could pin on your new rank insignia during a formal event." When she did not answer, Dunmoore said, "How about a sunset ceremony tomorrow in front of what passes for my mansion? Could your troops manage that at short notice?"

"By now, they can handle just about anything at short notice, sir," Salminen replied with more than a hint of pride, "as you may have noticed."

"Done. Ask Sergeant Major Haataja to let Chief Guthren know when and where, and ask him to pass along whatever regimental or Army protocol I should follow to avoid insulting *Iolanthe*'s newly appointed infantry company."

*

"Governor?" Mikhail Forenza intercepted Dunmoore as she left yet another pointless and mind-numbing meeting with the settlement mayors the day after Devine's confession.

She gave him as much of a smile as she could muster. "Ser Forenza. I trust you're well."

He smiled. "Tolerable. I've received my instructions and must leave within the hour. *Leopold*'s captain is preparing to lift."

The news did not surprise Dunmoore. Forenza's orders had passed through the hands of *Iolanthe*'s signals division, and Holt had dutifully warned her. "Then I'll wish you Godspeed and good luck with your next assignment. Hopefully, it won't be as convoluted a mess as this one."

"They're all messy in one way or another. A shame that your investigation hasn't progressed, but I'm not surprised. In my estimation, there has always been less here than meets the eye. I know you had hopes of extracting more from Andrew Devine, but I understand your interview produced nothing of consequence."

"Sadly, no, other than him trying to convince me he had little to do with the recent tragic events. It turned out to be a waste of time." She gave him a disappointed grimace. "Anton Gerber's death likely means that this will stay a mystery for the ages, though my instincts tell me we were dealing with nothing more than pure greed."

"That would be my interpretation as well." He gave her an abbreviated bow. "With your permission, Governor, I shall give you my farewells."

"Take care, Ser Forenza. I realize a cleaning job is never fully done, not even in the Colonial Office."

A faint, almost knowing smile tugged at his lips. "Just so, Governor. Take care."

She watched him walk across the spaceport from her vantage point by the temporary Government House's main doors and climb aboard his aviso. A sense of relief lifted some of the weight off her shoulders when the small starship vanished among the clouds though a few regrets and more than one unanswered question remained.

"Governor?"

Dunmoore turned to face her nervous aide. "Yes, Hector?"

"The Chamber of Commerce is expecting you in half an hour. That gives us just enough time to fly to Valance."

"I suppose you have the requisite briefing note ready for me to read on the way there?"

"Of course."

"This one better not drag on like the previous meeting. I have a ceremony to attend at eighteen-hundred hours, and it's more important than whatever blather they'll toss at me."

"I'll make sure you're back for it, Governor."

*

Hector was as good as his word, rescuing Dunmoore from the meeting before it went into double overtime. She was, therefore, ready when, a few minutes before the appointed time, Chief Petty Officer Guthren, wearing his dress uniform complete with rosewood cane of office tucked under his arm, knocked on her door.

"*Iolanthe*'s infantry contingent has assembled, Governor."

After a last glance at herself in the mirror, she stepped out onto the veranda of the Doniphon spaceport guesthouse that had been turned over to the colonial administration until the government complex was rebuilt. Guthren examined her with a critical eye to make sure her dress uniform would appear as spotless as those of the troops she was about to review.

"Do I pass muster, Cox'n?"

"Aye. You'll do, Governor."

She fell into step beside him, and they made their way around the building to the tarmac, where E Company, 3rd Battalion, Scandia Regiment, minus the stockade guard detail, was drawn up in three ranks, assault rifles at the shoulder with officers and command sergeants at the front. Guthren came to a precise military halt the edge of the strip, but Dunmoore continued until she found herself a mere three paces in front of Major Salminen.

"Company, to the governor of Toboso," Salminen shouted, "present ARMS."

Dunmoore was surprised when the first five bars of the Commonwealth anthem rang out instead of the usual ruffles and flourishes, then remembered that it was indeed the proper greeting for a planetary governor. Strangely enough, receiving a salute in that manner made her governorship seem more real than all the meetings, petitions, and bureaucratic nonsense put together. After the music had died away, Salminen put her company at the shoulder arms, followed by the order arms position before reporting.

"Sir, E Company, 3rd Battalion, Scandia Regiment, one hundred and three on parade, thirty-two guarding the stockade."

"Thank you." Then, raising her voice so all could hear, Dunmoore said, "It is my pleasure to announce that your commanding officer has been promoted to the substantive rank of major in recognition of her outstanding professionalism."

A roaring cheer rose from the ranks while almost one hundred rifle butts stroked the hard concrete in a rattle that echoed over Doniphon.

Dunmoore reached up and removed the captain's insignia from Salminen's dress uniform shoulder straps, replacing them with the oak leaves and four-pointed star of her new rank.

"Well deserved, Major."

"Thank you, sir." Salminen turned to the right, took one pace forward, then pivoted to face her troops, allowing Dunmoore to address the company unobstructed.

"By now," she continued, "you'll have been notified that you are officially members of *Iolanthe*'s crew until such a time as you're rotated to another duty station. As her captain, I could not be more thrilled about being allowed to keep such a group of dedicated, professional, and disciplined soldiers under my command. We've already accomplished great deeds together, and I can promise you we'll continue to seek out and destroy the Commonwealth's enemies wherever they might be."

Dunmoore glanced at Salminen who asked, "Would the governor care to inspect her infantry company?"

"I'd be delighted."

Trailed by Guthren, they marched to the formation's right flank, were Sergeant Major Haataja fell in beside the coxswain. Dunmoore had asked that the ceremony be conducted under Army protocol and they delivered. At a barked command from Lieutenant Puro, all heads snapped to the right, those in the front rank looking straight at her. Then, when the inspection party stepped off, Salminen's troops burst into a heartfelt and rousing rendition of the Hakkapeliittain Marssi, claimed by the

Scandia Regiment's mainly Suomi speaking Third Battalion as its own fighting song.

On Pohjolan hangissa meill' isänmaa
sen rannalla loimuta lietemme saa
käs' säilöjä käyttäiss' on varttunut siell'
on kunnialle, uskolle hehkunut miel'

Heads turned to the front in succession as Dunmoore passed by, but the proud soldiers continued singing until she finished her inspection of the third and last rank.

"Someday, you must tell me what the words mean, Major," Dunmoore said as they marched back to the front of the formation.

"Easily done, sir. In Anglic, the first verse would go something like this

Our homeland lies in the snows of the North
The hearth of the home glowing warm and strong
Our hand has grown sure with playing the sword
And honor and pure faith lies in our record."

"Beautiful. And your troops are just as beautifully turned out."

"Thank you, sir. They're very proud at having been selected to serve aboard a special operations ship. It is a rare honor."

They assumed their original positions at the front of the formation again.

"Please pass along my compliments. Your soldiers are impressive."

"Yes, sir. With your permission?"

"Proceed."

"Company, shoulder ARMS. To the governor of Toboso, present ARMS."

The first five bars of the Commonwealth anthem rang out again, ending the simple, but for Dunmoore deeply moving ceremony.

— Thirty-Nine —

The shuttle carrying Piotr Alexandrov and his staff settled on the tarmac, and the whine of its thrusters faded away. After weeks of dealing with a frontier colony's many problems, she experienced a profound sense of relief that it would soon be over. Major Salminen and her company were drawn up to one side, ready for the handover ceremonies, while behind them sat the shuttles that would take the soldiers, Dunmoore and the rest of her crew back into orbit. She had already given Alexandrov a thorough briefing via radio during his ship's approach, and Toboso's new administrator had declared himself ready to take over the moment he arrived. With the stockade now guarded by a contingent made up of members from each of the municipal police forces on Toboso and the future of the naval depot uncertain, there was no reason for any of them to stay after Alexandrov took up the reins of power.

When the aft ramp began to drop, Dunmoore stepped forward to greet her replacement. To her surprise, a tiny four-legged creature with black and tan fur appeared first, followed by a stout man with a pleasant, congenial face.

"That's my little buddy Pips," Alexandrov called out to her.

Dunmoore crouched and held out her hand for Pips to sniff. The little dog did so before settling back on his haunches to look up at her, head tilted to one side.

"He likes you, Captain, and he's an incredibly good judge of character." The governor-designate held out his hand. "It's a pleasure to meet you in person. Heck of a job you did here. I'm sure it'll enter Colonial Office lore as an example of how things can go off the rails."

"Hopefully it won't enter Navy lore. I cannot tell you how glad I am that you're here. The past few weeks have made me appreciate how relatively uncomplicated a starship captain's life truly is."

"I'll not argue the point," he replied, falling into step beside her as she led him to the table where the official handover documents waiting for their signatures. "It takes a special sort of masochist to want this line of work. Or someone unlucky enough to lose a bet. I can never remember."

"Which one are you?"

Alexandrov smiled at her. "That would be telling. Now, you said we would do this with the full military protocol. It's not usual, but then, having a serving Fleet officer as governor isn't either. Tell me what my part is to be, and I'll follow your lead. Don't worry about Pips. He knows when to stay quiet."

Twenty minutes later, with the scrolls duly signed, the outgoing governor having received her final salute and the incoming governor his first, Salminen and her company marched off to their shuttles. The little dog had indeed proved to be well behaved, staying by the table during the inspection and march past.

"With your permission, Governor," Dunmoore said, coming to attention, "I'd like to rejoin my ship. We're expected at Starbase 24."

"By all means. I'm hardly in a position to deny you." He stuck out his hand again, a warm smile on his round face. "On behalf of the Colonial Office, thank you, Captain. On my own behalf, I'm immensely grateful for your candor in preparing me. Toboso's always been a problem child, but no one back on Earth had any idea things had become this bad. I'll have plenty to keep me busy over the next few years, not least setting up a justice system capable of handling the charges you've laid and dealing with those you've arrested. Unfortunately, with your departure, Toboso is no longer under martial law, so it'll have to be in accordance with civilian rules, and that means enough red tape to keep several law firms in business for decades. Nevertheless, we do what we must, and with the evidence and depositions you've provided, I'm sure we'll work our way through the list before the rest of my hair turns gray. Godspeed and fair sailing."

"Thank you, sir. May you have a fruitful tenure as governor."

Dunmoore's hand rose to her brow in a parade ground salute.

As she turned away, she spied two police officers escorting Andrew Devine to the shuttle that had brought her replacement and his staff to the surface. He must have seen her glance at him because he raised a hand to wave while a self-confident grin split his face. She did not respond in kind.

Though not one to wish death on an enemy, Dunmoore would not shed a tear at news that fate had caught up with him, or with any of his cronies. Perhaps Forenza or one of his colleagues in the cleaning business already waited for him at the passenger liner's next port of call.

Behind her, thrusters whined, signaling that *Iolanthe*'s shuttles were preparing to lift. A quick look around the spaceport showed she was the last to board, something Guthren, standing on the ramp of the only one not buttoned up, confirmed by giving her the mount up hand signal.

A few minutes later, strapped in next to Petty Officer Purdy, she caught a final glimpse of Doniphon and the flurry of activity around the temporary Colonial Office building, proof that Alexandrov and his people were settling into their new surroundings. Then, with a roar, they left the ground, and she saw nothing but clouds through the cockpit windscreen while a giant hand pushed her deeper into the seat.

*

Holt, at the head of a two-dozen strong side party, greeted her on the hangar deck to the trill of the bosun's whistle.

"Welcome back, Captain. That was a beautiful ceremony. We watched from the bridge. You must feel a thousand tons lighter and thirty years younger."

"I'm not sure it'll ever be over," she replied, the weariness of the last several weeks seeping into her limbs. "But at least we can close this chapter. Governor Alexandrov will complete the work we started and make sure justice is served in full."

"Aye and good luck to him." Holt dismissed the side party with a nod, and then led the way to the hangar deck's inner door. "The wardroom would like to invite you to supper tonight, as a way of honoring one of the few serving starship captains who can also add colonial governor to her service record as well as marking another in a string of victories we all hope will continue. To misquote the most eminently quotable Winston Churchill, this may not be the beginning of the end, but it surly is the end of the beginning now that we've triggered some much needed cleansing of Commonwealth affairs."

"After eight years of war, some of it fought against our own side? I bloody well hope so, and yes, I accept the invitation. Then, I intend to sleep for a few days, confident that you can keep running *Iolanthe* and her consorts a little while longer."

He laughed with delight. "Horse feathers! You'll be pacing the CIC like a caged tigress by the forenoon watch, hatching new training schemes to challenge the rest of us."

"Probably," she confessed with a guilty grin. "Though it'll be a nice change of pace."

"Until the next murderous scum pop up on our sensors, but such is the everlasting struggle against sundry pirates, reivers, and marauders in this sector."

"Maybe we'll get lucky, and HQ will send us to the Shrehari front. That would be a true change of pace."

"Perhaps too much of one." She spied the soldiers forming ranks on the far side of the hangar out of the corner of her eyes. "But I know this — we'll be ready and able no matter what fate throws at *Iolanthe*. There's something to be said about the magic of avenging fairies, especially when they boast a battleship's broadside."

ABOUT THE AUTHOR

Eric Thomson is the pen name of a retired Canadian soldier with thirty-one years of service, both in the Regular Army and the Army Reserve. He spent his Regular Army career in the Infantry and his Reserve service in the Armoured Corps. He worked as an information technology specialist for a number of years before retiring to become a full-time author.

Eric has been a voracious reader of science fiction, military fiction, and history all his life. Several years ago, he put fingers to keyboard and started writing his own military sci-fi, with a definite space opera slant, using many of his own experiences as a soldier for inspiration.

When he is not writing fiction, Eric indulges in his other passions: photography, hiking, and scuba diving, all of which he shares with his wife.

Join Eric Thomson at: www.thomsonfiction.ca/

Where you will find news about upcoming books and more information about the universe in which his heroes fight for humanity's survival.

Read his blog at: www.ericthomsonblog.wordpress.com

If you enjoyed this book, please consider leaving a review on Goodreads, or with your favorite online retailer to help others discover it.

ALSO BY ERIC THOMSON

Siobhan Dunmoore

No Honor in Death (Siobhan Dunmoore Book 1)
The Path of Duty (Siobhan Dunmoore Book 2)
Like Stars in Heaven (Siobhan Dunmoore Book 3)
Victory's Bright Dawn (Siobhan Dunmoore Book 4)
Without Mercy (Siobhan Dunmoore Book 5)

Decker's War

Death Comes But Once (Decker's War Book 1)
Cold Comfort (Decker's War Book 2)
Fatal Blade (Decker's War Book 3)
Howling Stars (Decker's War Book 4)
Black Sword (Decker's War Book 5)
No Remorse (Decker's War Book 6)
Hard Strike (Decker's War Book 7)

Quis Custodiet

The Warrior's Knife (Quis Custodiet N° 1)

Ashes of Empire

Imperial Sunset (Ashes of Empire #1)

Printed in Great Britain
by Amazon